THE STANDING POOL

Adam Thorpe was born in Paris in 1956. His first
novel, *Ulverton*, was published in 1992, and he
has written eight other novels – most recently *Hodd*
– two collections of stories and five books of poetry.
He lives in France with his wife and family.

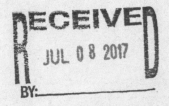

ALSO BY ADAM THORPE

Fiction

Ulverton
Still
Pieces of Light
Shifts
Nineteen Twenty-One
No Telling
The Rules of Perspective
Is This the Way You Said?
Between Each Breath
Hodd

Poetry

Mornings in the Baltic
Meeting Montaigne
From the Neanderthal
Nine Lessons from the Dark
Birds with a Broken Wing

ADAM THORPE

The Standing Pool

VINTAGE BOOKS
London

Published by Vintage 2009

2 4 6 8 10 9 7 5 3 1

First published in Great Britain in 2008 by Jonathan Cape

Vintage
Random House, 20 Vauxhall Bridge Road,
London SW1V 2SA

www.vintage-books.co.uk

Addresses for companies within The Random House Group Limited
can be found at: www.randomhouse.co.uk/offices.htm

The Random House Group Limited Reg. No. 954009

A CIP catalogue record for this book
is available from the British Library

ISBN 9780099503651

The Random House Group Limited supports The Forest
Stewardship Council (FSC), the leading international forest
certification organisation. All our titles that are printed on
Greenpeace approved FSC certified paper carry the FSC logo.
Our paper procurement policy can be found at
www.rbooks.co.uk/environment

Typeset by Palimpsest Book Production Limited
Grangemouth, Stirlingshire
Printed and bound in Great Britain by
CPI Cox & Wyman, Reading RG1 8EX

'Poor Tom, that eats the swimming frog, the toad, the todpole, the wall-newt and the water; that in the fury of his heart, when the foul fiend rages, eats cow-dung for sallets, swallows the old rat and the ditch-dog, drinks the green mantle of the standing pool . . .'

King Lear, III.4

'History is what remains when myth has left the room.'

Nicholas Mallinson
Saint-Simon and the Pre-Socialists (London, 1992)

PROLOGUE

The house is massive, three floors of trouble.

His father remembered its farming days, and it was trouble then. But all farms are trouble, Papa. We're not talking farms.

After the war, after the Germans had set fire to it and destroyed the wing that ran back towards the hill, the place was empty. Then it was lived in by mad Mamie Aubert and her goats, until she was found dead and rotting in her bed. Then it was empty again, and he used to come here with the gang to smoke and play records on a wind-up gramophone: the Beatles, Johnny Hallyday, rock 'n' roll and the blues. He kissed his first girl in the old kitchen, trying to work his hand around her thick bra, pressing her up against the stone sink full of cobwebs. They used to scribble slogans on the inside walls, doodle naughty pictures in charcoal on the lime-wash. Fire their air-guns at the outside stonework.

It was the gang that was the trouble, not the house. He loved the place. They'd squeeze through a hole they'd made in the attic, letting the rain in to rot and ruin it all, and lie up here like kings. Except then it was summer, and these very same tiles, cool and a bit wet now, burned their bare backs. They reckoned they were flying. He'd imagine staying here forever.

Then a bunch of hippies from Paris moved in, fresh from the noise in '68. They grew their beards long and pretended to be peasants, with a herd of goats scrawnier than Mamie Aubert's. It took ages to get rid of them. One of them was German: that was a cheek. They changed the name of the place: from Mas des Fosses to Mas du Paradis, carving it onto an old cart-wheel with an orange sun painted on the hub. They painted everything in the house orange – even the beams, even

I

the joists and the plaster between. Raoul and the other boys in the village gang would watch the hippies through binoculars; sometimes they danced about naked, flowers in their hair, one of them playing a flute. Half of them left after the first winter, straight back to their rich *mamans* in Paris; then the stragglers were dragged out by the police after a couple of years, sent scarpering in their beat-up hippy van. It was on the front page of the *Midi Libre*: the youngsters were trying to build a new society, the report said, but all they left was a mess.

Not that anyone really cared about the house: it was too big, too old, too dark. All it had was a south-facing view that made you feel you were flying.

Raoul thought, as he often did, how he might have bought Les Fosses at the time, dirt cheap. Just sat on it and all its land, while the prices shot skywards – he'd be laughing, now. Not stuck up here, laying tiles for foreigners. But Papa had said no. Bad investment. Wrong, yet again. He shouldn't have listened.

And now the old man's telling him to get down off the roof. Raoul can hear the voice in his head, going on and on, just as it used to when he was still apprenticed, when the old man was alive and strong as a bull. It's rained on and off this week and there's a mistiness in the valley. The tiles are feeling greasy, their curves slippery with damp – even through his gloves.

Get down off there, Raoul, you oaf!

What you don't understand, Papa, is that the new type of owner isn't the same as the old type. They're worse. They're impatient. They're beginning to panic, they've invited half of London and probably Her Majesty for the summer break: still more than four months away, and they're running about like headless chickens, just because there's no roof. They nag at him down the phone, like the others. You call them selfish and stupid, Papa, but it's because they're not on the spot, it makes them feel helpless.

And he doesn't cheat like a lot of the others, working for people too far away to know better, or too rich to care. Fixing a gutter in half a day and pretending it took three, or tiling a bathroom in two and chalking it up as a week. All he does is round off his hours a bit, half an hour here, forty minutes there. They can afford it. Wailing away on the phone as if they own him, talking in their three-year-old's French. Raoul! Raoul! Like kids.

I can't help the weather, he told them. I can't help the rain. But it'll be done. You'll have your roof.

And it's Monsieur Lagrange, to you. But he never says it.

He lifts his head and sends a shivery gob flying over the verge. The mist fills the valleys spreading away below, turning the blue of the farthest mountains very faint. They remind him of a girl's discarded see-through nightie, peeled off her and in a heap on the floor. They're not the Alps, though – those are beyond, invisible; on a very clear day you can see the snowy line of the Alps to the east and the silver line of the sea to the south, but today's not clear and the sea's just a brightness thrown upwards.

He wipes his face on his blue sleeve and removes his gloves and fishes a Marlboro out of his overalls' top pocket, flavouring his lungs as he contemplates the nearer view where the land drops away in overgrown terraces he remembers being tilled for onions, leeks, potatoes, when he was a kid. He aches, but he still feels strong. He was a good footballer, captain of the village seniors until he did his knee in when he was thirty-five. Ten years ago. Out on the wing at first, then in defence. Then cheering from the sidelines. *Allez, Aubain, allez!* He feels the strength in his body like a cloudy liquid as he rests his forearm on his upraised knee, boot firm against the timbers, leaning forward a touch, against the angle of the slope, the pitch you wouldn't want to fool about on. Working slightly against gravity, in case. Nobody can switch off gravity.

He takes a deep drag and lets it out in a perfect, expanding smoke-ring that floats up to where he's going to lay the ridge next week – then it melts into the sky. He's on a level with the birds. He's a big blue bird on the roof. A sparrow hops along the scaffolding that juts above the eaves below. The scaffolding's hugged this place for two years. Imagine the cost of

3

hiring that, that alone. And all those steel wall braces inside, keeping the old girl upright until they pin and cement.

Birds only fall if you shoot them. This reminds him of that joke big François cracked during the hunt last weekend. Two blondes walking along a beach, boobs like watermelons, arses you could disappear into. One says, 'Oh look, a dead seagull!' The other looks up at the sky and says, 'Where? Where?'

Contentment, suddenly. That's one thing you can say about this place, this area: no one really wants to leave, however much it gets you down at times. It's paradise. It's home. Off he went up north, for his military service, stayed on for a bit when they built all that concrete crap in Paris, then a spell in Lille, met the wife, passed his exams – and scuttled back home. Kids. Work. Papers. Life. A bit of hunting, though it wasn't how it used to be, when he was a kid. Who needs to see the world? He can see all he needs to, here. And business has never been better: Dutch, Swiss, Americans, the English. Belgians. Germans, even: keeping their heads down, this time round. There aren't enough days in the year, even when you work seven a week.

It's a bit more slippery than he expected, though. If he'd known, he wouldn't have risked it.

He remembers how his father used to say, when they first started roofing together all those years back, that no job was worth breaking your neck for. On the other hand, if he were to wait any longer then that Sandler woman would be at him again, pushing and prodding – wailing down the phone and making out he was diddling her and that she'd have to find someone else. Perhaps they don't have weather in England. They fly over from London for twenty-four hours just to check up, scratching the wall and poking the plaster and finding fault, squeezing out more unpaid hours, then disappear. Just like that American couple with the place in the big field the other side of St-Maurice. Even they come over for the day, over the Atlantic, just to poke and scratch! When the rains turned the field to knee-deep mud last year, blocking access, they wouldn't believe him. They phoned his mobile from New York and

4

moaned. He was in the café, it was late. What do you want me to do, he chuckled, winking at Louis behind the bar: hire a helicopter? Good idea, they said.

And she had her spies, did Madame Sandler. Jean-Luc Maille, for instance, supposed to be doing the grounds. Their lawn. Now that's a joke. A lawn! In the hands of Jean-Luc! That weirdo.

The fact is, the damp's got into the tiles that were stacked by the barn, and the misty air's settling on the tiles the moment he's put them on. Not yet a skating rink on a slope, but he wouldn't want to walk on it once the cover tiles are laid. There's a glisten on the finished part spreading away from him like a lot of overlapping thighs that makes his heart beat a bit faster when he looks at it, but he knows how to be careful.

And then again – you can take all the care in the world and tiptoe over like a ballet dancer, spreading your weight mathematically between each foot, and one tile will always break. Especially if the covers are the originals. There goes another, like a biscuit. Kneel on the battens, you clumsy oaf!

I'm boss now, Papa. I've three men under me, you only ever had one: me.

I made you too big and heavy, Raoul.

But the girls like it that way, Papa. They always have. Go back to sleep.

Five rows of pan tiles by ten across, then the covers. His men are up at the Swiss place today: foundation slab for a pool house. Only two on the job, with the new one sick. Yet again.

He's talking to himself, giving himself orders, hearing it. It can get lonely, when you're working by yourself. He needs to hire a fourth man, but it's not easy, you think you've got someone perfect and then they fall apart. They should be two at it, up here. He asked Marcel, but Marcel never helps; he thinks it's beneath him, these days. His own brother! At least they're talking, now. You can't not talk to your own brother.

The plastic sheets stir over the untiled third and make him think he's got company. The winds ripped the last lot off – twice over. He couldn't do much about it; he didn't fancy being

5

blown all the way to St-Maurice, he said to Madame Sandler. Who didn't laugh. She must have been an affliction to men when she was younger: he could just about imagine it. That luscious type, quite a bit of flesh on her. Blonde, but clever. Cooled down now, like lava. Just old rock.

He flicks his cigarette over the verge and gets back to work, conscious of the pale brightness towards the west, the gloomy shadows under the trees to the east. He's saved half his lunch for later, because he's going to work until he can only just see to get down. The wife's double rations, beef cut a bit too thin, stowed in the attic below him, in the dry. The coffee always tasting of the flask's plastic. But no regrets, when it comes to the wife. She knows how to turn a blind eye.

He's given the old, original tiles a hard scrub with soap and a bristle-brush, to remove the worst of the moss, the bird-shit, a century or more of soot. Lichen like fingerprints, bright green, like a kid's been at them with paint. Now he gives the tiles a last go with a softer brush, laying them on his thigh, feeling the weight. As if he's moulding them off his own thigh, like they used to in the old days: he can see the finger marks in most of them, long-dead fingers drawing themselves upwards towards the groin; smoothing out the clay. That's history for you. Long-dead fingers.

He's not sure why he does this cleaning business, he doesn't need to, but it's what his old man did and the old man was a true artisan, no one can deny that. He likes the swish, swish of his brush on the terracotta, as if he's polishing a shoe, a smart one of patent leather. It's to show the foreigners (though they'll never know it) that he's an artisan, not just a builder. A job well done. If they ever bother to look.

They might not have paid well in the old days, but at least they looked, Raoul.

I know, Papa. Now leave me alone, I'm in a hurry. It's cold up here, I have to keep moving.

He whistles softly through the gap in his teeth in time with the swish of the brush. It's never a proper tune: but it keeps him relaxed, even when he's fighting against time.

6

ONE

It was better than the photographs because of the air, the silence, the silent sweetness of the air, the sky, the proud beauty of the house. It was not as good as the photographs because the house no longer looked like a Mayan monument. Or a farm, all sweat and toil. Its tawny-hued, sandblasted stones gave the place an almost spruce quality.

But the view was the same, and stupendous. The slope descended from the building in a series of overgrown terraces. First there were the tops of bunched trees, both leafy-dark and wintry-bare, then the narrow valley falling away, then beyond that the flanks of hills and, to the left (they hadn't yet worked out their compass points), folding in ever-paler contours, the more distant mountains, blue upon blue like a screenprint. A far-off glow of light, they surmised, was the presence of the sea.

Nick Mallinson would have shouted for joy except that he had a voice complaint; his vocal cords had been thinned and inflamed, not by overuse in lectures (as people thought) but by acid rising from his stressed stomach, churned by college and departmental politics, his work as a member of the history faculty board, the dreaded Research Assessment Exercise, wranglings over everything from pay scales to information-communication strategies – and, above all, his failure to be appointed a professor. This was why he was here with his family. He hadn't been very good for the last year or so.

He'd had a dream a few weeks back in which his core lecture was invaded by the geography department – by the likes of Sue Jacobs and Jeff Michaels, scattering papers and turning over tables and backed up by their geography students who were screaming over his words, victorious, having the last laugh. What is history but the effect of the weather, the soil, the hidden minerals in the rocks, the relief of the land?

He pointed to the huge, oilcloth map of the Chad oilfield in desperation as they closed in on him with their drills, but to no avail. History was over. It was all to be biblical torment, now. He woke up shouting about geology.

Sarah had pushed him into taking the sabbatical early on grounds of ill health. He felt vaguely fraudulent, watching the poor and the sick scrabbling for survival in countries no one took any notice of these days, except to plunder. What did he suffer from? The affluent West's disease. It wasn't throat cancer, although he'd had all the symptoms as described on medical websites. It was 'life in the academic fast lane', as his departmental colleague Peter Osterhauser, newly-made Professor, put it. Not without a twist of ironic glee.

The five of them had set off from Cambridge on a grisly morning in early February and would not be back, if all went well, until late summer. The drive down the length of France, to the accompaniment of 'Oranges and Lemons' and other nursery favourites, was broken only by a dreadful night in a cheap hotel in a village somewhere near Limoges. The interior of the charming old building had been sucked out and replaced by a motorway motel smelling of wet paint in rooms with, instead of pictures, huge wall-clamped TVs tuned to global laughter and disaster. The girls loved it.

They reached the track that left the lane half a kilometre after the little stone humpback, as directed, and passed the American-style letter box on a stout pole: *Sandler*, it said.

'Checking the post should keep us fit,' Nick observed.

Two kilometres of bumps, the owners had said. A late, particularly fierce rainstorm in November had pinpointed the wood-covered valley at the head of which stood the house and the track had been badly mauled – criss-crossed by what were, effectively, the dry beds of flash streams. The three Mallinson daughters swayed and squealed in the rear seats as the car bounced along over hole, rock and rut. The car was the same age as Alicia: five and three-quarters. Tammy was a precocious eight. Beans was nineteen months. They were disco-dancing to the music of an unmetalled road.

'Girls, please,' Sarah pleaded, clutching the glove compartment and peering anxiously forwards, although she had her glasses on. 'Hey, this track goes on *for ever and ever*.'

Nick gripped the jittery steering-wheel and said, 'Nothing goes on forever except delusion.' He was fifty-four.

Sarah, eighteen years younger than her husband, laughed too loud – mainly from nervous excitement. 'And sleazy politicians!'

'Lord, spare us sleazy politicians. Youch!'

A series of metallic clangs sounded as loose stones – rocks, possibly – struck the chassis. The track widened into an open gravelly area and the house was sprung on them by the trees: it was like a great flat cliff, soaring three stories to a fretted verge.

'Please keep your seat belts fastened until the plane has come to a complete stop,' said Nick, pinching his nose with two fingers.

Alicia said she wanted to be 'let off' and blew a raspberry.

'Wowee,' said Sarah, peering up through the windscreen. 'Look at that. Here we are. Blow me away. Look, girls!'

Alicia yelped. 'Tammy hit me with her elbow, Mummy. Really hard.'

'Yeah yeah,' said Tammy, still struggling with her seat belt.

'Look, girls!' their mother insisted. 'This is it!'

'Likkel window,' said Beans, clouding the glass with her tiny nose.

'You don't even *love* me,' Alicia groaned.

Tammy unbelted Beans and waited for the child-lock to be neutralised, the gaoler to come with his keys. The three girls spilled out as from a helicopter in a war zone. The house was now an even higher cliff eaten out of granite, with windows for handholds. There was a cold wind, despite the southern-ness, and Sarah stepped straight into a spindly stand of heather.

Not a bad view, they all agreed, exhilarated and amazed by the blueness. The very air itself was blue, despite a whitish sky. Sheer, clear-eyed promise.

As the children raced off round the corner of the house, Nick Mallinson stretched his drive-weary spine and spread his arms out either side, as if embracing the infinite space before him. In a film of their adventures he would have leapt up and punched the air in slow motion, thought Sarah, already jogging gamely after her brood.

Who were skidding round the house and hurtling over weeds in what must have been the old farmyard, a considerable flat-ness half-enclosed by walls and outbuildings and overgrown with dried husks, tiny bristly weeds and matted tufts of grass in inter-mittent blotches. A long section of the back wall had tumbled, revealing a swarm of dry bracken spilling down the slope from the woods. A shard of porcelain sky had dropped into the middle of the yard and was framed by terracotta tiles. Sarah called out to the girls to be careful, vaguely wondering which one to save first if they were all three to fall in.

'Where's the garden?' Tammy shouted.

They were on the edge of the pool, which was large enough (Sarah calculated) to do about five breaststrokes per length. It was surrounded on only three sides by tiles: the fourth was rough earth to the concrete lip. The water was the colour of lime jelly.

'Yuk, it's ill,' said Alicia.

A set of metal steps descended into the murk and she gripped the rails and swung herself between them; the steps were slightly loose at the bolts and ticked. Tammy pulled off her shoes and sat on the edge and lowered a toe in.

'Freeeezing!' she announced.

Dead leaves were suspended inside the jelly, like bits of rind;

the ones still floating were huddled together in a corner. Alicia continued to swing on the steps' rails, panting excitedly as they ticked and tocked.

Sarah, out of breath, surveyed them all in one efficient glance – especially Beans. 'Well well,' she panted. 'So this is the pool. We've got to be very aware of the dangers, kids,' she added, with an apologetic lilt.

Tammy stirred the water with her hand. After a minute or so the filters started to cluck like the farmyard's missing hens.

Beans clutched her mother's thigh and stared at the liquified, wobbling light. Alicia had found a stick and was hitting a white plastic object clipped to the edge with an extension running into the water. It resembled a commode.

'Carry on like that, sweetheart,' said Sarah, 'and you'll be going straight back home.'

'Goody good,' said Alicia. She hit the object again.

'Oh, what a lovely little house,' Sarah cried, indicating the shed.

'Wowee,' Tammy said, drily, using her mother's favourite word. 'Let's get a postcard of it.' Nevertheless, she crushed her wet feet back into her trainers and ran to look.

The shed was padlocked. They could make out a giant vacuum cleaner nestling among half-deflated crocodiles with popping eyes; an enormous duck with a toothy grin (did ducks *have* teeth?); folded deckchairs; and something technological with dials and pipes.

'We'll have to dust that lot off in the summer,' said Sarah. 'Exciting. That must be the pool's pump thingie or whatever.'

The two older girls were already scampering away into the outbuildings – a big stone barn and something dark and low for animals; maybe a goatshed. Between these and a stone arch leading back to the front lay a long, wide strip of tangled briars with big charred stones among them. Sarah wondered if a wing of the house had burnt down.

Moments later they were back at the pool where Alicia leaned over the edge at an alarming angle, waving at her reflection.

'There's a frog!' she screamed. 'Yuk.'

Beans, still holding her mother's hand, exploded with astonishment when she spotted the frog, which was in fact a toad. Sarah told them. It had stuck its nostrils above the water and turned into a knot of slimy wood. 'Come on, you lot, let's help Daddy,' she said. Alicia threw a pebble and the toad vanished. Tammy was annoyed and belted her sister so she nearly toppled in.

'Tammy, don't you *dare* hit Alicia on the edge of the pool like that.'

'OK, I'll hit her when she's not on the edge of the pool, then.'

Alicia pretended to cry, balling her eyes with her knuckles.

'Fwog! Toe!' screeched Beans, pointing at a greenish bird in the sky as it passed over them calmly and into the trees.

Le Mas des Fosses.

The Mallinsons had advertised in *History Today*, the *Times Higher Education Supplement* and the *London Review of Books*:

> FRANCE: Two Cambridge academics and their three
> well-behaved girls seek quiet rustic house in South for
> six-month sabbatical, preferably in Languedoc.

They had received thirteen replies, and had fallen for the Mas des Fosses. A converted farm in a remote and stunning location; art-collecting owners; the fact that the swimming pool was mentioned in passing instead of, as elsewhere, being trumpeted as the main feature to which the house was a mere backdrop. In addition, the rent was very reasonable compared to the others: the owners wished to retain use of the master bedroom for the odd weekend, as needed. A minor compromise that dovetailed happily with the Mallinsons' meagre income.

Secretly, they were pleased there was a pool. They imagined post-meridian slumbers in the shade while the girls gambolled and splashed. They made vows to carve the water each morning. To keep fit. To grow more alive.

The owners were a Mr and Mrs Sandler; they lived in Chiswick, in a house full of ancient pottery. Visitors had to take off their shoes and select furry slippers from a linen set of shelves in the hall. Alicia and Beans were not present, in case they misbehaved. Tammy was old enough to understand: the representative Mallinson child. She tended to be either quiet (locked into her own thing) or extremely 'verbal', as her teacher put it, so she'd been told that this was a kind of interview and that if she wanted she could tell the Sandlers about previous trips to France but otherwise to let Mummy and Daddy do the talking.

This was early December, two months before the Mallinsons were to set off. The Sandlers had only spent summers in 'Les Fosses', but there were electric radiators and a 'fantastic' fire-place with simply 'heaps' of dead wood lying about. They'd had the place sandblasted last year, so it was even better than in the photos (which, to the Mallinsons' delight, had shown a beautifully unkempt place, whereas the others all looked blow-dried). And – the husband chortled – a great wine cellar, but the contents were *not* part of the furnishings, *naturellement*.

The Sandlers were dealers rather than collectors, but the Mallinsons, who were academics and knew no better, did not feel cheated. Alan Sandler was American and dealt, not in antiques, but antiquities. Lucy owned a print gallery in Chelsea. Alan found Sarah Mallinson small, dark and attractive, like a fine little chocolate left last in the box only because people are greedy. He asked straight out why she was so much younger than her husband. He liked her small, oval glasses. They were coy.

'Nick supervised my doctorate,' she replied, taking his candour as a colourful national trait. 'Usual story.'

Alan whistled. Lucy wondered what the doctorate's subject was.

'Fairly grim,' Sarah admitted.

'Oh go on, tell, tell,' laughed Lucy, whose beauty was taking affectionate leave of her features behind a screen of cosmetics. She had very short grey hair and fingernails painted dark plum.

Lucy tried to concentrate but was distracted by the way the tip of Sarah's nice nose was affected by certain consonants. 'M', mostly. Lips coming together. Something to do with Africa, ideology and technological development. The reticence of the French. Copying British engineering projects. Or not.

'Basically,' Sarah continued, noticing Lucy's intense interest, 'for fear of replicating the perceived despotism of the British Empire. So it's mostly about water control, forest clearance and oil. Any the wiser?'

Lucy raised her eyebrows and affirmed she was, miffed at the suggestion that she might not be.

'An under-researched area, both in the geographical as well as the intellectual sense,' Nick commented. The otolaryngologist had advised him to speak at low volume but never, *ever* to whisper. And to take a break. 'Basically lots of juicy, unread documents,' he added, as if this was the most exciting thing in the world.

Lucy looked sharply at Sarah. 'You don't teach, then?'

'I stopped for the kids,' she fibbed. In fact, the completion of her thesis, delayed by the usual part-time tutoring and an active social life, had melded straight into Tammy. She'd never really launched herself on a career, and this bothered her. 'I've spots of supervision and so on. I do plan to go back,' she added, a little too forcefully. 'I hope to turn the thesis into a book while I'm in France.'

Lucy turned to Nick. 'Which college in Cambridge?' she asked, somewhat querulously.

'FitzHerbert's,' he replied, trying not to sound apologetic.

'Never heard of it.'

'It's one of the smaller ones, founded in the sixteenth century,' Sarah broke in. 'Beautiful chapel and lovely little front court. I mean really exceptional.'

'So what're *you* going to be up to, Professor?' asked Alan, apparently wincing at Nick. 'Stirring the pool while your good woman slaves?'

'I'm not a professor,' said Nick. 'I'm a reader. My title is Doctor.'

'Sorry, I didn't mean to demote you,' said Alan.

'You did the opposite. A sensitive area,' he went on, candidly. 'Anyway, as a colonial and post-colonial specialist I'm editing a collection of essays written mostly by fellow historians, the theme of which is oil, oil in Africa. And working on a more popular book about reactions to Suez, targeted at students and people like yourself, which was meant to be done for the anniversary, alas. One will hardly be read and the other might earn me a little bit extra.'

'Oil, huh?' grunted Alan, eyeing Nick suspiciously.

'Principally.' The role of oil in post-war African politics and the dirty, viscous tricks of the United States: but Nick kept that to himself.

Alan sucked on a tooth, sizing him up. 'Do you know, Nick, that the energy in a single barrel of oil is equivalent to 25,000 hours of manual labour?'

Nick looked politely nonplussed – although he did know this, in fact. There was nothing he did not know about oil and its lamentable history. 'Well, that's why we're hooked,' he said, although he had not wanted to raise sparks. 'We're dependent on something that's destroying the basis of our existence, like a heroin addict.'

'So oil is heroin, huh?'

'Metaphorically, yes. For the last hundred years or so. A mere blink. There are analogies: potency, vicious effects, rapid decline of health.'

'And oil companies are the drug dealers?'

'In a manner of speaking,' said Nick, head cocked apologetically. They were being assessed, after all.

Alan smiled mischievously. 'Are you *walking* to Languedoc?'

'I know, I know,' said Nick, raising his hands as if surrendering. 'We're all addicts, whether we want to be or not.'

'Take out shares in biofuels,' said Alan, with a knowing sigh.

Nick and Sarah simultaneously, if somewhat murmuringly, protested. This conflictual debate was not what was supposed to happen.

'The thing is,' Nick insisted, crossing his legs and leaning forwards as he would have done in a seminar (the legendary 'Mallinson slant'), 'only the human race would dream up a solution that's even worse than the problem. Stuff like palm oil requires *massive* forest clearance.'

'Trees are trees,' said Alan, with a smirk.

Nick drew in his breath as if hurt and Sarah pulled a face. This is the enemy, she thought. We can't take this house. We'll be cursed.

Lucy, as if reading her mind, said the Mas des Fosses was an utterly fab place for kids. 'And what are *you* planning to do when you're not at school, Tabby?'

'Tammy.'

'Tammy.'

'Just being grateful.'

'Grateful?'

Despite her brightness, she couldn't quite remember what her parents had said she should be grateful for. She sipped her Coke to fill the gap. The ice rang against her prominent front teeth. She was worried about missing her friends.

'She's going to have some quality free time,' her mother filled in. 'In the countryside. She's ahead at school, anyway.'

'You're bunking school?' said Alan, provocatively again. 'That sounds neat.'

'We're not supposed to by French law, but I don't think anyone will bother,' chuckled Nick.

'We'll be home learning,' Sarah assured them, as if she needed to.

'They certainly won't bother,' said Lucy. 'No point in educating them in the midst of a ploughed field. As long as they don't play with matches. From May onwards it's a tinderbox. Bone dry. No barbecues, either. Look what happens in Australia.'

'Absolutely not,' said Nick, siding quickly with a phantom group of sophisticates against the mass of vulgarity she'd conjured. 'Actually we do know the Languedoc quite –'

'And *why* the south of France,' she interrupted, turning to Sarah, 'apart of course from the sun and the wine?'

Sarah told her, with an inward relish, that the Centre des Archives d'Outre Mer was in Aix and held original documents relating to major French engineering works in the African colonies. Apart from the sun and the wine, she added, pretending to laugh. She really wanted to pull out of this deal, to leave this awful couple.

Nick, battling his weakening voice, mentioned his sojourn at the Centre many years ago, rummaging in the archives for his paper on forced labour under the librarian's stern, owl-like gaze (the account exaggerated, of course). Tammy, having heard all of this many times before, rolled her eyes to the plaster grapes on the ceiling and began wiggling her feet. At her mother's whispered instigation, she settled down on the carpet to the felt-tip pen drawing she'd been told to do if she got bored, leaning on a picture book brought along for the purpose.

'What a genial family,' said Alan, eyes flicking from one to the other.

Possibly by association, he started on about the village mayor, who was a Communist. 'Organic farmer. He can't stand anyone earning more than him, and no one earns less. Up to his eyeballs in agricultural grants. That's Yurp for you. But what he hates most of all are you English folks.'

'And Parisians,' said Lucy. 'But don't let us put them off, Alan.'

'Perhaps he'll share my fascination for obscure Trotskyite splinter groups,' Nick chortled. The furry slippers at the end of his tallness made him look like a daddy-long-legs.

'Now I'll bet you're the type that uses words like *incommensurable*,' said Alan, leaning forwards good-humouredly and tapping Nick's knee.

'Oh, not always,' Nick grinned, a frown giving his irritation away.

Lucy hastily brought up the subject of speaking French. Hers was schoolgirl, it had got locked, it needed a kick-start and lots of axle-grease. 'I'm going to have to have *lessons*,' she grimaced, as if talking about surgery. 'How's yours?'

'I can read it for research purposes but talking isn't great,' Sarah admitted. 'Nick speaks it rather well.'

Nick waved a modest dismissal. Somebody had once taken him, after a brief exchange, for a Belgian. 'You've got some very impressive, er, artefacts,' he said, looking around him.

Alan was a specialist dealer in Near and Middle Eastern antiquities, it turned out. 'Only the best,' he says. 'I don't bother with anything else. No one's told this guy that the game's up,' he went on, confusing them. 'He's like a Jap in the forest who thinks the war's still being fought. The whole damn country of France is like a Jap in the forest who thinks the war's still being fought. "Come on out, guys! It's all over!"'

Alan laughed in wheezes, slapping the arms of the chair. Tammy paused in her drawing and took another biscuit, waiting a little before consuming it in rabbity nibbles.

'Do go ahead,' Lucy said to her, flatly. 'Eat as many as you want.'

'Thank you,' said Tammy, with her mouth full.

'That's a great drawing,' said Alan, leaning forwards with a grunt and turning it sharply towards him. It was of spindly horses under a tree with red apples and a volcano in the background over which flew a sinister black bird. 'You know, Tabby, in certain New York galleries you could give that a pretentious name and say it's by a recluse and you'd be into five zeroes. I'm thinking of going into that myself, as a dealer. It's called Outsider Art. I prefer the French term: *Art Brut*. Raw Art.'

Tammy looked faintly bewildered.

'Rubbish, in other words,' said Lucy. 'Not that your drawing's rubbish, of course,' she added, rather unconvincingly.

'She's really mad about drawing,' said Sarah.

'I'm not,' Tammy complained. 'It was your idea, Mummy.'

After an embarrassing pause in which everyone smiled, Lucy told them about the lawn. The lawn in embryo. 'I've wanted, since time immemorial it seems, a proper *English* lawn, near to the pool so you can walk onto it off the tiles without lacerating your feet. I've told Jean-Luc that if he can't do me a lawn, with proper soft grass —'

'A lush sward,' Nick broke in, smiling engagingly.

'Exactly – then he'll get the chop. I told him this two or three years ago, by the way.'

'This suggests,' Nick said, scratching his left eyebrow, 'that earlier attempts by Jean-Luc have been *unsuccessful*?' The last word was a hoarse croak.

'This suggests I am remarkably tolerant,' she said. 'Oh, there's always some little problem. The latest is climate change or something. Let us know of the lawn's progress, please. Have you got a throat?' she asked Nick, suddenly. 'The air's very dry down there.'

'Pseudopolyps,' he said, as if admitting to taking drugs.

'Too much lecturing,' said Lucy, sharply.

'Stress. I'm told. Unlike Ferdinand Lassalle. Who painted his throat with silver nitrate so he could carry on lecturing, heroically.'

Lucy frowned. 'Should I know this man?'

Nick tried to disguise his surprise behind a grin, but he was blinking too much: sometimes, Sarah thought, he really isn't in the real world, where no one knows anything much.

'The true founder of German socialism,' he said. 'Unlike Marx, he believed in brotherly love. Killed in a duel in 1864.'

'Good riddance,' chuckled Alan.

Sarah realised, concious of her feebleness, that there was no pulling out. Life was all about compromise, her mother had always said.

'What should we do about the telephone costs?' asked Nick.

'Oh, there isn't a *telephone*,' said Lucy, as if they'd asked about an indoor cinema or a sauna. 'Your mobile will work, but you have to stand on a stool in the bathroom. It's the countryside, you know. Undisfigured by cables. There is an Internet café in St-Maurice, full of saddos. Alan goes there and feels very at home. Don't you, darling?'

'I picked up the mouse and there was this damn *scorpion* underneath,' he chortled.

Nick felt dismayed: he didn't want to admit that, for ideological reasons, they had never had a mobile.

19

'Problem,' said Sarah, glancing at Nick. 'The thing is, we don't have a mobile.'

'Then get one,' laughed Lucy.

'It's rather against our principles. Given our field of specialism.'

'Coltan mining in the eastern Congo,' Nick clarified. The Sandlers still looked puzzled, as if sucking on something tart. 'Mobiles can't operate without coltan, and most of it's in the Congo forest. The local leaders use the revenue to buy arms. A third of the workforce are kids. Slavery, basically. And it's disastrous for the gorillas, too. The Conradian darkness at the heart of the mobile phone industry. Actually, it's also used in laptops and so on, but where computers are concerned I have no real choice, bar going for the more responsible names.'

There was an embarrassed silence in which Nick's own voice echoed in his head, sounding crazed. Lucy and Alan looked at them as if they were vaguely dangerous. There was, in fact, a sleek black mobile on the arm of Alan's chair. Nick banned them from his seminars, and was famous for it. It amused his students: Dr Mallinson's eccentric foible.

Lucy gave a little sigh. 'So the house is no good, then. Well, what a pity.'

They had no choice but to acquire a mobile for the duration of their stay. Purely for emergencies and to receive calls. Then they would bin it, they assured themselves, while Lucy and Alan gazed on them indulgently, as parents gaze on their naïve teenagers.

They were shown Alan's private collection in a locked glass cabinet: these items were not for sale. He put on a pair of white cotton gloves and opened the cabinet and took out a couple of treasures. A ram-headed jug from Ur. A votive cup from Uruk. Around 3000 BC: rescued from the rubble of ziggurats. They weren't allowed to touch. Sarah imagined them slipping out of his gloved hands and falling in slow-motion to the unforgiving stripped pine of the floor: it would only need a jab of the elbow in his large belly.

They were locked back in.

'My precious children,' he wheezed, tapping the glass with a gloved knuckle.

'Iraq,' Nick sighed, hoarsely: like a very distant army's battle cry.

'Great for crooked dealers like me,' Alan chortled, his white-gloved hand seizing Nick by the elbow and shaking it as if it were a cocktail. Nick smiled gamely, too flabbergasted to comment.

Sarah gazed into the cabinet, picturing each priceless pot being attacked by a hammer in extreme slow motion: the tambourine sound of it.

'Are your other children as "well-behaved"?' Lucy asked her suddenly, miming the inverted commas with a waggle of her plum-varnished nails. She was referring to the small ad placed in various highbrow journals, but it took a moment for Sarah to cotton on.

Sarah stroked her daughter's hair. 'Well I'm bound to say yes, they are,' she said. Tammy had red, claw-like felt-pen marks on her cheek. Sarah rubbed at them vaguely, but Tammy backed off.

'Children tend to know no limits, these days,' Lucy sighed. 'Their mothers are too fat to bother. They pass hamburgers through the school railings.'

'We try to establish firm boundaries,' Sarah reassured her.

'Your hair is loganberry,' admired Lucy, a touch wonderingly. 'The teeniest hint of dark red in the highlights. Lucky you.'

'I don't know for how much longer,' winced Sarah, very pleased. Her Indian grandfather had resurfaced in the hair (which she had always considered blue-black), along with large black eyes under smoky lids.

'Actually, Lucy is crazy for young Jean-Luc,' said Alan, as if it had been weighing on his mind. He turned and winked at Sarah. 'Happened all the time in the slave colonies.'

'Give us a break,' Lucy retorted. She said that Jean-Luc lived with his sick old mum. 'He's probably *gay*,' she added, with a peculiar wobble of the head. She gave a start and glanced down at Tammy. 'I'm not even sure he can read and write properly,' she added, floundering a little under the child's stern gaze. Tammy finally opened her mouth and informed her that, in Boulogne last year, they saw a sign on a restaurant that said *French Cock*.

Nick was lying on his back. He didn't move when the others approached from the side of the house. Only his head turned.

'You won't believe this,' he said. 'I've done it again. My back.'

The girls ran up and rolled on top of him, squealing. Sarah had to pitch in physically to throw them off, but this increased the fun. Like wasps, they kept returning: it was like the game they played every Sunday morning, clambering onto the bed and being pushed off. Because of his pseudopolyps, their father couldn't yell at them. He couldn't even yell in pain, not without damaging his vocal cords for good. Instead, he whimpered, pleading with them to stop.

'Daddy's hurt!' screeched Sarah as best she could over their frenzy. 'For God's sake leave him alone!'

They did, eventually. The house looked down on them like an old, disapproving nurse. The boundless view had absorbed the din and was now silent – even more silent than before. Nick lay there under his family's gaze and apologised.

'It's sitting too long in the car,' Sarah said.

'I hope it's not a slipped disc, that's all.'

'What's a slip diss?' asked Alicia.

'What a start,' sighed Sarah.

'I do apologise,' said Nick, drily. 'As a misbegotten blemish on the smooth order of things.'

'What's a slip diss?'

'Is blemish the same as a bee in my bonnet?' asked Tammy.

'Shush,' Sarah ordered, without thinking. 'Try to get up carefully, Nick.'

The children watched, fascinated and a little scared.

'I feel so daft.'

Sarah commanded him not to talk, giving him her hand. He winced and sank back.

22

'Daddy deaded,' announced Beans, pointing at his feet in their sensible English shoes.

'No, *actually* he isn't,' Alicia assured her, with an authority that sounded medical.

'Not yet,' said her father.

'Try rolling on your side,' Sarah suggested. Part of her was annoyed with him. He neglected his body in favour of the head. A terrible start to their stay. She could see herself doing everything, everything. She pushed up her glasses and sighed.

He rolled over and slid onto all fours. '*Now* what do I do.'

'I don't know. Pray to Mecca.'

This made Nick laugh, against his will. Sarah joined in. And they both laughed helplessly, Nick in the evening-prayer position, groaning between the monkey-like yelps. Tears ran down their cheeks as the three sisters gazed on them like indulgent adults.

'I think that's done it,' said Nick, eventually. He stood up in slow motion, stretched his arms above his head, then lowered them. He gingerly advanced a few steps, then stopped, like a waxwork of someone walking.

'Fuck,' he breathed.

The front door was on the side of the house, which made the side of the house the front. There was a dry flower nailed to it, like a big blind eye with golden eyelashes. Sarah slotted the black key into the hole. The door opened directly into the kitchen. Nick crawled in, inch by inch. He was crippled (it was his right hip's swivel joint), but it was an old problem arising from a student drama exercise thirty-odd years ago. It had happened before and usually lasted a week. The only remedy was to lie on a firm surface for as much of the day as possible. It was maddening, especially as the girls' favourite game was to ride him like a horse. He could just about go upstairs, but as little and as slowly as possible.

'This is so incredibly predictable,' he sighed, lying on the rug in the sitting room and feeling chilly under the blanket. 'I'm so sorry.'

23

'So you should be,' said Sarah.

But he still shared in their awestruck excitement, the analysis initially conducted in subdued whispers.

There was a pleasant woody smell in the house, along with a hint of mice. It was cold in a flat, fridge-like way. The sitting room had two long windows facing the front and huge, thick beams. Low-slung sofas which were useless to bounce on, a fireplace the kids stood in pretending to burn in agony like Joan of Arc, a bookcase full of what the Mallinsons assumed would be light holiday reading, apart from the large expensive art volumes, but turned out to host a decent, spine-creased smattering of mainly American and Irish literature, including a Complete Yeats and an annotated Collected Shakespeare bearing cigarette-papers as bookmarks. Lucy, they assumed.

The dining room was across a narrow corridor from the kitchen; it had a huge antique oak table and numerous porcelain statuettes of shepherdesses, clearly valuable. Sarah opened the dresser and saw a small scorpion on the side, its pincers wincing at the intrusion. 'I think we'll give this room a miss,' said Sarah.

'I *love* it,' said Tammy, naturally.

A low door off the corridor led down uneven steps to an interior *cave*, in which some thirty bottles were ranged on ancient wooden wine-shelves, the dark glass blessed with pale dust. The oldest – a Bordeaux – dated from 1982.

'I think we'll give this a miss, too,' said Sarah.

Upstairs had to be described to the afflicted: the bedrooms had white walls which left powdery traces on their clothes if leaned on. The walls were thicker than Beans's outstretched arms (Tammy tested her protesting form against them). The windows only opened inwards, which meant nothing could be put on the sills: this struck Sarah as bad design. There was a sweet little table in the bedroom, painted yellow and stencilled with grapes, which she earmarked for her desk. The small room at the back, with its miniature window overlooking the pool, could be Nick's den: it vaguely reminded her of his book-lined outpost at college, dark and woody.

24

Right at the top was the attic, reached by a narrow wooden staircase and lit by a dirty Velux: it was huge, bare and dusty, with old newspapers from the 1940s and 1950s, a box of pine cones, some venerable spindle-shanked spiders, a heap of dried bracken, a crate of bottles, and nothing much else.

After hauling everything out of the car with almost no help from the girls, Sarah began to prod the kitchen into life. It was long and had a butcher's block flecked with saw- and blade-marks, with a tell-tale depression at one end where the cleaver had worked over generations. Stools stood round it. There was what Sarah termed a 'catering-industry sink' of stainless steel, deep enough to drown someone in. Apart from the large fridge, there was a small, independent freezer. There was no dishwasher, amazingly.

No one had cleaned the house in preparation, as had been promised; or not in the last few weeks. The attic spiders' comrades were evident in all of the rooms, but the industrial-sized hoover dealt with them briskly as the girls watched, pretending to feel sorry as the frail, unsuspecting forms were whipped away by the hoover's grin.

Sarah was fed up, despite being here. Her fed-upness was deeper than travel weariness. For eight years she had bustled from one toy-strewn, high-decibel environment to another, sitting on rugs while infants battered her head with bright moulded plastic or flung themselves from side to side in her lap while she tried to engage in grown-up speak. Now, despite Nick being freed of commitments, she was still the domestic skivvy.

To her husband's annoying commentary (he now lay prone on the longest sofa), she prepared the fire with balls of the *Daily Telegraph*. There was something propitiatory about coaxing flame, she thought. Above the fireplace was an African mask fringed by hundreds of hammered-in nails that Tammy identified as its beard; it made her mother think of a mournful Victorian with mutton-chop whiskers. They were unable to identify its provenance. A crack went through one eye, blinding it; the upper lip was chipped and worm-holed.

'How's it going?' Nick asked, yet again.

He had brought along a Complete Sherlock Holmes for diversion and now he was working his way through it, tale after tale, interspersed with the odd dip into Habermas.

The room was opaque with smoke. Beans coughed. Alicia copied her. Tammy outclassed them.

'I think there's a blockage,' Sarah said, peering up into the flue.

'If you don't mind me saying, you need to use smaller bits at the beginning.'

'Crap. Girls, that's enough or you'll end up like Daddy.'

'Oh, what a dreadful fate,' groaned Nick, genially.

They would have to phone Jean-Luc, but not straightaway. They didn't want to look helpless. The girls went upstairs and carried on coughing: it was fun pretending to be tubercular.

The volume control was dicky on the telly and the reception was poor, but the old video machine worked. The girls eventually sat down on cushions to watch Postman Pat driving up and down his Yorkshire hills and dales while Nick dozed and Sarah leafed through *Exciting Things To Do with Nature*, an old-fashioned book she'd found in a jumble sale. She'd pictured the girls turning branches into animals, painting pebbles or making pomanders out of oranges and cloves. She could have done all these things at home, of course, but there was never enough time and Nature wasn't quite what it used to be, somehow. Now there was bags of time.

The girls settled with difficulty, bouncing about on their beds and then promptly getting scared the moment the light was switched off. Even Tammy was scared. Without the shutters closed, it was as black as ink outside, the stars glittering through rents in the cloud. At home in Cambridge, comforting yellow streetlight defeated the curtains, accompanied by the ambient wash of urban noise.

Only one of the bedside lamps worked, and Sarah briefly assumed the intricate skills of a film-lighting engineer, moving it about on the floor until a compromise was reached and they were neither dazzled nor plunged into gloom.

Tammy was allowed to read for another twenty minutes. She was very bright: even (at least in reading and writing) a 'prodigy'. She had finished *The Sword in the Stone* and was now deep in a book about the sea and had reached the chapter on tide gauges. Her parents' chief terror was that she might run out of books, as an aquarium shark might run out of meat. She reassured them that she could always consume what she'd already digested: following her starring role in the school version of the *Odyssey*, she had read T. E. Lawrence's translation twice. Although not all of its meaning had sunk in, it had given her many useful words: 'steading', 'wainscot', 'cleave', 'merchantman', 'perforce', 'bloom'. She did not mind a third go, if the spine held out. Or a ninth reading of *The Jolliest Term on Record* by Angela Brazil, near to disintegration on the top of her pile, and which had Grandma's name written inside in italics. Or a second of *The Myths of the Norsemen*, a thick old book which had belonged to Daddy and had frightening black-and-white illustrations.

'You looked so like a horrible monster doing that, Mummy,' she declared, idly flicking the book on the sea to find her page. 'Like at Hallowe'en.'

'Nightie-night you lot,' Sarah said, having smothered their soft, smooth, sweet-smelling cheeks in kisses. 'Sleep well.' She was trying her best to sound dully managerial, despite suddenly feeling full to the brim with love. She marvelled at the beauty of their lustrous fair hair, a blondeness that was temporary because their eyelashes were dark. Tammy's was already turning – autumnal, Sarah smiled inside herself.

'Like a skelington,' Alicia lisped, pushing her bedding down to her waist. The word *heronshaw* was embroidered on her nightie, a cream garment reminiscent of Edwardian illustrations. She lifted it up to reveal a rather corpulent stomach. Sarah was trying not to be too worried about Alicia's roundness: Tammy was bony, if anything, while there was still something minia-turist about Beans (three weeks premature).

27

Who now picked up the word 'skelington' and repeated it with an ear-shattering shriek.

'All you could see was your mouth and glasses,' Alicia went on, sitting up in bed and pulling the duvet back to her chin. 'Like really thin people.'

'Like ghouls,' Tammy added, relishing the rare chance to use the word, and stretching the syllable as taut as it would go.

Sarah had another bash with the fire. Until she succeeded, they'd all have to wear thick sweaters. Smoke curled over the plaster chimney piece, curved like a huge clamshell.

'No luck?'

'Some of it's going up.' Her upper body was fully in the fire-place, twisted to look.

The small heap of tinder suddenly caught, flaring like a miniature oil-well. Nick gave a hoarse shout of warning. Sarah scrambled out and ticked him off for 'panicking'. There was soot streaked over her face, like a rescue worker's. The little blaze sent its ghostly fingers of smoke creeping up over the chimney breast and past the long-suffering mask. The room was hazed once more: gauzy levels wavered under the ceiling as though the two of them were submerged.

'I never panic,' Nick said, closing his eyes. 'I simply react.'

TWO

When the Sandlers bought the property back in 1995, the interior of the house was all orange: orange beams, orange joists, orange plaster. Orange beds, orange cupboards. Orange doors. It had been a hippy colony for a while, was the explanation. But they had fallen in love with it, and with the view. A *coup de foudre*, according to Monsieur Soulier, the bespectacled estate agent – with the customary hint of wonder, as if he had never seen such a love affair before in the whole of his life. Far more serious than the orange paint was the ivy, its knuckles dug deep into the stonework and straining even the capstones in the arches, but he kept quiet about that.

He had shown them the house reluctantly, insisting they wouldn't be interested, that it was too old and remote: an abandoned farmhouse, empty for years. 'Almost a ruins,' he insisted in his office, in his decent English. '*Almost* a ruin,' Lucy Sandler repeated. 'Like being *almost* avant-garde.' '*À peu près*,' laughed Monsieur Soulier, with a rocking motion of his hand. He didn't tell them that the Germans – the Waffen SS, no less – had burnt down part of it. You never knew what might put people off.

Monsieur Soulier waited for the end of the three-day search, when the evening light would be gilding the ivied walls. He showed them, with great enthusiasm, three modern villas of mounting ugliness, climaxing in a musty bungalow with a huge plate-glass window like a fish-tank, concealed behind a cypress hedge near the public toilets of a village *stade*. He cultivated an air of bemusement at their reaction. Then he drove them up the winding road to the Mas des Fosses, like an angler reeling in a fidgeting line, shaking his head all the while.

It had reared before them in the golden dusk, ivy-clad and impossibly lovely after the horrors of the afternoon. The door-less front looked out upon misty blue mountains and a glow that was the light bouncing off the Mediterranean. A forested hill rose behind, stuffed full of evening birdsong – including nightingales. Monsieur Soulier kept looking at his watch and pulling a face. He squealed open the shutters as best he could, apologising for the musty smell more than for the orange paint. Monsieur Soulier reacted to the huge, ghostly barn owl that flew at them in the kitchen as if he had never seen it before. Then he showed them the outbuildings – with a comically overdone air of shame. The barn, strewn with mouldering hay, revealed a threshing-machine, wine-barrels, hung tools cocooned in cobwebs, a two-wheeled carriage and a farm-cart with massive spoked wheels. Monsieur Soulier shook his head mournfully. On the end of the line was a very fat fish. All he had to do now was reach out his hand and grab it.

'It is normal they demand for so small a price,' he lisped. 'It is a complete ruin. And twenty-three hectares of savage land! Who wishes for that?'

There was only one snag, apart from the house's unfortunate recent history (about which, as about the fatal grip of the ivy, he also kept very quiet): a young French couple from Normandy wished to farm it traditionally, with the help of a grant. Organic mushrooms and onions, he believed, with a *gîte d'étape* for walkers. The paperwork was finished, the *compromis de vente* was to be signed the following week. But of course the owners were open to negotiation.

'Then we'll negotiate,' said Alan, with a relaxed smile.

'We want it,' said Lucy, who was tall and could look down on Monsieur Soulier's bald patch.

'But the young couple . . .' Monsieur Soulier began, his fingers all but touching the cool, scaly flesh.

'Can go to hell,' murmured Alan.

The scaffolding stayed in place for at least five years. The roof had lost many of its old, mossy tiles over the two decades of abandonment, and the subsequent rain damage was serious. When it rains in those dry mountains, the Sandlers were told, it can do so with a ferocity that is unequalled except in tropical areas subject to monsoons. The equivalent of half of Paris's annual precipitation might fall in a few hours, gouging craters in roads, turning paths into streams, swelling rivers, swirling over bridges, sweeping away houses and people, bulldozing heaps of cars through village streets with a strange grinding and groaning that, once heard, is never forgotten. Three of the main beams were, in places, indistinguishable from wet peat. An expensive red crane was hired. It became a part of the landscape, visible from far off; folk in their dotage will still recall it in decades to come, Lucy joked.

The picturesque ivy had made such appalling inroads that it was, to all intents and purposes, keeping the house upright. Alan compared it to his grandfather's hernia belt. An expert was called in, more expensive than the crane. Everyone underestimated, he said, the destructive powers of Nature, the need to keep her at bay. He gestured with his smooth hands as he described where the concrete had to go, tons and tons of it, keeping it tight. The house is a web of stresses and strains, he said: the beams and the walls are mutually interdependent. Ironically, Monsieur Soulier had been right. Even the orange paint was a stubborn distemper.

And the price they'd paid was, to any local, the stuff of madness. There, Monsieur Soulier had been misleading. But that price paled into insignificance before the cost of restoration. The house gobbled it up. Fortunately, business was brisk for Alan Sandler, dealer in antiquities: Sumer and Assyria and Babylonia.

Around 2003, there was a sudden glut. A pity, he would think, the site at Uruk was guarded, these days; but there were plenty others that weren't. And in any case, who was doing the guarding?

By the time the Mallinsons arrived, only the finishing touches were lacking. The crumbling drystone wall around the farmyard.

The pool's surrounds. The English lawn. All the province of Jean-Luc.

'Oh. Who's that man?'

The way he just carried on standing there, watching them, not moving from the edge where the big flat area in front of the house fell away in broad, grassed-over terraces like steps into the valley, made Sarah uneasy. She tried not to act uneasy. She was sure he was perfectly normal.

'*Bonjour!*' she called out, heartily.

She and the girls were returning from their first great voyage. They had taken their new 'sabbatical' camcorder and climbed the slope at the back of the house, through laurel-like bushes with glossy foliage and into the woods, proceeding through deep drifts of leaves fallen from trees they couldn't identify and deafening themselves with the rustling, and then on into a denser, darker forest of holm oaks interspersed with granite outcrops. Not being able to make headway through this, they'd turned back to join the main track. It narrowed and curled up and up through skeletal-looking chestnut trees in great skirts and swathes of more dead leaves (in which Beans all but disappeared), only to dip through a scented hollow of very tall pines, the ground soft with needles.

Tammy had asked if there were wolves in this forest.

'Probably!'

It almost helped that Nick wasn't with them, but she didn't dwell on that: Sarah felt truly happy at last. In the bright, low, prismatic light, the pines fell away to a bare moorland area of springy grass and rocks that dropped steeply down on one side, revealing a patchwork of orchards and meadowland, with a tumbling stream at the bottom which had pretensions to river status further along, snaking mercurially between creamy shoals. The steep hills on the far side of the valley – she called them 'mountains'– were draped in a dark-green pelt of woods, relieved by smoke-coloured patches of something deciduous and bare. There was a black streak they assumed was a fire's scorch, and the odd *mas*, the odd little fleck of humanity, with a refractory air of silent resistance under its barrel-tiled roof. Nothing else. They were entranced, even stupefied.

'There's too much space,' Alicia had cried, twirling about on the summit of a rock.

The rocks were great granite lumps inlaid with hornblende and feldspar, spattered with lichen and dried mosses. The mosses felt like toothbrushes. On some the moss was really velvet, Tammy noted, cloaking the boulders' northern flanks.

'We have to show poor Daddy how beautiful it is,' Sarah said, filming Alicia. She swung the camera round to catch the other two. Beans hid her face, which was annoying. Sarah panned slowly over the landscape and back to Alicia, still prancing on the pocked summit in which tiny pools of rain reflected the sky like eyes.

'Be careful,' her mother had called, conscious of how unyielding granite was, how unlike the woodchips under the climbing frame in their boring Cambridge park, its liminal safeties. Sometimes she would see her chosen discipline, history, as a park. No, as a curious kind of wedge, a carved artefact stuck in a nameless, aimless and boggy wilderness. It was all about limits, in the end.

Right now, however, back in the yard – back in the place that already, after three days, felt like home – she was wondering who this man was. There was also a very battered green van, its back doors fastened by rope. The children had stopped skipping about and watched guardedly as the man came alive and approached. He might have been a teenager in his long-limbed awkwardness against the light. He aged as he neared them, like a speeded-up film: his close-cropped hair began to grey over the temples, and the lines around his mouth deepened. The peppery stubble darkened a chin that looked as if it had been punched to one side and poorly reset. Or replaced entirely, even, his whole face reassembled from different bits, like a potato man with plastic stick-on features.

His grip was strong and very rough – Sarah felt this as soon as he shook her hand, explaining that he was Jean-Luc, the *jardinier.* Lucy had called him the 'handyman'. Large but rounded shoulders he didn't quite know what to do with. Early thirties, maybe. Bags under his eyes that added another three or four years. At this rate, he would soon wither and crumble to dust like an old apple.

Sarah's French was quite good, but Jean-Luc's syllables were tumbled along by the local accent like pebbles in a fast-flowing stream. He also had a faint stutter. She nodded, standing there and catching whatever she could, like a primitive freshwater mollusc waiting for whatever crumbs of sustenance flowed past.

One thing was clear, however: it would be better if no one walked on the area seeded to grass. The Sandlers must have their English lawn. Sarah turned to the girls and instructed them never-ever-ever to go on *that* area there (pointing, wagging a finger). '*Ils seront interdit, strictement,*' she laughed. They had walked all over it already: he must have been able to see that. The sprinkler system worked at night, he said, pointing to the yellow spider in the middle. As he talked, the children stared at him; they followed the grown-ups around in a little knot.

He began to clean the pool; that's what he was here for, today. The girls sat on the tiles and watched him. He didn't look at them much, he seemed slightly discomfited. He had an extendable rake and a net on a bendy pole. Sarah wondered with a sagging feeling if he came every day. She asked what the white object on the side was and he told her with a snort that it was an alarm, required by European law. It detected any sudden disturbance of the water. If the water was *perturbé*, for instance by a child falling in, its siren went off. Jean-Luc was raking the water while explaining this, so the machine was clearly not switched on. Sarah wondered aloud how it was *activé*. She could see the child dropping down and down like a plumb bob without a line.

Jean-Luc looked at her, puzzled. Then he pronounced something entirely incomprehensible: it could have been in Hungarian. The only major word Sarah recognised was '*anglais*'. He gestured towards the woods and pointed up at the surrounding hills then

34

back to the pool, as if '*les anglais*' came lumbering in heavy hordes out of the wilderness. Well, they did, in a way, at the purchasing rate (she had read this in a *Guardian* article that began with 'Sacré bleu!') of fifty thousand houses a year.

She felt good they were only renting. She would have liked to have revealed their meagre academics' salaries, their modest house with structural problems off Gwydir Street, distancing herself from the wealthy Brit hordes. Instead, she folded her arms and nodded sympathetically, his French weaving a pleasant web of foreignness around her.

She told him the chimney didn't work. It never has worked, he said. He was pouring in liberal quantities of a liquid from a large plastic canister marked *ALGICIDE*.

They went inside to have a look, Sarah carefully explaining that her husband suffered a bad back and had to rest for a few days on the sofa. Embarrassingly, he was lying on the floor under a blanket with his eyes closed and began talking before she'd had time to signal Jean-Luc's presence.

'The apposite phrase is helplessness,' he groaned. 'Which fatally encourages introspection. And envy of those able to embark on inspiring walks. Go on, tell me. I'm incredibly cold down here. We haven't even managed a bloody *fire*.' When he opened his eyes and saw Jean-Luc standing there with a shy frown, his face was a picture of astonishment. And by the time Jean-Luc had bent down cautiously to shake his hand, Sarah found herself burbling in a French that had completely disintegrated into sitcom Franglais, while fluttering her hands.

However, once Nick had levered himself onto the sofa, apologising profusely, he did a much better job than Sarah at the oral comprehension. Nothing could touch Nick's brain.

After Jean-Luc had left, his sharp sweaty smell lingering in the air like a faint reproach, it was all explained. There was a code to activate the pool alarm, but Jean-Luc didn't know the code; the Sandlers would. The fireplace was useless, but Jean-Luc would try to sort out the smoke problem (Jean-Luc had a key to the house, of course, which made them slightly uneasy). Even when the code was found, the alarm couldn't be switched on at night because of the boars, who came down to drink nocturnally. The water would be thoroughly perturbed, Nick added, grinning.

Sarah was startled. 'The boars? What, real boars? Or boring locals?'

'*Sangliers*. Wild pigs, with tusks.'

She clapped a hand to her forehead. 'I thought he was saying *les anglais*. I thought he was saying that loads of English people came in the summer and perturbed the pool by swimming in it, but I couldn't work out why he was getting so excited.'

Nick laughed, then clutched the sofa.

'Anyway,' Sarah said, 'we can switch it on until we go to bed. The kids aren't going to be on walkabout at night. Are you? Eh, you lot?'

They were too absorbed in *Thomas the Tank Engine* to reply.

'There's one slight drawback,' Nick sighed. 'If a burglar falls in and perturbs the pool by drowning in it, it's the owners' responsibility. The victim's family could sue them. Or *any* night visitor. A drunk, for instance. According to Jean-Luc.'

'The gospel according to Jean-Luc,' Sarah said, drawing a cross in the air. 'We won't *get* night visitors,' she added. 'No one's going to be perturbing us out here.'

The champagne bottle was found hanging inside the chimney a couple of days later, concealed from everything but a two-year-old's sight-line. Beans squealed with delight and thought it was a rorqual. That was what her word sounded like and no one took any notice of her bobbing on the polished slates of the hearth in time with the repeated word until, trying to concentrate on colouring in, Tammy investigated.

Sarah found it disturbing. 'What's he done that for?'

'No idea,' said Nick, from the sofa, as Sarah gazed into the darkness of the flue.

'It's hung on a wire,' she reported. 'Maybe it's a local tradition. A welcome.'

He must have hung it up early, while they were lying in. Sarah didn't like this idea at all, that Jean-Luc had been creeping about downstairs while they were all asleep. He did have a key, of course. They weren't sure whether to light a fire, it might crack the bottle, but she lit one anyway, feeding it old, cork-like logs scattered about in the barn. The fireplace smoked less. In fact, the bone-dry wood made it blaze ferociously, billowing a surprising degree of warmth over the room.

'Clever,' Nick commented. 'I think the bottle's creating some kind of mini-vortex.'

'Clever old Jean-Luc,' said Sarah, grappling with two Duplo pieces that had got stuck together. Beans clambered into her lap and stared at the fire, the moisture in her eyes glittering.

'Fireguard,' Sarah said. 'Add it to the list.'

'Along with firewood,' said Nick. 'I romantically assumed I'd be gathering firewood myself. Another delusion. It's getting rather long, our list.'

'I do think the Sandlers, for the amount they're charging, could have supplied *that*,' said Sarah, separating the two pieces at last, but splitting a nail in the process. Alicia said she didn't need the arch now, and turned to her doll, a black infant called Moppet.

Tammy's head was cocked over the Tate Britain colouring book as she kept perfectly within the complex of hem on the Tudor lady-in-waiting's dress. She asked, with a kind of weary air: 'Do you like this place, Mummy?'

'Of course I do, Tammy,' Sarah replied. 'I think it's very special. Don't you?'

'Sixteenth century or earlier, this house,' Nick chipped in. 'Same era as your colouring-in person.'

Tammy contemplated her work. The pretty young lady-in-waiting's face was a drinker's puce. She picked a dark blue for the dress.

'It's sort of a bit crazy,' she said.

'Crazy? The house?'

'A bit.'

37

'Only because you're not used to it, Tammo,' Nick said. 'It's a question of adaptation.'

'Rorqual,' said Beans, absently, tiny chin in tiny hand.

The fire had stopped blazing and smoke was once again seeping out.

'Maybe the bottle's a fetish,' Nick suggested, adjusting his head on the sofa's arm.

'What's a fetsheesh?' asked Alicia.

Tammy snorted at her ignorance, although Nick's reply surprised her with a new definition.

'Something they use in Africa to protect a village or a house or a person,' he said, gazing up at the old beams. He loved old beams. There were several magnificent specimens here, whole tree trunks barely squared off, with patches of bark like callouses.

'That's a fetish,' said Sarah, nodding at the one-eyed mask above the fireplace. 'See all the nails? It's not just his beard. Each nail's a kind of wish, like when you cut a birthday cake.'

'Poor thing,' said Alicia. 'Bet it hurts him.'

Tammy snorted again, even more derisorily. 'You're a living quirk,' she said, sadly shaking her head as her felt-tip worked its way up to the curving black line, like an incoming and unstoppable tide.

When Sarah had first attended Dr Nicholas Mallinson's lectures in her third year, she heard him use the term 'Festschrift' – cleverly, out of its usual context. It was his way to describe the territorial carve-up of Africa after Germany's defeat in 1918. 'The white man's Festschrift, printed by himself and stuck up in schoolrooms all over his various empires.' Or words to that effect: the image recurred in his published essays. She had no idea what that key, repeated word meant, and had noted it down as *fetish?*. When he became her supervisor the following year (after her top First), this tiny rent in her knowledge was still unstitched. He used the word again, in a discussion of what she was planning to do for her PhD, and she asked him outright what it meant. He was amazed.

'I've got these gaps,' she had said, blushing. She pulled her skirt forward over her black tights, wriggling like a schoolgirl. 'When you first used it in a lecture, I heard it as fetish.'

He had laughed. So had she. She was on top of things, with everything still to play for. She didn't yet know what a PhD was like. She had a vague crush on Dr Mallinson, imagining long discussions about Fredric Jameson or Michel Foucault, about the abolition of the historical oppositional metaposition or the demise of class analysis before jumping into bed. Then he'd leaned forward after a long, lingering moment, tossed his fringe aside and said, 'I'm thirsty, Sarah. How about we do this over a jar?'

And here they were now, with their children, a reasonably normal family with a small Victorian terrace back in Cambridge whose thin walls, built on a former cesspit, were cracking in half. The only house in England that hadn't been printing money just by staying upright: Nick had bought it twenty-five years ago, when Gwydir Street was impoverished and bohemian, suiting Nick's then-granitic Marxism, which remained like a worn, half-forgotten stele in the folds of his mind; like the embarrassing ponytail he'd abandoned after a year, but which he was always threatening to resurrect. An area which, though now full of earnest, middle-class couples like themselves and with one of the most active Natural Childbirth Trust groups in the country, plus a green-tinged steering committee committed to local issues who met over organic food in the family pub, and in whose expensive streets could be heard the faint drifting, like thistle-down, of evening piano practices, he still saw as impoverished, bohemian.

She had just got back from checking the post: they'd decided to do this two or three times a week, but there wasn't a lot. In fact, there was very little apart from the odd good-luck post-card. It was a lovely jog, though, if a touch oppressed by the thick holm oaks either side; when the sun wasn't out and glittering on their leaves, they went a kind of dark and foreboding grey-green.

Alicia was jumping off the windowsill over and over. Tammy sat on its twin, looking through the dusty pane; Beans was asleep in Sarah's arms, clutching her bottle. She was still on the bottle, but not on the breast. The breast was over. Soon there would be school for Beans. School, university, work, children, work, retirement. Sometimes Sarah felt she had stalled at the university stage. That the day she'd walked in to Nick Mallinson's room was the day the spring had started to unwind. A wholly unreasonable reflection.

The house had draughts that knocked on its stable-like doors. There was a certain scruffiness about it, apart from the dining room; a certain calculated impoverishment in its internal furnishings and equipment. A plump old radio with dicky dials; a lumpen-grey dialling type of phone that was, of course, unconnected; the old video machine and defunct television; a dusty hi-fi that only hissed. Sarah admired the dog-scuffed sofa with its lovely patchwork throwovers and the soft, lumpy easy chairs: the type that were impossible to buy, that were only inherited, squabbled over. Even the refurbished kitchen was full of rejects – knives with chipped handles, a cracked salad bowl, forks with verdigris on the tangs. One bottle-opener, a single piece of metal, like something out of a cracker. And the African mask, although possibly priceless, would have looked at home in a flea market. Lucy's taste, she thought; not Alan's. Lucy was definitely class. Only the flashy modern prints from her gallery looked vaguely awkward, although hung crookedly on the uneven walls. One was all orange with a tiny spot of red and the word *verdure* in splashy white letters. It drew Nick's eyes to it, for some reason. He found it comforting.

Alicia banged her head, inevitably, on the top of the window-space as she stood on the sill ready to jump. She held the hurt in concentrated silence, working out whether the pain dancing on her skull would fade. Of course, it didn't. It got worse, wedging itself in. Out of the silence came the cry, furious and sorrowful.

'Stupid girl,' Tammy said, as if reading her mother's unspoken words.

Beans stirred from whatever half-state she was in and dropped the bottle. Tiny spots of milk shimmered on the floor. Alicia's bawling had no scruples: it swept them all up indiscriminately and deposited them on a steel platform out at sea.

Sarah suggested she stop. 'Don't make such a song and dance, Alicia.'

'Shut up,' said Alicia, suddenly, out of her arrested clamour. 'I might have be *died*, Mummy,' she explained, making Nick's heart give a little salmon love-leap.

'Oo-er,' he said.

'Don't think so,' said Sarah, as Tammy laughed. 'You look very alive to me.'

'Doide,' said Beans, pointing at Alicia with wide-eyed certainty.

Sarah handed Beans over to Nick as if the child were still a baby and went upstairs to the loo. She sat on the wooden seat and felt a goldenness rising through her body and popping in her mind, as it would during childhood holidays in Wales with the horses in the field behind and the cat that slept in the lane. She was with her friend Madge and Madge's mother, not with her own parents, and she went there three years running and there was Madge's brother Mark and his school-mate Rolly, and that's when, aged eleven, a boy had first tried to kiss her and succeeded in the lee of a hedge: it was Mark, in fact, the experience marred only by his brace. And that's when, aged twelve, she'd sat on the quay at Llangranog nibbling a sticky chunk of honeycomb, discussing horses with Madge, or perhaps love (or what passed for love at that age), and thought life could only get better and better.

Alicia's wail began again, and she could hear Nick's rumble of a voice like a hoarse foghorn, telling her to stop. Sarah couldn't help resenting the guilt she felt, but it made no difference. This guilt was no one else's fault but hers.

That night, Beans woke up and afterwards Sarah lay awake

for ages. Nick snored gently. Otherwise, everything was quiet, that amazing quiet of the deep countryside in a country big enough to have such a thing. She crossed the landing to the loo again and heard a strange sound, a sort of insistent, repetitive brushing. She opened the small window and the noise grew louder.

She poked her head out into the clear, cold night. The sprinkler was turning and turning, a sporadic arc of glitter in the moonlight, sweeping the dark seed-bed. The pool was an ingot of silver, a wedge of mercury.

Oh, she felt good. The thought of all those long-dead engineers' unread reports made her heart rise. They would be spotted with tropical flies, holed by African moths. Their dry texts would be a voyage of discovery under her gaze, revealing the wonders beneath. To analyse was to dive deep in a pressure-suit of intelligence, to uncover what no one else even knew was there. Alertness and wit.

What was that? That sudden hump of a shadow? It crossed the brilliant pool on the bottom edge and vanished. The window knocked in a gust, echoed by the door on its iron thumb-latch. A branch? The shadow of a branch? Moonlight was so strange, so blue and tricksy, in its pure form. She shivered and hurried back to bed; Nick's warmth welcomed her like a summery bluff over a cold tide and she was asleep within minutes.

Alan Sandler was on the lavatory when the phone went. Ever since Syria, two months back, he'd had a gippy tummy and a bad skin complaint. He was expecting a call, an important call – as usual. He rushed out of the lavatory clutching his trousers to his groin with his left hand, grabbing at the cordless with the other. Sometimes Lucy would not replace the phone and he would track its muffled ring tone until, too late, the message service triggered. He would invariably find it under a drift of Lucy's material, the wild, silkscreened patterns hemmed up with pins. This was a sideline of Lucy's, her hobby, an offshoot of her dealing in modern prints. She even had exhibitions now and again: great drapes of cloth like frozen breakers, or rect-angles of silk pinned austerely to the walls, like paintings.

'Yeah? What?'

He sounded gruff. He *was* gruff. It impressed the clients. It made him look as if he was fielding several phone calls at once. It made him appear in demand and that he didn't really need the work. What he felt like saying into the hush was, 'Yeah? *So?*'

It was someone whose name he didn't recognise at first. Mallinson? Nicholas Mallinson? His memory was faulty. It was the malaria, or maybe the curse. Years ago, when he was dealing in Central African stuff – village after remote village wangled free of its sacred fetish, a chief or a chief's relative bribed and the worm-holed, ancient, ivory-fanged mask safely in his arms in the jeep, or swaddled next to him on the Pan Am plane bound for New York, mute and powerless – this guy had cursed him. So the guy claimed: a witchdoctor in flared flannels and with halitosis. Or maybe, if he took this particular one-eyed mask, *he would be cursed*. It was all in pidgin French. He took the mask.

He never stole anything, not outright. He *worked* to prise the stuff free. At times he worked alongside the God Squad, their beaming faces offering the snap judgement of the Lord instead of the slow, unnerving mysteriousness of the bush spirits. How could the natives refuse? Sucked free of its magic, the hidden ju-ju stuff was so much junk. Then it became art, pulsating with the glow of money, even before it had been dug out from its earth or hut or wherever it slept between cere-monies. How many curses had, in fact, rained down on his head? Not one of them so effective as his recurring malaria from that time in Dahomey.

Africa! He'd given up on her, on equatorial Africa. Wars, disease, corruption. It was Conrad minus the exciting story. You only have one life. So he closed down his gallery in Los Angeles and joined Lucy in London, turning his sights on the Arab lands.

Iraq. A goldmine for a year or so after the invasion. Now it was, frankly, debauched. The dealers – American, Arab, Indian, whoever – were lewd. Bloated on their riches. Some of them with half a museum in their safes and boxes. Old Saddam hands as middlemen. Clumsy, careless handling, as if the goods were plastic – or someone's limbs. Alan was not happy with the situation, it made the hairs sit up on the back of his creased, sun-flayed neck. That was why he was waiting for it all to settle down, for the snoops to lose interest, before dealing any more of his Iraqi stock. Two little gypsum worshippers from Tell Asmar, a white marble head from Ur, an ivory plaque from Nimrud, a stunning alabaster statuette of Astarte, goddess of love – along with some Babylonian cylinder seals from East Berlin that had crossed the wall a few weeks before it fell, like so much else. Coming up to five thousand years old, most of it. It was his investment, secreted in a metal box in the smallest of the cellars in the French house. Every day he expected a call from some newt in the Foreign Office, making enquiries.

So when he heard this Mr Mallinson's well-spoken English voice, Alan Sandler was momentarily hauled up by his nerves. When he realised who it was, and what it was about, he quoted poetry and yelled for Lucy.

Lucy had never really liked children. She'd had Walter and Suzie as adjuncts to her life as an artist, gallery owner and agent. She was always determined that the twins wouldn't 'take over'. Her first husband, Neil, was wealthy enough to enable them to be packed off to separate boarding schools at the age of seven. Now they were thirty, amazingly, and more trouble than when they were small. Suzie was an intensely miserable aid worker whom the Red Cross flung into places like Bosnia or Rwanda or Sierra Leone or Chad or post-tsunami Indonesia with a kind of cold, Swiss relish. After the Congo, over two years ago, she'd had a complete breakdown and Lucy had had to look after her. Suzie would not describe what terrible things she had seen over her Congolese stint, only admitting to their 'banality'. Chop chop. It was the 'banality' of the chop chop that had got to her. She sat about and smoked incessantly and laughed at inopportune moments, which led to ructions with Alan, who had only come onto the scene after she'd left home. Walter was either off heroin or on heroin in Vancouver, of all places. Whether off or on, he was a pain, writing long and rather poetic letters on yellow feint-lined paper that rustled and demanded an answer she felt unable to give, or give adequately.

Now these people, these tenants, were asking her for the code to the pool alarm. This ridiculous piece of EU-sponsored machinery was only purchased to avoid the Sandlers getting involved in tedious litigation. Its sole purpose, she felt, was to provide extra dough for some EU minister's business-crony: namely, the manufacturers of this apparatus. Now, apparently, it was required to work. If a burglar or local yob (not that there seemed to be real yobs in France) or one of those horrible hunters fell in and drowned, and the apparatus wasn't actually functioning, the chances were good of being screwed by the vindictive, money-grubbing family of the deceased. She half-suspected the locals were plotting to push in unwanted relatives deliberately, just to get the dosh off the wealthy foreigners. Smelly grannies; mumbling teenage simpletons. Peasants were like that.

The alarm had operated once, on the day it was installed, and made one of the most horrible sounds she had ever heard, leaving her with tinittus for a week. It was an insult to the glorious peace of the place. It was yet another attempt by the EU flunkies to destroy whatever opportunity remained of a decent quality of life beyond the European 'norms', which she always witheringly referred to as 'normans'. The invading European 'normans' to match the immigrants and their mafias. It was laughable. So she had ordered it to be switched off – shouting at Jean-Luc over the hundreds of decibels – and entirely forgotten about it.

Now this Oxbridge professor was badgering her to get it up and running, whereas only two or three years ago it would never have occurred to him because such things didn't even exist. One had a pool, one splashed about in it, one kept half an eye on one's progeny, and that was it. But no – the normans of this world were in charge. Creeping into every crevice, into the very interstices of the grain, where primitive fear lurked and a childish lack of responsibility rejoiced. It was like vaccines. Measles was actually good for you. You couldn't guard against every danger, or why live at all?

So she fobbed him off. It was somewhere in a drawer, she said. Really, she had no idea there was even a code to punch in.

'Sometimes, Alan darling, I think *you* might need a code to punch in.'

Alan, half-asleep in his chair, grunted. She twirled her third malt in her long fingers. There had been a very attractive young man in the gallery this afternoon, wearing a homburg and an equally retro coat. He was taken with the 'hydroelectric' sequence of prints by Philippa Wanberg-Ketch – faint, cutaway diagrams of inner organs superimposed on hydroelectric plants in silhouette with scribbled German words in pencil underneath. She had desired him in a straightforward, lustful way, imagining wrapping her thighs around his face, but he had remained imperviously young and himself. She was past it, at fifty-eight. Even the face-to-face gymnastics of it all.

She hoped that was the last of it, from the tenants. At least for a month or so. The whole point was for them to take over, to chivvy Jean-Luc, to enable the Sandlers (or at least, her) to take a break from the worry. The house was a big, ramshackle ship battered by storms; it apparently needed continual attention. It was vulnerable, far more vulnerable than they'd imagined. They had spotted the cracks on their first visit, even through the romantic ivy, and the estate agent had laughed dismissively, although you could have put a hand into one of the fissures if it hadn't been for the spider-webs in it. It's been there for five hundred years, he laughed, I don't think it's about to fall down now. Liar. The moment they'd signed the deeds, it started. It started to crumble, to weaken at the knees, to go all effeminate. Even the lovely ivy was catastrophic, wedging cracks wider with its hideous, nobbly strength. Of course, houses fell down like cliffs if you didn't continually maintain them, seal them, succour them.

And that poor, wretched man had slipped off the roof. What was he doing up there, when it was still wet? Why had they needed to replace the whole roof, anyway? Because half those great, immortal beams were rotten. The house had claimed its victim. Now and again she thought of him, over the six years since it had happened, seeing his face grinning at her, his deep-voiced dishiness above the blue overalls, his lithe body and huge hands that she had trusted with the work, with the walls and the roof. With their bolt-hole from London. Their refuge. Pure man, he was. One of those big Roman noses like Serge Gainsbourg's, rakishly broken on the bridge.

'Our marvellous builder's gone and had an accident,' was how she'd put it to friends. 'Oh?' they would reply, not very interested. 'Yes. Out of action. We'll have to find another one. We'll have to go all the way down there and start the whole process all over again. Meanwhile, the rain's coming in.'

Hardly anyone knew he had actually died. And so, oddly – at least until the widow started trying to blame them for her husband's carelessness – *she* didn't really know it, either. It remained a kind of abstraction. She refused to go into the village cemetery to check – that would have been morbid. And so sometimes she wondered if it was all another French ruse, a way to screw money out of the foreigners – that one day she would meet dear wotsisname, Raoul, walking down the village street, or strolling with his gun in the forest, and say, 'Bad luck, didn't work, did it?' But as time went on, and it dwindled into the past, she believed in it more and more. It became this concentrated point of intensity in her life, a point so tiny she could mostly avoid looking at it. And then suddenly, in the middle of the night, it would drift into view and she would wake up all but crying out in a kind of blind terror, as if she were the one scrabbling for a hold on the wet tiles, slipping inexorably towards the verge.

'I told them it was in a drawer somewhere downstairs,' she said again. 'Alan. The code. For the pool alarm. Alan!'

'OK,' he replied, nodding in his chair, his double chin like a spotted cravat on his chest. He scratched at his belly through the shirt. Something in Syria – maybe a prawn in Damascus – had given him this skin complaint. The doctor had examined his face and then asked him to lift his shirt and had proceeded to write his doctorish name in the skin of the belly. It was exfoliating as they watched. Crumbling away. *Cantab.*, the doctor added with his nail-pared finger, grinning.

'The young,' she sighed. 'They're so frightened of it all.'

There was a pause, embroidered by a faint police siren.

'He's not that young,' Alan pointed out, suddenly alert. 'I didn't even know it had a code.'

'Like a security door. Like a safe. Do you have to scratch? It's all over the sofa.'

Alan smiled. 'I need to put the cream on. The steroids are no longer working. Maybe it was the CIA. Or the Saudis. Maybe I've been poisoned. The radioactive Russians.'

'Alan, don't be so romantic.'

He chuckled indulgently. Nevertheless, he was afraid at times.

'I think they're going to be fussing,' said Lucy, with a sigh. 'They're that type. I asked about the cherry tree. He's going to investigate. I can't really believe Jean-Luc hasn't planted it.'

'Planted what?'

'The cherry, you oaf! I kept reminding him. It was one of his priorities, along with the lawn. He should have planted it in the autumn. Do you have to slump? Being an ex-ballet dancer, I don't know what it means to slump. We'll have to have a word, face to face. At some point we'll have to descend.'

'They're a nice English family,' murmured Alan, not moving, one eye half-closed like a toad's. 'They're genial. Filled the house up. An empty house attracts the wrong people. We agreed. We don't want that Trot mayor snooping.'

'If one of them drowns, clever boy,' said Lucy, leaning forwards tipsily, 'the police will come. It'll be in the papers. As with Raoul.'

Alan grunted and said, 'The guy didn't drown.'

Lucy's mobile rang.

'My Lord, no, wow, *frightening*,' was all she appeared to say for ten minutes, in various combinations.

He'd been offered two silver Assyrian lions the size of his thumb by a dealer from Dubai this afternoon: their provenance was dubious. He had said 'no-no', as he had said 'no-no' to the scarlet ware jar from Khafaje, *c.*2900 BC, because in two minutes he had found it on Google under 'Stolen Treasures from Iraq'. The place was an El Dorado no longer. Or at least, it was now minimally patrolled. Bedouins with guns guarded Uruk. Deadly guys. Dealers could be undercover agents. Sites were still getting bulldozed, but the guys doing it were terrorist killers, they were way beyond his remit. He may have to wait years before releasing his stock – releasing it piece by piece, like a leaked report, an elimination so gradual no one would notice. Geological erosion. The silt of gain. Vases, cylinder seals, statuettes. That white marble head of a woman, the most beautiful woman he had ever seen, five thousand years old. He was in love with her, this woman from Ur. She hovered over his dreams. You just had to *imagine* the half of her nose that was missing.

Suspicion was the watchword. He would sit it out, as still as death. Lucy came off the phone, looked glazed.

'You know what the Chinese say?' growled Alan, barely moving his mouth, his body still slumped like an overstuffed dummy's. 'Or used to say when they were civilised? *Have patience: one day the grass will become milk.*'

'Oh the Chinese,' said Lucy, coming back to life. 'Now there's where we're *really* talking scary.'

'He didn't recognise my name,' said Nick, up on one elbow on the sofa. 'He was basically unfriendly. He doesn't know anything about an alarm. He called it "the watch-dog's honest bark", twice. Is that Shakespeare? Sounds like it. He didn't strike me as the literary type. Anyway, she's phoning back. Lucy Sandler.'

He confirmed that he'd been recognised eventually. *The people renting the farmhouse. Your place in France.* Then Alan Sandler had whooped, as if relieved. 'Oh, it's the *genial* family!' he'd said.

'Oh,' Sarah sighed, wondering if there was irony in this; 'I thought you meant he didn't know who you were at all. I'd have felt really weird, if he hadn't known you at all. They did say to ring, didn't they?'

She remembered Alan saying as they were leaving, in a loud and hectoring tone: 'It's called le Mas des Fosses, but I call it le Mas des *Fesses*. You know why? Because it's in the butt of beyond.' And he gave a big American roar.

'*Fesses* means backside,' Lucy had explained.

'Oh I know,' Nick had assured her.

Lucy then gave him the keys; the main key being black and enormous, like something stripped from a steam engine.

'There won't be,' Sarah recalled her saying, 'but if there are – problems, I mean – don't wait.' They were descending the porch steps. 'Mobile, if I'm not in. Just buzz.'

Sarah also remembered the fuzzy, hemmed-in image of the house she'd had then, the impossibility of imagining themselves there at all. And now they *were* there. Here. A simple translation in the mathematical sense. She'd be in Sainsbury's right now, feeling anthropological. Or trundling Beans through the Grafton Centre in a short-cut to FitzHerbert's, navigating huge dogs and hoodies, beleaguered under the endless thrash of what passed for public music. Or walking back home under the grey lid of an East Anglian sky, negotiating the cracks in the pavement with those wretched little pushchair wheels swivelling backwards at every opportunity.

Nick was wondering aloud why Alicia had her giant, inflatable hammer down in the sitting room. It was called Boris. Boris was a present from Alicia's half-brother, Jamie – difficult Jamie giving the difficult present for Alicia's fifth birthday. It was not only enormous, this hammer – almost the size of an adult – but undeflatable. Jamie, apparently at Alicia's request, had dripped Superglue around the nozzle so that the hammer wouldn't 'die'. Alicia used it mainly to bash the rest of her family on the head with; Tammy put up with this only because she found it quite fun pretending to have a serious head injury – keeping up brain damage for several hours and frightening her sister until she'd plead with her to be normal. Alicia had insisted on bringing it, which involved dismantling ('deconstructing', as Nick put it) the luggage-stuffed car at the last moment. 'Insisted' was a euphemism: Alicia's wails made passersby pause, wondering whether to call the police. The hammer grinned through the rear window all the way down like something out of a Jacques Tati film.

Alicia now lay sprawled across the hammer in a star shape, thumb in her mouth.

'She's not doing anything with it,' Sarah observed, sitting with a shopping list in the scruffy wing chair by the smouldering fire. 'She's promised to be very careful.'

'I'm *sure* she has,' said Tammy. She turned a few pages of the Tate Britain book and reached Holbein's *King Henry the Eighth*. She studied the black-lined, colourable version, its appetising white spaces.

'Shut up, or I'll hit you wiv it,' mumbled Alicia around her thumb, staring at the ceiling.

'Blairite,' Tammy replied, reaching for her father's arsenal of insults. 'Tory by another name.' She toyed with 'Porkie' but decided that would bring down trouble on her head. Alicia was on the podgy side.

'By *any* other name,' corrected her father, already deep in a report about Chad, his favourite subject.

'Please, kids,' said Sarah. 'Beans is trying to nap.'

'Not,' said Beans, from under a blanket on the rug. Sarah crouched over onto her hands and rested her lips for a few seconds on the silken cheek under the wood-shaving curls. A tell-tale smell emanated from the blanket's recesses.

After a few minutes Alicia made a raspberry noise as she propelled herself and the giant hammer in a circle with her feet, catching the colouring book and sending the felt-tip pen's reposed progress awry. The King's face had a green streak across it, now, leaping from the half-done collar like the record of a massive earthquake. Tammy stood up and, with the colouring book, began to hit Alicia about the head, silently, with the stapled end first. The victim made a squealing noise. Sarah told them to stop, as ineffectually as ever.

Nick crawled out from the kitchen. He was crawling more easily. They hadn't even noticed him disappear. He had one half of a plastic blue salad-shaker wobbling on his head. 'Here's the UN,' he cried, in a silly voice. 'Here's the UN come to save the day. Stop quarrelling! Be nice to each other! Oh, please do! I'm the UN!'

The helmet fell off his head and bounced and then rolled to Tammy's feet. Only then did they laugh. Nick's face was bright red and his thick grey hair was wild behind his ears. He neighed and whinnied. His pseudopolyps were already better, along with his back.

Now he stood up, inch by inch. '*Et voilà*,' he said, towering above them at last. 'All is not over with the republic.'

'Excellent,' said Sarah. 'Just in time to change Beans, my Caesar.'

Jean-Luc hoovered the pool, which was now less green near the surface but was opaque towards the bottom. The girls were sailing their boats of stick or leaf and had to stop. The wide-snouted monster had a long, flexible neck that travelled to its squat body confined to the shore. It cruised beneath the girls' frail craft, stirring the muck; it was famished and deadly. Jean-Luc smiled at them as they tried to tell him about the toad. His mouth was as wide as the monster's, and his teeth were crooked and probably never brushed.

He didn't take them seriously. They went *ribbit, ribbit, ribbit* in unison; he didn't understand. Tammy ran into the house but her father was on the mobile in the bathroom upstairs. She asked her mother what 'toad' was in French. Sarah searched through the drawers in her head and came up with '*crapaud*'. Tammy laughed, not believing her, and checked in the French-English dictionary for confirmation.

By the time she'd made it back to the pool, Jean-Luc had finished. No toad, it seemed, had been swallowed. She was out of breath.

'Crappo?'

He laughed and shook his head. '*Pas de crapaud.*' His singlet smelt of sweat, with a patch on his back the shape of Chad.

She went back to the house with her sisters to look for more words in French that sounded rude. Their father came downstairs as they entered the sitting room; he was holding the mobile. He turned to Sarah, reading in the chair.

'She claims she's remembered that the code's written down on a piece of paper in a drawer, somewhere.'

'Somewhere. Oh. Grrr-rreat!'

'And I've got to ask Jean-Luc about a cherry tree.'

'Are we allowed to look in *all* the drawers?'

'The ones downstairs.'

'Can I?' yelled Alicia.

'Fine,' said Sarah. 'And supposing it's upstairs?'

They opened every drawer, downstairs, pulling a few right out to sift through on the floor. Nothing that might have been a code. Scraps of paper with numbers on that Alicia squealed at, but they were telephone numbers with country codes and names. Sarah went especially carefully through an old clerical cabinet in the hallway. Some of its twenty drawers, small and square but deep, smelt sweetly of wax. In most there was nothing more than rusty clips and drawing pins. A scrap of serge with a set of needles stuck in. An epaulette trailing black thread, as if torn from its owner's shoulder. The usual ephemera of trapped insects, reduced to tiny black knots or varnished hulls.

They did find a few maps, including an official one of the property from the 1930s, showing the extent of the farm's *terrain* and the buildings marked in italics with their functions: *grenier, bergerie, poulailler, écurie, remise, soue, pailler, maison principale, caves*. Several of these had disappeared, mostly sited where the charred stones now lay. It was an entire universe that had vanished, in the end, with all its voices, its sensations, its smells. Stretch out and you touch it, thought Sarah.

They checked the attic and Nick got caught up in the old yellowing newspapers, redolent of the war and *l'après-guerre*. There was a strong breeze outside and it whistled in the roof, as if someone was trying a tune through their teeth.

Sarah hauled him down to help her poke through the five *caves* under the house: one of them was fastened by no less than two combination padlocks, which was intriguing; Nick reckoned it was the passageway down to the centre of the earth. The others, dusty and unlit, reached by a few stone steps from the outside, were full of rustic rubbish and rather heavy scuttling noises.

'This is bonkers,' said Sarah, back in the sitting room. 'I mean, to buy an alarm and not even know how to use it. They're just so incredibly casual. Like the non-existent heating system. Did she sound as if she cared?'

Nick reflected for a moment. 'No,' he admitted. His hands were dusty, although he hadn't scrabbled about that much.

The girls watched another video over tea, Alicia draped over Boris the inflatable hammer as Thomas and Gordon puffed up and down the branch line, bickering like lovers. It was four o'clock. The hammer's toothy mouth looked stretched back in pain as Alicia's bulk made the trapped air denser, squealing the taut plastic. They had all got up late this morning, their parents letting them bounce around on the high parental bed.

'It's Sun – day – to – day,' Alicia had announced, bouncing on the unsteady mattress.

'It's Tuesday, in fact,' said her mother. 'It just feels like Sunday. We ought to start classes soon.'

'That'll be fun,' said Nick, without irony, stroking Beans's hair as if it were a pelt.

Tammy asked to be pushed off the bed. Sarah pushed her, but not hard enough.

'*Push* me,' she insisted.

Sarah gave her a shove and immediately tried to grab her as she fell backwards. Of course, Sarah thought to herself: they are cats. They fall backwards and land on their paws. All part of the weaning process, to shove them off the bed to the ground – from where they will always clamber back, laughing like pretend ghosts.

'Why did you try to catch me?' Tammy demanded, nursing her wrist, which Sarah's Duplo-split nail had scratched. The whole point was to let them go and let them fall.

She snatched a few moments on her own after hanging out the washing. It was a perfectly clear day. The light was almost severe and certainly pure. Nunnish, she thought. Sacred's better. An infinite blue hazed into haloes of a green-tinged white along the gauze rumple of the hilltops. The sun was warm – almost burning – on the back of her neck. It was delightful. The whole thing was delightful. She felt as if she were being carried tenderly by the sacredness, her entire body uncoiling in the day's arms as she knelt by the pool: the contentment of sunlight, the silence, the hints of earthiness in the clear air and the shifting shapes in the pool water. The smooth, warmish tiles under her hands. It was all so simple, really: happiness.

After tea, the girls went outside and played at the front, with an order not to go round to the back on their own.

Their parents were listening in the kitchen to France Inter on the old Sixties radio with dicky dials. This was intended to be a teatime routine, to loosen up their hidebound French. Now and again it was France Musique or even France Culture. It took some getting used to, after a unique diet of Radios 3 and 4. It was like visiting a trendy, younger aunt with a smoky voice after the comfortable, older one called Beeb who gave you your favourite biscuits and poured unsurpassable tea from under a knitted cosy, wittering on about her cats one minute and Kierkegaard the next. Blasts of rock or jazz interrupted the trendy aunt's earnest discussions: she lived in Paris. The more intellectual she got, the more they understood. Nick and Sarah had great fun with this simile.

Today she was discussing Tadeusz Kantor. Whenever she grew particularly Left Bank, whirling her outrageous beads, they looked at each other and sniggered. The air was thick with the smoke of imaginary Gauloises. Words ended on a sigh.

Meanwhile, outside, Alicia was chasing Tammy around on the rough, gravelly area in front of the house. She was slowed down by her shorter legs and by Boris the inflatable hammer, although Tammy tantalised her by adjusting her speed or stopping altogether for a few seconds. Beans was stacking pebbles near the big pine tree with fierce concentration.

Tammy had stopped by one of the windows – catching her breath while Alicia was momentarily distracted by a sharp gust of wind that had hauled the inflatable from her grip. A noise grew in the corner of Tammy's eye and for a fraction of a second concealed the view and her sisters in a dark flash. She was too surprised to cry out, let alone move.

An explosion, like the giant snapping of a jaw.

The huge black vehicle, as it disappeared up the track, reminded her of Sophie Cartwright's four-by-four, always nearly squashing them in the playground as it delivered its golden gobbet on fat legs, and which had now been banned, like the taking of photos, from the school grounds. Beans had vanished. Tammy saw the green shoe, small and rubbery, but not the owner. She assumed she was run over, and frowned.

She had not caught up with the moment; she was still in a dream of it.

Then she saw Beans emerge from behind the big pine tree. She was sucking her thumb in fright: she had not been killed. She'd run away at the first sound of the vehicle, her shoe falling off. Tammy could hear the beast crashing away up the track as it climbed the slope behind.

Alicia stared down at the torn remnants of her inflatable.

The wheel had gone right over it and it had burst. Hammer Boris was no more. He lay in surprisingly tiny fragments, shrivelled and torn.

'Mend him, Mummy,' she ordered, tearfully, after an account had been given to their mother in the kitchen: a din of overlapping narrative chords obliterating the earnest voices on the radio.

'There are certain things you can't ever mend,' said Sarah, with an air of significance. She felt more disappointed than shocked, partly because the girls tended to embellish. 'Are you sure it was going that fast? I can't believe anyone would go that fast with kids around.'

'Completely crazy,' said Nick, who had been enjoying the Kantor discussion, having known nothing about him.

'Stupid Jean-Luc,' said Alicia.

'It wasn't him driving, was it?'

'Of course it wasn't,' Tammy said, the possibility having never occurred to her. 'It was a manic. Jean-Luc's not a manic.'

'A maniac. And it nearly ran you over?' she asked, with an ironic, unbelieving air.

'Beans was almost raspberry fool,' Tammy confirmed, breathlessly. 'Me too. Alicia wasn't, she was miles away. Just as well or she'd have made a real fat mess.'

Alicia glowered at her. 'I was nearly gnashed all up to bits,' she said, 'more than *you*.'

'We'll have to complain,' said Nick, turning the dial on a whiplash of static, reducing the child-free aunt to a mutter.

'Who to?' Sarah asked, rhetorically. 'It'll be just like at home with our feral youths.'

'Spoilt yobs, you mean. That's different.'

'Feral youths' was usually an expression other mothers used, not Sarah, which was why she'd given it an ironic colouring. It meant not being able to go to the local shops after dusk. It meant hurrying past the bus shelter and looking the other way. Sarah liked the word 'feral'. Maybe because she suspected that a universal state of feralousness (was that a word?) lay just round the corner.

'Stupid *cars*,' said Alicia. 'Why do we have to *have* stupid cars?'

'A dose of the real world,' Sarah sighed. 'How really depressing.'

'*Course* we have to have cars,' Tammy groaned, shaking her head in despair.

'Ah, but not necessarily,' said Nick. Unexpectedly, like a bubble released from a lake-bed, a perfect globe of happiness popped in his chest as he looked at his girls. 'The internal combustion engine was never historically determined, in fact. Not much is. The whole disaster, in this case, goes back to the moment James Watt tightened the last bolt on his steam condenser in a damp yard in Glasgow. Blame the Scots,' he added, jovially, turning to the young and lovely woman he loved and was bound to for life by these three perfect ribbons.

But the girls had already wandered back to the sitting room, where they were noisily pretending to be squashed.

Three gooey splats on the sofa.

THREE

Jean-Luc Maille taps the nails into the doll with exquisite delicacy, using a glazier's hammer. Tap. A navel. Tap tap. Another nipple.

The doll is tiny and legless and half-bald, a little bigger than his thumb. He found it in one of the Sandlers' cellars last year when he was digging into the crusted layers of goat dung for garden fertiliser.

The doll lay in a spread of straw and ancient dust on what he guessed was a kind of oven: a great slab across two stone uprights next to the fireplace.

This cellar at Les Fosses has a fireplace in it, and two waist-high stone basins embedded in the walls, so worn that the bottoms, where the water ran out long ago, are wafer-thin. The floor, once he'd dug down to it, turned out to be cobbled, not tiled. He knows that makes it very old, maybe as old as the Romans. It hasn't always been a cellar, obviously. It was once a house, carved out lower than ground level to keep an even temperature – warm in winter, cool in summer. It still keeps an even temperature. Maybe there was a whole village up there. Or at least a hamlet. All gone, now.

Jean-Luc lives with his widowed mother in the main street of Aubain, the commune's principal village of some three hundred souls – two hundred in winter. Their house is slotted into a row that dates back to the Middle Ages, but which has suffered so many vicissitudes – burnings and floods and rebuild-ings – that their skew walls face the thin street with a kind of dun amorphousness, an ashen neutrality not helped by the odd, garishly painted set of shutters. Jean-Luc's shutters are varnished the colour of chocolate: his late father's taste. On the front door is the cardousso flower his father nailed there for good luck thirty years ago: dry as cigarette paper, it beams on the street like a very old and gap-toothed sun. Jean-Luc won't touch it: it is the only defence against all the dark forces of bad luck.

Like the others, his house has one continuous staircase with a worn lino runner. It rises from the kitchen to two pinched rooms on each floor, without a corridor to join them. The door straight ahead in the kitchen opens to the little backyard and stepped garden – the households used to cultivate the hill's terraces: onions, potatoes. The bathroom also lies off the kitchen, housed in a lean-to put together thirty years ago by Jean-Luc's father, Elie Maille, out of breeze blocks roofed in transparent corrugated plastic, tinted a urinous yellow.

For almost all of his thirty-six years, Jean-Luc has had to pass through his mother's room on the first floor to reach his own. Except for a year in the army when he was eighteen.

He's had a dream for years: to clear one of the attics, insulate it with plasterboard, and knock out a window under the eaves. His mother thinks he's mad. During the storm in October – the storm that drowned twenty-five people in their *département* and washed away hundreds of homes – the rain poured down the slope at the back and Jean-Luc had to open the yard door to let it through. The kitchen became a turbulent pool, emptying out into the street through the front door, where people were wading up to their knees. There was that much water it bunched up on the roof and moved uphill, seething under the cover tiles and finding every crack in the rafters, sheeting through onto the stuff stored in the attic, welling on his own ceiling and leaving brown tree-rings of damp. The house still stinks of damp. His dream will have to wait until they can scrape enough together to sort out the roof. The insurance won't pay for that. And Jean-Luc hates heights. He can't do it himself. He'll just feel himself being dragged over the edge. He can hardly climb a ladder beyond a man's height without it turning his head. Look at what happened to Raoul Lagrange, who wasn't even scared of heights.

Aubain lost its school and its shop back in the 1990s, and

its café hangs on by a thread. The bread van and the butcher's van come round twice a week, hooting in front of the church. The farmer, Edouard, his vegetable stall a meeting point for the gossips every Saturday morning, has had a row with the mayor and no longer comes. The row was over the one euro the *mairie* wanted him to pay for parking his big van all Saturday morning: it was because he was a commercial enterprise, it was the law, it was not them being cussed. A matter of papers, forms, ticking boxes. Edouard left in a rage, one morning. He was never coming back, on principle. He was a sodding charity, *putain*: he was up before dawn on his land and got nothing for feeling knackered all day. The women drifted away, resigned. The mayor organised a weekly trip to the supermarket in Valdaron, using the *mairie*'s clapped-out minibus driven by Serge, under whose seat rolls a perpetual bottle of half-consumed local red.

The village is all but dead. This annoys Jean-Luc. He blames the foreigners, the second homers. He blames the Parisians. He blames all those who profit at the expense of others. But he keeps this rancour to himself. He has never been to Paris. He doesn't see the point.

The legless doll has a hole each side of its groin where the hips swivelled. It's like a Barbie but much smaller, it fits on the palm of his hand. Shreds of what might have been its clothes fell away as he was blowing it clean in the Sandlers' main cellar. It has starry blue eyes and long dry dusty hair on one side of the scalp, exactly the colour of meadowsweet, and a rosebud mouth like a pimple. He guesses it must be old, maybe from the 1950s. He was startled, and not a little frightened, once he'd taken it out into the light, to see a tiny rusted nail embedded in its head, and another in its pointed right-hand breast, just where the nipple would have been.

He took it home with him.

He makes sure it is kept hidden from his mother. Since she's pretty well bedridden, this isn't difficult. Sometimes, however, she'll recover her strength for a day or two and hobble about the house on a stick, bothering him, back to her old nagging

61

self; a short barrel of a woman and very powerful again. Today she is definitely unwell. Or at least weak. When he's tapped four more glazier's nails in, the last in one of the miniature hands, he puts the doll in the cardboard box under his bed and unlocks his door. Apart from Oncle Fernand, this lock is all that keeps him from going insane. He likes the feel of the key as it turns and slots the bolt into place: he is back in his own realm. She can shout through the door as much as she likes.

She is dozing. She dozes a lot, these days, especially in the afternoon. A nurse comes round twice a day and deals with her legs and other more intimate areas that Jean-Luc doesn't want anything to do with. Her room has the close sweetness of a sick-room, like sticking your nose in a mouldering bowl of fruit, along with something medical. He creeps past her and goes down-stairs. Despite the creaks of the floorboards, she doesn't wake up.

He was worried that the hand would break, but it didn't. It's a different kind of plastic, better quality than nowadays. Tapping one of the nails into the left-hand breast, matching the other, was extremely satisfying. It was something about the tininess, the deli-cacy, the beauty of it against the fatness of his thumb. The tit's sharpness, like in the old films. The way the old-fashioned film-stars' tits were always sharp and high, as if offering themselves, as if asking to be stroked and – unimaginable delight! – kissed.

That's enough, says Oncle Fernand.

It is nearly time to eat and his mother will soon be calling him. She's a stickler for keeping time, even though time for her is an unrolling nothingness, a boredom between dawn and dark, dark and dawn and dark.

The clock in the kitchen shows a quarter to seven. He unwraps a Marie frozen lasagne and shoves it in the microwave. Sometimes he pretends he's made it himself. When his mother has one of her good days, she rustles up something nice; he goes out and buys vegetables and fresh meat and soon the smells fill the house as in the old times. And he loves her for it. He'll watch her hobbling about the kitchen and love her all over again, every-thing sizzling and bubbling away as in the old days. The most he can rise to is broccoli, and then he always overdoes it. He's always liked broccoli, but in his clumsy hands it turns to mush. And yet he can hammer tiny, pin-size nails into a doll. The true artisan, my boy!

Jean-Luc blows on his lasagne. The microwave makes everything too hot and for too long – the plate, the meal, the innards of the meal. He keeps burning his hands on microwaved dishes, on the underside of a cup's handle. But there is no point in using the oven for a Marie meal, it isn't worth the time and the electricity. He's watching Marie-Sylvaine Vidal's show on M6, *Tout N'est Pas Entre Nos Orteils*. The clever gabble allows him to forget his own silence. It is all rubbish, what they are saying, but it allows him to forget. And he fancies the presenter: she has a dark mole on her left breast, just above the low-cut top, that his eyes are drawn to. She flaunts it, this little fault in her perfection. She flaunts everything, she draws millions of eyes to her and loves it. Each week her outfit is a little more daring and then, suddenly, she'll go all prim, like a Catholic schoolteacher, with a lace frill at her neck. That's good, because the next week she'll have a plunging neckline you can almost bury your head in. She'll lean forward, laughing at some stupid joke one of her stupid guests has cracked, and Jean-Luc will all but crane his head to see deeper down into the shadows of her cleavage.

It is Marie-Sylvaine Vidal in *Tout N'est Pas Entre Nos Orteils* that he imagines whenever his little frog begins to swell its cheeks, wanting to croak. He travels out, out and away into her long, naked arms on her tropical island under the coconut trees. Apparently she is off with some junior minister. A bloke in a tie and jacket and shiny black shoes, poncing in and out of some government building in Paris. He has to throw this ponce off a cliff, in his imagination, before travelling to see Marie-Sylvaine on her private, palm-fringed beach. Every time he has to boot him over the cliff, hear his screams. The crunch. Stamp on his fingers, sometimes, as they clutch the edge. And Marie-Sylvaine thanks him. She hates being what she is on the telly. Laughing, grinning, gabbling on about nothing, about nothing at all. Putting up with her ugly, greasy guests that hardly anyone has ever heard of. That's why she loves me, Jean-Luc thinks. She can be herself with me. Completely natural. And when I kiss her mole on her left breast, she strokes my hair and says, 'I love you, because you love my faults.' Even Oncle Fernand approves. And she kisses his frog each time, amazed at its size.

His mother is calling him. They've had lasagne already this week, and she is not happy having it again. It was the same story last week. Each week is a rerun, like the films on telly.

'There's nothing else in the house,' Jean-Luc always tells her, placing the tray on her lap. She lies against the pillows like a shipwreck.

'You don't think ahead,' she moans. 'Men never think ahead. If it wasn't for my legs, I'd go shopping myself.'

'No shops,' Jean-Luc always reminds her.

Tonight was just the same, almost word for word. His technique is to stay calm, to sound bored. He blinks at her from behind an impassive stare. She can't get him worked up: it increases her sense of paralysis. Her legs are swollen, her heart dicky, her body filled with damage. But her mind races. She's always been robust, efficient, active. She carried a yoke on her shoulders with a bucket at each end up the slope to water the top field every day, when it was all potatoes, years ago. Fifty years ago.

But to Thérèse Maille it isn't fifty years ago. It burns in her mind as if it happened last week. The field is no longer theirs. It was swindled out of them by the Lagrange family in 1982, who built a house on it and made loads of money after the Maille family were told by the old mayor that it wasn't building land.

She burns with rage in her bed: it scorches the pillows, her rage. Then come mornings when, suddenly, she knows she can move, and she is out of bed and limping about, elated. Then the damage returns, she feels her body being swallowed up by it, her legs won't communicate with her head, she feels exhausted again just sitting up in bed. But she's never lost her appetite.

She'd eat and eat, if she could. But Jean-Luc can't cook. He just brings her rubbish. At least that's stopped her getting too fat, because she's hardly able to stomach it. She reviles it. Factory food, she calls it. Pigswill. No taste. No goodness.

'Yes?'

Has she called him? She must have nodded off. 'I feel like an orange,' she says.

'There's apples.'

'No oranges?'

'I'll get some tomorrow. I'm going to Champion tomorrow.'

'I'm stuck with an apple then. Cut it for me. My teeth won't take it, otherwise.'

'Yes, Maman.'

'You're like a robot,' she says, grinning. 'That's what you're like. A robot. What are you watching downstairs?'

The noise of television laughter underneath them, like the rumble of a lorry filled with imps. Jean-Luc seems to be considering it.

'The news,' he says.

'The news? It's not time. They don't laugh on the news.'

'Then why ask, if you don't believe me?' says Jean-Luc, as he takes the gleaming plate away. Its mush of lasagne has been wiped clean by the hunk of bread that has also gone – swallowed up like everything is swallowed up, in the end.

Maman asks him about the English people up at Les Fosses.

He has brought her the apple cut in eighths, white newish moons that are already browning as they rock on the plate in a circle. He bought a crate of them a month ago, fifteen kilos for ten euros, and has kept them in the stone shed in the yard, but they're looking faintly wrinkled now, like amputated bollocks. There are loads of them left. They were off Monsieur Bernard's trees. He'd been hoping his mother would make an apple pie, but she's been up and about too little since he bought the crate.

'The English people are nice,' he tells her.

He knows this will get her going.

'Nice? How can they be nice?'

'Just because someone isn't French, doesn't mean they're not nice.'

'It's not that. The English helped us in the war. It's that they're friends of the Sandlers.'

He sees the English woman briefly appear in his head, but not clearly. Staring at him beside the pool as he explains about the boars coming down to drink and setting off the alarm. Nice smile. Bright black eyes, like a squirrel's or a bird's. Small and slim, not plump and red-faced like the other English. Dark hair loose, if a little thin, naturally curled below the ears. Not blonde and bobbed like Marie-Sylvaine Vidal's.

'Maybe they aren't friends,' he says. 'Just tenants.'

He is chewing on an apple himself. He peeled the skin carefully in one spiral with his Opinel, then bit into the flesh. They look tasty, but aren't so good in the end. The skin lies like a bedspring on the plate.

'Why don't you cut it up, Janno?'

'Cut what up?'

'I've never seen anyone peel a whole apple then eat it. It looks queer. It's too white. It makes me feel like making the sign of the Cross over you, I don't know why.'

She laughs her hoarse, weak laugh. She has already swallowed all of her apple sections. She often asks him why he does this – a hundred times in his life, if you count it all up. That's why he enjoys eating an apple in front of her. The part he most enjoys is popping the core in his mouth and crushing it with his teeth. It sets her own teeth – not that she has many real ones left – on edge.

'You'll get appendicitis doing that,' she says.

'No, Maman, I'll get an apple tree growing out of my arse.'

He's lying in bed, now. He has managed to coax the image of the Englishwoman out from the blur of inattention and given it flesh. He isn't sure of its accuracy. Her face has a soft, motherly vagueness apart from the gleam of the eyes: an elder sister's lack of definition. He's always been envious of those with elder sisters, like an extra mother; not having a brother, older or otherwise – or a younger sister – doesn't bother him so much. He might have ended up with someone like Marcel Lagrange! Marcel's boy, Serge, although almost as nasty as his father, is quite a few years younger than Jean-Luc, so he can't picture Serge Lagrange as an elder brother. A younger brother, maybe.

Imagine: he might have been buried in brothers, like the Lagrange family. Big, vicious brothers (not that the Lagrange brothers are all vicious, of course; but the vicious ones dominate, most of all Marcel – and the nicest of them, Raoul, is dead). He's better off, being on his own. There's no one to nag him, to hit him about the head. To kick him out of bed.

But he wouldn't mind a soft, kind, gentle elder sister. Marie, she'd be called. He indulges in a brief fantasy in which Marie, looking very much like his memory of the Englishwoman up at Les Fosses, is reading to him at bedtime. A picture book. Stroking his forehead, because he has a little fever. He even hears himself whimpering. In fact, it is more than a little fever. He is very ill. He is possibly dying. No, he *is* dying. His invented sister, Marie, cradles him, lies in his bed next to him and cradles him in her arms. His face is buried in her nightdress, he can feel the hem of the neckline against his mouth, the smell of her warm, brown flesh. But he won't die; onto his brow fall her salt tears, and her tears have healing properties. Marie's tears cool his brow, dribble down over his cheek to the corner of his mouth, where his parched tongue licks them and feeds on their saltiness. He is already recovering, miraculously, although Marie doesn't know it, she is weeping over him silently, weeping for her little brother, squeezing his hot form to her soft and giving body that smells of talc and strawberries and sweat in the dim candlelight.

Jean-Luc gives a shuddery sigh as he lies there, the sheet drawn up to his chin, his head straight on the bolster; a faint smile has settled on his face, its eyes closed and staring up into their private dream. When he opens them, he is back in his own, unsatisfying present. Oncle Fernand hasn't talked to him properly for days. Just a glance now and again, a rattle in the throat.

The bedside light is on. His eyes creep over the walls. Years ago, so long ago he can scarcely recall it happening, his father smoothed the rough walls and hung patterned paper. The paper has faded, its green splashy dots now blue, its red zigzags a fleshy pink. The water from the leaks in the roof crept down and found its way into his old bedroom, carrying with it tannin from the chestnut beams; so now there are dark vertical streaks along two of the walls, some of them making it all the way down to the lino, like long icicles the colour of dried blood. His eyes can't help straying over these streaks: they are like faults in his own life, somehow deathly. They say: no matter how hard you try, we'll dirty you. We'll smear your dreams with our shit-coloured filth.

One of the streaks disappears behind his old, black-and-white poster of Johnny Hallyday, its trace visible on the paper as a raised, cancerous welt that cuts right across the pop star's face. He's still where he always was, in the same narrow bed with its oxidised brass rods, staring at the same poster he'd stare at as a youngster. And he sees in it decay, his own decay. He is thirty-five. Or is it thirty-six? His elder sister would have known his age. Marie would have known. He could have buried his face in her body and still remained unblemished, completely inno-cent. The Englishwoman looked at him as he was talking by the waters of the swimming-pool; a lovely, lost expression he can't quite recapture in his memory, her eyes shyly sliding away from his. So very different from the way most women look at him, with their hard, closed faces; or mocking faces; or faces filled with only one animal thought. Her look was not like that. He struggles, lying there in bed, to recapture it. He switches off the light and curls around the expression, nestling it back into life.

But he can't. He sees the green, leaf-crowded water and his dipping rake more clearly than he can see her. But this doesn't bother him; the English family are there for six months. He will have plenty of time to fix her in his mind. An expecta-tion wells up in him at the thought of it. He can go there whenever he wants – every day, if needs be.

'Marie,' he murmurs, stroking the cool, hard bolster between his fingers as he has always done, even as a child: 'It's all right. I'm well again. I'm right as rain, Marie.'

Sarah spotted the plaque first.

They were on their way to the nearest weekly market: there was a Champion supermarket recommended by Lucy in St-Maurice-de-Cadières, the nearest proper town (which she'd affectionately called 'Saint Morris'), but one of their aims was to shop small and local. Supplies were very low after several days of meals, including the freezer-kept bread. They'd been in virtual retreat, like monks or nuns. It was the first time they had gone anywhere and it felt adventurous. Nick's back was much better, he just had to avoid sudden movements. They had decided not to bring the camcorder, as it would make them look like tourists.

The car was bumping and swaying along the track between the house and the lane when she noticed the plaque, discreetly embedded in a flat-topped stone.

'Look, what does that say?'

'It's a milestone,' Tammy suggested, having recently done a project on the Romans, bringing back a vitrified, paint-splattered lump meant to be the Pantheon and returning to school on Monday with a detailed felt-tipped map of the Forum at her parents' insistence.

'Kilometres in France,' said her father, peering forward at the track as they struggled on.

'I was only joking,' Tammy fibbed.

'We'll stop and check on the way back,' said Sarah, pushing her glasses up when they didn't need to be.

The market was in Valdaron, about fifteen minutes' drive away. There was a broad and surprisingly green river-valley in the hills which abruptly narrowed to a kind of gulf, and Valdaron was squeezed into the gulf. It had a narrow main street that wound on and on, pressed either side by gaunt, unbroken houses. The market was in the square which bordered the river, busily foaming between its smoothed rocks like a mountain stream.

The one modern note was an old people's home, berthed like a vast cruise-liner near the school the children were not going to, despite the law.

It was half-heartedly raining and the shadowed street felt damp and cold. The market filled the square with awning-covered stalls, diesel-generated meat-vans and redolent bread-trucks that were open all along one side. And people.

The people were badly, even clumsily dressed: Sarah remarked on it, although she was no fashion parade herself. She approved, in fact: it was a sign of authenticity. There was a host of fur-lined anoraks, long dull coats and baggy trousers. Some of the older women had consigned themselves to the identical type of blue, mid-length working coat (with lots of pockets) that Nick recalled from old French films. Spotted skirts or thick-stockinged legs protruded, finishing in the modern equivalent of clogs. Their owners had staunch, browned faces, rather closed. Both men and women were on the short side, with some very wrinkled specimens only coming up to Tammy's chin as they passed – or that was her impression.

There were hippies, too. Or what Sarah called 'ex-hippies'. She could tell by their ponytails (the men) and long beaded skirts (the women). One of them stood behind a trestle-table selling organic jams and pickles. She had piercing blue eyes. There were even some younger people with piercings and dread-locks and combat trousers who would get on well with Jamie.

'There was a kind of youth revolution in 1968,' Nick explained. 'And some of the youth came down here from Paris to make pots and look after goats, after they'd lost.'

'Why did the goats lose?' asked Alicia.

He explained in more detail but they weren't listening. They were subdued, for once. The bustle, the smells, the colours had shut them up: Beans pegged herself to Sarah's skirt with white-knuckled determination, refusing the pushchair. The hocks of meat on the butcher's stall looked dauntingly raw. The multi-tudinous cheeses, the tender heaps of greens, the peppery smell of dried sausages hanging like fat tentacles, the shouts of the burly stall-holders – it was peculiarly loud and confusing after their four-day retreat.

There was a stall full of shiny fossils and dim skeletons of prehistoric fish, tens of millions of years old. A small trestle-table with a clutch of orange and yellow gourds and three tired salads. A very long stall bursting with plenty, apples and lemons rolling carelessly over the ground every time a huge lettuce was fished for. The Mallinsons wandered about in a daze past plump, glossy fish heaped up in polystyrene boxes, a small, twisted mouth in a sole's white flatness drawing Tammy to touch it. How cold and wet it felt, as if drawn from the unimaginable depths!

The familiar sound of bongos floated over the market chatter; two men pounding away as a girl played vague scales on a wooden flute. They were dressed in patchwork minstrel attire and their faces looked dirty. In Cambridge, they would have been perched in front of M&S and Sarah would not have given them a second glance; here, they delighted her. One of the drummers caught Alicia's eye and started juggling three coloured balls. He looked as if he had been out in all weathers. Almost a gargoyle face, with frizzy hair. He glanced at Sarah, who responded with a look of elation.

'I'm going to get the bread. You can watch this with the kids,' said Nick, from under his floppy hat. He looked different from everyone else, and might as well have had a sign round his neck saying ENGLISH PERSON. In Cambridge, she thought, he looked tall, handsome, even debonair.

'You don't need your hat,' she laughed, although she wouldn't have wanted him any other way, right now.

Beans, affixed to Sarah in two different places on the skirt, refused to take one of the balls when offered and caused the minstrel to cry – to pretend to cry, knuckling pretend tears.

'Go on, Beans,' Sarah encouraged in a sing-song tone, 'take the ball. Don't be clingy,' she pleaded, unpinning a small and complicated hand.

'*I'll* take it,' said Alicia.

'It's not to keep, stupid,' said Tammy.

'Didn't say it *was*.'

'My name ees Coco,' the minstrel announced, settling on his heels.

'His name's Coco,' Sarah explained to Beans, who was gawping at him with her fingers in her mouth, still pressed against Sarah's thigh and with her bean-frog, Wally, pressed in turn against her own. '*That's* a nice name. What's yours?'

'You *know* what it is, Mummy,' Alicia said.

'What's ees your name?' asked Coco the juggler.

Beans mumbled something through the bean-frog, now squashed to her mouth. Coco smelt as if he could do with a wash and wasn't a very good juggler. The other two performers had stopped playing and were rolling a fag. Coco offered the ball again. It was a bean-ball in coloured leather, to go with the bean-frog. He had white hairs in his frizziness and red spots on his neck.

He said something funny and poked Beans's tummy. They left, waving goodbye, as Beans screamed in apparent agony, making people look their way with troubled expressions.

Nick was also the subject of glances; talking to a rat-faced man selling bread, his height was exaggerated by the need to keep his fragile back stretched. His floppy hat shook as he laughed. Tammy gazed at the stall next door, hung with plastic gewgaws: mini bagatelle-boards, water-pistols, butterfly hairgrips that would break at the first go. The *Made in China* stall. Beans had calmed down, looking at it with her.

'Don't even think about it, Tammy,' said Sarah.

'I was just telling him how we were escaping English weather,' said Nick, coming up with a grin, a week's worth of baguettes and chunky loaves in the basket. 'Weather a bit like this!'

'No wonder he was splitting his sides,' Sarah said.

'You never buy me *anything*,' Tammy grumbled, as they headed back to the car.

'Let's redirect that one to the Truth Department,' Nick said.

'Nor *me*,' said Alicia, seeing the advantages of a sudden, unusual alliance.

'Actually,' said Sarah, as they passed a stall with stitched-leather slippers and shoes, 'you do need new casual footwear, Alicia.'

'What?'

The young Moroccan woman behind the stall cooed over her, all smiles. Alicia chose, naturally enough, the pinkest and least handmade pair there, with buckles that were bound to break.

'*Ve-ery* trendy,' said Nick, gallantly.

There was a shop in the street full of bric-a-brac, which included a fireguard with brass knobs. It was, Nick thought, over-priced and fake-looking, but Sarah insisted. Apart from the child factor, sparks could pop out a long way and burn a house down.

'Coco,' said Beans, in the car, as if a penny had dropped. 'Touch Beans *here*,' she added, lifting her top and thrusting a finger into her rotund belly, then bending her head and investigating the pressure point with a concentrated gaze.

Tammy reminded them about the plaque. They had some difficulty in remembering where it was, because the overgrown woods either side made one length of the track look much the same as another. 'My plaque's on my teeth,' Nick joked, so they all groaned. Alicia spotted it on a curve.

'There!' she screeched.

The car stopped and they all got out. The plaque was embedded in a large boulder at chest height, near the flat top.

'*Ici le 28 février 1944 le jeune Fernand Maille âgé de vingt ans a été assassiné par les Nazis,*' Nick read out. 'Which means, girls: "Here on the twenty-eighth of February 1944, the young Fernand Maille, aged twenty, was, er, murdered by the Nazis."'

'Am I one of the girls?' asked Sarah. She had taken off her glasses to examine the words chiselled in, bending to them as if they might have other words hidden inside them.

'Nasties!' shouted Alicia.

'Alicia, quietly,' her mother remonstrated, as the cry echoed through the trees. Alicia had an extraordinarily loud voice, when required.

'Was it right actually *here* they killed him?' asked Tammy, stabbing her finger towards the leaf-strewn ground in front of the boulder.

'Oh, I guess so,' said Nick. 'Right on this spot.'

'Oo-er,' said Alicia, stepping back and looking at the ground, fearful of her new shoes. 'Lots of goodgy blood.'

'Why did they do that?'

'Now thereby hangs a tale, I suspect, Tamsin.'

'For oil,' said Alicia, which made her parents laugh.

'A very simple tale, I should think,' suggested Sarah. 'Fernand Maille was in the Resistance.'

The term beat dully in Tammy's head, but would not take flesh. 'What's that?' she asked, reluctantly.

'A kind of cupboard,' said Alicia, nodding. 'Like my Frosties are in the cupboard.'

'Good guess,' said Sarah, as Tammy covered her face in dramatic despair.

'Not *necessarily* in the Resistance,' said Nick, raising a finger. 'Let's not jump to conclusions on the basis of slender evidence.'

'Very likely to have been,' Sarah insisted, a little piqued at being treated, yet again, as if she were still one of his students.

He explained the term as they got back into the car.

'Coco *here*,' interrupted Beans, as Sarah strapped her back in her car-seat for the half-kilometre left. Beans was poking her round belly again. 'Coco touch renisance *here* tummy.'

'And Charles de Gaulle, in London –'

'That's not renisance!' squealed Alicia, snorting into her palm. 'You blinking fat *pussy!* That's a big fat –'

'Alicia,' Sarah broke in, 'where on earth did you get that word from?'

'What word?'

'It just means a cat, sweetie,' Nick said. 'So when de Gaulle, in London, Tammy, gave a speech –'

'Cats kill stupid little mice,' Tammy said, spreading her claws wide and baring her teeth.

★   ★   ★

74

They had got the Sandlers' stereo to work, despite its outdated Jumbo Jet console, flashing and winking and bobbing green-lit levels that meant nothing, even to the initiated. Troubadour music: all harps and girly voices, Sarah thought. It was Nick's choice. She had brought along Bach and Sibelius and Ravel and he had brought the Smiths, the Cure and Joy Division as well as his difficult jazz, so she counted herself lucky. The former trio dated from his early teaching years when he sported a radical's superior gloominess, nudging thirty and desperate not to be. Helena, the parti-coloured New Ager, had fallen for his all-black look. The fusion was Jamie. Or confusion, as Nick would put it.

They were having a candlelit supper, the kids in bed. They had started with fresh oysters. Tomorrow they would definitely start work, and lessons for the girls. The fireguard looked fine, if a touch flimsy. Nick looked a lot younger in the soft light.

'I'm quite pissed,' she said, although she wasn't. They'd been talking about Fernand, the 'man on the plaque'. Sarah couldn't get him out of her head. Only twenty years old!

'You can ask around, I suppose,' said Nick. 'What exactly he did to upset the Boche. Maybe nothing. Then you can check all the oral stuff against the documentary evidence. Archives, the town hall files. Then you'll find, to paraphrase Anatole France, that the evidence is, as ever, contradictory and irreconcilable. Then you'll write your report.'

'Like a war report. A field report.'

'We're heading towards the bottom of the bottle, look.'

'We're English,' Sarah observed, looking up at the ceiling, the knotted cross-beams, whole thick branches with curves in them. 'The English drink like fish. It's the only way we can let go.'

'Tell me why this very ordinary wine tastes so much nicer than its equivalent would over there,' Nick said, swilling it a little in the glass.

'Over there,' Sarah repeated. 'And far away.'

They were sitting near the fireplace at a round metal café table they'd rescued from the goatshed and covered in a Provençal-yellow tablecloth. The dining room was too cold, too frigid. The one-eyed mask gazed blindly at them, un-identifiable in its mournful dignity. It certainly wasn't Benin, although Nick hazarded a guess at Anyang or maybe Bakongo, while Sarah went for Dogon.

Nick emptied his glass. 'Beats off the cold,' he said, only warmed on one side, like a flitch of bacon, by the blaze of the fire over the last of the dry wood. It made the shadows dance in the corners and Sarah look even prettier. She was smiling, drawing her hand through her loganberry hair.

'I didn't think the south of France *got* very cold,' Sarah said. 'I guess that was slightly dunce of me.'

'Must ask Jean-Luc about logs. Oh, and the cherry tree.'

'If you were a real man, you'd be hewing and sawing away in the woods.'

'I know,' Nick sighed, bowing his head. 'I'm top heavy with mind. I've got a bad back. And I'm in my mid-fifties.'

'At your intellectual peak.'

'Fugh.'

She placed her hand gently on his. 'Love you, you old goat,' she said.

'God knows why.'

'Because you're incredibly special.'

'Blimey,' he said. 'And you,' he remembered, cocking his head to one side.

'And the girls.'

'Yup, they're not bad either,' he nodded. 'And not forget-ting, in our loving embrace, the son of me and my ex.'

'I'll give it a go,' Sarah laughed, although she felt he'd squirted a touch of lemon on her brain.

'Basically,' he added, in Alan Sandler's American twang, 'we're genial. We're the genial family.'

'Did he mean that in a totally nice way?'

'Oh, why? Do you think it might not have been?' He looked genuinely surprised.

Sarah had prepared the supper with exaggerated care. Even including the market oysters (such a pain to open) it was nothing fancy, but she was determined not to mistreat the fresh market veg, or the roll of pork tied up in string like a gladiator's muscular forearm. She underdid the greens, if anything, and was careful to place quarters of tomatoes in the oven dish the pork sat in, for their moisture. She'd kept edging her knife into the broccoli stalks, consulting the potatoes before setting them around the meat to roast; she'd docked the courgettes and sliced them lengthways, cut the indigo aubergine as thinly as possible and laid out the divisions on paper towel before frying them in what Françoise, her cookery teacher in Cambridge, would call 'no small garlic amounts'. The garlic bits had been sliced thin and were nicely browned.

The girls had partaken first, and spent most of their meal holding the garlic bits to their faces and pretending they'd extracted them from their noses, which all but put Sarah off the dish entirely. They'd been favoured with two oysters each, relishing the pained retraction of the flesh as they squeezed their quarters of lemon. Inevitably, an eyeball had been hit: Tammy's, fortunately. She was very grown-up for her age, most of the time.

Sarah hadn't attended the full twelve classes, for various child-related reasons, which meant that the series proved somewhat expensive in the end, but it had been a stimulating preparation, a crash course not so much in 'what to do' but in 'what *not* to do' – what never, *ever* to do, in fact, if you were not to embarrass yourself in front of your French guests. Nimble-fingered, slender-legged Françoise was from Paris, and her anecdotes conjured a chic Parisian dining room quivering to the haut-bourgeoisie and their elegant reign of terror.

If nothing else, Sarah had learnt to keep greens *al dente*, beef bloody. And to make *crème brûlée* with a crust that was fissile and all but snapped at the pressure of a spoon, subsiding into the light, buff-coloured custard (though never *call* it custard, please), like a tectonic plate into lava. She'd followed the oysters with avocado, filling the hollows to the brim with balsamic vinaigrette.

'This is a feast, and not even that expensive,' said Nick, who worried about money. 'Ten out of ten, sweetheart.'

He had put the girls to bed himself, as usual. A bath had been in order, which had resulted in the bathroom floor getting wet; Tammy slipped and knocked her head on the basin. The Sandlers had not laid the bathroom with non-slip tiles, but with something marble-like and no doubt very expensive. Wet, it glistened like fish flesh. Nick found a herbal salve in the medicine cabinet and let Tammy rub it into the bruise. He noticed, while searching through the cabinet's crowded contents, the same blood-pressure pills his father had taken before the end.

'Look, Poppa's pills,' he said, although they hardly remembered Poppa except as a grey mass of smells. It surprised him to see what it took to keep a holiday couple alive, if not well, when they were not that much older than himself. Not much more than five or six years older, maybe. He pictured himself as a cartoon figure walking out on a beetling cliff-edge that stretched over the sea and grew thinner and thinner, hollowing out under him, under the innocent, solid-seeming turf until the edge was pencil-sharp.

He tucked them in and read them *Winnie the Pooh*, entertaining himself in the scent of their clean pyjamas and washed hair. Beans made sucking noises on her bottle and it whistled, surprisingly empty. She will wet herself in the night, he thought, despite the nappy (changed by him): she'll wake up with a sodden pack at about six. She dropped the bottle ruminatively over the edge of the iron cot as he delivered an Eeyore monologue in suitably lugubrious tones. This, he thought, is what their deepest memories will be founded on.

Now all that was blissfully over. He emerged from bedtimes as after a particularly difficult academic colloquium: tousled, the begrimed survivor, weary of limb and in urgent need of a Scotch and its uncompromisingly adult deglutition. The sheer *outrance* of a straight Scotch.

The light was down to a flicker of firelight and the honeyed candles they'd bought at the market from a smocked woman, her hair dyed an erratic ginger. The music seemed to hold each moment rapt – although, as Nick pointed out, the style of playing and even the basic count 'is always guesswork'. The candles, which were not cheap, burnt down surprisingly quickly and smelt slightly acrid under the sweetness. The crimson Fitou, giddyingly reasonable at under five euros, had subsided in the bottle with like speed.

'What I wish,' said Sarah, 'is that life could be more – no, that life could be *guaranteed* to be like this for the foreseeable future.'

'It's going to be.'

'For six months?'

'That's quite a long time,' said Nick. 'Half a year. No, that sounds less.'

'Yes, but we always complicate things, it's bound not to stay this simple,' Sarah insisted, puzzled by her own pessimism.

She sighed and went for it, pouring herself more wine, imagining the disapproving look of Françoise the teacher of *haute cuisine*. Françoise seemed odd and vaguely exotic in Cambridge – out of place, like an actress playing a Frenchwoman. Today, in the market, in the swirl of French locals, it had been Sarah's turn to feel odd. Nobody seemed to be acting French, they *were* French. *Very* French. That had suddenly struck her, in front of a cheap shoe-stall, as an extraordinary, even dislocating fact. She had felt a dislocation of her own Englishness, its reticular complexity tearing.

Now the medieval harp was weaving her into a heartfelt past she had never known – she honestly had the feeling, as Nick was taking out the dishes with a thoughtful expression, that she might travel back weightlessly into this far past, seeing no reason not to, because the far past was in fact only a transparent soap bubble's thickness away, it was simply a matter of yearning. Of will. No, just of yearning. It was all just a matter of yearning, pressing against the bubble's wall. That's what this music was saying, plucking its simple twelfth-century melody, its impossible love song. If you allowed your yearning to carry you, it would carry you, back and further back and through the wall, popping it. Popping the separation, the division. Nothing really died. How could it? What would be the purpose of anything, if everything was allowed to die?

'I think I'm rather sloshed,' said Sarah, as Nick came back with the cheese.

'Sloshed,' Nick repeated, laying the board on the table. Sometimes he repeated what Sarah said as if rolling it in his hand, marking it out of a hundred. They had decided to eat cheese before dessert, the French way.

'Sloshed is good. One better than tipsy.'

'I haven't really drunk much for ages and ages. I shouldn't have had the whisky.'

'It's a five-course celebration,' Nick smiled, parting dried leaves from the peppered, mould-coloured pat they enclosed. To be honest, the oysters had made him feel slightly surcharged from the beginning. 'There's this tiny little window of opportunity, this very narrow gap, this kind of potholer's cleft, between the kids being put to bed and one of them coming down babbling of monsters. And we're *going* for it, babe.'

He had to admit that he was a little bit merry himself. They started on the salty chèvre, melting onto the board despite the chilliness still in the air. Sarah mentioned how Françoise had told her that if a cooked goose-bone turns blue it means rain. The four-by-four incident was circled briefly and then left alone, obscured by affectionate remarks about the kids, the daily music hall of their growth and change, before the conversation drifted onto work, inevitably. It settled for some time on Nick's prospective capstone to the essays he was editing: a long piece on the Chad oilfield. History nudging current events, as he put it: the urgency of the times, the world wasted by corporate crooks, political conmen. Sarah would sometimes picture the Chad oilfield as a sticky black meadow in which the odd gooey horse or cow forlornly stood, surrounded by desert and a swarm of evil people in dark glasses. She preferred it when he remembered Lake Chad as it was some thirty years ago, waving its reeds all the way to the horizon. The nomads who lived beside it, ignored by the world, watching the waters shrink to cracked earth.

Alicia had buried the remains of Boris under a holm oak, while Tammy helped her plait a cross out of twigs. Which Sarah had found touching.

'If only we could somehow *take over*,' she said, equally worked up now, her face flushed, still upset by the incident with the four-by-four. 'All the right-thinking people like us. There are loads of them out there and we don't *do* anything. I mean, Bush is completely . . .' She wanted to say 'evil', but knew how ontologically dangerous that was in front of a rationalist like Nick. 'Look at his expression, OK? It's barely *human*. He's exactly what clones are going to look like. And we *allow* him to do anything he wants. It's just so annoying. How can we? How can we allow him? We don't *do* anything. Look at us now. We're not doing anything while they're just ransacking the planet, it's just so *annoying*.'

'The Genial People's Revolution,' said Nick, nodding calmly as if all his rage had been siphoned into her. 'And who has all the guns?'

After their fancy supper, they removed the fireguard and stared into the flames. They lay on the rug together. Nick whispered into Sarah's ear. The heat from the fire had temporarily banished the chilliness.

'My back's ace,' he said, to her voiced worry.

'The girls?' she murmured.

'We'll hear their door open. It's got one of those old iron thumb-latches on it.'

Their words turned into sighs and giggles. Nick kissed the knuckles on Sarah's neck, undoing her buttons from the back, unthreading the cord that bound her skirt, revealing the long and miraculous flesh of her. He ran his hand along its landscape, its proud hills and hollows, until he reached in to find the place that always reminded him of the spot between his pet rabbit's ears when he was small. His fingers crept under the hem of her knickers, finding the warm, invertebral pulp as she let out a tell-tale sigh.

'Mummy?'

'Oh shit,' Sarah sighed. Apart from the knickers, she was completely naked.

Alicia was at the top of the stairs, peering down at them like an inquisitive old lady. They were nestled into each other like a pair of spoons in a drawer, the firelight stroking their flanks with complicated shadows and golden tones. As Nick slid his hand out little by little, with a deliberate languor, he ordered Alicia back to bed.

'I can't *sleep*,' she said, as if they were stupid to think otherwise. She leaned forwards from the curve of the staircase, one hand on the creaking banister, dangling her bare foot over the next step down. 'Why've you gone all nude?'

'We were fast asleep,' said her father.

'Especially me,' Sarah added. 'Darling, go back to bed and I'll come up in a minute.'

'I can't,' said Alicia, lowering her foot arthritically onto the next step and bringing her hand to her mouth.

'Why not?'

'Monsters. Like that one.'

She pointed to the one-eyed mask.

'Alicia,' said Nick, 'go *straight* to bed and stop that monster nonsense.'

She considered this, as if it were an intricate argument on which she had to adopt a viewpoint. Her parents did not move, not even reaching for their clothes. The shadows fumbled over them as the flames danced. His hand was free. He rested it on her thigh, the forefinger slightly glistening.

'I *really* can't, Daddy,' she said, finally; and lowered herself onto the step, sitting there in her nightie and shivering slightly, looking at them slyly out of the corner of her eye. 'What's Ram-a-dan?'

'What?'

'It's in my book.'

'Oh God, Alicia,' said her father. 'Please, *please* go back to your nice warm bed.'

'Or,' said her mother, 'we won't buy you any nice things at the market next week.'

An inadequate threat. Alicia cupped her chin in her hands and rocked her head from side to side, like a doleful guardian in the flickery gloom.

'I want to go *home* next week,' she said. 'I don't like monsters.'

'The monsters were in your dream,' said Nick, Sarah's warm heat salty on his lips, the top of her vertebrae beaded with sweat. 'Now go to bed.'

There was a short, victorious pause.

'Not without *Boris*,' Alicia said, looking to the side and splaying her hands as if rebuking a diffident companion on the stairs.

'There are definitely no monsters here, Alicia,' said Nick, suddenly sounding very tired, a wave of tiredness taking him beyond desire.

'I'll come up in one minute exactly,' Sarah promised, shifting her rump minutely against Nick's groin, reviving him a little. Too much, in fact: he had to concentrate hard on other things: reinforced concrete; the last department meeting; the question of wheelchair access to FitzHerbert's library.

'But first you have to get into bed.'

Alicia stood after a moment and asked them when they were going to get dressed.

'Go – to – bed,' her father intoned. Around his data-driven, precision-debated professional realm, where every error was magnified a thousand times (he had once muddled, during an academic conference on Suez, General Chehab and President Chamoun of Lebanon in a passing comment – and suffered an imaginary ignominy for years), his children's mental world swirled like the confusion of a frivolous, waking dream.

'Very quietly,' Sarah added, with a kind of stuck-on weariness.

The latch socked its clasp like a gunshot as the door was manhandled shut by Alicia.

Inevitably, after a few seconds of thought, Beans began to wail in short bursts. It was intensely annoying, because there was studied reflection behind each burst. Then she started to drone softly like a distant air-raid siren, without much conviction, but with all the time in the world.

★ ★ ★

The next evening, the monsters made noises again.

The girls watched from their bedroom, shielding the subdued light behind in the tunnel of their hands. Their bedroom looked out onto the pool. At first they saw nothing, brows cold on the glass. The water was lighter than the ground; there were stars, but not yet any moon.

Then Alicia gasped, fisting her mouth. A shadow, a shadow detaching itself from the darkness and becoming something alive and big. They yelled for their mother. Their mother arrived, breathless, from reading downstairs. She was astonished to see something dark and monstrous down below, as terrifyingly indistinct as the Loch Ness version. The mercurial water in the swimming-pool rocked and rippled as the shadow, bulky and ogre-like, dipped towards it. Something glinted on its face, like a toothy grin. It craned round and stared up at them, still grinning, its head eyeless and twisted. A terror and tribulation.

Tammy opened the window, nevertheless, and the cool wind brought with it the faint, sweet smell of night, tinged with dung. The shadow was making noises – human snuffles, old-man grunts. The toothy grin turned into a giant curved horn.

'They're very cute really, boars,' said Sarah. 'Even sharks are pretty harmless. We're the ones to worry about. We human beings.'

She closed the window as her girls stared up at her. Alicia was kneeling on a chair. She waggled her bottom. 'I know the names of *three* sharks,' she stage-whispered. 'Great white, basket, and blue.'

'We'll just keep one as a pet,' Tammy said, quietly, bypassing any higher authority with that assurance Sarah sometimes, at weak moments, found disturbingly unassailable.

Nick wasn't certain whether boars were generally dangerous, or only so if cornered. Royal boar-hunts were not, as far as he remembered from the records, without their danger. A composite image came into his mind, drawn from old paintings filled with saliva-whipping, canine snarls and a vast hairy bulk in the middle, impressively tusked: it wasn't reassuring.

Boars had long disappeared from Britain, he told them, hunted to extinction and becoming somewhat mythic, even primeval. The fact that they were using the swimming pool as their watering hole seemed almost surreal.

'It'll be lions next,' he joked.

'God, don't.'

He and Sarah were lying in bed. While the Sandlers' bed was a modern double with a state-of-the-art chiropractic mattress, the guests' bed was an antique: aesthetically satisfying but nothing else. Too narrow, too high and too creakily bouncy, it had a bedhead of dark wood, with a primitive carving of grapes in the middle, that rocked slightly and knocked the wall at the slightest movement. The horsehair mattress sloped inwards and, if a couple were not to end up kneeing each other in the middle, necessitated a counter-balancing force in the body. The Sandlers' bed next door spread like an inviting island. Could the Mallinsons sneakily move to the hallowed master bedroom, until the Sandlers came for their possible visit? Would the Sandlers know if their bed had been used, as the Three Bears had known?

Probably not, but there was another factor. Small kids are not only unreliable confidantes, they have Pavlovian tendencies. When the Sandlers visited – they were planning to do so at some point towards the end of the sabbatical, after some major sailing trip or other – Beans or even Alicia was likely to toddle sleepily into the familiar nest and find Alan snoring there and scream. Worse, they might run out of their bedroom into the shuttered morning gloom and leap onto the cuckoos, heartily pummelling their bodies. This happened from time to time, usually much too early, back in Cambridge. Reading the clock correctly was neither girl's forte.

Their parents kissed each other 'nightie-night' in the usual ritualistic way and Nick had walked through the sleek bubble-wall of sleep before he knew it. He dreamt he was placing an old tile over his own thigh. Perfect fit. The mould of a dead man's thigh over a living thigh. The weight of it, of the hump of the tile. Always heavier than you expected. It made you think. For instance, how this tile would probably outlive us all, not just its maker a hundred years back. His shoulders were nice and large, he could feel his hard dorsal muscles like the shell of a tortoise, his thick neck. He hadn't been aware of this until now, but really he was very strong, he'd spent his entire life underestimating himself and overdoing his age. He was, in fact, forty-four.

He grunted and told himself to shut up and lay the tile, slipping it under with that high, scraping sound he liked. Then he cracked it. Hammering in the nail, he cracked the tile. The bastard tile cracked, for no good reason. Like biscuit. That didn't outlive me, he thought.

He chucked the two halves over the side, without checking, and woke up to a dreadful scream from far below that might have been one of his girls, visiting her daddy and getting brained by a tile.

The scream hung in the blackness that he couldn't quite shape into their bedroom in Cambridge: it was too dark. Then he remembered. The scream was repeated, but very distantly: some sort of bird or animal, some raptor or raptor's victim. The secret life of the night. All those protoplasms shaping up for the next million years. His mouth was dry.

His neck was stiff enough to hound him through the rest of his troubled sleep, as if some linkage was out, though his swivel joint was now fine.

Woken again later by his neck, he knew straightaway where he was, from the lumpy horsehair mattress: the dorm at school. Second time round. The first time he'd won a scholarship, propelled from the grammar to Hilmorton Academy for Boys, long closed down. Now he was back, and the bed still fitted, squeaking in the same way. He'd written an article about his old school, once, which they wouldn't have liked. *Set up after the war by a rich eccentric who had discovered to her amazement, via a batch of urchin evacuees, not only how the other half lived but that there was actually another half, leaving her Lincolnshire manor house to the Ministry of Education and retiring to Cassis, Hilmorton College was a public public school, an anomaly, a melting-pot of the classes.*

Nick was bang in the middle of the scale, and therefore nowhere: not like his best friend Duncan, Duncan Haighley, the son of a leftish judge. For some reason, despite the idealism, bullying was a problem. It went on secretly under the benign, Ministry-approved surface. It was peculiarly vicious, and classless. The posh boys were no better nor worse than the pale, gifted cockneys, the runtish scousers who could do long arithmetic in their heads. Renton-Parr was the worst, with his cricket-thickened wrists, his malevolent gaze: he was no doubt out there right now in the darkness, plotting to leap on him and twist his nipple. A vicar's son. With bony, painful knees.

No, Nick realised, surfacing further: he was in Cambridge, he was an admired Reader in History, he was thirty – no, *fifty-*four years old! Hilmorton Academy was now a residential centre for business courses. His legs were sweaty with fear. It was never usually as black as this. A thin, small voice reminded him that nuclear conflict had taken out all the street lights. Correction: the collapse of the climate. Desert winds blew beyond the broken glass, swirling about the shattered carcass of King's Chapel where wild boars nested among the elaborate fallen fans of the vaults. His hand strayed towards the bedside lamp and knocked a wall instead. There was no bedside lamp.

Sarah was stirring as he surfaced entirely and remembered with a playful skip of his heart that everything was fine, that he had six months of his sabbatical in front of him, that the sheets were softer for a good reason. Their faint scent of lavender was happiness. Lavender was good. Shepherds kept it in their pockets to rub between their fingers, he'd read: it was the thin line of happiness running through the obdurate human story, as crude oil was the line of evil. *Define evil.* A philosophical, not a historical, question.

He kept very still until he reckoned Sarah was fully asleep again. He could hear the night wind whistling softly in the rafters, merging with her breath.

By which time the darker clouds had moved in. He was on the downhill half of his life. He'd wanted, at nineteen, to become an archaeologist, to study the mute mysteries of Bronze and Iron Age Britain, in love with tussocky, windswept hillforts and ancient nettled ditches. But this was politically otiose in the 1970s; he followed the banners, embraced the clamour of names and dates, the harsher materials of great men, of social forces and ideals instead of pottery and tombs. He concealed his real self under the guise of the rebel. He fell for absolutes, gigantic dreams, the overarching system, dialectics and determinism. Thesis, antithesis, synthesis: simple, really. He transferred his sensibility to the post-colonial, to power rather than settlement patterns. It was all a huge mistake. He would have liked to have knelt in grass in the rain, scraping and brushing. His entire career had been a mistake. He could have been an antiquarian.

He thought of the boars returning to the trees, to the inscrutable blackness of the forest. He thought, inevitably, of poor Duncan: Duncan, who went up to Cambridge with him but did English, not History. Who one day in their second year had shyly shown him some poems. Oh, how he blushed to think of it now, picturing his own mouth with the sound turned off, moving around the syllables of those few, terrible words in the revolutionary lexicon, trampling Duncan's frail verse under the heel of righteous polemic.

Privileged. Middle-class. Precious. Detached.

Individualist.

And Duncan left the room all but in tears. How easy it was to destroy a friendship! To cut down a great and spreading tree!

To massacre in the name of love and progress. Except that Marx rejected brotherly love, so there could be no illusions there.

In the panned-out curve of her professional life, there would be a book on the history of isonomy, with particular reference to its survival, or otherwise, in the emergent African states after independence. The isonomic basis of otherwise oppressive systems, with an analysis of the abuse and distortion of their constitutions. Even Stalinism was essentially isonomic, her intro-duction would suggest. The word was one of the keys to her and Nick's domain. Even some of their Cambridge colleagues did not know what 'isonomic' meant.

Equality of the citizenry before the law. The most cherished, and the most abused, of all ideals.

Not even a tattered mask, now. The winds were whipped up. She dreamed of the waving reeds of Lake Chad, glimmering to the boundless horizon; of the Teda nomads fishing in their hollowed pirogues. Nick had given her this. She was grateful. But she sometimes wondered what might have happened had she not walked into his room that first tutorial, unbearably naive.

She woke up almost every night, these days, and worried about the future. Nick said that when he was a student no one really believed they would escape a nuclear holocaust, that humanity tends towards apocalypse when confused. But she didn't find this at all reassuring. She tried to picture the worst-case scenarios, but it was always like a bad epic film: squalid, tormented extras clawing at each other, parched and hungry, over-acting, amateurish. No, she thought: we'll still make light of it all, when we can. The English will stick together, though no notion of a nation will remain, and we'll queue at the river or the lake and be laughed at, tormented by a kind of exaggerated species of gnat. We'll make jokes and gossip, veer between embarrassment and sudden bursts of what used to be quaintly termed 'yobbery'. We'll keep our chins up and pass the time in hope. My children will be there among the hordes: they'll be rumpled and prematurely old, wondering what happened to their childhood. The halcyon days.

Then she'd want to cry, each time, and would feel the beginnings of a real terror threshing in her stomach, as right now, while Nick snored gently beside her in this strange bed in this strange house in this strange country. And even in Cambridge, in her own home, she had felt this.

Nick had gone back to sleep, having woken her up. A kind of see-saw, she thought. One up, one down.

★   ★   ★

'What?' she asked, tapping and scraping Beans's toast free of carcinogenic cinders. She felt as though her eyes had been twisted in their sockets. The toast ended up too thin, almost membraneous.

'Want them ones.' Beans pointed at the *biscottes* bought on the way down.

'Temperatures today are expected to break all records for February,' Nick repeated.

'I've got *three* records,' Alicia informed them, a moustache of hot chocolate giving her a raffish look. 'No, *four*. And you can't break them cos they're special and anyway they are *still* CDs.'

Tammy snorted into her cereal. 'Who was responsible for your birth, Ali Baba?'

'Mummy,' Alicia complained, 'Tammy called me Ali Baba.'

Tammy's nickname for Alicia was forbidden, on grounds of compassion: the victim hated it, which was the whole point.

'Tammy,' said her mother, wearily, surveying Beans's attempts to spread her *biscotte* with the wrong side of the plastic knife, 'you know you're not supposed to.'

'Supposed to what?'

The *biscotte* exploded like a letter-bomb in Beans's hand.

'Lots and *lots* of honey,' her mother reassured her, spreading another one. This *biscotte*, too, splintered under the mild pressure of the knife. 'Oh for God's sake, how daft!'

'Stupid bikset,' said Beans. 'Want toatsie *now*.'

'Please, Mummy,' instructed Sarah.

Beans smiled wickedly at her, not saying it. The toaster was operated again, nevertheless, on a lower number.

'Beans is really rude,' said Alicia.

'Not like *you*,' said Tammy.

'I know,' said Alicia, too young for the dose of irony.

Tammy covered her face in her hands, stricken with mirth.

'You make *us* say please,' said Alicia. 'Or else.'

'She'll say it next time,' her mother reassured her, like a pathetic negotiator at some intractable peace conference.

'*Wanna toatsie now*,' Beans shouted, through a goblin smirk.

'Shush,' said Nick.

He was leaning to the old, bulbous radio on the kitchen windowsill, trying to catch the weather over the family noise. The newscaster seemed delighted by the record temperatures. Nick wanted some comforting signal, some boffin to come on air and say it was all fine, his kids were going to have a good life, not some Old Testament visitation craved for by crazed Americans.

'Want *toatso*!' Beans repeated, banging the table.

'Can't you help a bit, Nick?' said Sarah, fishing Beans's toast out of the toaster with a knife.

'What?'

'Ali Baba,' Tammy murmured, catching her sister's eye.

'That's asking to be electrocuted, sweetie,' Nick pointed out, unplugging the toaster.

'She said it again, Mummy,' Alicia moaned.

'Is it so interesting?' asked Sarah. 'The radio?'

'About gay marriage,' he said, in a low, depressed voice.

Beans's toast shot, apparently of its own volition, out from under Sarah's probing knife and onto the tiles. Beans leaned over the side of her chair to examine the damage as someone might look down from a biplane.

'Stilboesterol,' she remarked.

'I hope you like authentic French dust on your toast,' said Sarah. What she had wanted to say was 'Oh, fuck.'

'You look tired,' Nick observed.

'You woke me up,' she replied, flatly.

He was hurt. 'I dreamt I was back at school.'

'I dreamed of Pooh,' said Alicia.

'Ugh,' Tammy said. 'In your nappy.'

'Pooh and Piglet, stupid.'

'And before that,' said Nick, turning the radio down as it entered into a jingle, 'I dreamt I was tiling a roof.'

He repeated the information, as no one had reacted.

'That must have been exciting,' said Sarah, scooping the fragments off the kitchen's ancient floor.

★   ★   ★

Nick did wonder sometimes whether he had somehow missed it. That's to say, he had the feeling he was living just next to the real Nick Mallinson, who *was* experiencing the excitement of being alive. That he was this entity's shadow or blurred double. Everything he might have been if he'd been a little more courageous. Was it Aristotle who believed that courage was the supreme virtue, as all other virtues followed from it?

Cambridge, where he had spent his entire adult life, save the odd semester in Africa. FitzHerbert College, in particular. He felt sometimes that he had gelled over to one of the college's time-moulded stones, one of its lintels scooped by countless bottoms. Fitzherbert's was small, discreet and ignored by tourists unless they were lost. Three fifteenth-century courts leading to the modest, shrub-lined garden at the end, which was enclosed by a huddle of old flint walls and shaded by a vast yew on one side; the Gothic chapel 'uninteresting only to the jaded', as the last President famously put it; the dining hall boasting three full-figure paintings by Van Dyck and a mysterious, unnamed portrait of a woman from the sixteenth century which, though darkened by age, moved its eyes at night. The girls saw it move its eyes whenever they visited, but (despite the intensity of their squeals) they were evidentially unreliable. They'd made similar noises on their recent visit to Loch Ness, which Tammy had pictured as a large pond.

'There's the monster!' they'd kept squealing, pointing at the flux of dark wavelets. It was like the study of the past, living or no. You saw what you wanted to see.

'There's the monster!' cried Alicia. She was pointing at the lawn-to-be, this time. It had been trowelled up, hacked and cratered. Small clods of soil were scattered over the poolside tiles.

'I think they've left the field of battle long ago,' said Nick. 'Welcome to the Somme. No, the Zone. Post-explosion.'

They were very impressed. Tammy asked why they did it. Her father told her they were looking for their supper.

'Strewf,' said Alicia. '*I* can't see any chips or yoghurt.'

'At least, I'm assuming they were. They do like rooting about, do pigs.'

Beans threw her plastic cup into the middle of the mess with a sudden, violent thrust of her arm. Sarah retrieved it, ticking her off. The soil, sticky from the watering, stuck to her shoes in clods.

'I've a feeling,' said Sarah, 'that Lucy's going to blame us.'

'Jean-Luc, I thought.'

'We're the new arrivals,' she explained, cleaning her shoes of mud with old tissues from her pocket. 'The immigrants.'

The girls disappeared into the barn. Sarah asked if someone shouldn't keep an eye. Nick volunteered. 'I'll kind of hover,' he said.

'I've got a letter to post.'

She'd jog up to the letterbox at the end of the track once or twice a week, otherwise they'd check *en passant* in the car. Sarah regarded it as 'me' time, and it kept her fit.

Nick didn't like jogging: it jolted, and felt a shade naff. He wandered pleasantly about the old farmyard and noticed a low tumulus of builders' sand behind the scrubby growth on the edge, just in front of the collapsed wall. The sand was old, with tufts of grass and weed growing out of it; a few sacks of some chalky white substance – lime, presumably – lay burst and no doubt rock-hard next to the hummock. Several stacks of old tiles, spotted with the scars of moss and lichen and clearly hand-made, pretended to be a landscape-art installation.

It reminded him of his dream and he picked up a tile. They'd had their roof redone in Cambridge; he knew a bit about roofs, but from down below. Strangely enough, it was not only the right weight for the dream (heavy for its size), but it was correct in every detail: the moss-spattered, terracotta mould of a long-decayed thigh, tapering to a thickness at the ends, the tracks of smoothing fingers visible. A beautiful object of utility.

He thought of the Sandlers and their projects, the feeling he had about this place – that something had been abandoned halfway, despite the bright zinc flashing and guttering, the neat *génoise* cornice under the eaves, the walls knocked back to stone and sensitively pointed, the proud finials at either end of the handsomely ridged roof. It was a peculiarly poignant sight, that builders' debris, but he couldn't quite think why. A kind of intrusion onto the empty farmyard's rusticity, yet beaten back.

The future stalled, grassed over. A strange concept. He breathed in the clear air's present and felt firm with the moment, even joyous. He was looking forward to work, oddly. All this was such a good idea. Through the stone arch that led to the front he could see a castellated line of cloud over the invisible, far-off sea: thunderheads, he thought.

He sauntered in a broad arc over to the barn, just to check, high-stepping through the strip of briar and charred stones that they'd conjectured had been a wing of the house, destroyed by a blaze.

He and Sarah lived with this proleptic worry, this attempt to anticipate and thus cheat the gods, every day since they'd had kids. The kids were tiny, and the world was huge. They'd eventually get bigger (though he found this hard to imagine) and then they'd get boyfriends with motorbikes and go to parties where drugs circulated. Look at Jamie, who'd wanted to be an astronomer once. Jamie, the one great failure of his life. The guilt he couldn't dilute.

This was why he was blinking into the barn's darkness: it was a maw that had swallowed his girls. He considered the unseen rusty tools, their sharp flanges and points, the heights and the wheels and the places that were rotten. Then his eyes adjusted and he saw them squatting in a tumble of old, blackened hay in the far corner of the barn. In between lay a huge beam, strangely orange, with dark welts of decay. And thin hoops of rusty metal, piled one on top of the other, like a giant's discarded bangles. He had this suspicion that the cart and the waggon, belonging to an age as lost as the Palaeolithic, might creak and inch forward at any moment, rumbling out of the gloom.

He had spent time yesterday explaining to the two older girls how this was what the western world used before cars; their first home lesson. Tammy had drawn a wheel with *hub*, *rim*, *spokes*, *felloes* and *iron tyre* marked in different colours, and Sarah had suggested they take a rubbing somewhere interesting on the vehicles' planked sides with their chalks. It was a hands-on educational triumph, despite the rubbings not quite working out.

A thick slice from a tree trunk, like a giant cheese, was criss-crossed with nicks and blade marks. That's what they chopped wood on, he'd told them. That's what we'll chop wood on.

They pretended not to have noticed him, now, only glancing up as he approached.

'Look, Daddy,' Tammy said, pointing to a large circle cleared in the rotted hay, 'it's our fatherlands. Towers and swift-eddying rivers and all our golden fields' bounty,' she added, reciting breathily from her starring role in *The Odyssey* at the end of the last school year.

'Motherlands is better,' Nick suggested.

'Tammy's got the morest,' said Alicia.

'Me Disneywhirl!' shouted Beans, thumping the edge of the circle with her heel.

Alicia sighed. 'I wanted Disneywold, but Tammy give it to Beans.' She stood up, spreading her hands like a believer at prayer. 'I've just got *fowest*,' she explained, bending forward at the waist in emphasis.

'Forest is really *ace*,' Tammy insisted, losing patience. 'You can have a tree-house and a lot of the trees grow *brussels sprouts*, Alicia.'

She was imitating the strained, diplomatic tone their mother used as a last resort before the heavy stuff.

'Hey, brussels sprouts,' said their father, nodding. 'Cool.'

'I don't *really* like brussels sprouts,' said Alicia. 'I was only pretending.'

'Too late. They've been planted.'

'I don't care,' Alicia said. '*She's* got the sweet factory, *of course*.'

'Brussels sprouts are far more nutritious,' Tammy pointed out. 'You'll be still alive when I'm stone dead from too much sugar and coloureds.'

'Colourings, Tammy,' Nick corrected, hastily. 'Short-term gain, long-term loss. Sounds pretty good to me, Alicia.'

Alicia stepped into the cleared circle and dropped onto her knees and brushed their sweet lands out of existence, all the towers and the swift-eddying rivers and the fields' bounty, the long-settled hay-particles rising in sour and suffocating clouds around her. Beans wailed. Tammy clasped Alicia's hair in her fist and tugged as if on a heavy door. Nick was rendered *hors de combat* by a fit of coughing; he'd swallowed a wedge of fruit-cake made from dust.

'*Monsieur?*' came a voice from the far glare of daylight, oddly commanding. '*Monsieur?*'

Jean-Luc looked a lot bigger in silhouette.

He didn't seem to care much about the ruined lawn. Instead, he pointed to a small heap of gravel on the edge of the pool. Jean-Luc told Nick that gravel is very bad for the pool, that it would *abîmé* the filters. The water was no longer green but a cloudy white.

Nick asked the girls if this was their doing. Tammy said they were pretending the stones were sweets, because they weren't allowed sweets at home. Or not many. Not enough.

Nick explained this to Jean-Luc, who nodded.

Although Jean-Luc had said nothing of the sort, Nick quoted him as stating that 'Never, ever are you to bring gravel near the pool, or you won't be able to swim when it's hot enough. I hope you didn't throw any in,' he added.

Tammy sucked her upper lip before saying, 'Who do you think we are, Daddy?'

He sighed, unconvinced. 'When was this, anyway? You're not supposed to come near the pool without adults around.'

'Yesterday. Mummy was with us.'

They had to pick up the gravel and place it in their palms stone by stone and return it to the front of the house. They looked like a procession carrying offerings to the gods. The gravel leaked from their hands and left a trail like breadcrumbs.

Nick tried to turn it into a game.

'Empty your loads!' he cried, with his hand in the air like a crane. Beans threw hers up and it hit her face. She screamed just as Sarah came back from her run, red and sweaty in the face.

'It's nothing,' Nick reassured her, having checked for any damage to the eyes. 'A case of friendly fire.' Beans stumbled to her mother, who picked her up with the air of a superior humanitarian service. 'By the way,' he went on, 'don't let them take gravel near the pool again.'

'What gravel?'

Beans was pointing to her woundless forehead while a minis-cule bead of blood welled on her chin. 'They said you were with them,' he pointed out. 'When they were taking this gravel to the pool.'

'Beans is bleeding,' Tammy observed. 'He gave us blood to drive our hearts, our souls to drive our minds.'

'Don't exaggerate, Tammy,' said Nick, pained by the religious guff – the legacy of her new, young, possibly born-again teacher. Beans, of course, looked panicked.

'Goody-good,' said Sarah, bouncing her up and down, clearly energised by the jog, 'we can put some French-style iodine on it. I saw some in the medicine cupboard. It'll look incredibly spectacular, Beansie!'

Beans sat on the bathroom chair and stared at her with huge glistening eyes, holding the precious wad of cotton wool stained with iodine. Sarah kissed her on the forehead. Immaculate little clutch of hatchlings. Everything working as it should behind the soft envelope of skin. The brimming personality behind the eyes: the innocent, open-eyed promise.

'Mummy,' said Alicia, 'I really need that on my finger where I cut it.'

Tammy laughed in the echoey room.

'You cut it last year, sweetheart,' Sarah pointed out, creasing her eyes up. Where her glasses usually went on her nose there was a red mark.

Alicia winced, insisting it still hurt a really lot.

'Just a bit. It's not a game.' Sarah stained the red thread of Alicia's scar where her forefinger had been caught between two supermarket trolleys, a miniature digit versus a web of metal. That was a drama. 'From what you've told me, we're lucky it wasn't severed,' the hospital doctor had confided to her, after planting three stitches. Sarah nearly fainted, watching the needle ply the flesh like an oar. 'But as long as you stop the bleeding and pick it up intact, there's a good chance we can sew it back on.' It was as though it were bound to happen again, only worse.

There were no angels guarding the doors. No all-seeing God, unless it be the wicked, creator God of the Gnostics. Yet she still offered up little goodnight prayers, as if someone good beyond cognition might be looking after them. A guardian spirit with wings of white goosedown. Sometimes she preferred the old gods and their tantrums, their jealousies, looking like humans in the flaring torchlight of their high-up abodes.

'I'm hungry, Mummy,' said Alicia.

'That's because you left your hot milk at breakfast.'

'I wasn't hungry *then*, stupid.'

'Alicia, don't be rude.'

'I'm defnelly gonna starve to *deaf*,' Alicia asserted, covering her face in her hands.

'I think you're going to be an actress when you grow up, mate.'

'Can I have some hot milk now? With honey and cimmen?'

'Missing word?'

'Beans didn't say it,' Alicia pointed out.

'Cinnamon,' Tammy joked.

'Alicia,' Sarah chided, feebly.

Poor Alicia, she thought. Hard to be in the middle, but everyone has two elbows.

'I'm a prodigy,' said Tammy, looking through the bathroom's small window, 'and you're a podgy.'

Sarah joined her at the window. Jean-Luc was raking the messed-up Zone. 'Tammy,' she murmured near her child's small ear, 'that was totally unnecessary and arrogant and cruel.'

'Why?' demanded Alicia, who had excellent ears.

He could have done it himself with a sweep of the broom, he doesn't want the girls turned against him. They kept looking at him as if he was an ogre. It wasn't that serious, the gravel business. They're only kids. The Sandlers have provided him with a hoover for the pool, he's supposed to hoover up stuff like gravel before it gets into the filters or damages the lining. The fact is, the pool is crap; installed by a firm of overcharging cowboys, it'll begin to crack and buckle in a few years' time, squeezed or pulled by the ground. The ground moves in the heat and the cold, millimetre by millimetre. Fifty-degree shift between summer and winter. Everything gets pulled about.

Nothing is certain in life. Jean-Luc knows this. Not even rock. Not even the North Pole.

He stands by the tormented-looking, gouged-up lawn and feels contempt for the Sandlers. At the same time he knows what the consequences will be of this disaster. Madame Sandler is as tough to work for as a Parisienne: oddly, Jean-Luc doesn't mind her ways. He knows where he is with her, he humours her as he humours his own mother. She shouts and stamps her feet, and he measures his response in careful nods and shrugs, in moments of reflective silence. He'll let her get to the edge of hysteria, and then sweeten her back again to sanity.

She is totally dependent on him. He'll talk technically minded rubbish and she'll go to her *con* of an American husband and repeat the rubbish, but get it so wrong that it comes out as sense. It is fun, this game. A pity, in a way, that they are here so little, these days. Now and again she'll phone him at home, sounding anxious under the bossiness, and he feels a strange sensation of power, that he holds all these people in the palm of his hand, that he can close his hand into a fist and crush them to pulp.

Once, when the rains swept away some planting project or other, she threatened to hire a professional gardener from one of those firms that charge a fortune and advertise themselves in fancy websites on the Internet. He pulled a face. The problem, he said, after a thoughtful pause, is that you never know which firm to trust. Some of them are in league with the crooks, who are hand-in-glove with the antique dealers. Some of them *are* the crooks. They have all the time in the world to survey the house, knowing in advance the times when it is empty, the times when their mates can arrive with a furniture van and suck it dry. They're no better than the blokes who sell rugs from the backs of vans, or the firms who pretend to be timber special-ists, or the ones who phone you up again and again with some prize or other, seeing if you're at home – going for the foreign-sounding names, the rich pickings. He knows builders who'll nick keystones from arches (Marcel Lagrange, although he mentioned no names from sheer fear of the consequences), who'll strip empty houses of every original door, who'll steal the old capstones off stone walls, the slabs from a hearth, even the chimneypiece itself, if it's fancy enough.

'They are locusts,' he said, and Madame Sandler frowned. 'And if you make a mistake and you're at home, they'll knock you on the head. They wouldn't even bother with the DVD player, the telly, the computer; we're talking big stuff,' he added, as a garnish. 'Mafia. Organised crime. Not even Frenchmen. Russians, Chinese, Sicilians. It's enormous, it's international, because the rich love old stuff, don't they? Quality stuff, stuff no one can make any more, because we live in a world of rubbish.'

He was sweating, by the end, and he imagined Lucy Sandler on her knees, trembling away, looking up at her house as if it were a helpless virgin surrounded by lusting old men, like the other employers he'd given the same spiel to. But she wasn't kneeling. She had this little knowing smile on her face.

'I understand what you mean,' she said, in her decent French. 'You've got to be very careful.'

Whatever, he's become the guardian angel. It has never crossed her mind that he, too, might be in on the game.

But he isn't, of course. That's Lagrange territory. Dangerous. As dangerous as crossing the hunters. Not even the President of the Republic dares to cross the hunters. Jean-Luc keeps out of all that. Which is probably why Marcel Lagrange has called him a pederast, a homo. It is a Lagrange world, this world of ours, and Jean-Luc keeps his head down. He likes the woods, when they are left to the animals, the birds. In the woods he can think, in peace. He can work things out, where it is all quiet, where there is no one to judge him. He's always liked the woods.

He looks up at a window from the edge of the smashed lawn, seeing something move, and is surprised to see the wife and one of the children looking down at him through the panes. He turns away, embarrassed. He was probably muttering to himself, pulling faces, moving his hands about. He's got used to being the only person here in Les Fosses. The only living person, anyway.

He squats on his haunches and pretends to examine the disturbed soil. A boar's droppings lie snugly in a crater, like a badger's – only bigger. He is always surprised to see how deep those snouts can dig, the amount they throw up. He feels the Englishwoman's face in the corner of his eye, like a warm pad on his cheek. He doesn't want to lose his job here. Before, he couldn't have cared. But now he does care. And he doesn't want to be humiliated in front of her.

The husband comes up to him and says something he doesn't understand, in French so bad it might be English. To Jean-Luc, it sounds as if he wants to close the lawn down, like a factory or a brothel. Then he understands: the husband is suggesting they put a fence around.

Jean-Luc makes out that he's thought of this already. It is a good idea, because it gives him an excuse to spend a whole day or even two here, erecting a chicken-wire fence. He will tell Madame Sandler that the lawn is doing well, but that it needs protecting from animals. Then, when the fence is erected, he can resow the lawn. It's late to sow a lawn, the dryness will be starting soon, or the April frosts might come early in a month or so and shrivel the seedlings, but at least there is very little risk of rainstorms now. The idea is crazy, anyway; these people are full of crazy ideas, but that isn't for him to judge. The world itself is crazy. She will have her damp green English lawn, and the water table will be too low for the pipe, eighty metres down. Sucked dry.

The Englishman asks him if the boars are dangerous. Jean-Luc snorts. He folds his arms and recounts how the official hunting body introduced pigs to the indigenous wild boar population to bump up numbers some time back and the result is a lot of big hairy pigs because pigs breed faster. There are hardly any pure-blood boars left, he says, like you got in his father's day. The type that'd gouge out a dog's stomach just like that. He clicks his fingers. Intestines everywhere. He slipped in a dog's intestines himself, when he was a boy, out hunting. His father's best dog.

These new boars are soft, nothing but sweet little girls.

Nick felt good about this conversation. It appeared that someone, perhaps Jean-Luc himself, had suffered from a stomach-ache after drinking and tripped over a dog belonging to someone's granddaughter. He smiled and asked about logs. Jean-Luc knew a man in Aubain. The wood was a year old, holm oak, the best for burning. Sixty euros for two tons. Then Nick remembered about the cherry tree. Jean-Luc nodded without saying a word. He was at the pool now, holding a plastic canister marked CLARIFIER and pouring its liquid contents into the cloudiness, which foamed a little as it was struck.

Nick strolled round to the front view, satisfied. Small stone steps built out from the wall led down to the terrace below, which was choked with leafless brambles. A hyacinth pushed up out of the leaf-mould at his feet, and there was a scent of violets. The deciduous trees' buds were faintly swollen, encouraged by the warm, wintry sun. The trunks of the holm oaks, covered in lichen, were a sign of clean air, something one hardly ever saw in England. Perhaps before the Industrial Revolution all tree trunks were painted in these complex patterns of green and grey. Halcyon days! Like his youth!

Clarifier. That's what we all need. A dose of clarifier.

His life seemed ridiculously short, incomplete, as if it had only just got going. Always a terrible shock, in bed, to wake up to the fag end of middle age, into the later years of the empire and its crumbling frontiers instead of the dynamic beginnings of its apogee. He had never had an apogee! Day had followed day, tutorial after tutorial, lecture after lecture, exam supervision after exam supervision, paper after paper, meeting after meeting, holiday after holiday – and somehow the whole process had cheated on him; it had eaten up most of his working life, without him really noticing. He was pure product, in the end. Fragment of some vast time-and-motion study. Everything, *everything* had to be accountable, these days, even in the cosy antique splendour of FitzHerbert's.

He settled himself before the view's immensities and took a deep breath of the clear air, as if to re-establish his own reality. He had the kids, which was something. He was still celebrated (was that the right word?) within the narrow confines of his profession, as a Suez Crisis specialist; his fresh interpretation, circling as it did around concepts of power, control and hegemony, caused some controversy twenty-odd years back. But who now cared about Suez? Who now talked about power and control? Or used words like 'hegemony'? His book was almost certainly a waste of paper and ink, although he could write it with his eyes closed. And he was planning to.

He'd already wasted too many years on Suez. He'd poured his life-blood into that wretched canal and watched it flow away into the shimmering heat, just as now he was pouring it into the dry scrubland of the Chad basin, its vast, mostly concealed pool of viscous dollars – billions and billions of them, while thin-ribbed goats snuffled about the pylons. Suez meant nothing to his students, it was arcane – more so, even, than something chronologically further back: the Balfour Pact, the Congress of Vienna, Peterloo. The Third Crusade. Suez was impervious to the electroconvulsive shocks of gender studies, or queer theory, let alone the faded glories of post-structuralism. Suez was a black hole of foolishness, like the invasion of Iraq, with a whimpering and anti-climactic end (unlike Iraq, which was monumental tragedy). And Chad? He felt outnumbered by the grim faces in dark glasses, the scuttling rats of power, the melancholy elephants of the wells.

Oil was his heffalump trap, and he was falling into it again. The mammoth in the black tar-bog.

Nick dug his palms into his eyes and rubbed: an old habit, with him since student days, the years spent writing essays in the early hours because his days were full of fun – the fun never to be admitted to, though, in the thaumaturgical theatrics of the hard Left.

He saw it all differently, now. A man crouched over a brass engine in a Glasgow yard, shrouded in steam. Threads, threads. Spinning all the way to the future: the skeletal longshoremen, the toothless hags, the scrabbling in the dust amidst clouds of thistledown. The hoarded, precious sheets of paper. The terror they'll have of the sea.

This was not yet history, it was only on the very marge of history, merely approaching through the fog. But they were already shouting at him from the future, from behind the thick pane of unbreakable glass that surrounds the present tense like a bubble. Help! they were shouting. Do something! Now! While there's still time, for pity's sake! Do something!

The pressure of his palms on his eyes left his vision blotched and blurred.

There was a growl of engines and a thumping of wheel on rock from the direction of the track. He turned, but all he could see through his blotches was soldiers and invasion:

half-track troop carriers coated in dust; slit-eyed assault vehicles; the Krupps 1,500-ton tank powered by four massive submarine engines roaring like a miracle from its design stage; a howitzer bouncing on its panzer chassis. Strange, for a man of peace, this expertise in armaments. It dated from his boyhood: the massed ranks of Airfix models, the carnage caused by a fired pencil, the care with which he crippled his Junkers' wing with a match: that evil plastic stink, that elation.

He watched like that small boy as the hunters passed. A convoy of twelve four-by-fours with chrome nudge-bars like gates; some were the polished black of a hearse, others ivory white, one – monstrous, like a nightmare pastiche of itself – completely silver. An ordinary white estate van bumped past in the middle, looking miniature. Off into the forest like outlaws, one Little John towing a cage full of bouncing canine muzzles. He glimpsed stubbled, bloated faces topped by fluorescent orange caps or the odd stetson with a bandanna wrapped round of the same shrill primary-warning colour; more snouts poking through bars; slim rifles. Surprisingly, his hand went up in greeting. Equally surprisingly, several of the hunters waved back. The others glanced at him with a blank, faintly contemptuous air. One laughed. He was left standing in a swirl of diesel fumes.

Sarah came around the house with Alicia and Tammy as the last vehicle disappeared between the trees.

'Who on earth was that?'

'The local warlords.'

He had to be careful not to strain his throat again, because he felt like yelling.

'Did you say anything to them?'

'Oh yeah,' he laughed, feeling soured. 'No problem. Flag 'em down and take their numbers. A little too nippy there, sir. Blow into this, please.' He glanced at Sarah. She wasn't finding it funny. Neither were the girls, who were clearly nervous about stepping out in front where the huge tyres had rutted the gravel back to the original ground. 'How's Beans? Still in the land of the living?'

'Daddy kissing it better would make her even better. She's in the kitchen.' She strolled past him to where the ground dropped away. 'Oh shit,' she called out, over her shoulder; 'I've left the milk on to boil.'

'I'll see to it, I'll see to it,' Nick called, making silly siren noises as he trotted past the two girls at a dignified speed on his long legs, diluting his anger and humiliation by playing the genial dad. Embarrassingly, Jean-Luc was kicking his mobilette into life near the door; he sped off up the track in the lane's direction with no more than a glance. His lack of expression annoyed Nick.

The kitchen was dark after the bright sunlight. He heard a faint bubbling and then Beans's dwarf form emerged from the aqueous uncertainties; she was standing by the cooker and reaching up on tiptoes for the milk pan. Her fingers were touching its wooden handle. It had begun to rock in a satis-fying way, the boiling milk spilling over the rim already, but she couldn't quite bring it all the way down before her father hurled himself forwards, advancing against the air at what seemed to be the speed of an Ice Age glacier.

FOUR

Jean-Luc stops off at the café on the way home. The café, on the end of the main street, is not his favourite haunt: it belongs to a distant branch of the Lagrange family and the nastier blood-members are almost always inside – or (worse) sitting at the dented metal table in the street, under the faded Drambuie parasol, ready with their quips. He did, however, spot Marcel's massive silver Cherokee in the hunt convoy passing in front of Les Fosses and so knows that the worst member, at least, is absent. Also, he needs some advice about fencing. He's never had to keep boars out: some posts and a roll of chicken wire might not be enough.

As it turns out, it's a dead time and not even old Pierre is there in his usual spot, let alone the *doyen* of the village, Léonard Vallet, who knows all the traditional ways of doing things.

Louis Loubet, the youngish owner – a cousin of the Lagrange brothers via his aunt's marriage – is alone behind the bar, settled over the day's *Midi Libre*, his big shoulders rearing over his head as he peruses the sport. He looks like a tortoise, Jean-Luc thinks (not for the first time). Louis has yellow teeth and a sallow skin stippled by black warts, and smokes a lot of roll-ups that have given his nostrils a charcoaled look and turned his voice deep and hoarse. His favourite subject of conversation, these days, is the forthcoming ban on smoking in cafés and restaurants.

'So that's the Republic,' he sneers, when the topic has been exhausted yet again. 'That's our famous sodding Republic.'

He wears the same faded blue tee shirt day in, day out: *Helsinki City of Delights*, it says. Somebody must have given it to him, because he's never been to Finland. Louis Loubet has never been anywhere, in fact. Not even Toulouse, or Marseille.

When Jean-Luc comes in, the rain-swollen café door scraping over the lino, Louis lifts his head to check who it is. Jean-Luc feels annoyed and somehow ashamed by Louis's indifference: the café-owner returns to his perusal of the paper with only a grunted greeting. So Jean-Luc settles on the stool and waits, both dismayed and relieved by the café's emptiness.

He pretends to watch the television. The volume is low and the usual compilation is playing over the stereo – top hits from the Eighties that go round and round one's head. The telly's chatter is audible under it, like knobbles under a blanket. The wordlessness between them presses down on the blanket and grows heavier and heavier, but Jean-Luc isn't going to be the first to break it. It is a duel, played out many times before.

Some kind of terrorist atrocity in India or maybe Pakistan, with shots of bloodied shoes and men running with their arms up and their mouths wide open; Sarkozy, looking even more like a cartoon wolf; an advertisement for an intimate female article he'd rather not think about. It all washes through his head without leaving a trace. The pictures flicker and sway, reflected in the one big glass window that gives onto the street, the world, the universe.

Louis looks up at him, finally, as if he has walked in without asking permission. Jean-Luc keeps his gaze on the telly, pretending not to notice he's being looked at in case it shows that he cares about not being looked at. This tribe is all the same. Fuck them.

'Beer?'

'Why not? Yeah. A *boc*.'

'A *boc*,' Louis repeats, heaving himself away from the paper. He reserves a special contempt for people who order *bocs*: if everyone did the same, he'd go out of business. Jean-Luc knows this, but he can't drink coffee here: it is the worst coffee in France. He'd like to know just where Louis buys his coffee from. The sewage depot, probably. Dried and powdered shit, it is. And it's not yet midday. Jean-Luc, who never drinks much anyway, can't contemplate a *demi* at this hour, let alone anything stronger. And what else is there? Petrol-flavoured wine.

Chocolate with tepid milk. Fluorescent syrups. Coca-Cola five times the price of a bottle from Champion, and totally flat.

If Oncle Fernand hates this place, it's for other reasons.

Louis Loubet fills the small, stemmed glass, wipes its base with a cloth and places it in front of his only customer with the hint of a thud, the beer rocking up to the rim. Louis reckons Jean-Luc is one of those types who'll go off his head one day and kill half a dozen people in the village, including his mother, before doing himself in. It'll be on the news. They'll film the café, where the owner was found bleeding to death behind the bar, and then the *mairie*. Louis has thought this about Jean-Luc ever since primary school, when he saw Jean-Luc, at the age of nine (Louis was the year above, although three years older) stroking a flower. It was a big purple iris, half-wild on the edge of the meadow where the villas now stand, and Jean-Luc was stroking it with the flat of his hand and (from the look of his lips) talking to it. Louis and some of the other lads watched him secretly from the verge, on their way to school, and reckoned this was the weirdest thing they'd ever seen anyone do, at least at that age. After that, they took to teasing Jean-Luc mercilessly, without giving away the fact that they'd spied on him. They were just trying to make him normal.

Now the school is closed and some foreigner is living in it, making pots.

The café smells, in its emptiness, of bleach. This always surprises Jean-Luc, as the place is filthy, especially in the corners. Most evenings, in defiance of the forthcoming regulations, a litter of cigarette butts lines the floor at the base of the bar, as if a tide has washed them up. Jean-Luc can never believe so many have been smoked in a single day, just dropped there so casually, and wonders if Louis has a bucketful behind, scattering them himself when no one's looking.

Jean-Luc once made a good joke about this, in fact: 'Ah,' he said, looking down beyond his feet, 'I see you've been scratching your scalp again, Louis.'

The others, or some of the others, chuckled. Louis asked

him to repeat it: the noise had drowned it out, he claimed – although that was a lie. And Jean-Luc repeated it but not well, and felt stupid. Then Louis made a low, obviously cutting remark to Marcel Lagrange, further along the bar, and Marcel guffawed in his usual high-voiced way, slapping his knees and glancing in Jean-Luc's direction. Jean-Luc felt his stomach collapse like a house in a flood.

It took a lot of courage on Jean-Luc's part, to make that joke. He still doesn't regret it.

The *boc* glass has what looks like detergent stains on the side, a kind of chalky smear. Louis has always been a lazy sod: at school he'd lounge in the back row, rolling ink pellets or dismembering a cicada. He's not bothered to rinse the glass. Jean-Luc makes sure he drinks from the part of the rim that is clear.

The silence presses onto the blanket like a corpse. Louis lights up and returns to reading the sports without saying a word.

Jean-Luc wishes he smoked, sometimes. It gives you something to do. The beer tastes good, it oils his mind. The first sip is always the best.

'I need some fencing,' says Jean-Luc.

Louis chortles. 'To keep you in, or everyone else out?'

'Big pigs,' Jean-Luc replies, ignoring it.

'Boar?'

'Yeah. Up at the English place.'

'Les Fosses?'

Jean-Luc nods. A chill descends at the mention of Les Fosses, as it always does. Jean-Luc quite enjoys the effect; it makes him feel powerful, in some way. Like someone who has ventured into the deepest, darkest part of the cave where no one else has dared to go. Alone. He's spent hours up there, alone. Nobody else in the village will stay up at Les Fosses alone, not even for a few minutes. Especially over the last six years. As if Uncle Fernand had anything to do with it! Coincidence, that's all.

Louis pours himself a small *pastis*, the first of the morning. He never drinks before eleven o'clock, then keeps it down to no more than one an hour, with a break for lunch. This gives him the illusion that he is hardly drinking at all, that he won't go the same way as his father, who gradually dissolved into a puce-faced, flabby sot behind the bar, insulting customers and belching fumes until his sudden death the day before France won the World Cup. (The fact is, Louis drinks around ten *pastis* a day, half of them offered by customers. When he was small, running around the clientele's flared flannels or playing with cigarette butts between the stools, his father was on exactly the same dosage. But Louis does not know that; he was too young.)

He takes a sip of the *pastis*. The first sip is always the best.

'Electric,' he says, smacking his lips.

'Eh?'

'That Australian stuff the other American's put round his place, wired up to a transformer. Where we used to walk. Perfect for big pigs.'

Jean-Luc nods, thinking of when he was small, before things turned bad, when Louis and he would walk with the gang up over the hill through the woods and scramble to where the stream went wiggly over the rocks, to what was now the property of the other American, the younger one, the millionaire with the Chinese wife: a hundred hectares or more. There is a cave there, and a ruin. Paradise for boys. The millionaire has fenced it like an Australian cattle ranch, blocking a couple of old rights of way on some technicality. Or because he's greased the mayor's palm. Or both. Even though the mayor, Robert Papel, is a Trot. Jean-Luc hates him. In fact, the whole village hates him. But it is either the mad Trot, or Marcel Lagrange. Nobody else wants to be mayor of Aubain.

He's always let the hunters in, though, that American. He's smart enough to understand that. He's smart enough to know how not to die.

His wire is cutter-proof. His wooden posts are rot-proof. The gates are metal and massive. It snakes over the hills, the land clear-cut for a ten-yard strip behind the wire so that the American can tour his territory in a fat-wheeled buggy, pretending to be Clint Eastwood.

Where *we* used to walk. That's what Louis said.

Jean-Luc nods again. 'We used to have good times up there, didn't we, mate? The cave. The ruin. The field. That stream.'

Louis nods in turn, leaning on his hands on the bar. The music is disco, but slow and soft. 'Good times,' he says. It's as though nothing has gone wrong, since. 'That bastard of an American, spoiling our fun. No one ever used to put fences up. It's only the foreigners who put fences up.'

'That's because no one has goats any more,' says Jean-Luc, whose own father had a small herd up to the 1970s. In fact, there are still three flocks in the commune – two of goat and one of sheep – but both men remember the twenty or so flocks of their early years.

'Yeah, that's true. There were no fences before because of the flocks,' says Louis Loubet, who knows this already; who's had the same conversation about foreigners fencing a thousand times before, but feels each time as if it's a fresh wound, and that if he says it enough times it might turn the clock back to what it was all like before.

Jean-Luc thinks: It wasn't the American who spoiled his fun – he only bought it five or six years ago. It was the others in the gang, including Louis. But he doesn't comment. He just says, smiling faintly, 'That time you slipped and fell on your arse in the stream.'

And Louis smiles in turn and prods Jean-Luc's arm with a plump, yellow-nailed forefinger. 'Hey, the time we cooked the badger's turd.'

Jean-Luc laughs, squeezing his eyes tight and nodding. And so does Louis, with a wheeze in his laughter from his short lifetime of smoke.

'Good times,' he says, as a ginger-haired walker with a rucksack on his back struggles to enter, the swollen café door resisting his efforts halfway. 'Very good times, Jean-Luc.'

Hard to see how badly Beans was hurt, at first: she had mutated into a kind of red ball of agony in a pool of steaming milk.

Nick yelled, Sarah ran in and shrieked, and Alicia and Tammy looked mutely saccharine until, in a demonstration of sangfroid that was bound to be recalled long after in the oral annals of the Mallinson family, Tammy produced the local doctor's number as out of a hat.

On the very first day, the piece of paper pinned to the peg-board in the kitchen had attracted her attention: 'She loves words,' her bewildered teachers would always say, as if excusing her precociousness. *Emergency Doctor – Dr Roger* DEMARNE. The word 'emergency' had drawn her, like the word 'schizophrenia'; or 'torture' in the newspaper.

It seemed the only area hit was the hand. There was an ice tray in the fridge that required the percussive force of the stone wall to release its load, and the plastic shattered in sympathy. The ice melted quicker in the burn's heat than it could soothe Beans.

The doctor's surgery was in Aubain, located in a low, faded house off the main street, its windows blurred by tatty net. Beans stopped crying as soon as they stepped out of the car.

Sonnez et entrez svp.

The bell rang huskily somewhere within, but the door wasn't locked. It opened straight into the gloomy waiting room, which had a sagging Sixties-style sofa and highbacked easy chairs; it smelt of wet animal fur and vegetable soup. A faded poster showed the evolution of a melanoma like the birth of a galaxy, and another implored parents not to let their kids stay up late beneath a picture of a boy with spirals for eyes and flies circling round his head. The only reading materials were four-year-old numbers of *Le Point* and a slew of fishing magazines. The back of Beans's plump little hand was swelling and reddening as if a toadstool was pushing up. Alicia kept talking in stage whispers and was told to pipe down, while Tammy surveyed in silence, sitting on her knuckles and moving them interestingly against the pressure of her thighs. It had been quite an experience for her, driving fast on the empty lanes in the front seat and on the wrong side of the road until her father realised. Her eyes were full of rushing trees.

The one other person waiting – an attractive, sharp-faced woman in her forties, soberly dressed in brown coat and jeans and with long hair dyed a discomfiting raven-black – asked them a couple of polite questions about the incident. Sarah couldn't be bothered to participate, she was too caught up trying to turn a man holding a fishing rod, or a blurry shot of a prize-winning trout, into something remarkable enough to divert pain.

'Look at that, Beans,' she virtually whispered. 'Look at that beautiful fish!'

'Deaded,' sighed Beans, with the pathos of a dying soldier.

She extended her hand and gazed upon it. The woman made a sympathetic remark, then turned to Nick with an alluring smile and asked him if he was English. He confirmed this with a comic shade of contrition.

'*On reste ici six mois.*'

'*Six mois! Où?*'

Alicia tugged her father's sleeve and asked, in a stage whisper, what the lady was saying.

'She's asking us where we're staying.'

The woman smiled indulgently at Alicia, eyes searching over the child's face as if truly interested. '*Qu'est-ce-qu'elle vous demande?*'

This could go on forever, Nick thought, as he opened his mouth to explain, sweaty from the effort, his legs suddenly shaky from realising that they were all still alive only by some incredible stroke of luck or act of God that had removed all vehicles from the entire length of the lane.

'Le Mast di Vos,' Tammy provided, in a shy, velvety voice her parents were entirely unfamiliar with.

'Le Mas des Fosses,' Nick repeated.

The woman's eyebrows, plucked and carefully painted, rose up as her mouth tightened at each furry corner. She nodded and went silent, flicking again through page after page of outworn political events, long-forgotten disasters and once-fashionable faces as if decorum depended on it. Nick guessed that the Sandlers had not made themselves popular. It occurred to him only then that the woman might think that they were the Sandlers themselves, darkened by reputation.

'*Nous ne sommes pas les Sandlers,*' he said, forgetting to pronounce their name in a French way.

The woman frowned at him, as if he had interrupted her sequence of thought, or said something peculiarly stupid, and returned to her magazine. This did not surprise him: he had particularly disliked Alan Sandler, but Lucy Sandler was also pretty objectionable. A mere association was tainting.

Suddenly the woman, without raising her head, mentioned someone called Monsieur Maille.

'Monsieur Maille?'

'Jean-Luc Maille.' She said he worked there, at the Mas.

Nick felt stupid. He over-compensated, repeating Jean-Luc's name while slapping his forehead. She did nothing more in response to this eccentric display than nod with a demure half-smile. The woman's mobile growled and she answered it, chirruping in high-speed, sing-song French that made Nick feel thick-set.

He had never actually known Jean-Luc's surname, but it rang a bell. Maille. He knew a Maille already.

'It's the name on the memorial plaque,' Sarah said, wearily, when he murmured the question to her. 'Look at that carp, Beans! France came fifteenth in the world carp-fishing championships! Wowee!'

'Where's the doctor?' Alicia demanded.

'In his inner sanctum,' said Nick.

'I've got a pain in my inner sanctum,' Tammy joked.

'And this one's *really* special, Beans,' said Sarah, pointing at a blurred photo of a man holding his catch. 'Look at that incredible trout!'

'Deaded,' wheezed Beans again, her throat full of tears.

She extended her arm and gazed on her hand once more,

her lower lip projected right out, reminding Sarah of those indigenous women with huge discs in their mouths: another school project Tammy over-rose to with the help of her parents, providing a detailed coloured chart of Amazonian kin groups. The woman's call finished. Alicia had begun to read a magazine; she was trying the French aloud, word by word. From the photos, it appeared that an entire family had been shot dead, one by one, in the Alps. Sarah suggested she read something else.

'I haven't *finished*, stupid.'

An elderly woman with a face like a badly wrapped brown-paper package emerged from the inner room, followed by the doctor. He looked at them over his spectacles, something Sarah was always telling Nick not to do. He spread his arms and said, '*Toute la famille?*'

But it was the raven-dyed woman's turn. She was in there thirty minutes. They thought she would never emerge. Nick imagined being a doctor, receiving attractive women who allowed you to investigate their intimate parts. When the woman finally appeared, she looked faintly ruffled. Perhaps she'd been told she had cancer.

The inner sanctum was miniscule, shrunk further by an enormous Alsatian stretched out on the examining couch with its chin on its paws, as if at the vet's. They all squeezed in, somehow. Dr Demarne was in his early sixties and mournful, with a moustache like a thatched roof that almost hid his lower lip. He spoke very slowly. He even had a few heavily accented English phrases like 'Well, do you see?' which he dropped in at odd moments like a marble into blancmange. He advised them to go straight to the hospital, seeing the burn as possibly too severe for him to deal with safely.

'There is always the danger of infection,' he said, his French somehow coinciding with English homonyms for most of the essential points so that even Tammy could understand.

The dog grunted, releasing the meaty whiff of its breath as she stroked its coat; it had exactly the same feel as the purple hair on her mother's childhood troll, which Tammy had requisitioned. Sarah told them not to bother the dog – Alicia was poking its vast flank, checking it wasn't dead. It opened one bewhiskered eye. The doctor told them it was called Rondpoint, because he was found on a roundabout.

'Very funny dog,' he said, again in English. It was as if he were two different people, one behind smudged glass, the other behind an open door. He was tapping their details into his laptop with studied effort: there was confusion when they explained, in both French and English, that 'Beans' was actually called Fulvia, the nickname derived from the expression 'full of beans'. He had no idea what they were talking about. An unbridgeable linguistic gulf. When Sarah gave him the French address, his eyebrows lifted but his gaze remained on the screen.

'Le Mas des Fosses,' he repeated, in his ponderous manner, typing with two fingers. He sighed. 'It is OK? Hm? Not roubles?'

'It's beautiful,' said Sarah.

'*On loue*,' Nick hurriedly explained. He didn't want to be regarded as a rich Brit.

Alicia and Tammy sniggered in unison. The doctor examined them over his spectacles as the snigger threatened to spread into a virulent fit of giggles.

'*Pour six mois,*' Nick went on, anxiously.

'Loo means renting,' Sarah whispered, which didn't help at all. Their small forms were racked by the effort of stifling themselves. Dr Demarne said something in French and Nick translated: the doctor says he has this bitter syrup for such serious cases of fever. 'It's not a joke,' he added, in a jokey voice.

As they left, the doctor shook the grown-ups' hands and said *bon courage*, and stroked the children's hair.

'Yuk,' said Alicia, back in the car, brushing violently at her head. No adults were allowed to touch her, normally, except her parents. It was as bad as taking photos of her, outside her family.

'He's a pervy,' Tammy whispered in her ear.

'What was that thing about roubles?' Nick asked. 'Or was that just my ears?'

'Troubles, dumbo,' Sarah explained. 'He asked if we had *no troubles*.'

'Dumbo!' the kids chorused in the back.

Things were looking up, Sarah thought. The family had survived yet again, and genially. Her hands stank of wet dog fur.

'Why should we have troubles?' Nick asked, in a troubled way.

Jean-Luc turns the little nail-spotted doll over and over in his hands, deep in thought in his room. Until Marcel Lagrange came in, he was having a good time in the café, with Louis and their memories. Soon, he guesses, the *Café de la Tour* will close down. Half the houses in the village are shuttered, most of the year. The *vacanciers* don't come to Louis's place very much; it isn't very welcoming, it isn't their image of a picturesque French café. In the morning, under the coffee, there's always a smell of wet mops.

The ginger-haired hiker (who'd had a German accent when ordering a beer) sat on his own in the corner, writing in a notebook. This reminded him, Louis Loubet said, of the time when the English *mec* on a horse had come in. On a horse? Louis laughed: no, he'd left the horse outside, like in the old days that neither Jean-Luc nor Louis were old enough to remember. Then the *mec* had sat down where the hiker was sitting and got out a polished wooden box and produced a quill with a real goose-feather, a leather notebook and a bottle of ink. The *mec* was dressed like a smart cowboy, with a dark leather hat, a leather waistcoat and leather riding boots. He'd written there with his quill for an hour or more. Louis had dared to ask him a question or two, when serving him: crossing France on a horse, he was, from top to bottom. Six months or more. When he left, everyone had felt a bit, well, disappointed. Disappointed with themselves.

Jean-Luc had never seen Louis Loubet like this: quietly telling a story, sharing something intimate. It wasn't really intimate, but he made it sound as if it was. And Jean-Luc felt proud to be part of it. He felt almost happy, sitting there in the near-empty café, with Louis and his bloodshot eyes and yellow skin leaning towards him, elbows on the bar, talking like a brother, a friend. Even though Jean-Luc knew the story already, in its rough outline.

Then Marcel Lagrange came in with one of his hunter mates (an enormous barrel of a bloke with a sour expression called Aimé, whom Jean-Luc had once caught skinning a baby boar). He must have sensed, from wherever he was, that Jean-Luc was having a good time. The air turned cold, like outer space. Outer space without the stars. The swollen door shrieked over the lino as Marcel encouraged it with a violent kick, the German hiker looking up in alarm. And Jean-Luc was surprised to see Marcel; he should have been hunting. It was like a bad dream, because unexpected.

The hiker was even more alarmed when Marcel shook his hand and said *bonjour* in that high voice – always a shock. Marcel is one for the formal niceties. As long as the café isn't too full, he always shakes everybody's hand when he comes in. Not everybody's: those he has some grudge against, he ignores. It's a signal. If you're one of those who don't get Marcel's lifeless handshake, you have to start worrying. Unless, of course, you're a complete stranger. But he'll shake a complete stranger's hand before he'll shake yours, if you're on his grudge list. It's been known to get men wetting themselves, that signal.

He shook Jean-Luc's hand, though, the watery eyes skating over the younger man's face without settling. Marcel's hair is vigorous and messy, turning grey, and his head is bucket-shaped from the back. It tends to lean to one side, as if he's being hanged. But his face, with its large mouth full of grey teeth and its fleshy lump planted instead of a nose in the middle, is not really wicked-looking. It isn't mean-looking or rat-like. It's a hearty, fifty-odd-year-old's face, especially when spread over by a smile. It isn't the face of evil, even when it gets angry.

Then it's a frightening face, but only in the way a bull is frightening. It isn't a devil's face, except perhaps in the eyes, because those watery eyes flash and spit when he's angry. And his mouth expands, displaying the gums of his bottom teeth. And his skin looks as if someone has ground some black pepper over it, as over a slab of fish. He usually has a cigarette or cigarillo stuck to the bottom lip, but today it was a toothpick.

Apparently, old Gérard Rodier had a bad turn getting out of the jeep and the hunt was called off.

'Heart,' said Marcel, glancing over the front page of the *Midi Libre*, which featured a terrible earthquake somewhere in South America.

Louis asked if Gérard was OK, now.

'They don't know,' Aimé said, in his throaty bellow. 'It was a bad one. He went blue.'

'Thousands dead,' said Marcel, huge head bent to the photograph. He sucked on his toothpick, making a squealing noise. 'Terrible. Women and kiddies. Nothing left. We ought to send money. We could do a collection. Put a jar on the bar, Louis.'

Louis grunted, only half-listening. They talked weather: it was going to rain this week, maybe a storm, Marcel announced. To the German hiker, Marcel Lagrange must have looked like a colourful local, something off a calendar, or out of a Pagnol film. He probably noted it down in his book, in his neat German hand. What the hiker would never have believed was what Marcel Lagrange had once done to a German of about the same age, back in 1977. It might have been empty rumour, of course: the kind that hopped from door to door like a crow.

When Jean-Luc pictures the hippy they found on the side of the road, shot in the head, he could actually smell that sheepskin jacket, because it was so pungent. The hippy was part of the druggy, whacky group up at Les Fosses; no one warned him not to fall for one of the village girls, let alone plot to elope with her to Morocco.

The police put it down to accidental death. It was the hunting season, it happened, his sheepskin and dark trousers made him look like a – what? A boar? But the crows cawed from the tree-tops: you know those hotheads from Aubain, relatives of the girl? Caw! Lads like Marcel Lagrange? Well, we'll say no more. Caw caw!

A kind of honour killing, a hangover from the war. All those German atrocities. Sins of the fathers. The police conveniently lost the file. Washed their hands. Heil Hitler.

Whenever someone goes to their successors in St-Maurice-de-Cadières and makes an official complaint about Marcel Lagrange, all he does is laugh and ask: 'Who built the fucking police station? *I* built the fucking police station!' It's as if, having laid the foundation slab and cemented the breeze blocks and fitted the plasterboard, it belongs to him, that he's above the law. Anyway, most of the police in St-Maurice are his hunting mates.

He *is* above the law, in a way.

Jean-Luc has no idea which girl it was had wanted to elope with the hippy. A dozen candidates, back then, most of them related to Marcel. His mother won't ever say. Even his mother is scared. Sometimes, he feels the whole village conspired together. The whole of Aubain. Or, at the very least, it took a vow of silence, like a village in Sicily or somewhere. It was only a German, after all; wasn't it the Germans who had shot poor old René Dessilla by the stream: stone-deaf René, who couldn't hear the armoured car and the soldiers' shouts to get out of the way? *Rausch! Rausch!* They threw the bullet-peppered body over the bridge. Poor old René. He was much loved in Aubain. Even Jean-Luc's mother feels tearful, when she thinks of René Dessilla. Even more than when she thinks of Oncle Fernand, because Fernand was only her husband-to-be's brother, and quite a bit older than her. She was only ten when he was shot.

Over sixty years back, now!

Jean-Luc was even younger, back in 1977. He didn't even notice the crow hobbling through, with its nasty, biting fleas. He'd already been rejected by the gang, that's why. He was already a loner, dreaming and miserable. He was already fucked up.

As a result, whatever the actual facts, there's this general idea among the villagers that Marcel Lagrange can kill. It floats around him, like a cloud of gnats. He has this temper, this sudden temper. It flares up in seconds.

Jean-Luc knows all about it. When he was nineteen, Marcel was a powerful oaf in his early thirties: once, in the café, he knocked Jean-Luc's tooth out when Jean-Luc had physically objected to being called a pederast. Jean-Luc told his mother he'd fallen off a wall.

'Like a picture,' his mother sneered.

Marcel Lagrange can't stack five bricks straight. All he does is throw in concrete, tons and tons of it. Concrete: his solution to everything.

Unlike his brother, Raoul. Craftsmanship, not concrete. And so Raoul Lagrange had been getting more of the lucrative jobs than Marcel, right up to the accident. But Jean-Luc prefers not to think about Raoul Lagrange. After all, he has to spend days up at Les Fosses on his own. No one else in the village will do that. They're a superstitious lot. Jean-Luc is used to being alone, even in the company of phantoms. In which, of course, he doesn't believe. Not for a minute. If the house is troubled, it's not because of Raoul Lagrange's ghost. It's more thick-skinned than that.

He turns the slim little doll over and over, like an expert examining it for faults. He'll call it Bibi. Everything has to have a name. The twelve pieces of gravel are in a neat circle on his table. The little girls pretended they were sweets. It pleases him, seeing how white they are, even in the dim room. They watch him as he examines the doll. Little white eyes, watching.

When he takes a break, he reaches under the bed for his pile of *Spirou*.

They feel different, these days; they feel like dry leaves. The yellowing pages turn with a dry rustle and tear easily. His father bought them for him in the flea market in St-Maurice when he was nine. It was the one and only time his father bought him anything, as a kid, outside his birthday. He just walked in with a pile of old comics and said, 'The complete set from February 1957 to January 1958.' Jean-Luc was so pleased he didn't know what to say, and Maman clipped him on the ear for ingratitude, but not hard. She was pleased, too. She could read them, and she did. She still told Papa off for bringing back rubbish, though.

He knows them back to front and sideways, every comic strip in them: each cartoon square, each speech bubble, each black line. Buck Danny. The Knight Without a Name. Tom and Nelly. Alain Cardan. Gil Jourdan.

They were only twenty-two years old, then. That already seemed more than a lifetime. Now they are fifty years old. They look it. They're disintegrating, the edges are fraying, the colours are going. They can be buried with me, he thinks.

He finds the one with the page on 'Curious Little Facts' about the Elysée Palace: 'a resident clockmaker deals with its 130 clocks'. He remembers wanting that job, as if it were yesterday, and his father laughing at him. Laughing and laughing.

'Jean-Luc wants to be the President's clockmaker, and he can't even get up on time!'

His mother's calling him. He ignores her and searches for the *Spirou* for today. What is the date today, exactly? He glances up at his St-Maurice firemen's calendar with its glossy photo of a horrible car crash. The shock of the number punches him in the chest. Oncle Fernand never spoke a word about it all morning, staying sad in a corner. That's the trouble when someone else dies close to your date, however long after: you get overlooked.

'I didn't forget all last week,' Jean-Luc murmurs. 'It's what happens when you have too much to do.'

He'll just have time to buy the flowers before the place closes for lunch. The last lot were nicked – probably by the Lagrange widow, who's kept herself to herself ever since, gone a bit funny in the head. At some point you have to pick yourself up.

He doesn't even look at Maman as he whips through her bedroom, her shrieks following him all the way down the stairs.

FIVE

The hospital was in St-Maurice, which was circled by scrubby hills and announced on a tatty, peeling board as the *'Centre Mondial'* for portable fire extinguishers. If the town itself looked impoverished, down-at-heel and about as interesting as tarpaulin, its hospital was immaculate, nicely decorated and hummed like a well-oiled, technological marvel. They hardly waited more than ten minutes, with only a bruised young man and his furious mother for company. He was leaning forwards and nursing his wrist. He had fallen off his mobilette. His mother kept shaking her head and snapping at him. The girls watched as if it were on television. The odd stretcher passed down the corridor, bearing its obscure load while the bearers chatted gaily.

Although the burn was superficial, the nurses sighed a lot over Beans, giving her a magnificent dressing which Alicia envied. And rubbery crystal-sprinkled sweets, not one of which Beans gave away. Sarah was vaguely annoyed with the nurses for creating an inevitable scenario of division and fractiousness. She found it thoughtless of them. Nevertheless, she tried to chat away, all smiles. The portable fire extinguishers were now made in China, they were told. This area had the highest unemployment rate in France.

They decided to kill three birds with one stone and not only 'pop in' to the supermarket recommended by Lucy, but check their emails in the Internet café, which they did as quickly as possible – given the dejected interior with its one sheepish customer riddling Russians to a bloodied dismemberment under the girls' fascinated gaze. Still, it took them an hour, at the end of which Nick felt the residual lump of undissolved FitzHerbertitis had grown like an ulcer; despite having put up an Out of Office deflector with the appropriate snailmail address before they'd left, certain messages were unignorable. Professor Peter Osterhauser's, for instance. Minute, barbed tangles of fuss. The latest news from the Vice Chancellor's Guild of Benefactors, that circle of millionaire largesse to which he was bi-annually tied by some obscure administrative duty, and whose natural popularity quite unfairly irked him.

'We'll make that a monthly visit,' he said. 'Maximum.'

The supermarket's layout, being unfamiliar, foxed them into using up another hour of their lives while the girls squabbled under the quilt of lights; the two oldest were conducting frenzied negotiations for the last of the rubbery sweets, enforced by threats of shootings and bombings. It would end in some corporeal brutality or other. Beans's face wore an expression of benign munificence, like an oligarch's, as she clutched the treasure. The queue was almost motionless and Sarah imagined spending the rest of her life there, chronically embarrassed by the girls and their loud, English voices, emphasised by Nick's stooped tallness. Packets of lollipops were handed out like aid packages the moment they quit the cash-desk, toppling Beans from her throne.

'They're called *sucettes*,' Sarah informed them.

'Which literally means *suckies*,' Nick footnoted in a small voice.

'Likkel window,' said Beans, urgently, pointing to the huge plate-glass front.

As they drove out of Champion's car park, Sarah scribbled something on an old envelope fished from the detritus in the passenger well and stuck it under the sun-shield on Nick's side.

AM I DRIVING ON THE RIGHT?!?!?

Nick found the parade of exclamation and question marks unnecessary. It fell down a minute or two later.

'Leave it,' said Nick. 'It's burnt deep into my cerebellum.'

'Hey, a great title for my book,' said Sarah.

'What? *Burnt Deep Into My Cerebellum*?'

'No. *Am I Driving On the Right?* A book about our six months. Light-hearted, comic. Awesomely bestselling.'

'You have to be joking.'

'Have to be? On whose orders?'

'Oh no,' Nick groaned, checking Sarah's seriousness with a quick sideways glance. 'Spare us.'

All he wanted, though, was for life to be just that, light-hearted and comic. History was far too dark, a damn dark candle over a damn dark abyss. As some wretched historian once wrote.

The plaque on the track had sprouted big flowers set in garden pots on the stone.

'Of course,' said Nick, stopping the car this time; 'it's the anniversary. It's the twenty-eighth of Feb. Those could well be Jean-Luc's doing. He's got the same name. He's probably family. Ergo –'

'Oh they're really pretty,' Alicia sighed, pointing with her glistening *sucette*. 'I bet it's his Mummy and not Jean-Luc. Jean-Luc's too ugly.'

'Alicia,' Sarah snapped, 'that's enough! Anyway, she'd have to be about a hundred. Fernand Maille would be well into his eighties, now.'

'But he's dead,' Alicia said. 'They shooted him.'

Tammy groaned dramatically. '*Would* be, she said!' The conditional had begun to interest her, although she didn't have that term for it. It seemed to multiply over her like a canopy of leaves.

'Plastic,' said Sarah. 'I'm afraid to say I find them pretty lurid. Bathroom mauve and yuk yellow.'

'Mummy,' Tammy said, 'let me put the window down.'

Sarah released the window-lock. The glass slid down and Tammy leaned right out of the window, taking a deep breath.

'They smell really sweet,' she fibbed.

A shot, with a little comet-trail of echo. She knocked her chin in surprise. Then a second, spraying invisible pellets of sadness through the trees.

'Oh no, it's the Nazi men,' said Alicia.

'The Nazis have long gone,' said her father. 'It's just the hunters.'

'Or a squirrel with a really bad cough,' said Alicia, making her parents laugh admiringly. She tried to think up something else.

'Bung,' said Beans, through the plastic spout of her cup.

'Horrible hunters,' Tammy called out into the air — but not that loudly, she was not bold enough. Nevertheless, she was told off.

'We're guests here,' Sarah pointed out, cleaning her glasses. 'We should show respect.'

'Respect for the fascists,' murmured Nick.

'Like Mr Elephant banging on the ground,' said Alicia, but there was no response this time and she settled back into her seat, dejected.

The woods indicated no sign of human activity. Instead, there was a numbness about the aftermath of the two shots, as if even the trees were taken aback but were pretending not to show it. If trees could hear, Sarah mused, they would have heard the shots that killed Fernand, too; the shots that had thudded into him from some nasty German weapon, or weapons. As they drove slowly on, she pictured it quite clearly: the young man with his pistol or hunter's rifle, taking pot-shots at the advancing soldiers, then running up the track to warn the others, then falling as the bullets tore into him, his body rolling to a stop where the memorial stone now stood.

Nick made tea as soon they got in. They had brought along six months' supply of good, strong, builder's tea. 'I don't know how anyone copes without tea,' he said.

'Shakespeare coped,' Tammy observed, sitting down at the far end of the table, lingering while the other two watched something babyish next door.

Sarah was wondering to herself why the plaque said '*assassiné*'. Murdered. That implied he wasn't fighting them. And why '*le jeune*', when his age was marked anyway? Because of the anger, the emotion, the grief. In any historical analysis, one had to take account of the anger, the emotion. She could see the material of the boy's shirt or country jacket pock-marked by the bullets as he ran; it was as clear as a film. She could even hear his grunt, the thump as he fell. Perhaps he fell on his face and cut his lip. She felt she was in contact with the death in some way, probably because of the coincidence of the day, the anniversary that a relative – yes, most likely Jean-Luc – had obediently, touchingly marked. It made her feel more positive towards Jean-Luc, even tender; she liked to think it was him, although he couldn't possibly have known the dead man. One day the flowers would stop coming and the plaque would be forgotten, an occasional curiosity to a hiker. That was sad. But that's what happened to history; it congealed. It dried up to facts and opinions. Occasionally it withered to a lethal little point, used by troublemakers long after, stirrers full of hate and prejudice.

'The thing is, Sarah sweets, you left the handle sticking out.'

'Sorry?'

'Sticking out and on the front ring. Asking for it.'

Sarah said: 'Whip me, then. Go on.'

'No, sorry, but I thought I ought to mention it. Prevent it happening again.'

'So sorry. What a useless mother.'

Nick spread his hands. 'Look, why do you have to get like this?'

'Get like what?'

'All this overdramatic business. You know perfectly well you're not a useless mother, so why say it?'

'Nick, if I want to say it, I can say it.'

'Fine. Go ahead. I don't care what you say, actually, as long as you put the pan on the back burner next time. You learn from your mistakes, it's not a judgement. It's empirical progress.'

'Oh put a lid on it, grumpy.'

'I'm not in the *least* bit grumpy,' he declared, raising his voice and straining it.

'Sounds it,' said Sarah, recovering old tea leaves from the sink.

Tammy left a little pause and then said, 'Please don't shout at Mummy, Daddy.'

'Tammy,' snapped her father, 'this is none of your business. Go on. Leave us alone, please.'

'Why *is* Lake Chad drying up, Daddy, in fact?'

And then, for some mysterious reason, they both flared up at her and she had to bury her face in her folded arms.

Sarah wiped the kitchen table with a sponge as Tammy read *The Sword in the Stone* for the third time, just as Sarah had at the same age. Her family was not particularly intellectual. She always said she came from Kent, because more precision would have been pointless – her childhood consisted of trailing after her army father: Germany, Aden, Hong Kong, Belfast, Bahrain. The family had a small *pied-à-terre* in a development near Ashford, looking out on flat, undistinguished fields once teeming in the summer with hop-pickers from the East End and now put to desultory cows or slashes of yellow rape. She would stay there for weeks in the holidays with her mother, getting bored, while Colonel Allsopp did whatever he did with tanks far away. She read masses, uncorking book after book and shovelling the contents down past her eyes as her mother did with the whisky.

Even when, in Bahrain, there was a swimming pool as warm as a bath and secretive cocktail parties and young red-faced men who would finger her shoulder-straps under the scissor-like shadows of palm leaves, she read more books than her father thought healthy. She was reading Tolstoy at fourteen, and then again at seventeen, because she remembered nothing of what she had read before. She was plodding diligently, not flying, towards her single aim, which was to read History at Cambridge. Her parents never talked, or not about anything beyond the terrible, tight purgatory of their mutual recrimination. So – unlike Tammy – almost everything she knew was from books, not discussion. It was all printed in tiny letters she digested in swarms, like gnats flying into a great mouth.

Beans and Alicia were having a nap, still worn out by yesterday's hospital drama.

'I'm *assuming* this table doesn't object to getting wet. Lift your T.H. White, Tam-Tam.'

'They'd have protected it,' said Nick. 'They're that type. Anyway, it's only a butcher's block.'

'Not if he's really into antiques. That type just wax.' She studied some worrying circles where the kids' drinks had been. There were no coasters in the house, only antique iron rests for hot pans. The circles might have been there before, like marks of ancient enclosures, but she couldn't be sure. The wet sponge seemed to leave a pale comet-trace after it. Tammy pointed this out, but was not thanked for it.

'Don't worry about it, Sarah.'

'I'm trying not to.'

But he was worried as well. It was like staying with your parents. He had never been a real rebel. His only vice these days was watching High Stakes Poker on his laptop. He was too terrified of the consequences even to touch any porn, quite apart from the ideological angle. It was as if sleeping with the odd student and eventually marrying one had blown all the naughty fuses. He looked aghast at the viciousness of the world's powerful and went limp. Being genial wasn't enough. Stalin was fairly genial, behind his Dunhill pipe and yellow eyes. Bush, too, behind his spellbinding lack of the grey stuff, his creepy smirk.

'I just think we're all here to chill out,' he said, 'and not fret so much over minor things.'

'Maybe *minor* things are all we have,' Sarah said, nettled. She was attacking a recalcitrant mark on the catering sink's placid steel. 'Maybe everything else is just concept. Hm?'

Nick grunted and opened *Le Monde*, bought yesterday in St-Maurice, and pursed his lips, as he always did when facing the world's cupidity and suffering. This is difficult French, he thought. There are no eye-catching, over-egged stories. *Everything* in England is story. Instead of analysis. Infantilism, really: keep 'em hooked. What isn't a fleshy yarn is ignored.

This, however, is bony, holding back on the fat, the extraneous stodge. He struggled to feel nourished by it. A child had been murdered, but it was dispassionately recorded, without the lip-smacking details that what passed for British journalism would have conjured (conjured being the key word). A bit of a busman's holiday, he thought, working his way through the multiple classical arches of the words, the steady murmurings of the long, comma-stitched phrases. But he felt his intelligence was being addressed. That made a change.

Sarah squeezed the sponge out firmly and settled it behind the tap. She leaned back on the sink's frigid metal and folded her arms.

'I think I'm going to go to Aix *tomorrow*,' she said. 'And leave you with the kids.'

'We could all come. Aix is interesting.'

'Nick, it'll be a two-hour trip. I'll be leaving rather early. I'll need the whole day in the archives without interruption.'

'The world belongs to those who get up early,' Nick quoted, with a hint of irony, his finger in the air. 'No, correction: to those whose *workers* get up early.'

'And what kind of a world?' murmured Sarah.

'As long there's some lunch,' he said. 'I won't have the car to go and get anything.'

'You've got the car today.'

'Oh, I'm sure we won't starve,' Nick said, returning to the paper, its major things. A full-page article on Fra Angelico and the anti-Humanist influence of Giovanni Dominici on the young artist. Never a medievalist, what in fact flashed up was that awful scene in the film about the grisly Dominici Affair; he'd watched it, enthralled, as a teenager: the little girl running desperately away through the trees, the black-and-white shot taken from the axe-man's point of view, hand-held and jerky. Her parents had already been dealt with in their holiday caravan somewhere in the backwoods of Provence, and now it was her turn. At least this wasn't Provence. Run! Run!

'Supper?' asked Sarah. 'I'll be hungry.'

'Oh. Ah. Supper,' he intoned, turning the page. 'Omelette? I'll do an omelette.'

She had these moments when she wanted to take her shoes off and throw them at her husband's head. She was wearing soft espadrilles, today.

At least Jamie wasn't here. She had once screamed at her stepson as she'd never screamed at anyone in her life before and then left the house. All he'd done, Jamie had complained, with an air of bewilderment, was mention that the fruit had run out. Nick had asked (he later reported) if that was all. Jamie admitted to complaining about the loo seat being wet, but it had been meant as a joke. Nick had then asked if he – Jamie – had any idea what it was like bringing up two small kids, with a third on the way.

'That's her choice,' Jamie had replied, with irreproachable logic. 'Nobody forced her. You dig your own grave, man.'

One of the most difficult aspects of Jamie was that he was superficially a replica, or perhaps a pastiche, of his father as he was in his own student years: same language, same look, same smell, with a touch here and there of the new: an earring, a bead in his nose, the occasional variation into matted dread-locks or, as if a gremlin had gone mad with a miniature lawn mower, an erratically shaven scalp. So Nick found it hard to act the straight-laced, authoritarian father. Anyway, Jamie was a grown-up, at least officially.

As a result, Sarah had gone to a psychiatrist, to get her relationship with her stepson 'sorted' (in the stepson's words). She admitted that she could have done him bodily harm. The psychiatrist unravelled her difficult childhood and the general idea emerged that she was projecting an ancient animosity towards her absent father onto Jamie.

'How about he just learns some manners,' she said, embedded in a leather wing-chair that reclined in five positions, 'to start with?'

But the psychiatrist wasn't paid to discuss someone's manners, he was paid to go into the abyss. He'd repeated 'manners' with a hint of ridicule. Manners was probably the arch enemy of psychiatry: a bourgeois relic. Sarah felt herself turning into a starched Victorian maid.

'I reckon manners,' Sarah persisted, 'is about thinking of other people. Manners are actually quite deep. Manners maketh man. Or woman.'

'Ah,' said the psychiatrist, who was in his forties and quite dishy, 'now we're getting somewhere.'

Nick had asked how it was going, after the first three sessions. Sarah had told him that she was, essentially, a starched Victorian maid and it would take a lifetime to unstarch her. No more sessions.

'I'll phone the Centre on the mobile to let them know I'm coming,' said Sarah, already moving towards the door. She wondered what the Centre d'Archives d'Outre Mer would look like, already seeing herself mounting a flight of stone stairs into a beamed and panelled hall, with French intellectuals in scarves and rimless glasses dotted about. She didn't feel like asking Nick, who had been there many years ago.

'Don't fall off the bathroom stool,' Nick muttered, while unravelling a never-ending sentence in the editorial that appeared to have no object or main verb, with the flash of the Dominici Affair not quite sluiced away.

With Mummy off for the day, the girls plunged into the Daddy-only scenario with exceptional zeal. It took him back to the days after his divorce, when he would take Jamie to the park every second weekend, joining other sad-looking single dads at the swings. The girls weren't like this in Cambridge – when, in fact, he was hardly ever with them alone for more than half a day. Sarah would be back at about eight tonight. He worried about the drive, whether she'd remember to stay on the right, and kept involuntarily picturing a wreck, fire engines and ambulances flashing – much like the accident they'd passed on the way down, between Le Puy and Brioude. How would he tell the kids?

How were such things even possible, he mused, as he made faces out of the bits-and-pieces lunch, disguising its salady nature; how did they fit into a world of minor, everyday things, burning into them like that heavy knuckle of shell fragment he'd spotted, years ago, perched on a furrow in the Somme?

'Ugh,' said Alicia, grimacing at her plate, 'don't like cucumber *or* vegetables.'

After lunch he read to them from Tammy's 'lavishly illustrated' book of Greek myths, a present from her godfather. Beans sat on his knee as he started on the chapter dealing with Persephone, snatched down to Tartarus by Pluto. He read to them about Tartarus, about Charon and the Styx and the ghosts waiting to be judged, about the pool of memory and the pool of forget-fulness called Lethe, and how the clever ones drank from the pool of memory. Why? Because it was vital to remember: that's what historians do, he added. They remember that we should not forget and do stupid things over again.

It was quite a grown-up book, he realised, but they listened without a murmur. Beside the pool of memory grew a white poplar, with fluttery leaves. Alicia said she wanted to see one, and Nick suggested they go in search of one – he had seen what he reckoned were poplars down in the cleft of the valley where the river ran, although the leaves weren't yet out. The white poplar's male catkins turn reddish, he informed them excitedly, looking it up.

Never had he experienced such a perfection of fatherhood: they were behaving like children in an Edwardian novel. He thought of Sarah crouched over documents two hours' drive away and felt vaguely guilty at his suspicion that all this was due to her absence. Next week he would start on the Norse myths, thickening their knowledge, laying the cultural sediment. He'd had to discover it all by himself.

On the walk, Tammy asked him whether praying hard to Jesus can take you out of 'Taratarus'. He emphasised that it was just what the Greeks believed and that it wasn't true, anyway. This Jesus thing bothered him; it was the new teacher. Beans leaned over to one side in the backpack and he told her to keep straight, but she was in fact asleep, her hand clutching a *sucette*. There should be a law against preaching religion in English schools, he thought, as there was in France.

Alicia said she didn't want to die. Nick began telling lies, stuff he didn't believe. Reincarnation rather than the afterlife, but still. He was a confirmed atheist, but could hardly tell them that. Tammy reckoned being reborn was frightening, you might be reborn as someone really fat like her school enemy Lucilla Bales or a beggar or someone without legs.

'Oh I don't know, I think it'll be pretty nice being reborn,' he said, unable to find a decent eschatological rejoinder to her remorseless logic. 'It'll make a change.'

Strange, to think of his kids dying. Of being able to die at all.

It was a bright day, with a peculiarly sharp, cold light that blanched everything and gave it a kind of varnish. They were heading for the granite rocks on the heathy stretch from where you could see the river valley and a row of leafless but poplar-shaped trees, like a painter's fine brushes. On the way, in the chestnut wood, a brown-and-white troop of goats came towards them like a flash flood, bleating and jingling. The shepherd, walking in the middle, had a jacket over his shoulders and a crook that had a nobble instead of a curved top. His dog padded about at the back, rounding up stragglers. One of the goats had a limp. Nick regretted not bringing the camcorder, then realised it would have been embarrassing, the wrong image entirely.

It was the same shepherd they'd seen passing the house, but had never met. He was somewhere between thirty and sixty, a lined, browned but boyish face with moist eyes that seemed to have two silvery points in the middle from the bright light. He stopped to talk to them, for the first time. He reminded Tammy of the funny man who would stand outside the swimming baths back home, humming to himself. Beans insisted on getting down to meet the goats.

Afterwards, Nick refused to give Tammy a précis of their conversation. The girls had been rubbing the goats on their hard, bristly foreheads: they were slightly scared of their horns and their jostling nervousness.

'Oh, it was just a chat. About the weather,' he said. 'He can tell what the weather's going to be without watching it on the telly.'

'So can I,' said Alicia mockingly, looking up at the clear sky. 'It's going to be all sunny.'

'Wrong,' said Nick. 'He said it'll rain tonight. Coming from the north. He can smell it and he says it's too bright. That's a shepherd for you. It might rain heavily, so let's hope Mummy's back before it does.'

'That's *only* what you talked about?' confirmed Tammy.

'Yup. All we talked about, pretty well.'

Tammy didn't believe him. She'd picked up the word 'accident' in its French version, repeated several times, and the fact that her father's face looked shocked at one point. What her father did add was that the shepherd was called Bruno and his greatest wish was to visit Greenland.

'Weirdo,' Tammy said.

'Not really. Not that weird. Shepherds are traditionally a little on the strange side, spending so much time on their own.'

The girls' palms smelt sharply of goat: they made him smell it.

'Ah, the smell of Pan,' he intoned, still in the classical swim. Alicia snorted, smelling hers again. '*That's* not like bread!'

'Daddy,' said Tammy, after Nick had explained about Pan, 'didn't the shepherd say something about an accident?'

'Not really, no.'

'That's what I heard.'

'You don't understand French, Tammy.'

'*I* do,' said Alicia. 'Ang, doh, twa, craa, sank . . .'

'It wasn't Beans's accident, then?'

'Oh, probably,' said Nick. 'Sorry, yeah, it was.'

They were growing like speeded-up coral. He was fading away.

'You're not telling the tru-uth,' Tammy chanted, and Alicia joined in.

'Sorry, you don't always get the right end of the stick when you're seven.'

'I'm eight.'

'I *mean* eight,' he said, starting to walk on with Beans in one hand and Alicia in the other, their faces turned back to smile triumphantly at their sister.

As they entered the yard on their return, Nick saw what looked like a mysterious stack of broken white crockery or perhaps crumpled balls of paper against the back wall next to where the zinc guttering finished in a stone drain. Alicia ran up to it and yelled so that her voice bounced back off the barn: 'Look, someone's brung us nice flowers!'

The white and creamy lilies, roses and chrysanthemums were set against dark glossy leaves and lighter sprays of fern. A pale, silky ribbon bore the single word REGRETS, which Nick assumed was to be read the French way, without sounding the last two consonants, although he mentally failed to.

'Oo-er,' Tammy said. 'Someone's died again.'

'Why?' asked Alicia.

'No doubt,' said Nick, somewhat rattled, 'Jean-Luc will throw light on it. Don't touch, Alicia.'

Alicia cocked her head like a bird and asked if it was like the thing on the track with the name in it and them flowers on too, her mind almost audibly whirring.

Nick nodded. 'Sort of.'

What Bruno the shepherd had revealed was that his brother had fallen off the roof of Les Fosses exactly six years ago today, but not that flowers had been left. Maybe it was another relative. Or the wife.

'When did *this* one die?' essayed Alicia again, all but breathless with excitement.

'I think it's very pretty,' said Nick, stalling.

'Film it,' Alicia suggested. 'What's regrets mean?'

Nick demurred. 'Something too sad to film,' he explained.

'Maybe it was Jean-Luc again,' Tammy said. 'He's pretty strange.'

'Is he?'

'He's nice,' said Alicia.

Beans broke into earnest chatter, like a little bird, tugging his trouser-leg. Nick nodded and repeated *really?* but couldn't be bothered to make out what she was saying, although the word 'cruck' kept appearing.

'Or maybe someone conked out on this very spot,' Tammy interrupted, also excited now. 'Not Fernando but someone new, Daddy.'

Nick looked at her uncertainly. This was no doubt the very place where the builder had landed with a thump, a crack of neck-bone. He looked up. The edge of the roof was a long way up, falling slowly backwards against a small, complicated wisp of dark cloud in the blue.

'Or in the house,' Tammy went on, tossing the hair out of her eyes. 'Of something like choleric or turbo locust. And whoever left this couldn't get in, or didn't even want to.'

'Why?' asked Alicia, lost.

'Likkel window,' said Beans.

'We can go on speculating forever,' Nick said, eyeing the barn. *Turbo locust* was good. He would tell Sarah about Tammy's turbo locust, but not about the accident.

'We can throw the flowers away when they walt, Daddy.'

'When they wilt. Of course, Tam-tam.'

'Hope it doesn't upset Mummy too much. She doesn't like deathie thingies.'

'No, she certainly doesn't,' he agreed.

And thought, as his daughter stood there in her diminutive pensiveness, how much could be crammed into the small-size sock of eight years.

Alicia nodded when she was told not to tell Mummy because Mummy 'doesn't like deathie things just as she doesn't like hamburgers'. Nick found his explanation as unsatisfactory as the subterfuge itself.

Away from the others, Tammy was instructed in a whisper to carry the floral offering not too far into the trees and hide it respectfully. She was proud of the responsibility.

The flowers were stuck in wet sponge that soaked her sleeves, and were heavier than she'd expected. She laid them at the foot of a tree, in undergrowth, and scratched her ankles. It didn't feel good, though, doing this. She thought she'd gone quite far into the woods but when she turned round there was the house beyond the washing-line. There was something big and round at her feet, like a big root. She brushed the prickly stuff to one side with her foot, bravely. The root carried on until it came back and met itself. She suddenly saw it as a cartwheel, like the ones in the barn. Its spokes were broken and its orange paint was peeling off and there were words carved on the rim, almost overflowing its thinness: *MAS DU PARADIS*.

She threw dead leaves over the flowers and pricked her finger. Like in a fairy story, she realised, and hurtled back before the wheel rose up with a grin and rolled on top of her.

Sarah came back from Aix a little earlier than expected, at seven-thirty. The return trip had been very quick, but she'd also been warned about the rain. The air was wet-smelling and close, despite the coolness.

The Centre d'Archives d'Outre Mer was a dull, modern building with a municipal look to the pine and metal shelving, but the librarians had been highly efficient in finding what she was looking for: records relating to the forced dispersion of French-colonised West Africans to French Guyana as labourers. She was expanding on a footnote in her thesis: Nick, who'd been her supervisor, had advised her to do so nine or ten years back.

'You found proof that it wasn't voluntary?'

'Kind of. I'll show you my notes. It's not straightforward.'

Nick had used the Centre several times both before and after he'd met Sarah, and he now recalled finding the records of the Bureau de Recherches de Pétrol's subsidiaries in Gabon and the Congo, with the usual story of corruption, displacement of locals and so on; and how the files were warped and stained by the African climate, with tiny red splotches of squashed mosquitoes; and how, since the Bureau de Recherches de Pétrol was now Elf-Total, he'd expected a visit from hitmen in dark glasses, almost as much as he had when digging up details about Chevron in Chad – *in* Chad itself – a few years earlier, which was quite another story (Sarah had, of course, heard it many times).

'You'd have been so lucky,' murmured Sarah, fully upstaged.

'My paper wasn't completely ignored,' he went on. 'There was some disgruntlement in the trade mags and one or two annual reports. Esso's, for instance, mentioned it.'

Sarah had enjoyed her few hours away, especially the drive there with the CD-player blaring out her Dylan (not Nick's favourite); what she omitted to tell him was that she had not been able to stop herself worrying about the girls. You either worried or you didn't: you couldn't worry a bit, like you couldn't be a bit pregnant, or a bit Nazi. As it turned out, on her return the girls were deep in a board game with their father in front of the fire and had barely looked up. She'd felt redundant. She'd expected them to run towards her and fling themselves at her skirt.

'We've had a *great* time,' Nick had confirmed, just in case she was in any doubt.

The Smiths were playing on the hi-fi: 'Suffer Little Children'. A song she didn't like at all – about the Moors Murders. Inappropriate. It was on quite loud, too.

'I'm starving,' she said. 'How's the omelette?'

'As you can see,' said Nick, 'still in the project stage.'

'And the girls not even in their pyjamas?'

'French time,' he murmured, trying not to show his own irritation.

'By the way,' he told her, pouring out more wine at the end of supper, 'I met the local shepherd. Bruno.'

The omelette was fine, in the end. The only flat note, as usual, was the bread: thawed out; fresh each day was impossible. It was a round trip of about three-quarters of an hour to the baker's in Valdaron, including the wait as folk chatted. Sarah had put the girls to bed and was only now unwinding after a couple of hours of appeasement. Nick felt exhausted.

'The kids told me, yes.'

'Fascinating. His greatest dream is to visit Greenland.'

'You don't say.'

'So I said to him, "Well, if it's for the glaciers you're going, you'd better hurry up."'

'That's pretty advanced, if it was in French.'

'I paraphrase,' said Nick. 'It's simpler in French. *Si c'est pour les glacières, il faut aller vite là-bas.*'

'*Glacières?* You're sure that's right?'

Nick groaned. Sarah looked it up in the French-English dictionary, tipping the page towards the candle-flame.

'*Glacière* is, I'm afraid, an ice-box. Glacier is *glacier*,' Sarah announced, looking pleased.

'No wonder he laughed,' Nick chuckled, gamely. 'Actually, he didn't laugh, he was too polite. He just looked puzzled for a second.'

'Eef eet ees for zee ice boxes, you must go qweek to there,' said Sarah.

'Better than zee ice burgers, I suppose. Or buggers, even.'

They were in fits, worse than Alicia and Tammy in the doctor's surgery. They polished off the wine, still laughing, and that was that. It was good to be back, thought Sarah. She told Nick about the dishy young Arab guy in the reading room, looking up registers of military recruitment in colonial Algeria; he wasn't allowed to reproduce it in any form, he'd whispered to her.

'In your ear?'

'In my ear.'

Nick pulled a shocked face, pretending not to be bothered. He did not broach the other matter, about the builder, about the builder's accident and the anniversary flowers. He saw no need. Now she was happy, he felt he could be disgruntled, anyway. Rain began to spatter against the shutters like bursts of typing. Then, after stopping to think about it, the storm broke. At least, they reckoned it was a storm. It drummed on the roof all night, as if it would rather be inside. It made the track into a temporary collection of streams and gouged channels through the gravel at the front. It smacked on the pool and appeared to have raised the level by several centimetres. Sarah, squeaking the shutters open slightly and looking out at the wall of water in the middle of the night, was reminded of Africa, and all that she had not, after all, achieved or (more to the point) dared.

Logs were brought the next day and deposited next to the barn. Some rolled into the strip of briar and charred stones. Everything glittered after the rain, and they thought they could see the snowy flanks of the Alps: a suggestion of whiteness like little teeth, that wasn't cloud.

The ancient lorry looked much the worse for wear, with broken wing-mirrors and a dented bonnet, and made a terrible din as it bashed its way along the worsened track. The little 'log-man', as they called him, was almost perfectly square (Tammy's description), with a squashed nose and huge leathery hands. He showed Nick how best to stack logs, each layer crossways on the previous layer, so that the air might get in and dry them quicker. He admitted the logs were a bit green and may need splitting. They were certainly wet. The stack was begun inside the barn, just to the left of the entrance.

Nick couldn't find gloves and the wood seemed to sap all the moisture from his skin, despite the wetness. He initially enjoyed the unthinking task, although it seemed to take ages before any inroads were made on the sprawling heap outside. The two older girls intermittently helped, clutching a single log to the chest or choosing fat sticks, which they stacked separately for kindling. The air was washed clean but not cold, although the log-man assured them that April could be frosty.

His body engaged, Nick's mind kept returning to the shepherd's grim tale. He toyed with the idea of not telling Sarah at all. Of trying not to dwell on it, let it float away as most things did in the end, but it remained obstinately moored in his head.

The poor man had been working for the Sandlers. He'd landed just there. He felt bad, now, about the memorial flowers.

Thump. Broken neck. Rabbit punch.

There was something vaguely distasteful about the way the Sandlers hadn't mentioned it, but he could totally understand their position. It had nothing to do with them, the Mallinsons, it was something that had happened in the past, a few years back, and it could stay there. His instinct was to probe, but he fought it. This sabbatical was about living in the present. It was about dwelling on what mattered, letting time run through his fingers without trying to hold it, to clasp what couldn't be clasped. Because time was above all a liquid. Time was the historian's worst ally, like the ultimate peer review.

Time had surprised him, especially by dissolving his Marxist foundations. He had drifted from Habermas and Jameson to the unlikely port of Gilles Deleuze, a thinker for whom everything is displacement, contingency and indeterminacy, like worrying medical conditions. For several years he'd been taken up with domestic problems: his hyper-active first son, Jamie; his aged mother – who'd gone from benevolent sharpness, deep in her whist and bridge in Crowthorne, to blunt recalcitrance and dementia. (She was, he'd say, a paradigm of the West.) He left Helena and met Sarah – not in that order, come to think of it.

He rarely read his contemporaries in the field, there was far too much thanks to the research ratings nonsense: everything was seething – teasing proliferation instead of debate and reflection. It was the fundamental sign of Deleuze's unsynthesised present, he once wrote (adding to the seethe): experience undergone, not yet passed into memory. None of it, then, had meaning: it was a disparate jumble. Only the cocaine of virtual communication had meaning. At times during this difficult period he had craved a simpler world, a world of mud roads and burning faiths. Simple, stark choices. He'd crave to be back in that world, to be a peasant in the chill plough-lines of feudalism, looking up at the God-filled sky. He had, in other words, become the precise opposite of what he was in his youth.

That's what time did, because it was liquid. It wasn't a sea, of course, but a river – as large and powerful as the Congo river, on whose banks he had several times marvelled in earlier years. He could find no more original metaphor for time. He wasn't a poet. What poetry he read, of the modern kind, he mostly found obscure and baffling.

Maybe he was more prophet than historian, he thought, stacking a large log cloaked in pubic moss, a soft pelt against his hands. The girls had gone in, bored.

The car. The computer. Mortgages and shopping. All of us have fallen for it – hook, line and sinker. Again and again. It won't be the bathing and anointing, the ewers of fresh wine, the cushioned recliners, the slaves to light our way; it'll be the toilet paper we'll miss.

He was enjoying the logs, the creaminess of the bared timber, the criss-cross layering, the woodblock strikes of it.

When Sarah was pregnant with Tammy, was it – his return to Michelet's history of France? His marvelling at it? The rekindling of Nicholas Mallinson! Dates, dates. His own dates fuzzed. Tammy, precocious Tammy, plus two more. Unruliness. Whole hours thrown into the air like confetti. The days and then weeks and then months, gobbled up. Years. His scholarly biography of Ferdinand Lassalle had taken five of them, and it was scarcely noticed. His more approachable book on the pre-war history of African oil exploration, *Tending the Reserves*, was remaindered after a year (he first knew of this in a second-hand bookshop in Brighton). His first major appearance in a TV documentary as a talking head last year, illuminating the build-up to Suez, dismayed him: he looked venerable, despite the strange, purplish light on his face.

Looking back from his sixth decade, he was astonished (particularly in the sleepless middle of the night, when whispering, malicious elves took over) by the brevity of what had been his life so far. 'The syncope of the long breath', as that young colleague in English put it in one of his published poems. The new man whose name he can never remember, and who expects you to have read him. Who has, in fact, been at FitzHerbert's for at least five years.

Yet, as a teenager, life had seemed to stretch out to infinity. The simple grasslands of life. The reeds waving to the boundless horizon.

All these logs will be burnt.

He supposed that, if he *was* insufferably ideological, it was not just in reaction to his own Deleuze period. A tiny handful of people in suits were looting the world. Ransacking it. Casino hustlers, tilting the tables. Consumerism as another, very subtle form of slavery. Founded on literal slavery, if you think about it, if you delve a little deeper.

Oil, too, was liquid. What could be as deadly dull, as viscously horrible, as that one word *oil*; or be as tediously monotonous as the repetition of that dry, flat, scrubland name, *Chad*? But the intellect's pistons had begun to move again in tune with his heart, and he'd seen how his life's work might, after all, cohere.

Sarah was suffering because of it, her own work obscured by his enthusiasm, his reborn zeal. For 'oil' had become his mantra, the thread that made sense of it all: of thirty years of scholarship. The two older girls would pretend to switch their ears off when he talked about his work. He was a gangly bore, and he knew it. When he looked at photographs of himself as a rebellious adolescent, all he could see was his trousers set too high and the absurd explosion of hair in which his pale face stared out like a mouse from its nest. He wondered who those creatures were, who loved themselves, and how contented they must be in their innocence.

By the time he'd stacked the last log, he'd covered an awful lot of ground. He was mentally exhausted, and the tendons around his right elbow burnt.

He stood by the clear pool for a moment, wondering why it had a deposit of what looked like snow or white ash covering the bottom. Maybe that's what happened when you clarified things: the fog just solidified.

Jean-Luc fishes under his bed and pulls out a cardboard box.

Inside the box is rubbish, including a rusty kitchen sieve, broken plastic toys, old spoons, lots of birds' feathers, silvery stones from the river, a plastic bowl split on one side, cheap paperbacks swollen by damp, and the doll. She jumps leglessly onto the table and then he fishes out the sieve and places it next to her. He touches the sieve, orange at the joins of the mesh, and it rocks from side to side. Then he lays Bibi inside it and watches her rock with it, like a naked girl in a round hammock, missing her legs but still beautiful.

She is stuck. Like a fly in a cobweb. He stops the sieve rocking and holds it still. He feels excited, now. All he needs, then, is a spider. A big black spider. He'd watch cobwebs for hours, as a kid. The spider wrapping up the fly in a white cocoon, the fly struggling at first, then giving up. He'd pretend to be the fly, lying on the floor and being wrapped up in sticky thread. He couldn't move his arms for ages.

In the corner of his room, a real cobweb flutters in a draught from the window, which won't close properly since the rains. It is an old cobweb, so old the spider is a bony white skeleton inside it. He considers using the skeleton for a moment. No, too fragile. It'll crumble to bits at a touch. He knows what he has to find: something like that bundle of tiny bones. He can look out for it. Again, he feels a surge of pleasure inside him. Bibi is the fly, despite her Jesus nails. But who is the spider?

Himself, he thinks. Everything is himself, from inside him. Even Bibi. Even the cobweb.

His mother is calling his name. She's beginning to shriek it out, only muffled by the door. She needs help to do her doings. But she can wait. He doesn't want to destroy this moment.

He thinks of the Englishwoman at Les Fosses, probably a little older than himself. Marie, he murmurs, my sweet sister

146

in love. He needs a photograph of her, he is sure about that. Of her cold face, and of her warm face. Then he will rub the cold face out. He has to have a photograph of her smile, her lost look.

A secret photograph.

Because if she knew he was taking it, she would not put on that lost look. She would not look like Marie. All he needs is a camera.

His mother has stopped, worn out by calling his name. Now she will wet the bed, deliberately. He will let her, so that he can scold her. Scold her as once she scolded him. He won't let her take over. He is the boss, here. Then he remembers there are no more clean sheets; he has neglected the washing. The nurse comes in the morning, but it's not her job to do the washing. The nurse, called Elodie, binds his mother's swollen legs in a tight bandage, gives her the medicines, chirrups and twitters to cheer her up. Jean-Luc quite likes Elodie, who is young and business-like with short mousy hair and heavy eyebrows, but he is always afraid she will find some fault in the way he does things. Then she might wrap him up tightly in her long white bandage, over and over, and sit on his face.

He studies the wall where the rain ran down during the night. Always in the same place: the dark brown streak glistens, that's all. And in the morning there's a big puddle on the floor where the old stain is. The old bruise.

Once, when Elodie found bruises on his mother's arms, blue as a tattoo, she gave him a suspicious glance. He made a joke of it: ah yes, I've been clobbering her a lot lately! And the nurse and his mother laughed. And so did he. In fact, it was when he had lifted her up off the bolsters to rearrange them: she bruised easily. He had strong hands. One forgot.

His mother was always older than other mothers, mothers of his contemporaries. She had him at forty-two. It wasn't normal, to have your first and only child at forty-two. Not around here, at any rate. Maybe there was some problem.

The excitement has passed. It comes and goes. It can be

triggered by pulling out the cardboard box of rubbish, but it's so easily dissolved. In a few minutes he will go downstairs and watch Marie-Sylvaine on her chat show while getting the supper together. That cheers him up.

He thinks he hears a laugh through the door. His mother is probably pissing into her bedclothes right at this moment, just to spite him. It'll go right through to the rubber sheet, which will stink unless it's taken off and rinsed. He gets up from the chair so abruptly the chair falls backwards and he's unlocked the door and has leapt into her room before the back hits the lino.

It happened when they were all watching television – French television – from various vantage points on the sofa or the rug or both at once. The show consisted of a panel of about ten guests laughing hysterically at their own jokes. They were all ugly. The audience members appeared to be watching a mildly depressing documentary. The Mallinsons, large and small, scarcely understood a word.

The other channels were umbrageous, shifting shapes in a blizzard. One seemed to be about the economy. They stopped on what was either a rugby match or a documentary on migrating caribou.

'Maybe the aerial needs adjusting,' said Sarah.

Nick grunted. 'What aerial?'

'Isn't there one? Up on the roof?'

'Is there? Haven't noticed it.'

'I don't know,' she said, feeling she was sounding like her mother.

They flicked back to adverts on TF1, the channel that worked: they understood those, at least.

'The semiotics of Omo,' said Sarah, although it was an advert for a car. She yawned. 'Nearly time for bed, kids.'

'We can ask Jean-Luc to check the aerial,' Tammy suggested.

'And then he'll go up on the roof,' Sarah said.

'So what?'

'He might fall off,' she pointed out, with a hint of a chuckle.

The sound fizzed abruptly and a dark bar descended over an image of a fluffy snow-white cat nestling in a washing basket. The bar, as it descended, compressed the picture comically, the bottom half appearing again at the top. The fizz was electronic and nastily harsh, as if someone was drilling nearby, drowning the voices. It was the perfect projection of what had just happened inside Nick.

'Stupid telly,' said Alicia.

'We can always read instead,' said her father, stretching. 'You know, that strange activity called reading. Or play a *brief* game.'

They waited in a lazy way, but when the interference lessened, it left another channel overlapping what was now the chat show again: a dim, X-rayed face, no doubt a newscaster's, took up most of the screen. He slid slightly to the left and then to the right, as if on a swing that had all but stopped. The pale lips were moving. He was looking straight out at them.

Obviously the dead builder, Nick thought, alarming himself.

'Pearl's on great form,' murmured Sarah, who had been on her mobile ten minutes ago, up in the bathroom.

'Really?' said Nick. 'How come?'

She looked mildly hurt. 'Why shouldn't she be?'

'Why *should* she be?'

'She usually is.'

'*Woman's Hour*, or something?'

She looked at him quizzically, with some concern. 'Er, what?'

He said, 'It's not everyone who gets on Radio 4.'

'On *great form*, I said.'

He stared at her for a moment. 'OK,' he said. 'Call me Professor Calculus.'

'Professor Calculus!' chorused the girls.

Sarah squeezed his hand. 'Professor Conquest, I say.'

That was a surprise. It didn't take much to cheer him up. He squeezed her hand back.

'You're like the stupid telly, Daddy,' squeaked Alicia, shoving her head between his knees as her mother rested her own head on his shoulder. The insides of his knees found Alicia's neck and squeezed it playfully. 'Cut my head off, *pleee-ease*.'

'Maybe we should put him in the recycling bin,' said Tammy, chin on her hands, staring back at the dim face on the screen.

Nick switched off the telly with the remote. The idea that he was looking at the face of the dead builder had not evaporated. He was reminded of the faces of the torturers, bullies and other apparatchiks in Budapest's House of Terror museum, about which he had written, for *Past & Present*, his last published paper: 'Re(In)formation in the Disney Age: Selective Trauma in post-Communist Hungary'. Despite not knowing a word of Hungarian. It was a sortie out of his field. A refreshment. He got clobbered, quite justifiably, by a revered Central European specialist in the next issue.

Sarah's head was heavy against his shoulder. Tammy prodded her elbow, presumably by mistake, in his stomach. Alicia was now trying to separate his knees further, exercising his flabby calf muscles. He pretended to complain. He loved them with a scattered intensity: not a single bright point but something dispersed that was still of the same property and energy as the single bright point. History had somehow escaped them all; had so far let them off. He'd heard it all his life, muffled, like a busy street through a closed window. Even in the Congo, with its street-mobs whirling chains and brandishing machetes, its bloodied faces and casually murdered neighbours, he had not felt the window open. He wondered if one day he would hear the high, unexpected smash of a stone in its glass.

Impossible, of course: history can never be present. It can never clamber over you and prod you in the stomach, exercise your calf muscles, lean on your shoulder. It is all words. It is only words. It has always happened, it is always a kind of ghost.

SIX

They found stale chocolate digestives in the back of a cupboard and rejoiced.

They decided to take them on a walk as supplies, and then decided not to, as they would go all gooey. When they got back! The weather was calm and spring-like. Yellow flowers, some like buttercups, some like small dandelions, had appeared in the woods in spread-out gowns, along with white star-shaped solitaries. 'We must get a flower book,' Sarah said.

She had noticed, while hanging out clothes, that the glossy-leaved bushes between the washing-line and the trees bore small globes of orangey fruit, even though the bushes' flowers were only just beginning to open. They didn't dare try the fruit, though. Anyway, they were hard, not yet ripe. Nick said that he had seen these laurel-like bushes in Ireland, where they were called straw-berry trees; they had nice white flowers and the fruit turned red.

'I believe,' he said, as if accumulating points, 'the Ancient Greeks made their flutes from the wood.'

'They're not strawberries, stupid,' Alicia scoffed.

'If they're actually *called* strawberries,' Tammy said, 'they're probably dee-lish.'

'Yum yum,' said Beans, reaching up with her right hand, which had entirely healed within a week.

'It might be a trap,' said Sarah, stopping her. She knew the names of hardly any wild flowers, unlike mothers in books. Her own mother's garden was mostly gladioli and hydrangea and a big ornamental birch. There were huge fields of rape beyond, and the bright yellow along with the bright red of the gladioli gave them all headaches in summer.

They took another path forking off past the granite boulders and descended to an unexpected stream. It fell noisily over rocks into large, smooth-cupped pools as clear as glass. They had to shout.

'Let's go back and find the digestives tree,' Nick joked. 'The Famous Five *ont faim*. Are famished.'

They climbed up to the main track and tramped along, having ventured further than they'd meant to. Beans fell asleep on Sarah's back. The others moaned like prisoners on a forced march.

'We could buy a caravan,' said Alicia, suddenly. 'Then we could *cook*.'

'Don't like caravans. Or camper vans,' said Nick.

'You don't like *anything*,' she whined.

'I like chasing you,' he growled, and she immediately ran ahead.

He pretended to pursue her as a wolf. She jinked like a hare along the path, squealing. 'Kill her and eat her up!' shouted Tammy from behind. Alicia was gurgling and squeaking in both delight and terror. The delight of terror, he thought, pretending to lope fast, pursuing the small, jinking form and unable not to conjure the girl in the Dominici Affair, desperate to save her life.

'Gotcha!'

When they arrived back, they found Jean-Luc nailing a new eye on the front door, just as dry but with all its lashes and still a coppery-gold colour. He left the old flower on, which now looked blind, wrinkled and jealous.

He told them that people round here called it a cardousso, and the old folk claimed it protected the house because it looked like a sun. It opened when it was dry and closed when it was wet.

'*Une symbole solaire*,' said Nick, nodding in approval.

'*Un baromètre*,' said Jean-Luc.

He hoovered the pool again while the girls watched. He sucked up the white stuff until the bottom was showing for the first time. It's not as good as when it was hidden, thought Tammy: the bottom had stains and tiny cracks.

Sarah trusted they were safe as long as Jean-Luc was with them, but worried nevertheless. *A child's drowning is silent*, she'd read on the Internet back in Cambridge. *A child can drown in the time it takes to answer the phone.* She kept peeping through the kitchen window. It was sweet, the way they watched Jean-Luc at work. They didn't need gadgets, telly or computer games.

Afterwards, while they were all having tea, they heard a knocking sound. Nick investigated. Jean-Luc was splitting logs in the barn with a huge axe. He was taking logs off the stack Nick had made, setting each upright on the giant cheese of a chopping block and swinging the blade down unerringly almost every time so that the log in question flew into two parts; then each of these were chopped into two more. Four from one. Nick marvelled at the accuracy, the ease. A split log jumped so far it hit his shin. He pretended it didn't hurt. He felt he should have been doing this himself.

Better for the fire, Jean-Luc told him. Then you put on the unsplit logs. As if Nick had never lit a fire in his life. But he nodded gratefully nevertheless as Jean-Luc swung the polished blade up high and let it come down on its own gravity. It was his grandfather's axe, he said. The bulky blade was hand-forged: its edge was fretted but razor-sharp. Only the red handle was new.

Nick asked him, in a pause, having mentally rehearsed the French, whether he was related to Fernand Maille, the man '*memorialisé*' on the track. The axe's blade was well bitten into the chopping block.

Jean-Luc seemed to give thought to the question, staring at the pale woodchips on the barn floor. Then he stated very firmly that, no, Fernand was nothing to do with his family. Nothing to do with his family at all. *Pas du tout, monsieur.*

The church in little Aubain was as cold as a fridge and decrepit. There were peeling eighteenth-century frescoes and the faded names on the backs of the choir-stalls were in thick-nibbed, italic script. A worm-eaten statue of a red-lipped Virgin with cheeks like pink marshmallows stood with raised arms in a piddle of water. Damp had etched, not just stained, one end of the nave on whose high half-dome a crude constellation of gold stars had been painted in a wash of deep cerulean blue. The windows were plain glass, with streaks of cobweb like thin leading. The echo was amazing.

A tiny woman in spectacles and blue frock was dusting the altar. Nick chatted to her while Sarah tried to stop the girls' natural impulse to whoop. The woman informed them that the Protestant rebels had burnt the church a hundred years ago, leaving nothing of interest except the outside stones. Nick knew that it was two hundred years ago, but kept mum. The kids' whoops, although parakeet-like, were undeniably English, but the woman gave them a friendly smile.

'*Elles sont mignonnes,*' she sighed, as if that justified everything.

They left at last and the outside flattened their voices like tin. The sun blinded and warmed: they had changed latitude in seconds.

'Aren't the French *nice* about children,' Sarah remarked.

'Even *us,*' snorted Tammy, screwing her face up into cartoon ugliness.

'Maybe I should ask her about Les Fosses,' said Nick.

'Why?'

'Historical interest.'

The girls crouched around a hapless invertebrate under the plane tree. From the church came the high, moaning hoover sound in which devils laughed and the innocent groaned. Or vice-versa. Where faith was concerned, one could never be sure. The front door was a cleft in a cliff: Nick disappeared into its black pitch. Alicia ran up to the front steps and sat on them, shielding her eyes while Beans and Tammy hid behind one of the plane trees. The air was cool when it shifted into a gust. Sarah sat on a low, sun-warmed wall and felt a moment of absolute repose; life was good, really. It was really really good, in fact.

Nick reappeared like Orpheus climbing back into the land of the living. He had forgotten his sunglasses at home and squinted as he approached them with news of the dead.

'Any lowdown on the house, then?'

'No. Well, she didn't react. I suggest we try the café. Girls,' he called out, with a ham note of irony, 'you don't want a *sirop*, do you?'

'No,' Alicia shouted back, unexpectedly – and meant it.

They were the only ones making a noise outside for one simple reason: they were the only ones. Aubain could have been a ghost village, apart from the vacuuming. No barking dogs, even. The neat *mairie*, with its capital A of steps and its French flag above the door and its glassed noticeboard full of official decrees (*Avis à la Population*), was shut for the day. The redundant words *Café du Louvre* were just legible in pale brown across a shuttered house facing the church. The hand-coloured poster pinned to its door announced an art competition; Nick was surprised to see the closing date still in the future instead of the far past.

Sarah studied the war memorial while the girls panted theatrically next to her. It was nothing more than a tapering slab of stone inside a chained-off square of tussocky earth. The stone had a dozen victims etched in under 1914–1918 (several of the surnames recurring), while there were six under 1939–1944. Alicia asked if these were people's birthdays. Sarah explained, while Tammy implored God to give her sister a brain.

'Shut up, Tammy,' Sarah uncharacteristically snapped.

'Look!' shrieked Tammy, regardless. 'Fernand Maille!'

Faded flowers, still in their plastic, lay on the plinth.

'There you go,' said Sarah, already contrite. 'Well done, Tamsin –' and Tammy greeted the cheering hordes with a sardonic wave.

'We'll check him out in the cemetery,' said Nick. 'Let's go to the cemetery, then, girls, instead of the café. We'll go on foot. It'll be a nice walk.'

'Yippee,' said Alicia, despite the mention of a walk.

'Are there drinks in the cemetery?'

'Erm, don't think so, Tammy.'

'You said we were going to the café and having a Coke.'

'Not strictly accurate. I proposed the café and was met with a thumbs down. I never mentioned Coke.'

'That's just stupid Ali-Baba,' Tammy scoffed. 'She can go to the cemetery and we'll go to the café and sniff coke.'

The hermeneutic key to this precocious joke consisted of one word: Jamie.

'Coke, Coke,' echoed Beans, slapping her hands.

Alicia said, tugging her mother's sleeve: 'Mummy, she called me stupid and a name.'

'Cemetery first,' Nick insisted. 'It'll give us a good thirst.'

'That rhymes,' Tammy pointed out. 'Mrs Foster says poems shouldn't rhyme.'

'Does she?'

'She gives you marks off if you rhyme. Oh, how grateful I am for jolly Mrs Foster. Especially her lovely smell, exactly like an old sock.'

'Tammy, that's enough,' Sarah remonstrated. 'She is your teacher.'

'She does her best,' Tammy sighed.

'Mummy,' said Alicia suddenly, in a worried, conspiratorial tone, tugging at her mother's sleeve, 'where's all the CVV cameras gone?'

Jean-Luc sees Marcel's big jeep pass below the window, going too fast as usual, the dogs yelping. It's not that Jean-Luc has never hunted. He'd go out with his father and a few of his father's mates from the age of ten, bouncing along in the old Renault van. But he was never a good shot, and something about killing animals doesn't agree with him, although at the moment of the hunt his blood can get up as much as anyone else's. He once shot a big hare and ran up to it and found it alive, but badly messed about in the rump. And before he picked it up to chop it on the neck and put it out of its misery, the hare looked him straight in the eyes – not accusingly, no, but wonderingly, as if wanting to know why. They'd warned him about that look: there's something bewitching in it, they said, as if animals were sorcerers. But he hadn't looked away in time, and after that he only hunted to please his father. He hasn't hunted at all for at least ten years. He is glad.

His father would tell him how, in the old days, when *he* was a boy, they'd pedal out on their bicycles before dawn, their bare feet in wooden clogs pushing at the pedals up the hill in the darkness, each dog in a wire cage behind the saddle.

He'd once got a double kill, his father said, soon after receiving his permit at seventeen; posted as the furthest look-out behind a clump of gorse on the high, lonely hills between Aubain and Valdaron, he'd watched the dawn come up, the sky turn milky, the first robin fix him with its tiny black berry of an eye; he'd watched the buzzards circle and the rabbits feed and the hills turn pink, 'like they were blushing, like they were pretty girls blushing'. He could have shot ten rabbits, but he wasn't there for rabbits.

Sometimes Jean-Luc believes that his father's whole life revolved around that morning just after the war. Elie Maille was four years younger than his brother, Fernand. Poor Oncle Fernand. Had a limp, worked in the stinking tannery in Valdaron, never harmed anyone or got involved in anything: murdered by the Nazis on the way back from Les Fosses. And we all know why that was! Only Jean-Luc keeps him company, now, in his sad wanderings.

Elie was different. He was wilder. He became a messenger boy for the *maquis*, and saw terrible sights. Then the war was over and he was no longer a boy and there was no longer an enemy. And he got two magnificent seventy-kilo boars in four shots. After that, it was all downhill. Too much drink, a nag of a wife, a useless dreamer of a son; and never any money, or not enough of it – not enough to do anything more in life than exist, apart from the hunt and his handful of goats and the telly. He'd point at the telly with its flickering black-and-white pictures and say, 'That's my window on the world, Jean-Luc.'

Poor Jean-Luc. He often thought about his father at that time, just after the war, aged seventeen, before the phone or the telly – and how he must have got stuck, somehow, at that age. Because the way he behaved, until he died aged seventy-one, was not as a grown man should behave. So Jean-Luc, although he was afraid of his father until he was on his deathbed, tried to picture Elie just after the war: with his lame brother Fernand dead, his father Gabriel assumed dead (in fact, he was taking his time to get back from labour camp in Germany), his grieving mother Clémentine seeking comfort in Léon the black-smith up at Valdaron, and nothing in the larder but chestnuts and old potatoes.

Jean-Luc can just remember his grandmother as a wasted skeleton, wandering about Aubain in black, muttering through toothless gums. 'Fernand, Fernand,' she'd mumble, as if talking to her eldest. Maybe she was! Maybe no one died, in the end. Maybe they all hung about like Oncle Fernand, just the other side of the glass, mouthing words at us, eyeless, with limbs like newts.

Elie Maille lived danger and excitement and sorrow too young, the priest said at his funeral. There was the massacre of the Resistance camp at Jallau, way up in the open hills above Aubain. It was a bush-camp, really: Jallau was just a few ruined walls and a shepherd's hut with a roof of slates. The SS surrounded it after a tip-off and there was a shoot-out, thirty boys against three hundred Germans. Jean-Luc found a book in the flea market with photos of the dead Frenchmen lined up on the grass against a stone wall. There was a German in there, too: a deserter, a Communist, gone over to the Allies. His hands were up to his chin, as if cold. The label on the photo said 'Karl Goldschmidt'.

This book was interesting, with a lot in it about Camp IV. It cost twenty francs and had a coffee-ring on the cover. He studied the photographs, linking the handsome, living portraits and the dead, battered faces. His father wasn't mentioned anywhere, but then he was only a boy who brought bread and messages, sworn to silence. Sometimes Jean-Luc wondered, in the periods when his father was behaving really badly and his son hated him, whether the boy messenger wasn't the one who tipped off the Germans. Only a local knew the way to Jallau, along the sheep-paths. But his father would cry real tears, sometimes, when remembering those men of Camp IV: and Jean-Luc never dared ask him where he was when the camp was surprised by the SS.

There were the twelve corpses, lined up neatly on the grass, some in bare feet, all in baggy trousers, blood coming out of their mouths and noses. One or two looked as if they were sunbathing, with little smiles. A German in uniform was crouched at the far end, his hand on a foot. Jean-Luc wondered what he was thinking. A separate photograph of the dead maquis camp commander showed something strange about his arm; it was bulging in the wrong places, connected to the body in a strange way, and the hand looked like a pig's bladder. And his face! In the unclear photograph, it was calm under the webs of blood, but the left eye had been blotted out and the nose was swollen and someone had wrapped a cloth around the neck, hiding the chin. Jean-Luc knew the commander, whose Resistance name was 'Villon', had been badly tortured before execution. But there was no sign of pain in his expression.

This fascinated Jean-Luc, and he would (up until only a few years back) lie on the floor of his room in the same way, his arm bent crookedly, and adopt the corpse's peaceful expression, trying to understand what death was. On bad days, he would also enact what came before the death, rolling about on the floor in dreadful agony, his testicles a bloodied mess, one eye gouged out, big SS boots stamping on his arm and then stamping again on the broken splinters. And oh, how sweet death felt, then! And how he understood that saintly expression!

And his mother would sometimes shout up the stairs,

wondering what the noise was about. Or the silence after it. If only one could live alone, with only the birds and animals for company. If only the whole human race could be wiped out, starting with his own mother; then Marcel Lagrange; then the politicians; then the rich, especially the foreigners with swimming pools. Then anyone who happened to be in his way.

But he always shakes his head after these terrible thoughts, and laughs out loud. Doesn't everyone have them? He doesn't dare ask.

His father knew these young men of Camp IV. They were like fathers or brothers to him – Elie's own father was a prisoner in Germany. The day after the massacre at Jallau, the bodies were shared out between the villages, to be put on display in the village *mairies*: Aubain had three of them, laid out on the council table, as stiff and cold as waxworks, their guts spilling from their shredded stomachs. The children at school had to file past, followed by the rest of the village. Jean-Luc's father was among them, determined not to show how upset he was. The pig-necked SS soldiers were watching all the time. Watching their reactions. Six of the kids, from the Vasseur's farm, were Jewish – they'd been swapped for six Vasseurs of the same age, farmed out to cousins since '42. No one knew, or maybe they knew and didn't say; there were so many Vasseurs, they bred like rabbits. Grégoire and Juliette Vasseur didn't even get a medal, after the war, let alone a thank you.

You didn't have to be a Jew, though, to be worried: this detachment had already shot dead ordinary folk for no good reason in the latest sweep – the Coutaud family in their isolated farm, five out of the full eight; Monsieur Bataille in his chateau up at Ardouillet, before chucking incendiary grenades into the lower rooms. They were angry, then, and now they were glad. But they were just as nasty.

It must have been that day, back in 1944, that his father got stuck.

Walking past the bodies in the *mairie*.

Or maybe during the beautiful early-morning moment of that time he had a double kill. Jean-Luc knew it off by heart; sometimes he felt it had been his own experience, that he was seeing it through his own eyes. His father's gun is down in the cellar; he should clean and oil it, he thinks. It's only right.

The hunt is running in the valley below, hidden. Then the music of the dogs (that's how his father would put it) grows louder. The hunt is turning out of the valley and approaching where Elie lies behind the gorse bush and then there's a panting and snorting and it's two big beasts followed by three little ones crossing the field in a line right in front of him.

He lifts his gun and aims at the leader's flank just in front of the groin and he fires and the boar squeals and stumbles and recovers enough to reach the trees and then it's the second running into the notch of his sights and he pulls the trigger and nothing, it carries on running. The first of the little ones comes into view and he fires again and it rolls over instantly, as if by magic; so wild with excitement is Elie that the rest of the pack – the piglet's brothers and sisters – vanish into the trees without another shot being fired.

All he has to do (and by now young Jean-Luc would all but mouth the words his father used, so familiar were they) – all he has to do is find the wounded animal and keep the dogs from ripping it apart. The other one is dead as a log, kidneys smashed. It's a very young female. They aren't supposed to kill them too young, but he didn't have time to think. The wounded boar is the male of the group: he finds it by the barking and the squeals: surrounded by the dogs, still strong enough to keep them off with its huge tusks.

One shot in the head finishes it. Seventy-two kilos ready to be tied up and carried three kilometres along the rough track on his back.

'It was a family,' Jean-Luc would pipe up, the first few times his father told the story. 'Like us. Papa, Maman, and three little ones.' (In fact, he was an only child, but Papa knew what he meant.)

'I just thought of them as Germans,' said his father, each time. Then he would grunt, a bit like a boar himself. 'Listen, Janno. We were hardened, back then. Nothing but chestnuts, chestnuts, chestnuts. Rough winters, almost no fuel: that had hardened us, not weakened us. We slept outside. We were on the alert. We were as hard as animals. It was war.'

At those moments, when his father talked like a real maquisard, the young Jean-Luc would feel weak and girlish. He almost wished there had been a war when *he* was growing up, that he might have become his father's equal. But he would have been filled with hatred, too, and that Jean-Luc was glad not to have inside him. That anger, that hatred. The thirst for revenge that could never be satisfied. Everyone having to forgive and forget, once a bit of cleansing had happened. Jean-Luc's father among them.

'Nothing can bring back our Fernand,' he would say. 'I'm not going to end up like Mamie. I'm not going to go mad.'

When Jean-Luc's paternal grandfather, Gabriel, returned from Germany, it was two years after the end of the war. He hadn't been missed, being a lazy, bad-tempered type. He walked into the village on foot, as he'd walked all the way from the East on foot, with the odd lift in a cart (or so he claimed – but he was also something of a liar, it was said). The first person he passed was someone working in a field. That person was Elie, his own son. He didn't recognise his own son, after seven years away. And Elie didn't recognise his own father, so thin had he grown, and so long was it since he had gone away. So each waved to the other, politely, but neither knew.

That's hard to imagine, Jean-Luc would think as a child, when his father had recounted this other story yet again. And Jean-Luc would pretend he was in the field, hoeing or planting, where a bright yellow villa has been built since. And he would look up and see Gabriel – who had become his father in his imagination, not his grandfather – lift his arm, waving, and he would not know him from Adam. All he could see was a thin man with browned, leathery skin and a drinker's pouches under his eyes.

A stranger. A stranger means trouble, most times. Gabriel found his wife, Clémentine – Jean-Luc's grandmother – had hitched up with Léon, the blacksmith from Valdaron. They had all thought Gabriel was dead.

Fortunately, Gabriel left within a fortnight. Vanished, no doubt taking to the road in a huff and disappearing into drink. But wicked rumours, started by the Lagrange clan, suggested he'd vanished more permanently: that the blacksmith and Jean-Luc's grandmother were behind it. Then the rumours swirled into all the other murmurings that followed the war and, by the time Jean-Luc was born, had become fossilised – and might as well have been millions of years old, for all the truth they told.

Even the Lagrange clan let go of the Gabriel business; they had too much murk on their own side. A lid was put on it all. The blacksmith Léon was killed by a horse's hoof in the head in 1953. Maybe that's when Clémentine went mad. Electricity came to the village, then piped water, then, in 1993, a proper drainage system that ended up in a huge circular septic tank that converted the shit to a clear stream. Aubain no longer smelt. It was a new era. Foreigners began to buy houses, the older and more decrepit the better. Swimming pools appeared, bright blue, flashing in the sun, more and more of them, a whole emergency fleet of them – until even the locals had caught the disease.

Towards the end of his life, though, Jean-Luc's father would talk about nothing else but the war: always the same stories, in the same order, as if he were burrowing back, finding the reason why it all happened. Over and over again, like a tape recorder with only one tape. Until he resorted to Oc, which Jean-Luc only half understood. Over and over again the stories were told, in a gabble of Occitan. No wonder Jean-Luc's mother had her husband put away in a home, where he could drive the nurses mad instead of herself.

'But that's their job,' she would say. 'That's what we pay for in our taxes.'

Not that she paid any tax; they earned too little. And anyway, his father withered away after a few months in the home at St-Maurice. Jean-Luc couldn't stand its smell. It was the smell of sickness and death: toilets, medicines, bleach and rottenness. No wonder Elie Maille fell silent in the last week or so, gazing into the distance as if through the wall of his little room. Jean-Luc was sure his father was back on that slope in the hills, crouched behind the gorse, hearing the lovely dogs bark and the whole hunt moving towards where he had been waiting with his gun since before dawn.

Maybe he's up there now, Jean-Luc would think. Maybe if I went up there on the anniversary of the hunt, before dawn, I'd see him crouched behind the gorse bush, just the same but aged seventeen and with eyes covered over in a film of white like the skin on old milk.

Like Nick, Sarah was 'worried' about Mrs Foster. After the school's nativity play (in which Tammy played a singing ladder up to heaven), Nick said that Mrs Foster was the type for whom Creationism was validated every morning by the mirror.

He was annoyed because he hadn't been able to take photographs, even after the play: there were other kids around and the Mallinsons might put the snaps on their computer and send them to paedophiles or cut-and-paste the heads onto naked children's bodies and so on. Nick fulminated at the fallen world and had a bit of an argument with Mrs Foster, who said it was nothing to do with her, it was health and safety. No photos whatsoever, Mr Mallinson. Sorry.

Mrs Foster was the acting head, now: the rather dull and crabby Miss Kearton had been killed in her car by a newly arrived Pole speeding the wrong side of the Cambridge ring road; he had claimed afterwards that, having realised his continental mistake, he'd been heading as fast as possible for the exit.

Miss Kearton's death engendered, with Mrs Foster's encouragement, a Diana-like flood of flowers in front of the school gates. Nick thought about this as they walked along the road to the cemetery. The whole thing had annoyed him, particularly as Tammy was very concerned about the size and expense of her own floral contribution in comparison with the others. He ended up spending far too much: Tammy virtually disappeared behind her showy mass of blooms as they approached the school gates and their huge blown-up photo, somewhat Stalin-like (he claimed), of a much younger Miss Kearton.

Which, of course, was defaced by obscenities within twenty-four hours, causing a mild spasm of despair in the community that surfaced in the local paper as quasi-fascistic rage. Photos were sent of the offending article, but it was decided that Miss Kearton would never have wanted herself to appear in public with blacked-out teeth, hairy nostrils, and obscene drawings all over her face. Tammy found it funny, but didn't say so. And afterwards, when there were the jokes – about Miss Kearton driving into a pole and bending it, or whatever – she always giggled.

After passing a villa rendered (in the girls' estimation) the yellow of sick, and then a stranded-looking, half-built one in breeze blocks next to a finished swimming pool, they came to the sign they'd noted on the way in, further from the village than expected. The cemetery was up a winding lane. The girls delayed their progress by treating the short hill as a Himalayan flank, plodding two or three exhausted steps then groaning, or sitting on the grassy verge like refugees. Contrary to their earlier enthusiasm – or at least Alicia's – they saw no point in visiting the 'stupid cemetery'; their father fell back on the limpest of justifications ('It's living history, guys') while their mother gave ineffectual encouragement, counterbalancing Beans's gravitational pull on the end of an outstretched arm. They gradually diluted into a straggly line; at one point the rest of his family were out of sight around the corner and Nick was alone.

He looked up at the sky, which was entirely without cloud or blemish. He might have been a fish at the bottom of the sea, with the bright, lit surface somewhere above him through layer after layer of blue. But the bottom of the sea is lightless, he reminded himself. This was more like the time he'd stood on the bottom of an outdoor public swimming pool as a boy, looking up, until his lungs were almost bursting and he'd had to kick up in a stream of bubbles. Here he was in the air and on the earth and sunlit, the warm photons settling on his face and making him happy. It is quite easy to be happy, he thought. It is a matter of simplification. Of cutting out what interferes in the appreciation of this. That glossed leaf, courageously itself against the depth of blue; a faint honey-smell of warming vegetation. He was actually alive. It's not often you realise you are actually alive.

The others rounded the corner of the lane one by one, preceded by noise. Nick raised his arm ceremoniously.

'Nearly there,' he called. Beans was on her mother's shoulders, bringing up the rear.

'Dad-dy,' Alicia whined, 'you're really horrible.'

'I'll give you a lift,' he offered, although Alicia was getting heavy these days – a compact five-year-old.

'What about me?'

'You've got huge long legs, Tammy,' said Sarah. 'Is it much further, Nick?'

'I said, we're nearly there.' Alicia settled on his back, crushing his upper vertebrae. Her hands were in his sparse hair, gripping his scalp like tiny suckers. Her pink shoes were not unsmelly, his fingers circling her ankles at chest-level. The hill felt steeper. He was too old for kids, at fifty-four. They exhausted him. They were unrelenting. He could have been their grandfather.

'Vroom, vroom,' he said, feebly, hoping he wouldn't suddenly drop dead like the Vice Principal last year. 'Formula One.'

And there were the gates.

The cemetery was surprisingly large for a small village, and had nice views from the crest of the hill it occupied. Four tall cypresses, black against the sunlight, lent a certain disconsolate harmony to the muddle of graves and crosses. The sun felt warmer up here, and beat off the stones in a blinding glare; it was hard to imagine it was still officially winter. The girls ran about between the tombs, gaily looking for Fernand Maille.

'Fernand! Fernand!' they called out, as if he were hiding.

Sarah hoped no one local would come, tolerant as the French were.

He was discovered by Tammy; carved on a simple grave he shared with other members of his family. The slab was scattered with miniature stelae and fake flowers, but no more clues were given as to the precise nature of his death. Sarah wondered if Jean-Luc could tell them more.

'Hello, Mr Fernie-Wernie,' Alicia joked, stroking the stone. 'Bang! Bang!'

'Let's go and explore more,' said Sarah, looking around her nervously. The three ran about again, making vrooming noises like boys.

A friend had told her that modern Western children, usually shielded from immediate experience of death, needed to visit cemeteries. Needed to have the truth gently introduced into their carefree, indulged lives. The way the girls were now, the picture of merriment between the slabs, seemed to rubbish the friend's theory. Or perhaps not. Perhaps this was how life and death should be brought together.

Death was rock-hard. Her children were tiny scraps of softness. One of them might already be harbouring a mortal decay, a cancer. She was frightening herself.

She saw Tammy had braked in front of a huge, thick, slate-grey slab with a wavy top, and joined her. It belonged to the Lagrange family, with a cheery colour photo of the most recently deceased, a handsome man called Raoul. Died six years ago, almost to the day.

'We saw the name Lagrange on the war memorial, didn't we? He looks nice, poor man.'

She asked them to calculate his age, swinging her glasses from the crook of her forefinger.

'A hundred and one,' said Alicia.

'Forty-four and three months and about ten days,' Tammy murmured, with a sigh. 'I don't know how many hours and minutes.'

'For someone who's not supposed to be good at maths . . .' said Sarah.

'I got more years,' complained Alicia.

'Hawo!' cried Beans, pointing at a large crow-like bird hopping about on the gravel.

'Tammy's right, but then she's older than you, Alicia. Now, how many years ago did he, um, die, Alicia?' She thought 'die' was more honest than 'pass away'.

She felt curious about him, about this sunlit, smiling face vitrified and embedded in the stone; he didn't look forty-four, he looked about her age. It was an old snapshot, chosen by the grieving family to show him at his best. A good choice, she reckoned. Other graves had photos, too, some of them sinister-looking or blurred or somehow unreal, as if the person could never have existed except as a waxwork, or a phantom from the past in a silly hat and spectacles. Always a phantom, even in life. But only Raoul Lagrange seemed impossible to imagine dead. So many of us do, she thought.

'He died eight and a quarter years ago,' tried Alicia, earnestly, in a full-on classroom way.

'Six,' Tammy said. 'Almost exactly. Just after Fernando, because March comes after February. That's really strange.'

'Slightly different year,' laughed Sarah, albeit amazed at her daughter's brightness. 'And if this poor man's year wasn't a leap year, which has an extra day, we're talking about two days after, because February only has twenty-eight days.'

'What're you *on* about?' wailed Alicia.

'Tammy's actually right again,' said her mother, compensating the news with a cuddle. 'Six years it is. Ten out of ten. But you got pretty close, darling.'

'I can have a Coke, then,' said Alicia. 'In the café.'

'Soon.'

Sarah put her glasses back on and looked about for Nick. He was on his back on the grass that bordered the cemetery, arms flung out as if he'd been shot. She wanted to call him, shielding her eyes from the bright sun and waiting for a sign of life. He'd looked quite puffed and red in the face, carrying Alicia up the last part of the hill. A mistake to come here, she thought. Living history! It was morbid.

Dishy Raoul, four or five years younger than Nick. If he'd lived. How kinky, to fancy someone through a photo on his grave! She walked towards the prone form in a relaxed way, so as not to worry the girls.

He didn't stir. She wanted him to stir. His arms were flung right out. He never lay like that, normally. Stretched out like that.

Then his head lifted up as she approached, her shoes scrunching on the gravel over the beat of her alarmed heart. He needed to trim his eyebrows.

'Isn't the sun *marvellous*?' he called out, head still up.

His neck must be almost dislocated. 'This grass seems OK,' she commented. She was so relieved for a second that she wanted to cry. Now she was back to normal and saying dull, inconsequent things, assessing herself as usual.

'Oh,' said Nick, taking a moment to cotton on, 'it's a bit prickly. There are prickly things in it. Not exactly a *sward*.'

His head was back on the grass. A wash of buttercup-like flowers shared part of the grass with similarly yellow flowers which were probably dandelions from the look of the leaves. She found the way he emphasised words a little cranky.

'We should get a book,' she said, sitting down next to him. 'A flower book.' Tammy had trailed her and was now hovering.

'I've always found flower books useless,' he confessed, 'like bird books. Very little ever seems to match up. They're gone before you've found the picture.'

'Flowers don't fly,' she said, leaning back on her elbows.

'No, but they wilt and die before you come back with the book the next time, because you inevitably forget the first time.'

'You've always got the following year,' she pointed out. 'Assuming.'

The crow-like bird flew up and disappeared over the trees.

'Tammy,' said Sarah, 'I think the others want you. Let Daddy and I have some *me* time.'

'Mean time,' Tammy murmured, moving off.

The three of them, golden sun in their golden hair, were planted comfortably on handsome Raoul's grave, their ceaseless jittery kid-movements casting long, nervous shadows over the slab. She wondered if this was legitimate, too liberal of her; whether a villager might come along and be shocked at the foreigners' behaviour. But she couldn't move in the warm sun, the first real warmth of the year. She felt spiritual buds burgeoning inside her.

Raoul was grinning at the girls from his gravestone as they chatted together. Tammy kneeled on the gravel and felt its painful impression through her jeans. The younger two were making roads out of the gravel between the stelae and the porcelain flowers, visiting each other for tea and cake.

Tammy glanced at Raoul and stuck her tongue out. He didn't react, except (she guessed) when she wasn't looking.

SEVEN

Jean-Luc studies the remains of the fish he has rescued from the kitchen bin. Fish is expensive. Just as well, then, that one of Jean-Luc's hobbies is angling. He took it up properly when he was a teenager. He has one rod and no permit. He knows the hidden, special places you have to scramble down to. He always fishes alone. He prefers it to hunting with a gun.

He caught the fish in the autumn and froze it for lean times. Yesterday he shared it in the evening with his mother, making sure there were no bones for her to choke on. He pretended it was fresh, but she could tell it wasn't. He insisted it was. 'Pffff,' she scoffed, spraying particles of fish all over the place. It was a smallish trout; where he fishes, up above St-Maurice, the river squeezed between rocks and forming pools as it descends, there is never anything big. He wants to eat all of it himself, but he isn't that sort of person. Anyway, his mother would have smelt it cooking. The white flesh came off easily and he served it to her, as ordered, with a scatter of capers, a knob of butter, and an overdone mulch of salted spinach.

She'd been well enough to come down to the kitchen to eat, although she groaned on the stairs and he had to help her. She peered at her plate when he served her.

'Is that all?' she complained, her eyes widening at it nevertheless.

'You've got half,' he said, taking the plate back, teasing her with it. 'But you don't have to eat it. It's fresh.'

She smelt of toilets. Her dressing gown needed washing.

'When did you catch it?'

'This morning,' he lied.

His hand was on her shoulder; he felt the shoulder blade as a sharp ridge, like the edge of a flint. He squeezed it gently, imagining the skeleton so close under the skin, getting closer and closer as she thinned until it popped out, cackling like a horror film, and that was that.

'I hope you've washed your hands,' she said.

He threw the bones away and now he's rescued them. They smell rotten already. His idea seems even better, looking at the bones. He cleans the skeleton under the tap, with plenty of washing-up liquid, then takes it upstairs to his room in a plastic bag, ignoring her snores.

It is all spine and a head with its gaping mouth. He tugs the head off and an eye goes flying, as round and white as the Sandlers' gravel. His fingers are oily with fluids. He runs his thumb down the sharp backbone. This is what we came from. Bibi, the little doll, is caught in the cobweb. The sieve is no longer a sieve. He rocks the sieve as it lies on the table, although cobwebs don't rock and make that noise, they just tremble in a draught. Bibi has a backbone, too. So does the Englishwoman. And Raoul Lagrange, once.

He bends the fish-spine back until it snaps, cutting his finger slightly on its sharpness. That's what happens when you hit a stationary object too fast. Backlash. Rabbit punch.

He shot his first rabbit when he was ten or eleven, and didn't kill it outright. He picked it up by the ears. It kicked feebly, although its rump was mincemeat. 'Like this,' his father said, making a chopping movement with his hand. 'That's why they call it a rabbit punch, when you break your neck.'

Jean-Luc held the rabbit tight by the ears and chopped onto the neck. The rabbit kicked again, feebly. He chopped again and the rabbit kicked. It must be stuck in a nightmare, Jean-Luc thought. The worst nightmare possible. His father shouted at him and grabbed the rabbit and down came his father's hard, calloused hand and the rabbit's neck snapped with a tiny click, the eyes losing their spark, the legs dangling after a little judder.

But his father was so angry with him! Jean-Luc had never seen his father so angry!

'Never do that again!' he shouted. He was upset, that was the thing. The rabbit had suffered. Jean-Luc wanted to chop his useless hand off; instead, he practised on sticks and planks of wood until the side of his hand was blue and bleeding. The next time, the rabbit's neck snapped straightaway and his father nodded, obviously proud of him.

What he needs now is a head. A tiny, shrunken head.

The excitement is deep in his belly again. Better than playing with himself, and not sinful (while he doesn't reckon God exists, these days, you never know, you can never be too careful).

It doesn't have to be a real human head: that would be hard. A chicken's or a rabbit's, say: he can ask at the butcher's for that, but it'll go off. Or a cat's head. He'd still have to shrink it, though.

Once, long ago, in the rubbish dump beyond Yves Dardalhon's farm, he and another kid – Matthieu Soupault – splashed paraffin on a kitten and dropped a match on its tail. They watched it run about, screeching and mewling, until it lay down in its own flames as if tired, raising a burning paw to its burning face as cats do when they clean their whiskers. Then they poured water over the little black corpse and studied it. Jean-Luc had only watched, it wasn't even his idea. It was mad Matthieu's idea. Matthieu now worked at the tax office, in a proper shirt and tie, at his own desk with his own computer, making sure people paid their taxes. Jean-Luc felt sick for a week, after that.

It doesn't have to be a head at all.

It can be anything that makes you think of a head. Something round. Or he can take a photograph and stick it on something shaped like a disc. Of course, he thinks of the photograph of Raoul Lagrange stuck into the gravestone. He looks over his shoulder, just in case. Although he never feels scared up at the Mas.

His room is in shadow, the desk-lamp pointed low so that his own form darkens whatever's behind him. His high, old-fashioned bed is made up, the sheet folded neatly back over the thin blue quilt, touching the bolster like a collar. No one can make up a bed like Jean-Luc, except his mother. Sometimes, for no reason, it won't come right, the folds and pleats and tucks not working, the top edge a few centimetres out, and he wants to scream. He does scream, now and again, when making up his bed: short, sharp screams, more like a puppy than anything else.

'What's up?' his mother always calls out.

'Mind your own business,' he yells back, each time. Or doesn't say anything at all and keeps very still, hand on the quilt, so she can worry for a bit.

He looks at the sieve and Bibi and the fish bone and the little white circle of gravel stones and feels something expand inside him, like a flower. It is going to be much larger, this flower, than he ever expected. He realises that, now. Will he be able to hide it, if it is that big? He looks up at the ceiling. There's the attic. But if it rains hard, his flower might get damaged. So he needs a big sheet of plastic. Everything is possible.

He pictures the Englishwoman, her small, untouchable face behind the teasing spectacles. He pictures that face as a flower, repeated lots of times like roses on a rose bush. He remembers a picture book at school, when he first went to school. A big book with scuffed, cardboard pages a teacher gave him to look at. There was a garden with a watering can and a green-eyed cat and all the flowers had happy, smiling faces encircled by petals. One of the faces had been changed by a naughty kid with a biro, perhaps a long time before. It had been changed into a filthy old woman with missing teeth and bushy eyebrows and hairy spots. Her name was written next to it with an arrow pointing back, but he wasn't old enough to understand the letters. Jean-Luc couldn't take his eyes off her. In the end, he had to cover her face with his hand.

He pictures that page right now, thirty years later. And all the flowers will have the Englishwoman's face on them, except one. And that one will be my mother, Jean-Luc thinks.

He glances out of the window and, like a miracle, *he sees*

her. Sees the Englishwoman, walking down the street with her husband and her kids, then turning off towards the café! His heart is thumping as if he's run up a hill.

It thumped like that when he went out hunting in the old days. When the animal cleared cover and the gun was tucked into his shoulder, all ready. She disappears with her family into the café, like a mother duck leading her brood to water. Now that, thinks Jean-Luc, is God operating. And all the angels.

He waits with his binoculars by the window, until they come out again half an hour later. Her spectacles flash the sun into his eyes, like a message, as she turns her head. The girls all have purple mouths. That makes him smile, as he follows them, closing one eye against the lens that is cracked.

A few days later, getting back home from a cultural expedition during which Beans left a stellar splat of sick on a museum step, they heard a regular thumping that juddered off the walls. It was Jean-Luc, knocking wooden posts in. He was building a chicken-wire fence around the Zone.

'I ought to give him a hand,' murmured Nick, neck stiff from looking up at roof bosses.

Sarah filmed him, although he did nothing more than hold the unrolled chicken-wire upright. The girls watched with a quiet, almost awestruck concentration, as though something was being burnished into their brains. Afterwards, watching on the camera's little screen, they noticed how Jean-Luc had his back turned almost the whole time, as if he couldn't stand being filmed.

He came the following morning to sow the lawn and fiddle about with the pool. He had passed Sarah jogging up to the postbox, and she had given him a polite wave. The chicken-wire had, rather surprisingly, kept out the boars – or maybe they couldn't be bothered with something they'd already dug over. Jean-Luc's French amusingly implied that the pool still had 'troubled waters': it was certainly a bit green again. They would be able to swim in June, in the real heat, but for now he must keep the water clean and clear or algae would deposit green-and-black slime on the sides and in the filters. He told Nick there were 15,000 types of algae, which Nick found hard to believe. He'd always had problems with numbers in French.

Jean-Luc tipped in granules of something called *Shock Chlorine*. The smell of bleach was suffocating, it actually burnt in Nick's nose. No swimming for two days, Jean-Luc told him: it was a joke, the water was still freezing cold. He explained to Nick how to test the pH levels, using a paper strip that turned from white to purple. The darker it is, the more acidic. The lighter, the more alkaline. He showed Nick which chemicals to use to adjust the pH levels. This was, Jean-Luc claimed, in case he was not around in a couple of days. Anyway, it needed testing at least once a week, maybe more if it started to cloud. Nick nodded, perturbed. He knew all about colonialism and its aftermath, but nothing about pools.

'Jean-Luc has Simon-and-Garfunkel'd the pool,' he joked in turn. His eyes stung. The song went round Sarah's head all day.

They hadn't yet found the alarm's code. Tammy put up a reward poster with a stubbled face and letters coloured with her new Caran d'Ache crayons: REWARD. $10,000. WANTED ALIVE OR DEAD. JIMMY 'THE DROUND' CODE.

'On purpose,' she stated, when Nick pointed out the misspelling.

'Shouldn't the code man look nice,' smiled her mother, 'rather than nasty?'

Tammy went off in a huff, and Sarah felt bad. They were so exigent as parents, she realised. Nick pooh-poohed this: they were softies, he reckoned. Over-liberal, if anything. Not everything kids do has to be praised.

Sarah tested a small key she'd found in an ashtray; miraculously, it unlocked a drawer in the pantry, full of technical-looking papers and old string, but nothing to do with an alarm. The pool's pump and filtration equipment were covered, as well as a food-mixer and an alarm clock, but the vital document was missing.

'It always is,' Nick joked. 'That's why everything's so approximate.'

Jean-Luc unhooks the chicken wire and rakes the earth, having watered it for an hour but not so much that it sticks to the tangs, then throws the grass-seed from a two-kilo plastic sack; he has gone to the agricultural merchant's in Valdaron and bought seed adapted to drought areas. He has done this at least four times before, but the difference this time is the amount. It turns the earth white, and the little English girls pretend – or perhaps believe – that it has snowed. Then he comes back from the tool-cellar with a fan-shaped leaf-rake, which he draws steadily across the area until the seed is reasonably set in.

Inside himself, he knows it will fail. It is too late in the year, however much he waters it. It will either burn in the frost (which can occur as late as April, in normal times) or in the heat of the sun. The little girls watch him silently through the fence, which is as tall (or as low) as the eldest. He likes them watching. He gives them a handful of seed each to sow for themselves. He takes the small claw-tool and grubs up a patch for each of them on the edge of the yard, where there are lots of tiny nissoun leaves. He digs up one of the nissoun's swollen roots and peels off the brown skin, then pops it into his mouth. The little girls look astonished as he crunches it up, its sweet taste of chestnut and hazelnut flooding his head with childhood memories, the aftertaste of spicy carrot as reliable as a moan from Maman. He explains to them, in the simplest French he can muster, snorting for the boars, that the yard was covered in these plants, and that's why the boars come to turn it over, because they love the roots. The girls like his snorting.

He keeps repeating the name of the plant.

'Neess-oon,' they reply, giggling. He peels them each a root and they bite and chew and swallow. Only the middle one makes a face and spits it out.

They seed their miniature lawns, the youngest throwing hers up into the air so that most of it settles in her hair. He imagines

177

their lawns as just big enough for their small bodies to stretch out on. Already the black ants are transporting the seeds one by one down a tiny crater in the dry earth. He could put insecticide in, but he is like his father, who hated all the rubbish they'd pour into the vineyards and still do pour, so that nothing lives that should live.

He fills the watering-can and dampens the kids' seed-beds; they chatter to him and he feels he can understand it in the back of his mind. They have a little hoard of nissoun roots, like a pile of marbles. They are very excited.

By the time he's finished, it is late enough to water properly. He sets the timer again and watches as the big sprinkler sputters into life. Swish, swish, swish, it goes. He likes the expression of wonder on the kids' faces.

The middle one comes up to him and smiles and he pats her hair and thinks how much he's enjoyed the day. Her hair is very soft, soft and golden over the hard skull. He can feel the wintry sun on it turning into spring.

He swivels and sees a face in one of the upper windows of the house, pulling back. It is her face, the Englishwoman's face behind its spectacles. His heart leaps in his chest like a salmon and his face burns. He knows her face is gone, now. He sees the small black window out of the corner of his eye, high up.

Why is she shy about looking down at her children? He folds his arms and looks out at the watering. She is watching *him*, not the children: he is sure of it. She gave him a big wave when she passed him on the track, running. A nice smile. All these foreigners run instead of cycle. Cycling's harder, he reckons.

The late afternoon light. Shy, she is.

He feels good about her watching him. She makes him feel good about himself. She is as perfect as a flower. He pictures her face stuck on a flower with petals all around, bare of her spectacles. Over and over.

The middle one takes his hand and they watch the sprinkler together. Her hand moves like a tiny baby rabbit in his.

★ ★ ★

Nick was attempting to read one of his oldest essays (on the Balfour Declaration) in front of the fire. It was too fresh to sit outside, despite the sun: March had turned cool, cooler than when they arrived. The essay's wince-count was pleasingly low – some of the Marxisms apart. They were like a series of rusty hooks.

He looked at Sarah over his reading glasses. She had short sight, he had long, like Jack Sprat and his wife when it came to fat. She was telling him that it may be her paranoia but they should keep an eye on Jean-Luc *vis-à-vis* the girls.

'*Vis-à-vis.*'

'You look about ninety doing that,' she said.

'Thank you.'

He had not been abused at his boarding school, unlike others. They didn't call it abuse, then. He was trying to remember what they did call it. The notorious Malcolm Fettlewick was said to do it: the slurpy Head of Classics, with the beard that ran down his neck. Malcolm XX, they called him.

'I don't think he's that type,' he said.

'No, it's probably just very sweet and touching, like an Edwardian novel. But I've suddenly gone anxious,' she admitted. 'Here I am, in Paradise, and I'm all nervy.'

'Might I make a judgement on the Paradise bit, as being a touch exclusive of reality?'

She didn't reply and Nick went back to his reading. Strange how his forehead took up most of his face in that position, as if it were a visor that could be drawn up when needed.

'Maybe Midgard would be ontologically better,' he added, all but murmuring to himself. 'The Eden of Norse myth. As being earthy rather than heavenly, I mean.'

'He gave them wild bulbs or something to eat,' she said, impatiently. 'I presume he knows what he's doing.'

'Wild bulbs?'

'Like little prunes. Nissow or something. The French name. They said he told them that's why the boars dug everything up. They understood his French, it seems.'

179

'If pigs can eat them, so can we.'

'They eat anything.'

He went back to his reading. 'You'll be fine,' he said, eventually, in a soothing tone. 'Old one-eye's looking after us.'

'Old one eye?'

He waved a hand at the African mask. Oh really, she thought, keeping her expression blank as she stared at the flames feebly licking the new logs. Oh really and truly just give me a long, wild night on the razzle.

Jean-Luc finds the baby pram while pissing in the underbrush behind the Mas, out of sight of the girls. It is nestling in the dead bracken, on the side of an animal-run (badger, most like). All that's left apart from the handle is the undercarriage, four wheels in rusted metal. He thinks it is a toy pram, but he can't be sure. The long handle has a pink bit of plastic on, moulded to small fingers, and a real pram is usually bigger, but it might be a very old pushchair. He's seen photos of women pushing babies in four-wheel pushchairs with long handles next to old-fashioned cars in Paris.

Straightaway he knows he will take it back home. He feels that excitement in his belly. Luckily, he has brought the van today. He gingerly reaches into the undergrowth, tugging at the metal struts, which are wrapped round by those thorny creepers he hates. Ugly scratching tentacles, thin as wire, much thinner than brambles. As they release their hold they whip over his hands, leaving beads of blood on his knuckles and the fat underbit of his left thumb. The scratches sting; there is something in the thorns that irritates the skin. But he's holding the find free, now. It's his.

The wheels have bits of rubber left on them, dried out and crumbling. Maybe this belonged to one of the hippy kids. Or even before, before crazy Mamie Aubert and her goats. Before the war. Before Oncle Fernand was shot on the track. When there was a working family and the fields were cleared and the terraces put to onions and potatoes and leeks.

180

But it can't be that old, not with the moulded handle of pink plastic, loose on its metal rod.

He's putting it in the back of the van and the English girls run up. From the sound of it, they think he's got the pram for them.

He slams the doors shut and fastens them with the rope. He shakes his head and says 'no', in English. It isn't a toy any more. He has the excitement in his belly. The girls pretend to cry, knuckling their eyes. Why do they like him so much? It's a kind of mistake. His fingernails are black from the day's work. He can smell his own sweat, the sharpness of it. He picks up the youngest one. She squirms, so he squeezes her tighter in the crook of his arm, then jigs her up and down. She likes that. All kids like that. He walks up and down by the van, jigging her. She's chuckling, her hands spread wide and moving in time. She's amazingly light, almost weightless. He wishes she was *his* kid. Her nose needs wiping, but he leaves it. The middle one wants the same game but not the eldest, who just watches with her hands on her head. The middle one is heavier, plumper. She squeezes his waist between her legs, squeezing him with her knees as he jigs up and down by the van making snorting noises. She throws her head back and watches the sky. She reminds him of his second cousin, little Priscilla. His back hurts from the raking. Their mother is walking towards them. He sweeps the one who is like Priscilla back onto the ground, her legs curling up so she rolls over, laughing. His face is burning, because the mother is coming up. He avoids her eyes, this time; he's already opening the driver's door.

'Teatime!' she says, stretching out her hands.

He knows that word. It makes him want to laugh. But when he glances at her face, it looks anxious. Her eyes meet his. His hand is on the door, he is ready to climb into the van. Her eyes are angry. He can feel it, as if they are spitting at him. She has dark, brown-black eyes and they are spitting at him over her smile, over her saying *teatime* in a stupid, high voice.

He has taken something off their land – off the land of the

Sandlers, at any rate. The children chatter to their mother, tugging on her trousers and her sleeves, no doubt telling her about the old toy pram he's taken without permission. It's just scrap, he thinks, but he feels shifty. He still avoids her eyes. The sun turns her black hair reddish. He climbs into the driving seat and closes the door.

'*Merci*,' she cries out, as the engine coughs into life, as his seat squeaks and bounces under him. '*Merci beaucoup!*'

Why does she need to say that, when she doesn't mean it? He raises his hand and nods through the open window. She has her arms around the two younger kids, as if protecting them from harm, pressing them against her and frowning at him.

They wave as he drives off. Even the mother waves. As if he isn't coming back tomorrow, or the next day. All this troubles him. He stops by Oncle Fernand's memorial and asks him for his advice. The flowers haven't been nicked.

'Just wait,' the low voice says in his head. 'Just wait and be patient, my little Jean-Luc. Go and have a pastis in the café. Have it on me.'

'Thank you, Oncle Fernand,' Jean-Luc murmurs, before he drives on too fast over the holes and bumps of the track, so that the rear-view mirror falls off onto his lap.

After he was cremated and turned into a ghost, people who saw him said he had a loose head, a dangling head, a head like a dead rabbit's or hare's, and he couldn't lift it up however hard he tried. That's what terrified them. Trying to look at them through his eyebrows, but he could never lift his head up high enough, or at all. His chin rolling against his breast-bone, but no noises, not even a moaning. Just his loose neck. Worse than a bull after the picadors have been at it and it can't lift its horns higher than its tail.

That's why no one local goes to Les Fosses, these days. Not even Gabrielle, the sister-in-law, who is supposed to be the cleaner.

But Jean-Luc knows it's all rubbish. Oncle Fernand has told

him so. It's all stories. It had nothing to do with Oncle Fernand, the anniversary. It was the wet, the pressure.

He goes to the café before dinner, as instructed. The usual crowd, a good dozen of them, and they make him nervous, even though Marcel isn't there. But once Jean-Luc opens the door, scraping its bottom edge over the lino, he can't back off. Oncle Fernand would be disappointed. Jean-Luc even thinks he can feel him in the back of his head, a vague brown shape; a bit like the only photograph of him (taken in front of the new tractor) that Jean-Luc has ever seen. Maybe there are more, but if so they can't be found – and Jean-Luc has looked in the cupboards, in all the suitcases and drawers. Oncle Fernand is thin and wiry in the photograph, with a sheepish smile, hand on the tractor's tyre. Half his face is in the shadow of his hat, as the sun was bright, so Jean-Luc has never been able to tell what he really looked like. The tractor was purchased in 1938, by the cousin Oncle Fernand worked for, so he couldn't have been more than fifteen. Jean-Luc never pictures him as young, though; just old and wise. Not as old as if he were still alive – he'd be in his eighties, now – but around the age of Papa when he died. Seventy. Still fit enough to work in the vegetable patch.

Jean-Luc feels proud of his relationship with Oncle Fernand. Sometimes, when he passes the spot on the track, there is nothing. Not even a wink in the back of his mind. He imagines Oncle Fernand out in the hills, hunting. Even though he was never much of a hunter, according to Papa. 'Fernand never liked guns,' he'd say. 'Too soft, soft as a girl. That's why he helped in the bakery before he worked in the tannery. Fernand liked making cakes. Made a change from the fields. Don't get blisters making cakes.'

Jean-Luc would always nod, then, because he understood why Oncle Fernand had preferred that job in the baker's to labouring in the fields or hunting with his brother. If only Papa had been the one shot on the track! – but then there would have been no Jean-Luc. Might have been better like that, he'd think. Especially after Marcel Lagrange had pushed him about;

because Jean-Luc, instead of seeing red, felt limp and useless, as if he didn't have the right to exist.

Now, though, he is an object of interest; they want to know about the English up at Les Fosses. The English have been seen in the village, they went to the church and the cemetery the day before yesterday – no, three days back, how time flies – and then came in here. Louis nods in confirmation behind the bar.

'They asked me questions,' Louis says. 'About the house. I pretended not to know.'

'We'll all be speaking sodding English soon,' one of Marcel's mates growls.

'In French,' says Louis. 'The husband speaks French. The woman never opened her mouth. Never so much as opened her mouth. Not to me, at any rate.'

Jean-Luc shrugs. 'They've got a problem with boars,' he says, to deflect them onto a problem that was shared by many. 'I need to put a proper fence up.'

'That's right,' says Louis.

'We can go looking for them,' says Petit Gaston, who used to work on the railways but now putters about on his mobilette all day, rifle over his shoulder, with some mysterious, state-supported invalidity. 'We'll take the dogs up there next week. The whole gang.' He draws deeply on his yellow roll-up and coughs. 'We haven't done Les Fosses for a while. Didn't think there was anything there.'

Jean-Luc curses himself for mentioning the boars. But it's usually Marcel who decides where the hunt is to be, not a little runt like Gaston.

'They were only babies,' Jean-Luc fibs. 'I saw them.'

'How big?' asks Gaston, creasing his eyes up suspiciously. He is a nasty, yapping terrier who never lets go. He starts drinking at eight in the morning; completely pickled inside, he must be. He floats in alcohol like a specimen.

Jean-Luc spreads his hands no more than a realistic metre. 'About so. They'll be fine in a year or two.'

'They'll have a mummy and a daddy,' Gaston persists, picking tobacco off his invisible lips. 'And big brothers and sisters.'

'Hey,' Aimé yelps, an enormous lump further down the bar, 'has she opened her mouth to you, Jean-Luc?' And Aimé, because it has taken him a few moments to think this one up, makes sure everyone understands what he meant by waggling his tongue.

They laugh. Jean-Luc blushes, unfortunately. Louis hands him his pastis, sliding it across the bar, and Jean-Luc blushes deeper and his hand trembles around the glass. Because everyone is looking at him. His left eyelid starts to twitch and he has to pretend to scratch it. All those private, naughty thoughts are dancing up and down for everyone to see. Scribbles, drawings like cartoons, a whole comic strip. The others, bunched in a line against the bar, wait for him to speak and make dirty remarks that trigger further laughter and cat-calls. Their smoke circles him, makes him crave a fag for himself. He sips his drink and lifts his eyes to the bottles behind the bar. One of them, almond syrup, has not shifted its level in twenty years.

Emile of the massive eyebags says that Jean-Luc has dug for all the Englishwomen in the commune. How many is that? someone asks. Others are snorting with laughter because of the age of some of these women. Louis, perhaps out of kindness, is having a serious go at counting. 'It's well into double figures,' he says, wiping the bar with a cloth and trying to be serious about the number in order to calm it all down, 'but they hardly ever come in here.'

This would have deflected the regulars into having a go at the English, normally; how they were too rich and too mean, while a defender would always put their case either because – like Jean-Paul Rohr the plumber or Yves Plantier the plasterer – they were making money out of them, or – like Jacques Evrard – they were old enough to remember the war. But not tonight. Marcel's mates make sure of that, even in his absence. It isn't often they have Jean-Luc Maille on the end of a fork. By the time Marcel himself comes in, Jean-Luc is ready to leave, although there's something about the attention that he appreciates, deep inside. Only Marcel would turn it really nasty – which he does.

'Here's to Jean-Luc,' he says, in his high, piercing voice, raising his glass. He stands two customers away, his huge, rough-cut face the focus of attention. Today his bottom lip has only the blister where the cigarette usually fits. 'And his dear old mum. Who still rocks his cradle too close to the wall.'

'At least I sleep in my own bed,' Jean-Luc replies, without thinking, oiled by two pastis. It provokes a nervous scatter of laughs. Oncle Fernand is clapping in his head. *Attaboy,* he's saying, *you tell him. Let's get our own back.*

Marcel drinks and puts the glass down with a click on the zinc. Jean-Luc feels his gut beginning to liquefy. He thinks of the German boy and the way Marcel kills stray dogs with his iron bar, beating their skulls in – or so the rumour goes. But nothing more is said. Marcel turns silent and thoughtful, lighting up and blowing out the smoke as if he's not fussed either way.

Louis changes the subject by bringing up the football results; and then nice Françoise, married to Aimé for some unknown reason, comes in with her well-educated friend Sophie, who works in a bank and never stops nattering about health scares. Tonight it is the dangers of batshit.

Jean-Luc slips out, pretending to look at the Ricard clock and be shocked by the time. When Marcel goes quiet, it's best to get away, as far away as possible – even if that's just a few houses up the street and not New Caledonia. Then hope it will all blow over.

EIGHT

A great plain, tiny figures waving desperately at the helicopter
for a moment of attention, even rescue. The helicopter most
often hovering over the wicked or the insane, rescuing them
from the oblivion they otherwise deserve while their victims
remain on the ground, largely anonymous. What was it Emerson
said? 'The first lesson of history is the good of evil.' That's a
mystical positivist for you. Actually, history is tragic. No one
ever learns from it.

But at least there is a helicopter.

Almost everything escapes attention. One forgets that, Nick
was thinking. Most of life falls off the edge like millions of ball
bearings on a continually tilting tray. The few little balls that
remain are formed into patterns, as people in families or firms
or villages make up stories about each other. Contradictory
stories.

He had become, despite his political rekindling, a relativist,
a near-total sceptic incapable of trusting the evidence.

Once, as a boy, on holiday in a windy Lowestoft, he'd walked
across the flat sand against a brisk wind that stroked the incoming
tide to molten pewter against the light, and he'd pretended he
had the power to walk across water: you couldn't tell from the
brilliant, rippled surface whether it was an inch or abyssally
deep. He'd think of that moment – the salt air in his mouth
tainted with the stink of fish and lumpy wrack – when toiling
in the dismal, obscurer reaches of history. It remained one of
the key moments of his life, even more than the birth of his
first daughter.

He'd scanned all of his own essays back home and was now

scrolling through, the years flashing past, all those thousands of hours of furrowed thought. He would include two of his more relevant efforts in the collection, as the editor's privilege – one to introduce and one to conclude, like bookends. A definitive review of the field.

His three distinct periods were too distinct, smelt of fracture and intellectual confusion. One of his more Deleuze-style pieces took Stalin's statement that the Soviet people were too perfect to need jokes as a basis for analysing the records of various of his drunken meetings, where jokes had flown all night. This followed, in terms of publication, an earnest comparison of Peterloo with the miner's strike of the 1980s: the last effort of his Marxist phase, it still resembled polemical juvenilia, riddled with methodological errors. Not much worse than the ensuing period, though, wracked by icy, polysyllabic mumbo-jumbo, like scientific formulae, and peppered with French words like shots of Drambuie. Even the term 'imperialism' now looked hopelessly faded.

Oh, this was a stinger: a brief look at the Muslim Brotherhood during the Suez Crisis, his lofty rejection of claims they were being trained by ex-Nazis, late of the SS. Paddling about in jejune references to 'ideological discourses of power', he'd never once investigated the fact that the claim might have been true. The Brotherhood's roots, its early allies, the links between vestigial Fascism and mullah-brand nationalism –

There were sudden shouts outside. A wailing? He nipped to the window, which looked out onto the doomed lawn and the pool. Following Jean-Luc's instructions, he had tested the pool's pH levels after breakfast and the strip had turned the deepest possible purple, almost black. An acid bath, anyone falling in would dissolve. He didn't tell Sarah. Instead, he'd poured in an entire bottle of *pH Decreaser: sodium carbonate*. He felt he was dealing with something alive, like a crafty, bone-idle and generally impossible student.

He listened. Muffled high-pitched voices from the front area. All fine. Let kids be kids. And then he saw, the other side of the arch, the stream of goats passing. The babble of their bells. The dream of Greenland. Poor Greenland of the melting ice-trays.

This was his third bash at work since their arrival, and he was finding it difficult. He opened the file marked *Contributors* and rubbed his neck, crouched to the screen. His neck was stiff, as it would sometimes get after swimming. It came of thrashing through this confused swirl of facts, the names all demanding to be brought alive again, made sense of. People briefly swept into historical play, then mostly forgotten. Reconstructing a voyage from snapshots of the barnacled wreck on the ocean floor: the music, the affairs, the quarrels. At least two of the contributors had disappointed, their efforts feeble or out of date. Others were still to deliver. One had died, her husband sending a draft that would need revision. Several were superb, and made him feel faintly obsolete, as their authors were mostly young. Peter Osterhauser's was, alas, a corker.

He wobbled his tooth with his tongue, remembering the day his father bit into a raw carrot and said, 'Blimey, my tooth's gone.' His father then fifty-four, of course, or thereabouts. Totting up figures in a British Rail office, proud of the computer that took up an entire room calculating timetables. To his son, home from university, he was already an old codger, part of history's detritus. He didn't wear jeans, for a start, and had his hair buzzed away an inch above his large ears every fortnight. And believed in the Red Menace, despite his son. Or because of, it suddenly occurred to Nick. So hard to interpret correctly. Motivation. Reasons for. He envied the Anglo-Saxon chronicler in his draughty cell, setting down the handful of facts picked up from passing monks knocking the mud from their boots.

The door shivered, as if someone was trying it. It wasn't locked, though. It was only kept shut with a drop-latch.

'Hello?' he called.

The draughty cell. The silence. Despite the ever-surprising antics and noisy demands of the kids, there was a smooth quality to time here, an unruffled surface that was on the verge of being dull. Dull only because he was not yet adapted to Eden. Midgard. Whatever. On the other side of dull, he felt, was wisdom.

That night he had one of the most vivid, meaningful dreams he could ever remember.

He was in a kind of purgatory, perhaps the gloomy plains of Tartarus, all asphodel flowers and misty pools. The Sandlers were wandering about, naked and with split knees. 'What we need is a ladder to the Lord!' shouted Alan Sandler, shaking his fist in a crack of light. He reminded Nick of a faded rock star in a bad musical.

He looked down. As in waking life, his own big toes had curved inward but even further, it was hideous, he had to limp everywhere – it was not just the sharp stones. Alan Sandler was worrying and worsening a huge groin scab like the shell of an old hermit crab into which his manhood had retreated, overlooked by the folds of his withered belly. His nails were shattered. Nick was half-aware this was a dream, a tremendous one, and deliberately turned his back on the daylit mind. He was dressed for a moment like d'Artagnan. He swirled his rapier about and called Alan Sandler names: Uncle Sam, Washington, Exxon-Mobil, Saudi-sucker. Alan laughed and nodded his head like a madman. Lucy, with her withered breasts, seemed to have vanished.

'Too right! Too right!' yelled Alan Sandler. 'America fucked up the entire world!'

Nick told him not to exaggerate, to remain faithful to the facts, to recall that the Industrial Revolution started in Great Britain, with a restless man bent over a boiler in a Glasgow yard; except that he could only sing it in a kind of plainchant. Alan said he was talking about *casino* capitalism, about crookery and oil, sounding weirdly like Nick himself, who was now intent on finding his own father in the humming swarms. The mist thickened briefly so they became phantasmal to each other, even though they were squatting together on a pool's littoral, the water stretching into the mist like a sea. The stench of bad eggs gagged them, then a breeze blew through and the light silvered on the water, glittering here and there where the light shafted.

'That light must come from somewhere,' Nick's father mused, suddenly present and as young as in the photos.

The hordes were by the pool of forgetfulness, scooping the brackish water in scrawny, pustuled hands, elbowing past in their coming and going, eyes hazed by amnesia.

Nick made for the pool of memory, dragging his father. They sat under the shade of the white poplar by the lapping water, the hordes despising them for it, throwing them angry glares and pointing until Nick dismissed them with an effort of mental will. Burning his mouth on the scooped-up water enabled him to talk of the old times. Nick had a need to talk of the old times. But his father had gone, pushed away by Alan Sandler. Sometimes it was better to dive straight in. Not here, of course: whole crowds ran into the brackish shallows and waded out to where the water reached their necks in a bid to drown themselves, but they could not drown themselves. No one died twice. Their lungs were phantom lungs: water passed straight through them. Were they to suck the bitter, burning waters of memory up through their noses, as he had once done with apple purée through a straw when he was five, they would only feel the pain, they would not succumb. The white poplar fluttered its leaves in a pale shimmer.

'What I miss is the power shower,' Alan croaked, with a wet mouth. 'It's right there in my head again.'

'A soak in a hot bubble bath,' sighed Lucy, who had materialised as if she had never been away, as if it were Nick's memory that was faulty.

The brackish pool of Lethe was actually the remains of Hendon Reservoir, Nick's father told them, having been around all along. Nick laughed uncontrollably. What does that make the pool of memory, he screamed? The Ruislip Lido? He woke himself up laughing, which reality translated into a mute juddering in his throat.

They made their presence known at the tiny *mairie* – a mixed experience. The secretary was a charming, attractive woman in her thirties, with impeccably cut hair that curled below each high-boned cheek; Sarah recognised immediately that Nick was taken by her, but didn't mind that much. An attractive woman is an attractive woman. The President grinned at them from the shadows, his charisma reduced by being hung crookedly. The chugging of a photocopier in the back was the sole sign of activity, despite the slew of papers (mostly forms) on the desk.

They introduced themselves and the secretary seemed pleased, admiring the girls and giving them each a flat, grown-up's sort of toffee from the drawer. 'A present from the State,' she joked. When they asked about the origin of the name of the farm-house, she fished out a thick, stapled little pamphlet from a wad in the bottom of the cupboard behind her desk, and blew on it. It had a dim picture of Aubain church on the front, and a hand-drawn map of the commune on the back. The house was marked on the edge with a dot and *Les Fosses (ruine)*, which impressed them. It must have been very romantic in 1992.

'The previous mayor was a great intellectual,' she explained. 'He knew *everything*. A great loss.'

Then the present mayor appeared on cue from the inner room, holding a sheaf of papers; short and stout at the hips, in his late fifties or early sixties, wearing baggy jeans, a dismal old sweater and half-moon glasses, his crumpled, brown face under the straggly hair and droopy moustache never strayed far from its expression of profound distaste. The secretary introduced Monsieur le Maire and told him who they were. He didn't even shake their hands.

They were glanced at over the half-moons, given the briefest sign of recognition that they existed, and then granted a view of his mayoral back. Sarah was struck by how incredibly like their local Cambridge bag-lady he looked from the rear. She felt a peculiar anxiety at the rejection, however. When Beans pulled a box-file off the desk by mistake, Sarah rescued it in a flustered way, as if she were a flunkie at the court of a tyrant.

She left the *mairie* feeling unwanted and unloved, which was stupid. Her notion of a tubby little mayor with cheeks rosy from wine and a fund of amusing stories had gone up in smoke. It didn't seem fair.

It was oddly misty, today, and the village resembled a daguerrotype. An elderly man was coming up the steps. He asked them if the mayor was in and they said yes, he was. *Anglais?* Yes, they were English. They were staying, etc., etc. He commented on the extreme prettiness of their girls (who were skipping about at the foot of the steps) and the parents thanked him without showing their discomfort – which in any case was, for some reason, negligible.

His face brightened even further when he learned they were Cambridge professors and he insisted they come over to his house opposite, a perfect little eighteenth-century place set back next to the church, to look at his books. They did so, thirsty for approval.

His name was Georges Chambord and he was a retired engineer. He had designed motorways: his chief pride was the motorway that curved on concrete columns between two places they didn't recognise and did not retain. It was a work of art, he said. They could have no idea how long it had taken him to design it thirty years back; he'd studied the landscape and now it was part of that landscape. His hands swept the air in his small front room lined with books and, although they disapproved of motorways, both Nick and Sarah felt inspired.

The girls were running about in the little square, safe as houses, as Georges Chambord swept the parents up in his scholarly enthusiasm for motorway design, Charles Dickens, Victor Hugo and the philosophy of Hölderlin. He showed them a book of de Musset's poems signed by the author: he had picked it up for twenty francs years ago. His neatly dressed wife arrived and shook their hands and seemed equally at ease with the heady heights of literature, philosophy and concrete engineering. They drank tiny coffees laced with some ancient family-distilled liqueur and laughed and chatted, while the Mallinsons' French soared as it had never done before; this was because neither Georges nor Claudine seemed to notice its lack of fluency, and their own French was so clear it was almost transparent: the English visible at the bottom. The only flat note was Georges Chambord's scathing view of the locals. Nick told him, in a neutral manner, about the hunters passing the Mas.

'The hunters are onion-heads. They feed, sleep and reproduce, like my onions in the garden. That's all.'

'And hunt,' Nick laughed. 'Not quite like onions.'

Pas tout à fait comme les oignons. It was the first successful joke he'd made in French, ever.

Georges said he was a Parisian and, for Parisians, everything was a joke except revolution. For him – Georges – revolution was also a joke. Around here, he claimed, they were mostly inbred peasants with nothing in their heads but how much money they were hoarding under the mattress. That's the Midi for you. And Protestants. Don't trust *anyone* in the South, from around Clermont Ferrand down. As Hugo said, *La moitié d'un ami, c'est la moitié d'un traître.* Not that anyone's heard of Victor Hugo, down here!

The liqueur softened the content of these acerbic reflections to an acceptable mush in Nick's head – and he was still smarting from the reception by the mayor. A Trot, pickled in ethyl. The only great Trot was Leon himself. He idly spun the image of his old, wild-haired hero opening the door to the assassin's alpine axe. Georges may be a neo-fascist, he reflected, but at least he's welcoming: friendly and civilised.

They asked the Chambords about the history of the Mas des Fosses, but all Georges knew was that it had been a Resistance camp in the war. 'Like most other places!' he laughed. 'You won't find any family here who didn't have a heroic relative in the Maquis! Strange, *hein?*' From the way he said it, he was clearly being ironic, even cynical. They nodded knowingly, although really they didn't have a clue. But at least it vindicated Sarah's interpretative reading of Fernand Maille's plaque.

They only beat a retreat – a somewhat hasty one – when Georges began to tell them about the British Club in Valdaron, run by someone calling himself *Dezerez*, eventually disentangled by Sarah as 'Des the Res' – an amusing character, according to Claudine, if a bit loud. They met fortnightly over tea for gossip, discussion, and the occasional talk or film. Georges was privileged to be an honorary member, improving his English as their French was almost non-existent. He was sure they would be *joyeux* at having two newcomers – they were all a bit long in the tooth!

'Thank you, but no,' said Nick, instantaneously guillotined by depression. 'We're very busy, you see.' He pretended not to have a telephone number of any kind.

Driving home, the liqueur no longer romping, he felt remorse. The mush had now hardened to something salami-like in his forehead. Sarah kept muttering 'Right side' at every junction. Fortunately, there weren't many. The kids pronounced the mayor's title like a sheep noise, exaggerating in the car, going over the top, hungry.

'I guess,' said Nick, 'you can't blame the Trot. Rich Brits called Des pushing up property prices beyond the reach of locals. Swimming pools draining the water table. We're the class enemy. The lackeys of imperialism. Turning farmhouses into fun palaces.'

'They'd fall down,' Sarah pointed out, 'if we didn't do that.'

'Phew, that was close. Thank God for us Brits, then. Saving France's heritage. Phew. All power to your elbow, Des.'

Nick drove on with his head tilted back and his mouth open, anticipating a response. Sarah should never have made such an elementary mistake. A few years ago she would have crawled out of the wreckage with broken wings; now she ignored the momentary press on her heart, as if her head and her heart were in separate compartments. Anyway, she was a little tipsy.

'The mayor doesn't even know us,' said Sarah, prodding the point on regardless. 'Right side.'

'*We* don't know any of the locals.'

'Jean-Luc. Georges and Claudine. We tried in the café, but they weren't exactly friendly.' She pushed up her glasses and recalled the café visit, the telly blaring above their table, the big hairy man with the cigarette stuck to his lip, who was nice at first but then turned cold when they mentioned where they were staying.

'Georges and Claudine aren't locals, they're Parisians. We've known them an hour and a half. And that's probably enough. Jean-Luc is the handyman, not a friend.'

There was an awkward silence full of little wormy things they couldn't say in front of the girls.

'The grass is *not* coming up,' she said, as if rebuking herself. 'No sign whatsoever. Lucy Sandler won't be happy. Right side.'

'If she asks, we'll pretend it's hirsute. We don't want him to lose his job, do we?'

Sarah turned round, frowning. 'Tammy, what's happened to your seat belt?'

'Broken.'

'Rubbish. Put the end thingie back in. Or you'll go flying through the windscreen.'

'Wheeee,' yelled Alicia. 'Fun.'

'It *is* the mayor's job to welcome people to the commune,' Sarah continued. 'Alicia, that's enough!'

'I'm parcel deaf,' she explained.

'How do you know that's his job?' asked Nick, rhetorically.

'I'm assuming. Right side.'

'Please don't keep saying that,' he snapped, still nettled by the sour face of the mayor and his own political spinelessness in the Chambord house. 'It's become meaningless.'

They bumped past the plaque with its gaudy offering and Alicia made gunshot sounds as best she could. Tammy's sheep now made feeble, dying noises. Beans was asleep, head lolling like a drunk. It was still strangely misty today.

'Nothing sourer than a sour Trot,' Nick said, trying to make up for his burst of temper. 'Except a bitter Leninist. As we used to say. And I should know. We're the vanguard, comrades, not the guard's van!'

'That photo you had in your passport when I first met you,' said Sarah, as the house swung into view through the trees, 'it looked *so* like one of the Baader-Meinhofs. That hirsute one whose beard looked like a giant bow tie.'

'They were all pretty hirsute.'

'He was by far the hirsutest.'

'What's hirsoot, Daddy?' asked Tammy, head thrust between the front seats.

'Hairy.'

The girls exploded. The car growled to a stop.

'Did mine really look like one, in the photo? A giant bow tie?'

Sarah nodded. 'Uh-huh. Well, it was sort of on each side of your chin. A floppy bow tie. Thank God you'd grown up by the time I met you.'

Whiffs of pine sap, warm pine needles, sticky pine cones: always that flash feeling of bliss from pine sap, as if heaven or its equivalent was just round the corner. He had found a helpful, if rather heavy, field guide among the novels in the sitting room, concealed in plainness behind its lost dustjacket. A field guide to heaven would be thinner, he considered: he couldn't quite think why. He was introducing the girls to the local flora and fauna in the part of the forest that was mostly pine.

He explained to them about what botanists call 'litter fauna' – the forgotten centipedes, slugs, worms, ants and so on who eat up what drops down onto the ground and then make fresh soil out of it.

'Yuk,' said Alicia. 'Does it come out of their bottoms?'

'Kind of,' he admitted, turning a page of his crib.

Alicia shot to her feet and expressed disgust. From now on she'll have a soil phobia, he thought. She'll live her entire life in the city.

'I was only joking,' he fibbed. But it was probably too late. She'd end up in New York or Shanghai. 'Let's make a documentary about it.'

They scraped with twigs at the soft forest floor of pine-needles and instantly discovered creepy-crawlies, which Tammy filmed, using the zoom to make them bigger. Unfortunately, Beans enthusiastically stamped on a large, newly emergent snail and they spent several minutes trying to mend its shattered hull. Detergent-like spume began to ooze from its writhing, muscular slime.

'That's medicine to mend itself with,' Nick lied. 'Now it needs to be taken to the hospital and covered up.'

'Antibotticks,' Tammy nodded.

'Anti *bottoms*,' giggled Alicia.

'Not quite,' Nick said. 'This is one-hundred-per-cent natural.'

He placed the broken, pulsating snail in his palm and carried it ceremoniously over to the next tree. The foam issued forth from its chilly bulk in surprising quantities, like the contents of a fire extinguisher. He hid its agony in the pine-litter under their innocent, enquiring gaze. Beans seemed not the slightest bit troubled. A moral lesson had been missed.

'I used to put leaves and stuff on slugs, because I thought they were homeless,' he told them. 'That they'd lost their shells.'

'When you were our age?' checked Tammy.

He nodded. 'A long, long time ago.'

A gunshot sounded, making them jump.

'Whoops. It's the Wild Hunt of Odin. We'll have to whistle, kids. To let them know we're here.'

'Don't like Odin,' said Alicia, for whom Nick's bedtime reading of the Norse myths was a luminous swirl of incomprehension.

'Can't whistle,' Tammy admitted. 'But I'm in training to.'

'Sing then.' Nick cleared his throat. He'd been told by the doctor to avoid singing for six months. But this was an emergency. '*Frè-re Ja-cques, frè-re Ja-cques* . . .'

Another gunshot, closer. It echoed dully and flatly through

the tall pines. The song hiccupped and then continued, louder. They sang, raggedly, between the trees.

Sarah was at work in the bedroom while they were among the pines, using the little yellow table with the grapes painted on the drawers. She had reorganised and expanded a single paragraph from her thesis (which had been generally regarded as 'exceptional'); it was so hard to fit everything in and yet keep order and sense.

> The grand irrigation scheme of the *Office du Niger* in West Africa, its engineers inspired by the hydraulic works of British South India, was hardly consonant with contemporary conceptions of an 'associationist' rather than 'assimilationist' French empire (as illustrated by Normandin's narratives of hydraulic decline and fall outlined in the previous chapter), and remained the exception. As Raymond Betts and Alice Conklin have argued, continued French rule would be assured by decentralised adaptation to the interests of native societies and economies on the part of modernising colonial developers. The *Office du Niger*'s vast waterworks were attacked by the Sorbonne geography professor Charles Robequain as being 'a waste of time and money . . . [resulting] from an intense desire for assimilation, into which certain factions hoped to force not only people but climate and soil as well' – unfavourably contrasting that scheme with the development plan he had drawn up for post-war Indochina.

She looked again at the paragraph and felt it needed major hydraulic works itself, perhaps preceded by a development plan. The laptop's keyboard yielded again to her quick fingers – a spatter of rain on glass, a stormy gust of concentration. It was even worse: poor Normandin would have to be relegated to a footnote. She groaned hammishly in her throat. How odd, to make a private sound, to be completely alone.

On a strange whim, a kind of amusing feint, she opened a new document on the screen and began something entirely fresh:

Nobody is sure why Le Mas des Fosses is thus called, since there is no indication of any 'quarry' or 'burial place' in the records held at the two-room *mairie* in Aubain (the commune's only village lying some five kilometres away by narrow road).

A local publication by the previous mayor of Aubain – a well-read ex-teacher and amateur archaeologist – suggests that, given its superb position, the site was a sacred place in the later Iron Age, marked by now-obliterated sacrificial pits or ditches before the ilex trees took over. His only evidence for this is a nineteenth-century discovery (recorded by the village priest but now lost) of an iron sword-blade folded back on itself, recovered during the laying of a terracotta water-pipe behind the house. The blade was dated to pre-Roman Gaul.

Scraps, she thought. We cannot always choose what we carry with us. A shopping list. A supermarket flyer. An iron sword.

Even if most of the above was lifted from her reading of the 'local publication', it was still good, objective history. Sarah did not yet know how to introduce her own memory into her account. She was too well trained, and history undoes memory, picking it apart and reducing it and reassembling it. No memory – organic, self-constructing – is ever reliable. It is easier to forget, or to reinvent. That is the role of the historian, she thought: to remember, and not worry about being despised for it. She was enjoying herself.

She turned over another page of the pamphlet and tapped gaily on, scarcely noticing the vague percussives of gunshots from the woods.

NINE

Jean-Luc has waited several days to carry the toy pram to his room, even though the van is parked almost directly in front of the house. If anyone were to see him, it might result in teasing that would ripple out until it got to Marcel's ears, or one of his mates. Not a good idea. Not good at all.

Now he's ready. He did supper in the microwave, took it up, pretended it had been hours in the making instead of five minutes flat, then got out to the café. He came back and was told in a whine that the phone had kept on ringing; she'd been bad all day and couldn't get down to it; if she'd tried she'd have fallen and bled to death while he was having fun in the café with his mates. Then she nagged at him about not having a phone upstairs. He told her the caller was bound to be Tante Juliette, which calmed her down.

'You can throw the phone in the river, in that case,' she snarled.

He sits in the kitchen until he is sure she's asleep. She usually nods off before ten, then wakes up in the early hours, moaning. The handful of young lads left in Aubain do their evening bit on their mobilettes, setting his teeth on edge, up and down, up and down like wasps in his ears, before being tucked up in bed. He switches the telly off, slips out, opens the van, checks the coast is clear both ways along the street and that all the shutters are closed and then lifts the treasure, wrapped in a filthy, oil-stained blanket. It is easier than he expects, though his heart is hammering. The clattery bang of the van's door reverberates up and down, but no one opens their shutters as he fastens the rope on its handle in one quick twist, not even nosy old Lucille two doors up. It's the semi-finals of *Star Academy*, that's why. He isn't interested. Not now that sweet little Céline has been knocked out.

He lays newspaper on the kitchen table and gives the toy pram a wipe-down with hot water and paper towels under the bright neon strip. The metal struts and spokes are hardly dirty. Rust comes off on the paper, orange-brown. The rust has nibbled all the paint off. He could give it a new coat, in all the colours of the rainbow. Or just pink, like the handle. A glossy pink. At least three coats, after an application of that black, anti-rust stuff. A picture comes into his head of the English kids dancing around the pram, laughing at its bright pink shininess, happy as larks. But this isn't for them. This is for him. Or no one at all. No one. Oncle Fernand, maybe.

Maybe it wasn't ever a toy. Maybe babies were smaller, in the old days. He read that, somewhere. But not that small, surely.

He creaks up the stairs, tiptoes past his mother's bed and makes it safely into his own room. The smell in hers is getting worse. He wonders if the nurse even bothers to change the commode each time she comes – twice a day, it should be. But Elodie is sometimes replaced by Colette, who is lazy and drinks. It makes him feel ill. He isn't about to change it himself. He opens his window a little.

He clears his table and puts the treasure on it. Its four wheels fit easily inside the edge. The toy pram seems bigger, now. He moves it slightly, though it doesn't move easily: rust has seen to that. Then, as he's thinking hard, the phone rings downstairs in the kitchen. It is the old phone, so old it doesn't even have a push-button dial and the mouthpiece sits on a cradle. Before the storm, they had two cordless phones and he ran one of them all the way up here. The storm did for them, as it did for the previous set. Now they're back to the old one in the kitchen. They tried to sell him a mobile in the shop, but what would he want one of them for? People you don't know ringing you all times of the day and night. Stupid messages. He read somewhere that there are 20,000 germs on each square centimetre of mobile. It made him feel sick.

Anyway, in Aubain mobiles only work on one spot outside the *mairie*, or in about half of the houses if you go upstairs – or into the attic, in some places. He'd like to be the last person left in the world without a mobile, sticking out to the end. Then the telly cameras would come round and he'd have to shout at them.

'Go away! Piss off!'

Lots of reporters in the street. Fame at last. But he'd still shout at them to go away. And if they didn't go away, he'd pick them off one by one with Papa's hunting rifle and then there'd be floods of reporters, keeping a safe distance, until the specially trained police bods would come smashing in through the roof to fill his body with lead from their machine-guns while Maman called out next door, wondering what was up, desperate for her commode.

The phone stops. Hardly anyone phones them up, except for Tante Juliette. And she's off her rocker.

He places the sieve carefully on the pram, where the baby-basket part would have gone. Bibi is in the sieve, legless in the spider's web, next to the fish-bone; the little nail-heads on her naked skin are like warts. He has to find the spider, but it isn't in his box under the bed. He knows that without looking. The fish-bone is a dead fly the spider has forgotten about. No, the fish-bone is the spider, the dead spider. It is Raoul the spider, dead. It is still after Bibi, though, being Raoul: it is a resurrected spider. I am the Life and the Resurrection. He doesn't need a head for the spine, after all.

He pinches off some of the tiny bones until there are eight left, roughly. He places the eight-legged fish-bone on the edge of the sieve, just under the edge of the web. He doesn't like the way it looks as if it's about to gobble Bibi up. It will have to work its way slowly towards her. Give her a chance.

And growing up the handles of the pram will be the rose-bush, full of faces. The Englishwoman's face, all warm and smiling. He feels the excitement so strongly, this time, that his hands shake. Wire. A camera. Paint.

Under his fingernails is the earth of the Sandlers' lawn. He planted a cherry tree today, the buds already swelling on its thin, twiggy branches. He dug a big hole next to the fenced lawn and watered it in with the hose until the earth was squelching underfoot. A bit late to plant a fruit tree, but at least he's tried, carried out his orders. He should have put compost in, but he was behind with the stone wall up at the Swiss place, so he wasn't about to go off looking for some. He should have bought some when he bought the tree at the nursery outside Valdaron, where the Sandlers have an account, but he was thinking about other things. More exciting things.

He picks at the black under his nails as best he can, given his excitement. Then he uses the point of his Opinel. He stares at the pram for a long time, hoping to share this moment, but Oncle Fernand is away.

Unless that's him phoning, Jean-Luc chuckles to himself.

He lies on the bed and reads a *Spirou* through the squeaks and groans of the springs – his favourite, from 23 May 1957. Sonny, in *Buck Danny*, battling through the storm in the plane with the evil Japanese. He turns a page and it leaves the others, comes away from the rusty staples. He stares at it, stricken. He's read it too much. Nothing goes on forever. He sees his father grinning in the kitchen over the pile in his arms, twenty-nine years ago.

'I dropped him five francs,' he said. 'What do you reckon, Janno?'

Jean-Luc feels hungry. He tiptoes past his snoring mother and creeps downstairs and looks in the fridge, which has nothing much in it but some old vegetables lying in their juices and a Petit Suisse past its sell-by date. He's been busy this week, thinking too much to shop. He eats the Petit Suisse and cleans the spoon with his mouth so that it shines and then catches his face looking up at him out of the spoon's clear little mirror. He looks even uglier in the spoon, he thinks, like a fat clown;

he moves the spoon slightly and his face, distorted by the curve, makes him laugh. And then he has an idea. It bursts into his head like a bird. No, like an angel.

He scuttles upstairs and pulls the box out from under the bed and scrabbles eagerly for the old green-tinged spoons. There are six! He found them in a broken cupboard thrown out onto a tip, years ago. Soup spoons, with shorter handles than modern spoons. He holds a couple of them next to the pram's grip. All he needs to do is attach them. This is the best idea he's ever had! It is how Oncle Fernand works: secretly, in silence. Six roses on the rose bush, Jean-Luc.

And the bowl of each spoon will bear a face, like Mary bore Jesus Christ.

Not that he believes in all that junk. And then the phone goes again. It almost scares him.

They found the lights didn't work, on their return from the pine wood. There was a strange silence in the kitchen, which came from the fridge not operating. They went upstairs to find Mummy.

She was working in the bedroom. She didn't even know the electricity had gone, just like that – her laptop had switched to battery mode and she'd not noticed the dip in the screen's contrast. She hurriedly hid what she was writing by lowering the laptop's screen, then snapped at Alicia for trying to peep.

They tried the fuse box immediately. Nothing. There were mice droppings on top of the box, like black husks of rice. They had three candles left. 'This is how,' Nick told the girls, 'people used to live. Before electricity. No television. No light-bulbs. No radio. No computer. No fridges. They went to bed when it grew dark and got up at dawn. For thousands of years.'

'Millions,' Tammy corrected.

He reckoned it was the damp. Yesterday's mist had blinded the house: it was warm and swirled about, it must have got in and shorted something. The wind would dry it all out. He went up to the bathroom and stood on the chair and tried to phone a few numbers in the phone book, but they were all finished for the day. He returned downstairs and Sarah suggested he phone Jean-Luc after making a big pot of tea, not realising the latter was impossible. Only then did they sense the gravity of the situation. They searched for more candles and unearthed a couple of stubs.

Bathroom locked, this time. Alicia. Beans and Tammy were downstairs, drawing houses – in Beans's case, a manic jumble of marks they would all have to coo over. Tammy's was King Solomon's palace, plus a tennis court.

'Are you going to be long?' he called.

'Go away.'

Tammy came up to observe.

'Alicia, honey, I need to make an urgent phone call and there's only one spot where the mobile picks up, and you're in it.'

No answer. Alicia had been known to spend an hour in the bathroom. Preening herself, probably. At five years old! It was all a mystery to him.

'Alicia, as you are aware we've got an emergency on our hands. No electricity. In fact, no *telly*,' he added, in a fit of inspiration.

'Telly's bad for you. You said.'

'OK, no lights. Night will fall and there'll be pitch darkness everywhere. Creepy.'

Pause. He would pay for that tonight.

'Go away, Daddy,' came the confident order through the door. 'I don't care. Anyway, I'm parcel deaf.'

'Where the heck did you get that idea from? Hm? What are you doing? Are you going to be long?'

'Say please.'

'Please.'

Then there was silence. Tammy kept mum. Her father paced up and down for at least ten minutes. The only signal in the entire house was that spot below the ceiling in the bathroom, seven feet up, between the loo and the basin. At six feet it was dodgy. But at seven feet it was clear.

'Alicia, I'm going to explode.'

Some clinking noises issued from the bathroom, then nothing. Sarah was on the stairs. 'Have you got through, Nick?'

'I haven't even managed to get into the bloody bathroom!'

'There's no point in getting annoyed with *me*,' Sarah complained, her face returning to the point of anguish in which they'd found it an hour ago. Already an hour!

'I'm not annoyed with you, I'm annoyed with that incredibly selfish girl in *there*!'

Sarah talked through the bathroom door. 'Alicia darling, Daddy needs to phone Jean-Luc about the electricity right now. Could you open the door, please, sweetie-pie?'

The door opened and Alicia emerged with sparkly eyelids and lips, rouged cheeks and a ribbon in her hair. She walked straight past them and into the bedroom and started talking animatedly – presumably to herself or to one of her cuddly toys, because Beans was now present, holding Tammy's hand. Sarah said, 'There you are. It's called negotiation.'

'Jesus Christ,' he said. 'It's called being in a state of denial, that's what it's called. Dancing on the deck of the *Titanic*.'

He stood on the chair in the bathroom and knocked his head on the beam and said fuck several times. Jean-Luc wasn't in. Alicia was squealing in her bedroom at something one of her sisters was doing. He felt as if evolution was running backwards inside him, that he was short and thick and snarled a lot. Sarah would be fed up with him for losing his temper. His skull-bone winced from its contact with the iron-hard wood of the beam. Fuck.

Sarah wasn't fed up: she suggested he go back up and try the gods themselves, in London. Nick did so, and mentioned the flowers being left. It was a probe, but Lucy didn't react. Or rather, she pretended it was to do with a child dying a hundred years ago. He assumed she was inventing, anyway. He didn't have the courage to be more direct. After all, she was no doubt covering up for their sakes.

He came back from the bathroom with the deities' message:

phone Jean-Luc. It was a kind of loop tape. He tried every hour, on the hour, taking a candle up when night fell and searching for the numbers in the shadow of his thumb.

'Still no answer,' said Nick. 'Yet again.' He was standing on the chair in the bathroom's darkness, tall enough to have to stoop. The mobile's blue light made his face look artificial, thought Sarah. The wind had got up outside and added to the atmospherics of the lone candle with distant bangings and moanings. 'I think it's too late. We shouldn't have tried again so late. It's nearly eleven. Then our mobiles will run out and we'll be stuck forever. I should have driven over to Aubain.'

'Too many *should haves*. Anyway, I can't believe he goes to bed before eleven.'

'This is the country, Sarah. He hasn't even got an answerphone. I'm not trying again. Tammy, what're you doing here?'

'You woke me up. I want to stay with you for a bit.'

They went gingerly downstairs and sat in front of the fire, which blustered feebly in response to the wind down the chimney. Tammy was perched on her mother's lap, although neither of them was very comfortable. The logs hissed, turning black and bubbling sap without producing more flame than the smallest ring on the hob. Smoke puffed into the room. Nick said they'd have to go into the woods to collect heaps of dry stuff, to get the fire really going. They both had sweaters on, but Tammy was fine in her nightgown.

Each day it got colder; the year was going backwards, perhaps, despite the flowers.

The air was really smoky, now. He had reached a compromise of mild grumpiness. It was late – half past eleven. Sarah's glasses lay on the arm of the sofa like someone contemplating the heavens with their arms folded. The wind was saying *sassa, sassa*, picked up by the chimney. Amplified. Knocking noises.

'Maybe we should all go to bed,' Sarah said, tapping her daughter on the back.

Who coughed and sounded impressively consumptive,

exaggerating the rattle and prolonging each cough until her mother, hand on her back, suggested she stop.

Lucy Sandler's advice, when she took the call from the annoyingly helpless couple in Les Fosses, was to contact Jean-Luc. Otherwise an electrician, but of course she didn't have any numbers here. There was an okay electrician in Valdaron, but the one in Aubain was useless; she couldn't recall his name. Yes, he would have to wait until tomorrow if Jean-Luc was still no joy, but since mankind had done without electricity for thousands of years then one more day wouldn't threaten their survival, she didn't think – and laughed to take the edge off. Horribly, there was a delayed echo and she heard her own laugh come back at her faintly.

'Millions,' said the voice at the other end. 'Millions of years.'

She asked again if he'd pressed the black button or the red or whichever it was and he said yes, it was not a storm but the damp. It had been misty. She pointed out that a storm could have happened miles away and hit a main thingie, it was one of the inevitable drawbacks about living in rural France, their electricity system used some method peculiar to them and was not up to scratch and you couldn't tell them anything, they'd rather die than learn from the Brits, it was the same when they'd pulled out of NATO, they had to be different and superior, Alan knew all about it but he was out.

In fact, she was looking at Alan as she spoke, but he had received a death-threat by the ordinary post that morning, made up of words cut out of a newspaper, and had drunk too much as a result. He was ugly, today. He was onto his ninth whisky and zapping through rubbish on cable. She heard the ends of her sentences like someone teasing her: her voice sounded ghastly, high and affected.

She asked the professor how the lawn was getting on.

'Fantastic,' he said. Which was an odd reply. 'And the cherry tree's fine.'

She wondered if they were enjoying themselves, otherwise. Oh yes, he replied, none too convincingly.

But she groaned inwardly at the thought of five more months to go. The whole point had been to forget the blasted place. If Alan hadn't stuffed one of its cellars full of his blasted Iraqi art – stuffed was not quite the right word, since it was only a single metal crate with a label saying BOOKS – she'd have been very tempted to sell the wretched house. She had suggested a Swiss bank vault, but of course you couldn't even trust a Swiss bank these days: they were onto the police just like that, it was the latest fashion. There was that big Nazi haul of Impressionist paintings that had just been unlocked. Nowhere was safe. You had to go DIY, these days. Bury the treasure. Yo ho ho and a bottle of rum. At least it wasn't drugs.

The professor was going through what they'd done, and she was making the right noises, although she hadn't taken in a word, it was utter tedium, the usual stuff about the marvellous vegetables in the marvellous bloody markets, but the conversation then took a peculiar turn.

'By the way, someone put some memorial flowers against the house two or three weeks ago,' he said. 'Any idea why?'

She felt a sharp tear in her nervous system, all over. She said something about a child's tragic death a hundred years or so ago, how tenacious these peasants were at remembering, how important family was, and so on. Even that was a bit risky: why had she invented a child dying? She gave herself the shivers, just saying it.

'Must have been a special child,' he said, in that dry, half-mocking way his sort cultivated.

'Much loved, that's all.'

Which she thought would squash him. But after a little pause he bounced up again, wondering if anything had happened in the house, it seemed to have a totally undeserved reputation. Lucy felt an iciness creep up her back and she had to take a deep breath.

'Nothing's happened in the house that I know of,' she said. 'I've always found it a very happy place. But I can't speak for before we got it.'

She regretted this immediately. '*Got it,*' said the echo, before he replied. They would be bound to find out about that poor man sooner or later. Why was she hiding it? She wanted to backtrack, to tell him about the wretched builder falling off the wet roof, but he was already saying goodbye. She put the phone down on the snow-white arm of the chair and felt very unhappy.

'Well,' said Alan, shaking the ice in his tumbler, 'I guarantee that's got him confused.'

The television was on mute, showing a man blowing glass somewhere Scandinavian, from the look of it.

'I thought the whole point was not to have to worry about it,' she said. Her chest was a cavern full of bats.

'The whole point was to occupy the place,' Alan murmured. 'Empty houses get unwelcome visitors.'

What, she thought, if the unwelcome visitors are already *in situ*?

'Maybe we should retire early to New *Zealand* or some-where,' she said, not really meaning it. 'Though they say it's terribly philistine.'

Alan stirred and looked at her for a moment, his eyes almost regaining the blue lustre that had so attracted her once. 'Now that, Lucy, is the best idea you've had in a very, very long time.'

Sarah woke up, startled, unsure where she was until she surfaced. Her bedside light was on. There was a faint, manic sound of laughter from downstairs. She had no idea of the time and looked at her watch on the bedside table. *3.22*. Ugh. The laughter frightened her, especially when it subsided into a muttering. She didn't remember switching her light on.

Nick was on his back, snoring gently. She preferred not to look at him like that, and slid out of bed to find she was step-ping on Beans, who didn't seem to notice, her little form curled in a welter of sheet and blanket. Then Sarah remembered. The electricity had gone and the girls could only sleep with the shutters open to the stars and a sliver of moon, the suggestion of light entering their room like vapour. She wasn't keen on lighting a night-light, but Nick had put one into a jam-jar and it quivered in the corner. If it was precariously enough for Tammy and Alicia, it wasn't enough for Beans.

Now the electricity had come back on, by itself, or as if someone else was in charge. The noises downstairs were, she realised, the telly. One of the girls must have switched it on after the power-cut, forgetting. She padded downstairs to find the room constantly flickering in the telly's blueish light.

Bleary from sleep, she didn't spot Tammy at first. Her daughter was sitting on the sofa like a Buddha, blue-faced, legs curled up under her, staring at the screen that flickered white in her eyes. It was mostly snow, with dim shapes moving and laughing in the blizzard, the occasional close-up of a face through misted glass.

'Tammy, you should be in bed.'

'Can't sleep.'

'Why?'

'Cos lots of things are putting together in my head,' she said, eyelids blinking slowly.

'What things, darling?'

'Like motorbikes and French angry things and Alicia's being really annoying. I want to go home.'

Sarah felt a lead weight of dismay sink through her. She sat on the sofa and put her arm around her daughter, who immediately nestled in the crook of her waist.

'It's so nice being here; it's very special,' she whispered, as if persuading herself.

The morning was bright after the wind, and she had to put sunglasses on. The air was hardly warm, but the sun certainly was – she was very aware of it as a heavenly body, a physical entity with tongues of flame licking her skin; she wondered whether to begin to apply cream on the kids. The miniature clothes were pegged up one by one yet again, coming round so often she wondered whether the days had slid into each other, a temporal pile-up. Ladybirds, teddy bears, wizards.

She walked round to the back of the house as she always did after hanging the clothes and received a shock. The chicken-wire fence around the Zone had been pulled down all along one side, the side facing the barn. The boars had rotivated the seed-bed so thoroughly it made her want to laugh. The little cherry tree leaned at an angle, its roots exposed. It was as if they'd been visited by an English stag party.

She stood by the swimming pool and stared into it. Jean-Luc had certainly cleaned up the troubled waters; the bottom was waveringly visible, the filtering system purred, the surface had a silky vibration to it at one end. Nick had tested the pH levels yesterday and they were fine, to his delight.

She dipped her fingers in and was surprised by the cold. A brisk morning swim each day, that would be nice: but then the girls would want to and that would be complicated. Unless it was her secret thing. Her little vice.

Maybe it was *too* clean, now; she hadn't thought of this before. She'd almost preferred its greenness, its murk, in which the toad and various slimy plant-forms lurked. Then Jean-Luc had come along and poured his chemicals in, like an unthinking scientist, like all those unthinking scientists who dreamed up pesticides and everything else disastrous. A chlorine smell tinted the air around it, now. Sarah almost resented Jean-Luc for this: something no one else would understand.

When her father had been based for a few months in Aden, Sarah and her mother joined him, and the officers' pool was theirs. The officers hardly used it, although it had been made for them in 1973: the date was marked in the cement surround, with a heart around it, which made the cement seem still wet. The pool was surrounded by a flimsy rush fence and the water was full of frogs and huge drowned insects, a dark mantle she'd swim through, keeping her mouth shut, not thinking twice about it. She was only ten, but she loved it. She thought it was paradise. She sometimes found insects still struggling, and saved them. Even locusts. She couldn't see her feet in the murk, but felt the frogs nibble them. She assumed it was the frogs. The pool turned into a kingdom full of stories, of which she was the queen. She was surprised now that she hadn't fallen ill with some water-borne disease, but all she came down with was some type of whooping cough. Her mother had seemed very relaxed about it all; she'd let her daughter play alone by the pool for hours, not even bothering with sun-cream. Neglect, really. Then along she would come with a towel, smelling sweetly of drink, and lower herself in, wrinkling her saggy face under its flowery plastic cap, sweeping the insects from her so that the mantle darkened in a clear radius around her body.

'Dutch courage,' she'd always say, giggling, then launch herself forwards and swim two clumsy lengths, chin held high, eyes almost closed. Her daughter would laugh and feel pleased: her father would never swim in the officers' pool.

Now she felt almost sorry for her children, having only this sterility. She rocked the surface with her hand, sending out ripples that made the filters cluck and gobble. Almost a loud noise in this stillness, this held breath of the place.

The hunt came two days later, just after dawn, *very* much like Odin's bursting into Midgard.

A murmur of engines and shouts and tinkly bells, then a gunshot, very loud. Then another. Tammy was already awake, though tired. Beans started crying, joined by Alicia, calling out for Mummy. The darkness was still total in their bedroom except for a pencil-line of light either side of the window where the shutters didn't quite meet the wall at the hinges.

'Help,' Tammy whispered. 'I think it's the terrorists.'

Seven gunshots. Seven was enough.

They were all in their parents' bedroom within a minute. They stayed with their mother in bed while their father opened the shutters gingerly, because there were still voices below. He could see two men in fluorescent orange caps and with guns on their backs, chatting below. Another was peering over the drop to the first terrace. A huge, silvery four-by-four was parked crookedly in front of their car, as if to stop it getting away.

Their car had shrunk into itself, just as Nick did when one of the hunters glanced up. The hunter didn't wave, or laugh, or look surprised. Instead, he simply ignored Nick. The man's stubbled face returned to its former position, and carried on chatting.

'Just to confirm. It's the hunters,' Nick said, blearily, closing the window but leaving the shutter slightly open. 'Complete with hell-hounds. And they are not in the slightest bit bovvered, by the way.'

The room was dusted over with the grey morning light, re-assuring them.

'Didn't you say anything?' asked Sarah.

'Did you hear me say anything?'

'No.'

'Then why ask?'

'They can't be allowed to hunt in someone's garden. They were shooting in our garden.'

'It's not *our* garden. There was no point in me saying anything.'

'You know what I mean. It's private property.'

'Fox-hunters follow the fox wherever.'

Sarah didn't reply, cuddling Alicia and Beans. Tammy was too sleepy to contribute.

'Someone must have told them about the preponderance of boars,' said Nick, now reduced to the very edge of the bed.

'Boars deaded,' said Beans, still shuddering slightly.

'Sssh. I'm asleep, *please*,' said Alicia.

Once properly up, Nick evinced a sudden burst of energy, the type that hits everybody from time to time and in which an amazing amount can be done – houses cleaned from top to bottom, gardens dug over, curtains whipped off the rails and seamed into ball-gowns, revolutions sparked, the planet saved, the glaciers thickening up again and millions of creatures pulled back from extinction.

He fashioned signs. Three, to be precise. He was no carpenter, but a righteous anger gave him a sudden facility, the pieces of wood and the tools leaping into his hands and the black paint appearing out of the darkness in the first cellar he tried, and still usable through a rubbery skin. He was 'on a roll' (as he put it) all morning, and hammered the signs to trees on the track where, from the old map of the property, he'd identified the remains of a smothered stone wall as the unmarked edge of the Sandlers' land. The hammering echoed through the woods.

PROPRIÉTÉ PRIVÉ!
ATTENTION AUX ENFANTS!
PAS DE CHASSE ICI SVP —
MERCI!

The letters were a bit squashed up one end, but he considered the 'please' and 'thank you' necessary, if not meant. After he went off to have a shower (he was very sweaty), the three girls studied the signs with nervous pride, talking in whispers.

They were having their afternoon tea when the hunt passed on its way back. They all held their breath around the table. Shouts, a couple of bomb-like shots, more shouts, and then laughter. They looked out and saw boars strapped to the bonnets of several of the vehicles, and a couple more nodding from the open back of a small van as it bounced away, leading the pack like a tiny terrier.

Two of the signs were splintered driftwood on the track, printed with muddy tyre-marks and spotted by trails of blood. One was still on the tree but nicked into illegibility by gunshot.

'How charming,' said Tammy, glancing anxiously at her father.

'Wow,' said her mother. 'So much for the power of the word.'

'Bastards,' growled the sign-maker, no longer lord of the analytic phrase. 'Complete fascist bastards. *Têtes des oignons!*' he yelled, in a polyps-fretting addition that daringly bounced through the woods as if trying to catch the hunters up.

Jean-Luc hears about what the English have done from Henri at the agricultural merchants in Valdaron, when buying the electric fence. There are only two types of fence in the whole place, because this isn't the Auvergne, where cows grow faster than the grass grows fatter, as Henri puts it.

'Stones grow nice and fast here,' says another customer, whose small curving nose and big curving upper lip make him look like a budgerigar.

'They just have lots of babies,' Henri jokes. 'If they could stop stones breeding, then we'd be laughing.'

Henri has a ponytail, but that doesn't stop him knowing a lot about agricultural merchandise. He recommends the stronger voltage for boars. They have thick skulls. There are a lot of them. What sizzles us is a tickle to them.

'That's what my women say,' whistles budgerigar, leaning on the counter.

But they ignore him. The 6,000-volt-maximum type, running off a battery, is enough to give a large dog convulsions; it won't kill anything that doesn't have a weak heart. Henri exaggerates, usually, especially when it comes to prices; but this time he's believed.

'Just as well you told me, I was going to test it on my mother,' Jean-Luc jokes.

'I tested it on my missus,' says Henri, 'and now I've got to mend the hole in the ceiling.'

'Just stuff her in the hole,' cackles a bald oldie, looking for rat poison on the nearest shelf. But Henri doesn't laugh. Instead he tells Jean-Luc to test it with his finger, after it's erected.

'Unless you're a weakling,' he grins, winking knowingly at Jean-Luc. 'Unless you're a girl with a weak heart.'

'How much? And make sure you give me a receipt,' says Jean-Luc, quickly. But it comes out as a mumble.

The stronger voltage is three times as expensive. It has short green plastic posts with moulded hooks and a fancy blue battery made in Germany. Jean-Luc often emerges from Henri's store wishing he hadn't spent as much, but it's usually other people's money so it doesn't really matter. And the other people in question are filthy rich, anyway. It is only the Dutch couple who

217

fuss about how much he spends on their massive garden and its pool shaped like a kidney dish. He pissed in it, once – in the Dutch couple's pool. Probably helped the pH levels.

'Your English lot put up offensive signs,' Henri tells him. 'Marcel Lagrange gave one of the signs what for with both barrels.'

Apparently, he flipped and it was all the others could do to stop him from emptying both barrels in the English themselves and tying all five of them to his bonnet. That would have finished the hunt for at least the rest of the season, as the others could have been charged for not doing enough, or even aiding and abetting. The whole club would have been closed down. Imagine! Henri laughs in disbelief at his own words. It would have been worse than that time Marcel's young, trained-up dogs ripped poor old Madame Chaldette's legs when she was out walking, and if he hadn't hidden the dogs they'd have been put down. Two years' hard training down the chute!

Jean-Luc nods and feels ill. It would have been his fault, in the end, for telling everyone in the café about his problem with the boars on the lawn. Madame Chaldette dropped charges after someone, it was rumoured (one of the Lagrange tribe – Marcel himself most likely), had sent her threatening letters; she spent half her savings on her medical bills, even after the state had picked up most of them, and not got a penny back. She no longer went walking, and not just because of her limp.

Jean-Luc would have had worse than a limp, if the hunt club had been closed down.

From now on he's going to zip up his mouth. He carries the electric fencing out to the van, vowing to keep an eye on himself, on his own mouth. It's just that he sometimes can't stop the words from spilling out.

He crosses the street and buys a throwaway camera in Valdaron's *tabac*. It is cheaper than he expected.

'Going away on holiday, then, Jean-Luc?'

It is Cécile's joke, because she knows Jean-Luc never takes a holiday, never goes anywhere. She's run the *tabac* from when

Jean-Luc was a teenager, and he likes her. She is sixty-eight with dyed chestnut hair and looks about forty and sleeps two hours a night because her father was a market-stall fishmonger and that's how she was brought up. But then he died and she ended up in the hills, selling fags and papers and a bit of everything, along with rearing six lazy kids. Jean-Luc wishes he'd been one of those kids, because something about Cécile makes him want her to have been his mum.

'I never go on holiday, more's the pity,' Jean-Luc replies, pretending he doesn't know it was a joke. He doesn't want to say any more. He is burning with embarrassment.

'I know what,' says Cécile. 'It's to take pictures of your girl-friend.'

This is also a joke, but Jean-Luc stares at her with his mouth open.

'It's not,' he says, collecting himself when she looks un-comfortable. 'It's to take pictures of me killing my mum.'

Cécile starts to laugh, then turns all worried. 'I hope not. It does happen. I've seen it on the news.'

'Better call the police now, Cécile,' says Jean-Luc. 'After you've given me my change.'

TEN

The washing line in front of the trees bore a holed sweater, wan tee shirt, encrusted socks and faded boxer-shorts along-side a multi-pocketed, vaguely military pair of trousers, stiff with use, and an Arab burnous whose hood dangled like a head. They hung shamefacedly next to the kids' togs like those dead crows farmers suspend from barbed-wire fences, stinking and turning slowly to bone. Sarah recalled hanging those same trousers up when he was still in the sixth form, but that was seven years ago. Jamie was twenty-four or twenty-five. It was not her job to remember her stepson's birthday. Or maybe it was, because Nick *never* remembered.

Jamie was not visiting. He was staying. Since the girls thought their half-brother was good fun, they were happy. He'd always popped up like that, without warning. This time it was a text message activated only when his father had stood on the chair in the bathroom to check, as he did twice a day. Jamie was not only in the country, and not only in town, he was in a tiny hamlet three kilometres away. Nick and Sarah had to consult a detailed map from a drawer, trying to hide their dismay, their thumping hearts, hoping Jamie had his geography wrong and the hamlet lay at the other end of France or even the world.

'It's not in New Caledonia, after all,' sighed Nick.

'I don't believe it, shit,' Sarah murmured. 'I was just begin-ning to relax. This is unbelievable.' A vague sense of chaos invaded her, the empire's borders falling to wild hooves.

'It'll be fine,' said Nick. 'He won't stay long, it's too remote.'

'Hooray!' the girls yelled, when Jamie stepped out of the car an hour later. It had not been easy tracking him down, even in a hamlet. He was dressed in a long earth-brown hooded mantle and carried a huge stained ex-army swag shaped like a sausage; he couldn't even go round with a rucksack, like everyone else. He had a discreet butterfly tattooed on the back of his neck; Sarah thought it was dirt and tried to brush it off. They laughed. It usually started well, with Jamie.

For the last year, he told them, he'd been part of a Canadian circus without animals. This did not surprise the girls; nothing surprised them about their big brother. They didn't, however, know he had circus skills, since their father would complain (at bad moments) of his son's lack of any skills – basic, circus, or otherwise. He was short and wiry with small girlish features, a legacy of his now-plump mother. His hair was still the same, gathered in a plaited knot like those on Germanic tribes described by Tacitus. One of Nick's colleagues had pointed this out: an Iron Age specialist. Nick had assured him it was an accidental reference.

'I was a carer,' Jamie informed them.

'Of the lions?'

He went pffff, and said: 'That would've been a cinch compared to my job?'

One of the trapeze artists had fallen eighty metres two years ago: he'd swung over the void to meet his performing partner's firm hands but all he'd grabbed was air, the partner having left a fraction too late. He'd landed the wrong way in the safety net and broken his spine. Jamie had been this trapeze artist's official carer, running errands, feeding him, washing him, holding the mirror while he shaved, changing him, putting him to bed. The girls were disappointed but their parents were amazed: Jamie had never cared for anyone in his whole life. It was tea-time. They sat around the butcher's block in the kitchen, enthralled.

Nick nodded. 'Sounds good to me, Jamie.'

'It was shit. But we travelled all over the world and that was really agreeable.'

'Poor guy,' said Sarah, 'to go from high trapeze to wheel-chair.'

'Except that he was seriously evil?'

'Evil,' Nick sighed, resigned already to Jamie's high meta-physical colouration.

'A genius. Like the best and bravest trapeze artist in the whole world, a total perfectionist, always wanting to go that half an inch further? And unfortunately he also happened to be the Antichrist? The accident just made it worse because he couldn't go anywhere at all and it was like when you married Sarah it didn't change you one bit.'

His father raised a weary hand. 'Thank you for that, Jamie.'

'It didn't make you worse but it didn't change anything and I really thought it would? Kind of dilute the dictatorship?'

'Can't win 'em all.'

Sarah said she had to give the bedrooms a clean and trotted up the stairs while inwardly shouting abuse. She lay on the bed while the remaining members gave him a guided tour of the house and grounds.

Jamie carried Beans on his back, Alicia and Tammy squab-bling over his spare hand. 'Yeah, it's fairly phenomenal. I certainly like the fence knocked down like that.'

'Ah, yes,' said Nick, 'we've the inevitable problem with boars.'

'As in wild pigs,' Tammy added, in an eerie imitation of her father.

Jamie shrugged. 'Maybe you're the problem for the boars,' he pointed out. 'Like, you're getting in the way of their wildness?'

Nick conceded that Jamie looked better in a beard, despite its gingeriness. It made him look like a musketeer. His exposed ears were small and looked as if they'd been crushed against something: his mother Helena, probably, as she'd never put him down when he was a baby.

'This is *really* wild,' Jamie commented drily, looking at the pool, its crystal-clear waters like pewter in the ebbing light of dusk.

'Hey, it's great to see you,' said Nick, 'but in fact this isn't a holiday house. I'm on a paid sabbatical. Sarah and I are *working*, yuk. We're going to need quite a bit of help with the kids. So actually it's good timing, you dropping in like this. Baby Sitters Inc.,' he added, with a chuckle. 'Child Minder Corp.'

Miscalculation: Jamie's face did not fall.

'Whatever, yeah. I was thinking about families in South America and the extended families thing and how cool they are? And so that kind of fits in. How long are you in residence for?'

'Erm, nearly five months more.'

Jamie nodded slowly.

'OK, yeah, that's a deal,' he said.

'Sorry?'

'I like the hills here. I can take the kids up into the hills and have adventures.'

'Hooray! Hooray for Jamie!' His seated half-sisters bounced up and down on the sofa.

'The hills?' echoed Nick. His face had definitely fallen; he couldn't help it, the props had slipped away.

'Or swimming in rivers? I saw this wicked river where you picked me up. This one spot I saw was really wide and deep.'

'Only suitable in the summer, Jamie.'

He shrugged. He told them about a car crash in Peru involving a llama, with unpleasant details. On his lap was the dried flower with the golden eyelashes that had been nailed to the front door; he'd picked off the petals one by one onto his lap. The girls told him that Jean-Luc had said it was a golden sun, to protect the house and bring good luck. Jamie claimed the flower had fallen off by itself. All that was left by the end was the rustly centre, not like an eyeball or a sun at all.

He threw the petals in the air for Beans to catch. They scattered on the rug.

'What's the point of that, Jamie?' asked Nick, sounding exasperated at last.

'Your definition of history.'

'Which one?'

'The disproof of superstition,' Jamie sighed, lounging back

in the sofa as if he owned it and would not be rising from it for a long time.

Nick and Tammy left the shot-blasted sign on the tree and stacked the remains of the others neatly at the foot, as a subtle gesture of defiance. Then – unusually for him – he took a photograph, not for purposes of juridical evidence but because it looked like an art installation.

He had a splinter in his thumb, from stacking the signs. He tried to press it out as Tammy watched. He also had several splinters in his mind; in the months to come here they would work themselves out, he was sure of it.

They went back into the house. Beans was bouncing a small empty plastic Evian bottle down the stairs and shouting 'Coco!' This was because the sound that the plastic bottle made was incredibly like that of a bongo-drum. Jamie had spotted this, after an hour of bong-bong-bonging, and it was then they'd understood why Beans said 'Coco' every time she launched the bottle from the top of the stairs. The Congo Bongo Game, Jamie christened it.

He was sitting at the bottom of the stairs, retrieving the bottle and taking it up to her over and over for a relaunch. He'd finally relinquished his one set of outrageously dirty and smelly clothes to the washing machine and was temporarily dressed in his father's scruffiest gear: all-blue denim from Nick's trendy-lecturer days. The collar rode high on his thin neck and the trousers and sleeves were rolled up at the ankles and wrists. Helena's four-foot five had roped back whatever tall genes he'd inherited from his father.

He had been assigned the attic to sleep in, at his own sugges-tion; although it had required a full day of cleaning and sweeping out, laying the dust with sprinkled water and opening the Velux window and rubbing the glass free of the sky's deposits, he seemed very happy with the arrangement. In a remarkably short time, he was scrubbing the boards.

'It's because it's just for him,' Nick had said, when Sarah

marvelled at the change in her stepson. 'He's always pulled his finger out when it's just for him.'

Jamie had found a spare mattress under one of the kid's beds, and within two days had accumulated bits and bobs from here and there: a parachute cloth strung across the middle of the vast room, natural sculptures in found olivewood, interesting stones, old chairs with sagging seats, a broken set of drawers retrieved from the back of the goatshed. Nick had succumbed and bought a cheap paraffin heater in St-Maurice, with the claim that 'it would be useful anyway', lugging the heavy flagons of fuel into and out of the car and straining his tender elbow tendons. Although they didn't say it, he and Sarah were amazed at the attic's transformation: Jamie had turned it into a cosy den by the end of the week. It already smelt of naughty, smoky, sweetish things over the paraffin. All he complained about was the wind whistling in the roof, because it never made a tune.

'A natural melody,' Sarah joked.

'He's good at building nests,' Nick said, when Jamie was out. 'But they're always in other people's houses.'

'We're not other people,' Sarah had pointed out. 'We're family. We're blood. At least, I am by proxy.'

Sarah was at her little desk in the bedroom, writing her journal on the laptop. She had instantly minimised the text when Nick appeared so that all he saw was her screen saver of their girls playing on the beach in northern Portugal last year. Today's entry was about her secret dip in the pool, which she'd managed to interleave while the rest of her family were on a short walk to pick thyme.

The thermometer in the pool had registered sixteen degrees, well below her bearable threshold. Yet she'd done it. It had snatched the breath from her lungs, replacing it with ice, and guillotined her at the neck with its honed blade, but she'd done it. After a few moments her glaciated body, of which she had lost the sensation, had started to glow, and she'd dipped her head under. It was glorious.

She would try to do it every morning, in secret in case the kids followed suit. Before anyone else was up. Slip out of bed as she was always doing for one of the girls. Her private corner of the day. Ten minutes max. Ten lengths.

It steeled her for Jamie, somehow. If she could ritually immerse herself thus, galvanising her body and thus her spirits, she could even cope with Jamie for as long as he was around.

Nick left and her text leapt back. She finished her piece and lay on the bed diagonally for a read. One consolation of Jamie's presence was that he could occupy the girls, keep an eye on them if they were near the pool. She was reading an absorbing book on Grotius, Hobbes and Locke by an old and brilliant friend, Jennifer Wiles, who couldn't have children. She was allowing Jennifer's elegant chapter on the church debate between political and pastoral power to sponge her worries up when there was a sudden howl from downstairs, an unearthly howl of agony and despair that had her out of the door well before the terrible sound was interrupted by the need for its generator to take breath.

Alicia had stamped on the plastic bottle, which, like a broken violin, now refused to reproduce the sound of Coco's bongos, Congolese or otherwise. Jamie rescued the situation by taking Beans and going outside and whirling her around by the arms, higher and higher, the leather boots turning and turning on the gravel until they'd worn a hole in the earth beneath.

Sarah recalled something she'd read about unsocketing the arms of a child at the shoulders, doing that. Beans squealed with delight, virtually horizontal, the centrifugal force pulling her little arms dead straight; a small shoe flew off, and Sarah smiled anxiously from the door.

'Supposing he lets go?' murmured Tammy.

Jamie found something 'negative' about the house, something that wanted to be freed, something trapped and in pain.

'Negative,' reiterated Nick, flatly.

'In pain,' reiterated Sarah, just as flatly.

'Really kind of *needy*, yeah?'

'Maybe you shouldn't have removed the solar symbol,' said Nick. 'Protector against the dark forces.'

'Can't have it both ways, Mr Rationalist,' Jamie said, shaking his head.

'Maybe I was joking.'

'Hey, a real cracker.'

'No jokes in a dictatorship,' said Sarah, with an ironic lift of her eyebrows.

'That's what they say, but it's erroneous,' Nick declared. 'Take Stalin. He used jokes to trap people in queues. Someone would crack an anti-Stalin –'

'Hey, I like *this*,' said Jamie, interrupting as usual.

He lifted the fetish mask off its hook and placed it over his own face. His voice sounded deep and hollow behind and it was creepy; it was nothing like him, even though the mask was small and Jamie's ears stuck out behind. The fact that he was dressed head-to-foot in Nick's blue denim, familiar from ten or more years back, made it even stranger. The mask, as Jamie jigged up and down, tried to keep its dignity. The girls whooped and fled temporarily into the kitchen.

'Thanks, Jamie,' said their mother, raising her eyes to the ceiling.

The mask looked very fed-up, back on its hook. To make up for his tactlessness, Jamie promised to take the kids white-water rafting.

'That's a promise, is it?' said Nick, cheerily.

'You know me.'

'Your dad's togs suit you, Jamie,' said Sarah, in a half-involuntary flash of cruelty.

Jamie studied the rolled-back, frayed sleeves of the denim jacket that had once been Nick's tenacious lecturing gear. 'I'm not *really* struggling,' he said, 'to rip 'em off me.'

Waiting every morning in the woods, on the edge, for the last four days, where a clear view of the washing-line at the side of the house opens between the bushes, he has worn a little circle of presence in the dead leaves.

He's been arriving early because of what he has noted when working here: the Englishwoman hangs out washing in the mornings. Not every morning, of course, but it seems there is always new washing on the line whenever he comes: the miniature clothes of the girls, especially, and now, on the fourth day, some hippy clothes.

He is kitted out in his old frayed hunting gear, a camouflage of green and brown, military-style, a little tight around his waist because he hasn't worn it for years. He has waited three hours or more each time, settled among the thick arbutus bushes with their shiny leaves. He's always loved their little round red fruits, hanging like goolies in the white flowers. The local nickname, among his mates at least: goolie bushes. The fruits are sweet and rough in the mouth and he's gorged himself. They take two years to ripen. He and his father would help pick them for distilling when he was a kid, and the old folk would say, 'one is enough'. But Jean-Luc was different.

On the first day he stripped this side of the bush, waiting. The fruit went down as easily as when he was a little boy. Back then, Louis Loubert would hold two against his groin, then squeeze them to pulp and squeal and open his mouth wide in agony: a member of the Maquis in the hands of the SS. Louis was OK, back then. But Jean-Luc was always afraid because the others would say they were going to do it to him and for real, one day, just as an experiment. A medical experiment. So when the fruits ripened he always used to be a bit scared, in case it reminded them, and tried to eat them all up before the others remembered.

On the second day, a gusty day without sun which had him shivering a little, his patience was rewarded: but she looked tiny in the viewfinder, and her face kept being covered by the flapping sheets she was pegging out. He dared not approach nearer. And then he had a brainwave, based on experience: he's responsible,

228

these days, for much of the washing at home. She would have to collect them. He sniffed the air and judged its humidity. The sky was cloudy, the sun unlikely to break through and the gusts now dying down. Five, six hours?

He would come back in the late afternoon, after working on what was overdue at the Dutch people's place. There was an arbutus bush not five metres from the washing-line, more to the left and on its own: dangerous, on the very edge, but possible. It was overhung by holm oak branches and still in the shadows. He could darken his face with earth. If she spotted him, he would say he was clearing brush.

This is why, when he does return in the late afternoon, he brings the big curved knife with the twine-bound handle. It belonged to his grandfather: the old handle is smooth and polished, the blade-edge nicked with use but as sharp as a razor. His face is soiled, like a soldier's. He wouldn't have minded being a soldier, even if his year of military service was not all fun and games. Cleaning out toilets. Squatting in wet trenches in freezing winds.

She doesn't appear. The air is cool and damp because there are storms on the coast and the wind is blowing up into the mountains. The girls come out on their own, run about a bit, look at the pool, run into and out of the barn. Then he notices a suspicious-looking character, suddenly, at the side of the house. A hippy. There are lots of them in Valdaron, banging on drums and smoking cannabis and having sex everywhere, just like the old times. They must be the second generation and Jean-Luc hates them. This is a young type, in his twenties, dressed in one of those long Arab coats with a hood. A new wave to replace the ones with long grey hair and creased faces. Maybe he's a hippy Arab.

He thinks, as he watches the young no-gooder loitering at the side of the house, of Madame Sanissac up at Les Pins, who at the age of eighty-five was stabbed to death during her siesta. A passing hippy did it; in fact, he lived in the next hamlet, the one with all the ruins. He tried to burn her body and the smoke got people running, but he'd gone by then. The firemen took ages to come, it was so remote, and meanwhile the neighbours (all three of them) had a job keeping her blazing body in the bedroom under control, because there was no running water and the well was low and the bucket took ages to creak down and up. The room was black, afterwards; even the beams were scorched so badly they had to be pulled out, in the end. Jean-Luc saw it and wanted to be a fireman. And now Madame Sanissac's house is the Swiss place, done up to the nines with three bathrooms and a jacuzzi and not even haunted. It takes Jean-Luc half an hour to drive up there, but it's an easy job, keeping the lawn down on the sit-up mower.

He grips the brush-knife's handle as the no-gooder joins the girls in the yard. They appear to know him.

Jean-Luc crouches lower as they pass, their voices like twittering bats, except for their hippy friend. The kids might still be getting kidnapped, though. The hippy might have fooled them, given them sweets. You hear a lot about it on the news, these days. Jean-Luc is on full alert, as if the horns are blowing and the dogs are going mad, out on full stretch. They all go into the house.

He waits until it's almost dark, then makes his way back through the trees to where he's hidden his mobilette. All this military-style operation excites him; he's not too dejected. Staking out in his military togs. Better than watching telly with Maman moaning and shrieking upstairs.

He returns the next morning, at dawn, sure of seeing her now. His heart leaps when he sees the phantom shapes of the sheets through the dark trees. And then it begins to rain. Although the rising sun was a red ball and there were rays at the bottom of it, he didn't think the rain would blow all the way up here, but it does. She might run out and try to rescue the sheets, but she doesn't. The rain gusts against his face, pattering on the living leaves and the dead leaves. He shivers, beginning to feel the wet reach his skin. He doesn't want to be ill. He gives up.

It rains on and off all day. He watches the weather on the telly: little golden suns cover the south, the rain-clouds now over the Alps. His heart lifts. During the night he wets his hand and sticks it out between the shutters: a brisk easterly wind. A drying wind. He hears it skittering along the street like small kids.

He's waiting again behind the leading arbutus bush. From one side of it he can see a wall of white cotton and the door of the house: from the other, he has a view of the swimming pool, the trampled fence around the seed-bed, the half-uprooted cherry tree and the huge black square in the barn wall where the old doors creaked before someone nicked them: Marcel Lagrange, probably.

The side and rear of the house are tall and full of small windows like prison windows, so he has to be careful of his movements, even behind the goolie bush on the wood's edge. The brush-knife is tucked away safely under the bush's lower branches, in case he steps on it. The hippy's trousers and Arab coat are hung next to the sheets. Perhaps they've bumped him off.

Half an hour passes, the sun rising up just clear of the trees. The high clouds are the fish-scale type that mean good weather, and the birds are going mad as if he isn't there. It makes him want to go hunting again, the way he can lose himself, become like a beady-eyed animal or even a plant, watching nothing but the new light growing on the leaves, so slowly he can't see it move. Every sound as if it's not accidental. The ants on their business. The rustlings. The freshness. The little red squirrel not even realising he's there, snuffling away to itself. He hasn't done this for years. It's when he's at his happiest, he realises. His whole problem was being born human. The breeze bringing smells, including a smell of burnt toast.

Something swoops out of the side of the barn and he realises what it is: the swallow. The swallow's arrived. It's come back to the same nest ever since he was a boy, exploring the ruins

231

after the hippies had been chased out. It's a touch early, this year. It must be twenty-five years old, at least.

Once he watched a hedgehog for hours; he kept so still it sniffed his foot, making little grunts and snorts like an old man. He didn't find it again.

He shifts to release the cramp in his haunches. No one has yet come into the yard. The house stays silent. Usually, the little girls play in the barn or just in front for a while in the morning and the Englishwoman comes in and out to check, but it's still too early. It is just like waiting for a rabbit or a boar. He raises the throwaway camera to his face and looks through the viewfinder.

He has never taken a photograph in his life, except once when some hikers asked him to, with their own camera. It's like a gun: you shoot with it. Without killing anything. This is why he's wearing his fingerless hunting gloves.

He's surprised this time when the sheets swell in the little eye, look bigger, although not as big as they would in the binoculars hanging round his neck. His father found them in the woods after the war, a German pair still in their leather case, and only used them when out hunting. Apart from a rainbow effect in one eyepiece that surrounds bright objects like coloured fur, they're in good condition.

He's holding the camera the wrong way, that's why everything's swollen up. The lens is pointing towards him. The view-finder magnifies the view, in that position. He looks again the same wrong way round and amazingly, as if he's attracted her, the Englishwoman appears in the little rectangle. She has on a bright yellow sweater that makes her look about nineteen. His heart beats just as it did in the hunt. The sheets hide her progress. He waits for her legs to appear below them. Nothing. She disappears behind the sheets and he waits for her legs to show up, her feet. Nothing.

He takes little crouched steps to the other edge of the bush, where he can see the yard in full.

She's squatting at the edge of the pool, dipping her hand in

232

from the look of it. It's too far to take a picture. The sheets clap in a sudden gust and she lifts her head towards him. He stays very still. He's in the shadows, in camouflage.

He waits for her to come back and take down the washing. She stands by the side of the pool hut and takes her glasses off and puts them down next to a lump of coloured cloth. She puts her arms over her ears as if she can't bear some noise or other. No, she's taking off her yellow sweater – it comes off over her head, showing her tummy. And then she pulls off the top, too, which is a dark red tee shirt. And then she unbuttons her jeans, from the look of it, and steps out of them. Maybe she's a nympho and an exhibitionist and knows he's here: he saw something on the telly recently about people with strange compulsions.

She scratches her back with both hands and leans forward and her bra comes off, dropped on the little heap of clothes by the coloured cloth that he now recognises as a towel. He turns his head away for a moment, feeling guilty and full of sin, although he hasn't been to church since he was eighteen.

She's bending down and lifting each knee in turn: her underpants join her bra. She takes her pulse: no, she's taking off her watch. He has stopped breathing. He starts again. Her body is paler than expected: from this distance it might be covered in a pale body suit as tight as a toreador's, she might not be nude at all – except for the two brown eyes on her chest and the spot of black fur below her tummy, which he knows smells gamy because, when he was a kid, the others picked up an empty sardine tin they said smelt exactly like Francine Sellier's pussy.

She hugs herself in the cool air, turning her back on him to show two white uncooked chestnuts of buttock that, even from this distance, surprise him, because they look bigger than when they were inside her jeans.

He's sweating, giving off a stink from under his old gear, which itself stinks of boar's fur and smoke. His frog wants to croak under his trousers but he ignores it. Carefully, silently, as he used to do when out hunting, he backs off into the trees and makes his way round, losing sight of her for a few painful moments, to where the wood turns into bracken behind the tumbled wall.

He uses the standing part of the wall to creep even closer, as far behind cover as he can go, to the wild growth near the back of the hut where the builders dumped their sand. It is mostly spurge here, the heavy-headed type that starts off early and before you know it, before you've got used to spring, it's flowering at the height of your belly. He sees his father towering over a clump of spurge and warning him never to break it, never to cut it or he'd blister and burn on its bitter milk. He was about four or five. He misses his father. He doesn't like crouching in the spurge, he's fearful of spurge, but it's good cover, with its heavy toilet-brush heads, its fat stems full of their deadly juice.

A twig cracks underfoot as he shifts his big boots. He keeps very still, crouched, becoming vegetation, a shadow. Tiny black ants crawl over his boot, following each other up one of the laces and then onto his leg. It's a good thing his trousers are tucked into his thick socks, or they'd crawl inside. He's forgotten his brush-knife over behind the washing line.

She's squatting by the pool halfway up along the side, still holding herself with her arms. She's definitely naked as Eve. He's so close he can see a red mark on her back where the bra's strap must have pressed; a mole above the cleft of her back parts. He hopes the water's pH levels are not too high or too low.

He turns the camera round to take a picture and she shrinks; what he wants is her face, and he only has the side of her face, the breeze moving strands of black hair in front of it. He is only about five metres from her, but she seems very small in the viewfinder. He thought the camera would have enlarged her, her body being the most important object in the picture. But she stays small.

It isn't like pictures in a magazine, when the person being photographed is always large and clear. He doesn't press the trigger.

This is the greatest gift he has ever been given in his life. He is like God, seeing what normal people never see. He lifts the binoculars to his eyes and her pale, crouched body slides into view and obliterates everything else; he closes one eye to stop the rainbow blur covering her skin. The German binoculars are so good he can see a vaccination mark on her upper shoulder, a glint of moisture in her eye. That's sometimes all you can see of an animal, that glint. She'll get a cold just staying there, he thinks.

And then she stands up, as if hearing his thoughts. She turns towards him and walks along the edge of the pool in his direction, but looking to the side, at the water. The kitten clinging on upside-down between her legs is very black and has a thick coat. He lowers the binoculars and lifts the camera just clear of the spurge heads and sees her swinging into it and presses the trigger. The camera's little click scares him, sounding very loud. But she doesn't have the ears of an animal. Nor the nose. The wind, anyway, is very light at the moment and blowing in his direction. He thinks there might have been a flash when he took the picture, like the flash of sun on a gun-barrel that warns the quarry, but she hasn't reacted.

Her breasts are a lot smaller than in the shiny magazines, where they always look as if they've been blown up with a pump until they're almost exploding; they jiggle up and down as she walks towards his end and then turns her back on him. She crouches down yet again, so that all he can see is the white scuts of her buttocks and the back of her feet pressed against them, a circle of dirt on their heels. He takes another picture, despite there being no face. His hands are shaking so much that, if the camera were a gun, the shot would have missed.

He raises himself slightly to ease the big, swollen frog in his trousers but his foot has gone to sleep and he topples over, scratching his cheek on a dead spurge stem, hard as bamboo.

She doesn't notice because of the noise she's making herself, slipping into the pool bit by bit, sighing and gasping with the shock; the high sounds float into his ear like a shared secret, like she's sharing her secret with him, his ear warming against her lips. He watches her slip into the water, head sticking up above the edge of the pool with a look of pain, both hands raised above the surface until she disappears with a cut-off yelp.

Jean-Luc is happy. He'll have to wait a few days for the film to be processed – he sent off the camera to the enclosed address – but he's in no doubt of the triumph of his efforts.

The Englishwoman is like a ghost haunting him in a nice way, and he takes to drawing her in his notepad (the notepad he keeps for his jobs), over and over in blue biro. He draws her special jiggling breasts, the furry kitten clinging on between her legs, her expanding white buttocks released from their jeans. He draws her face crowned with the glittering crown of a beauty queen. He draws arrows to show his love for her, the gush of his ardour sometimes drowning her in seas of biro-squiggles that break the cheap paper of the notepad. *Marie*, he writes, *Marie of the Holy Pool*. He draws big fat frogs, croaking in their pools.

Measurements for the Dutch people's shelves and the Parisians' watering system and the Germans' concrete steps into their bathing hut; quantities of compost and grass-seed and liquid feed; algicide and clarifier and shock chlorine; ship-varnish for the Belgian couple's outside table and lubricating oil for the Danish family's barbecue set: the history, over several years, of Jean-Luc's odd-jobbing, all in cash (sometimes not even paid for when some clients' family crisis takes over), vanishes under these drawings when, because the notepad is full, he runs out of blank pages.

By drawing her, he finds she remains in his head: his queen, his love. Like measurements and quantities and what a client demands in bad French or no French at all.

She smiles at him secretly the whole time. She knew.

He ties the sieve to the baby pram. Bibi and the fish-bone spider are inside the sieve. They're on the cobweb. One caught, the other in charge.

He decorates the wheels – hiding them, really – with feathers he's picked up over the years, kept in the box under his bed. He uses the strong glue he bought for mending his boots, so the feathers lie against tiny brown pillows stuck to the rims and spokes of the wheels. Although they no longer move after he's fixed them with a wire, the wheels still have to be hidden. This is not a pram, he thinks. This is a monument, like the monument to the war dead in front of the church: on which the name of Oncle Fernand has always winked at him, right from when he was a little boy. But never spoken to him like the plaque on the track to Les Fosses, because the monument is not where Oncle Fernand died.

The notepad is full, so all he can do is turn the pages. He can't draw her on anything else. This is the one and only Bible. He has an urge to draw her on the walls of his room, but the wallpaper is too old and there are hardly any blank parts, so he starts to peel off one strip so that he might draw on the bared plaster, only to find it isn't bare but painted a sky-blue colour familiar to him from the older people's houses. He likes this colour. Why did his father hide it?

He begins to strip more of the wallpaper, talking to his love the whole time. She lies on the bed admiring his notepad, stark naked but for her crown.

He ignores the shrieked or moaning demands of his mother through the locked door. It is so pleasurable, peeling the wallpaper slowly so that it won't tear. Scabs and even large lumps of plaster sometimes come with it; he wishes for more rooms like this. For soon it will be over, as the making of the monument will be over. And it strikes him then, taking a pause to scrunch over the fallen plaster and shout to his mother that he is fast asleep, how like a bird the monument looks, squatting there on the table in its pride of feathers, with its long bare tail ending in a pink hand-grip that he will have to hide too, somehow, in case anyone thinks it is the handle of a toy pram.

ELEVEN

The two of them went on a little excursion that began at the *source* of the local river, leaving the girls with Jamie. He'd got the message about the pool, he claimed, nodding sagely. About never leaving the two younger girls alone outside, especially at the back, because of the pool. He'd loosened his Iron Age top-knot and it now poured like a frizzed-up horse's tail out of a red hairband, more prehistoric than protohistoric, Nick thought.

'Well, Romans invented scissors,' he joked.

They'd told Jamie about the danger so many times that he made his sisters laugh by turning it into an advert once the parents were gone. He wrote something out and then put on a baseball cap he'd found in a cupboard and read aloud what he'd written in a funny American voice, poking his elbows out and prancing from foot to foot like a show-horse:

'Hey, folks, introducing probably the Most Dangerous Swimming Pool in the World, with enhanced drowning levels and *no* operating alarm! With this state-of-the-art model you can lose your life in *two minutes flat*! No one will hear you, thanks to its *unique* location just far enough from the house to make it a true and *deadly* risk! Yes, folks, there's one name and one name only when it comes to choosing *your* family pool: *Death Trap Inc.*!'

Tammy cheered and Alicia squealed, Beans going over the top and slamming her fist onto her Petit Suisse pot, which seemed to explode in ectoplasmic globs.

'Death rapping!' yelled the girls. 'Death rapping!' Tammy pretended to drown in bubbling paroxysms and lay on the tiled floor, asking for the kiss of life, which Alicia granted by dripping cold cocoa onto her face. Tammy had to welt her with an elastic hairband, which was quite effective. Jamie said 'Whoa,' as ineffectively.

Their parents filmed their romantic excursion on the camcorder. The spring was a muddy whelm in a cave in the side of a rocky overhang, reached through a sloping field of silvered grass the wind kept switching from right to left, left to right. They couldn't work out exactly where the water came from in the rock behind. It just seemed to seep up, almost a pool, then to trickle through the grass and end up tumbling out of an ancient stone conduit at the bottom of the slope.

There were echoing drips in the little cave. Nick blocked the trickle with stones. '*Manon des Sources!*' he called out. He pulled a gruesome face for the camera, which made the girls laugh during the laptop screening that evening.

'It's that peasant, Ungulino or whatever he's called,' came their mother's voice as the image wobbled. 'Who blocks it first. Isn't it? With his dad.'

'They'll be looking at the parched fields down below, shaking their fists at the sky,' Nick declared, lifting a large stone into place. 'The coolants in the nuclear power station will be at critical levels.'

Despite the leaks in his dam, the muddy whelm became a pool quite swiftly. It was a dryad's pool, clear and lovely, nestled in the little cave with its strange, greenish light. It lapped at surprised ants on the dry edges: Sarah captured these on the zoom, but for too long and was photographed doing so by Nick. Then the water reached the top of the stone dam and trickled over. Nick pointed to this, as serious about it as a small boy. The pressure of the water had loosened the stones and the pool was diminishing. Where did the water come from? All they could see were secretive little whirls and turbulences in the sinking pool.

Sarah lay back on the field's tough, springy grass. It was cool but sunny and she didn't care about the insects, she'd let them explore. She opened her eyes and flicked a tiny winged thing off her cheek; it stuck to her finger, a broken biplane crashed into the giant whorls of her finger. For which she was sorry. She looked up and rejoiced in the puffy white clouds high up like a dream of elsewhere, scarcely moving, as the camera panned away and onto a revolving buzzard none of the others would be able to see on screen.

And the ants were too small to be interesting. The girls could hear their mother breathing behind.

'Don't I look unbelievably old?' said Nick, sitting on a cushion on the floor like a teenager.

Jamie was a fun big brother, quite a good child minder. Nick and Sarah returned from their walk to the *source* to find the four of them playing sleeping lions in front of the barn: an idyllic portrait, down to the sun playing in Jamie's wispy chestnut beard as he pretended to snore, his small eyes open just a slit. Sarah said nothing about the use of one of the Sandlers' magnificent Middle-Eastern blankets, which had picked up half the yard's natural detritus. Instead, she filmed him. The tiny break had done her good. Seeing her children again, intact: a decision someone had made in a shady heaven.

She also filmed the boat of dead flowers, circling in the water. Jamie had gone off for a pee and discovered it. Tammy had said nothing, feigning ignorance. They'd placed it in the water because a beetle had drowned. The ribbon saying REGRETS was still on it, pinned to the stems and just legible.

Sarah said how strange, to find a funeral bouquet in the trees. Dragged off the plaque by an animal, maybe.

'It makes me think of military burials at sea,' she remarked.

The flowers were completely wilted, like overboiled veg. Nick fished it out with a stick and carried it into the trees, relieved that it hadn't traumatised Sarah, in the end.

'All gone,' he said, on his return.

'We hope,' said Jamie.

He'd smoke his dope up in the woods, which meant he was out a lot. He only appeared, in any case, at midday: he tended to stay up into the early hours and emerge mid-afternoon with tiny, bloodshot eyes. He never had a meal with the others. He used the very low and cobwebbed back door which opened directly onto the yard and was reached through a kind of scullery, thus avoiding the kitchen entirely. Jamie's Door, they called it. No one else used it because no one else liked spiders, especially not the long-legged, hairy type that lived in the Mas des Fosses, so big you could see their beak-like mandibles muttering. Jamie could open the door without breaking their webs, which lay across the hinges and half hid the panels in dusty, Victorian swags.

He'd walk occasionally to Aubain (an hour on foot) and from there hitch to Valdaron. He'd met the Chambords, from the sound of it: Hugo, Hölderlin and concrete engineering. They sent their best wishes, he told Nick, and hoped he and his family would come to dinner one day. Nick's heart sank: what lies would Jamie have told the Chambords? Was his French even good enough? In Valdaron he had a favourite café in which (Nick and Sarah surmised) he was dealing dope. They assumed he'd brought back dope from South America in tight little high-grade wads of darkness to pay his way. This was all they could gather, and much of that was guesswork.

He ate quite a lot, compared to the others. He liked bread. The bread was cut in hunks (rather than slices) straight onto the table – adding to its cleaver-scars – then devoured with butter but without a plate, casually, anywhere in the house. You could trace Jamie's progress via the crumbs, but only the ants – miniscule, as if assembled through a microscope – appreciated it. Sarah didn't want confrontation, since any victory on her part would lead to something worse than Jamie the Annoyance: namely, Jamie the Avenger.

He helped a bit. 'Now you're here,' his stepmother said. He even hung out the washing one day, with Tammy's help. The trousers were the right way up, which was the wrong way up, legs expecting feet. Tammy showed him what she called the 'Irish strawberry' bushes next to the line, which now had creamy flowers, but the ripe fruit on the biggest and best had been completely stripped – by the birds, obviously.

'They're kind of rough and gooey at the same time,' she said, handing him one. 'They made flutes out of them in Ancient Greece. They look like mini hedgehogs, don't they?'

'Must have been messy, blowing them.'

'Not out of the fruit, stupid!' cried Tammy, creasing up.

Jamie ate one. 'Hey, I love eating foetal-sized hedgehogs. Now I'm going to die very slowly and in incredible agony, right?'

Nick suggested appointing him as pool manager, but Sarah said no: the idea of a stoned Jamie leaning over the troubled waters with a bottle of acid or whatever was not reassuring.

Unknown to the others, she was skinny-dipping every two or three days, just after dawn. The last time had been under a grey sky, and the pool was a grey slab. Deliberately lowering her body into a liquid grey slab was unpleasant, and she couldn't quite reach the glow phase before she emerged, as cold as a slug, the filters clucking their disapproval. Afterwards, though, she'd felt good – tingling with health as she towelled herself vigorously. It was a secret corner of her life, like lost ground rediscovered.

'The thing is,' said Nick, with his mouth full, 'we've got bags of time in front of us.'

'He might stay right to the end.'

'He can't.'

'I'm not clearing up after him. He never does his teeth. He never washes his hair.'

Nick shrugged. 'An anarchist. Or just absent-minded, like me.'

'Whatever else he is,' said Sarah, the prunes in her lamb stew swimming like blind eyes, 'he is not absent-minded. He's calculating. He's a schemer. He's like Peter Osterhauser.'

Nick groaned. 'Peter Osterhauser?'

'That's all just a mask, all that hesitating of Peter's, those ums and ers.'

'Ums only. He never ers. As it were.'

Sarah laughed and leaned across the little table and gave him a kiss on his high forehead; the smooth pale sweep seemed to dwarf his features, gathered between it and his jaw as if conferring.

The Bobo Stenson Trio were edging Swedishly through calm connecting lakes of jazz and making him feel forgiving and tolerant. 'Graffiti,' he said, miming it in the air with his knife, 'on the walls of Fellows' Court. Pffff! *Peter Osterhauser: he may, um, umm, but he never errs.*'

'Why does Jamie want to be here, anyway? He can't stand us,' he admitted, later, after they'd finished the bottle between them. He fiddled with his plum stones, rearranging them on the bread-scoured plate.

'Helena? Her suggestion?'

'*Probablement.* Knowing we were having a good time.'

'Mind you, he gets a good deal,' Sarah pointed out.

'A good deal of what?'

'I mean a good deal, period. Fed, watered, sheltered, shown affection. He does love his sisters.'

'Do you think the way he talks is the way he thinks, or is it a mask?'

Sarah didn't reply, not really concentrating. She found Nick's type of jazz tiring after a while, and CDs went on too long.

'Don't you think CDs go on too long?'

'He could've got into Oxbridge, you know,' said Nick, ignoring or not having heard her. 'If he'd pulled his finger out. Of course he could've done,' he added, draining the very last of the bottle. 'Instead, he didn't even manage more than a couple of terms at Chester.'

'That wasn't Chester's fault,' Sarah pointed out. 'Your brightest graduate student last year had got his first from Chester, if you remember. The one who did his thesis on the Brazzaville Conference and never stopped talking.'

Nick nodded. 'The one from Coventry who said he's going to be a city trader because money equals freedom.'

'Yup, 'fraid so.'

'At sixteen Jamie wanted to be a policeman,' said Nick.

'Because that was the one sure-fire way to annoy both you and Helena.'

Nick shrugged. 'We all need the police,' he said.

'Did you tell him that?'

'Yes.'

'Oh dear.'

'You OK, Sarah?'

'I'm OK. Thanks, Jamie.'

'Cool, yeah, I can kind of *imagine* what that's like?'

Sarah smiled sympathetically, spreading apricot jam on a slice of baguette for Beans. Nick was at work upstairs.

'I can just about imagine it,' Jamie went on, ''cos I have this memory of it from somewhere around eight years old? Eight and a quarter? Nine?'

'I'm *practically* nine,' said Alicia, wandering off into the sitting room with her plate of biscuits at a dangerous angle.

'Silly Bin-Bag,' chortled Tammy. 'Bin-Bag Ali. That's me who's nearly nine.'

'Don't spread crumbs,' Sarah called after her, her eyes flicking over the king of crumb-spreaders. Alicia came back into the kitchen and said, 'I'm nine in –' Here she stopped, counting on her fingers. Tammy laughed.

'Tammy, you're not nine for another seven months,' Sarah said, trying to seek equability between them, placing weights on the scales like a goldsmith.

Jamie's eyes narrowed, suddenly, as if peering through a bunker's slit.

'It's good you've made your life so comfortable,' he said, perched on the stool with his elbows on the table. 'With my old man.'

'Yup, there's good and bad.'

'There's bad then, is there?'

'I want to do some cookery,' Alicia announced, tugging on her mother's sleeve. 'Mummy.'

'That's an idea. We can make that choccie cake.'

'*Choccie* cake,' echoed Jamie, his head moving up and down like a toy sheep Tammy had. The two words buckled under the derision unfairly loaded onto them.

'Yum, Damie,' said Alicia, waggling her bottom as if she were desperate to go to the loo. '*I'm* doing it all, not Tammy one bit.'

Sarah announced, in a gay and carefree voice, that they were fatally short of flour.

The day the photographs come in a plastic envelope, his mother is down in the kitchen, watching his every move with eagle eyes.

'What's that, Jean-Luc?'

It has dropped through the letter box and sits in the wire basket hanging off the door. Jean-Luc can hardly believe it. It is like a miracle. It has only taken three days. He stands up slowly and calmly and retrieves the envelope, although his hands shake.

'Fishing stuff,' he says.

She snorts. Her eyes are like a young girl's, in terms of sight. She's noticed the pale footprints on her carpet and the stairs from the plaster-dust in his bedroom. She notices everything. 'That's photos,' she chuckles, as if she can see right through the envelope. 'Photos of your girl, my sweet?'

Jean-Luc wants to hit her. 'That's right,' he murmurs, too feebly. He puts the envelope into his jacket pocket and sits down and carries on with his hot chocolate, lifting the bowl with both hands and dipping his head with a stretching movement of the neck as he's done in the same way at the same table every morning since he was three, when he was allowed his first bowl, red and made of tin. He sucks it up and she tells him, as she's told him for three decades, that he'd win the Olympics for noisy drinking. And as usual he ignores her.

He's loaded the van with the kit for the electric fence and the bright-yellow outdoor paint for the Belgian couple's garden furniture, which he is overdue on because he got the wrong shade and they fussed. He'll look at the photos somewhere on the way to Les Fosses. The idea that he might meet the Englishwoman, with the photos of her nude in his tunic pocket, terrifies and excites him at the same time. His mother watches him, chortling to herself. She used to make everyone laugh, they say, with her Limousin humour.

'I wish it *was* photos of your girl,' says Marie-Thérèse. 'Instead, I've bred a Félix la Ponte.'

Jean-Luc is used to her calling him this. Félix la Ponte was an artiste in a travelling revue way back, before he was born, who dressed up as a woman. The revue went from town to town, and she'd watched it as a kid when she was still living in Dijon. Even though no one except his mother even remembers Félix la Ponte, it hurts him, it makes his chest pop like a roasted chestnut, but the one power he has over her is to ignore her insults. Everything that comes out of her mouth is not much different from what comes out the other end. It stinks, anyway. It's like her rolling Dijon *r*s that she's never got rid of, strange as Spanish.

He takes a sip of his chocolate and pretends to be watching the telly with great interest. It is a programme on parrots. No, on where to go for your holidays. Martinique, they suggest. Shots of lovely black and browned girls in bikinis, gleaming with oil. Palm trees and surf. Then another parrot.

'Your dad always said you were an odd one,' she continues, pulling out another cigarette against Dr Demarne's orders. 'No one but yourself to blame, I'd tell him. He can't even hold a gun straight, he'd say. Unless it's pointing at his foot,' she adds, in his father's rasping voice, chuckling again then bursting into one of her coughs that seems to seize her and shake her like a giant and go on and on.

Jean-Luc gets up and leaves the house, even though she is having one of her coughing fits. Let her die, he thinks. He's walked out like that before now, but she's always been right as rain on his return. Now, as he closes the door behind him, stepping into the street, he hears her trying to say something, begging him not to leave her like that. Of course his dad never said what she claims he said! Her tongue is not like a viper's, it is worse than a viper's. Vipers don't talk, for a start-off. They only sting.

He pats his packet of photos and starts the van. It coughs like his mother and dies. He tries again. Lucille's watching from two doors up, as usual, bent forwards on her front step. It fires, leaving its dark smoky trail all the way up the narrow main street of Aubain as he heads for Les Fosses, the posts for the electric fencing jiggling behind him. He hasn't been back all week, and he is nervous. He glances in the driving mirror and sees he still has a smear of chocolate on his upper lip, like a small boy. A kid he's never seen before circles on his bike in the road as if he owns the place.

He stops on the way, pulling in off the Mas's track where there's a passing space overgrown with low brambles. They rustle under the van and catch in the trailer-hook that he keeps meaning to unbolt because he hardly uses it. He high-steps into the acacia woods to where the slope dips sharply into a hollow darkened by a cover of holm oak. He opens the packet in a single blot of sunlight. His fingers are huge and clumsy and dirty-nailed. A smell of laboratories with technicians in heavy glasses replaces the scents of vegetation. Plastics and chemicals and city life. The faraway dream of Paris.

The first photograph is of her walking nude by the pool, but she's blurred into a ghost and everything is sloped, including the house in shadow behind. His heart sinks. The second photo shows her from the back, crouched to the water. Although he was standing behind the hut and felt very close, there's much more background than there is of her and her rear end is not much bigger than a bread crumb, you can almost blow it off. The right side of the photo is blurred by spurge leaves sticking out from their stem, huge compared to her rear end. He should have crawled even closer, snaked up closer as they used to snake up to the German sentries before garrotting them.

Then there are the two he took of her standing up, ready to go in. One is all blurred again because his hand shook so much. The other is better, her chest is outlined against the house – two swollen egg-shapes that make him think of the flowers of the *pétaro* around the old bucket on their little scrap at the back.

He squints closer. The sunlight and shadow muddles her arms and stomach and the clinging black cat is hidden by her thigh. Her face doesn't look the same, what he can see of it – she didn't know she was being photographed and her mouth is pinched in. Below her hair she is as pale as a shaved branch. Her hands are too big. Three useless ones of her swimming, her head a dark blurred spot in the water and then a final one of her that is almost completely blacked out by his finger.

He is disappointed, but not surprised, that the ones left are those he used up on the little girls. He was hoping he'd taken more of her, but knew inside him that he hadn't. When she'd come out of the water she'd trotted to her clothes with little happy gasps and he was scared of being seen, he'd kept still as a post. Really, there is only one of her that is any good. He feels ashamed of his efforts, looking at them again.

Tick tick tick. A robin hopping about in the hollow, ticking away. He studies the photo of the three sisters posing with serious faces in front of the barn and holds it up to show the robin, talking to it, and it jumps about excitedly.

He thinks he hears voices as he looks at the ones of the kids. Little girl voices as they run about, all blurred, or pose with serious faces, or put their fingers into the corners of their mouths and stick their tongues out like frogs. The one they took of him, tilted as though he's on a deck in a storm. He looks weaker than he'd expected, and his hunting gear seems as though it's not on the right person. His face is crooked, completely wrong. Nothing like what he sees in the mirror. He should've smiled.

Then silence, apart from the gusts filling the leaves. The patch of sun wobbles like water. The robin has gone further off in a burst of its wings. The holm oaks are twisted with age and their trunks are covered in pale green splashes of lichen. Oncle Fernand would have seen the same ones, probably. Trees live longer than humans, when left alone. He used to think he could talk to them and they were listening, but now he reckons they don't care.

The best photo of her begins to grow the more he looks: he's a look-out man on a hunt who after an hour or two starts to see more and more in the muddle of vegetation, slopes, far blue hills. The shape of her breasts is the shape of bells.

There's someone standing at the back.

Where the zinc gutter meets the drain, there's someone standing. He feels his heart lurch like a sprung rabbit.

It could be a set of blue overalls hung on a peg. It's in the shadows, because the sun never touches the back of the house.

He changes the angle of the photo in the sunlight and squints at it until everything fogs. There's a paler bit on top of the overalls, exactly where the face should be.

The gutter sticks out like one of his mother's varicose veins; his eye follows it down to the tiny smudge of blue and black. Surely he'd have noticed a man in blue overalls a few metres away, even if he was in the shadows! There are two dots that could be hands. He tries to remember if there was anything propped by the gutter and just to the left of the back door, the one with cobwebs like white bandages across the hinges because no one ever uses it. He's left a sweaty thumbprint on the glossy photo, that fades as it dries.

And then he shudders, despite himself: the person – if it's a person – might have seen him taking the pictures. Might have seen him doing much worse. The man – whoever he was, probably not the husband – might have been watching him with sharp, hunting eyes. Jean-Luc looks around, as if expecting hordes of police to erupt from the trees.

And then he hears the voice of Oncle Fernand. A calm voice, as usual, but cross underneath. Strolling about in the back of his head.

'Don't be stupid, nephew. You didn't see him there, out of cover, so how could he have seen you? Go and erect the electric fence.'

It makes everything easier, the silence of the empty yard.

He doesn't feel scared any more, either. He isn't ready to face the Englishwoman. He'd stammer and go into a sweat. He keeps expecting the kids to run out of the big black cave of the barn to watch him, he doesn't know why. His father could remember Les Fosses when it was a working farm; twelve hands, at one time. He'd say you wouldn't have known where to put yourself for the bustle, the voices, the carts. The hard work, the hay, the weeding between the vines. You could eat a lot of the weeds, chopped up in a salad. Or take them as medicine. You were taught from the day you could walk. These days, his father would say, they just pour in their poison. That's the world gone backwards, pouring poison into the earth. And everyone would laugh at him, including his wife. Backwards! You silly goat!

And he'd say: 'What about young Michel Renaux?'

Michel Renaux, back in 1913, sprinkling his father's vines with potassium, had taken a thirsty gulp from the bottle of wine he'd brought along for lunch. Except that it wasn't the wine: it was the potassium, the same colour through the green glass. Label hidden on the other side. Oh, how he'd suffered!

'You weren't there,' Jean-Luc's mother would scoff.

'But I know people who were,' said his father. 'Oh, how he screamed! And only twenty-two! He carried on screaming even after he was dead!'

But no one listened to him except to laugh, and so he just poured drink into himself until it killed him. But Jean-Luc knew what he meant, though he didn't say so. He'd once felt sick, standing over the pesticide-vat on old Pierre Lézinier's tractor heading up to the field; suffered a splitting headache for days after.

He works hard, dismantling the old fence, tapping in the plastic posts (short, only up to his waist) with their hooks ready-made to take the electric wire. At least someone's dealt with the cherry tree and put it back upright, although there's no sign of the buds breaking and the earth's not stamped firm enough around it. He takes a break only to test the pool's levels: a bit high, the pH, so he pours in a shot of acid. That'll be perfect for her, he thinks. It's like preparing a bed, smoothing it out, folding back the sheet exactly right.

The messed-up earth is already dry, as dry as the skin on his hands – as if dusted over with cement powder. He'll smooth out the earth and sow it yet again. It's much too late to plant seed, unless you water almost all day. And then the water will run out. The old boys in Aubain say it'll be a drought summer, the chiffchaff arrived early and the wood anemones were out a week too soon. They're always right, as his father was always right. There'll be none left for the pool, because he has to top up the pool – making up for the litres lost every day to evaporation once the sun gets going in June, the water melting into the heat and gone forever.

But the main thing is to show he cares. He needs to come to Les Fosses; he'd burst, otherwise. And he can't come if he's chucked out. They'd call the police.

Unless he sneaks up here early, to watch her. But she might never do it again. He can at least try, even if that was a lucky present from God, that time.

Maybe it was an angel, stood by the gutter.

He looks again at the spot. He walks over to it and studies the ground, as if there might be some trace. And then he feels a cold flush hiss through him from head to foot – he can hear it, hissing like the sea in his head – as he remembers something.

He remembers something and looks up at the roof. Raoul Lagrange always wore blue overalls, working. The Beau in Blue, he was known as. He'd wear them unbuttoned at the chest, so you could see his hairs. The women undid the rest, they'd say. Or: he hadn't had time to do them up to the top before the next round. Viper tongues.

He can hear the thump, like the thump of his own heart, as he stands by the gutter. He steps away, as if there's something there that might bite him.

The Beau in Blue, neck broken like a rabbit's, was curled up like a baby. Like a little baby, like a foetus in the mother's tummy, Dr Demarne said, who was called out and saw it for himself. It was normal, it was something called a reflex. Bruno found the body. His brother's body. Just here. Where tufts of wiry grass grow by the drain. That good-looker's face.

He ought to clear the drain of dead leaves: it smells a bit.

He turns his head suddenly and checks behind him and all around. For the very first time at Les Fosses, Jean-Luc feels his neck crawling. The Beau in Blue was watching. The Englishwoman is Raoul's woman, that's why. And Raoul watches her, invisible, from where he landed with a thump and a crack. Maybe he fell for her the very first time she entered the yard. He'd chase anything in a skirt, let alone nude.

Jean-Luc Maille and Raoul Lagrange are rivals in love.

But instead of running away, speeding off in the van, Jean-Luc stands his ground. Raoul Lagrange is dead. Jean-Luc Maille is alive. This is his one advantage. He feels the air whip and go colder around him, as if Raoul Lagrange is everywhere.

But he is nowhere, really. Because he is not flesh and blood like Jean-Luc Maille.

The fence operates off a battery unit that impresses Jean-Luc by its small size, although it's heavy. It can go up to 6,000 volts. It has six months of life, if the fence is continually operating. He runs two sets of wires through the posts. Henri advised him to string the lower wire about ten centimetres from the ground, to catch the babies. Baby boars can turn earth over just as nicely as their mum and dad, Henri said. The upper wire is only knee-height from the ground.

The baldie in the shop went on about protecting the battery unit from rain, as if Jean-Luc was stupid.

He finds some breeze blocks in one of the cellars and builds them up around the unit, roofing it with an old washing-machine cover from another of the cellars, and fixing that with a big rock from the tumbled wall. He works without stopping and in complete silence. He doesn't even drink anything. Something's filling him up with fuel.

It's all in place by midday. He is nervous about the connections: the two copper clips spark as they touch the battery. He hears a clicking in his head which is also outside. The fence is alive and its heart is beating in time to his own. The juice is flowing round and round and inside there is somewhere cut off from the outside world, but it is a mess. It reminds him of the mountains of the moon. Only the moon doesn't have a boar's turds perched on the rim of a crater.

He turns the switch to the highest voltage and tests the fence on himself, as Henri challenged him to do. Don't grip, Henri joked, or you might not be able to let go. He isn't worried; he's spent so long with the fence it has become what he knows best in the world for now. He taps the wire as lightly as he can with the pad of his forefinger and there's something about the shock, the way it takes on his arm, his shoulder and then the roots of his teeth without cutting out even after he's leapt back, that reminds him of the time he received the joke Valentine he thought was for real. He feels sick and shaky. He doesn't visibly shake, but he is shaken inside, and it is poisonous. It has bitten him. The boars must feel something like that when they're shot, he thinks. The air biting them before they even hear the noise.

He takes a seat on the top step of the cellar, until the nausea goes. He feels satisfied with himself, for once, looking at the powerful thing he has created, ticking with its poisonous pulse that still stirs around in his limbs and makes him want to drink a lot of cold water. At the same time, it looks like a toy fence, not a real fence. Everything he does in life is playing. He might be a small kid circling on his bike. He studies his hands, which are cut and bleeding in places and have grown-up blisters on them.

He rakes and sows the loose earth and sets the watering to two hours in the morning and two hours in the evening. He is hungry, damp with effort, sweat running off his nose in the cool gusts. He has burst one of the blisters.

Madame Sandler won't get rid of him as easily as that. He'll keep the voltage on the highest possible. He doesn't want to take any risks.

The six of them left the house on foot for a walk and a picnic. Jamie actually wanted to join in. Although it was cloudless, there was a coolish, frisky wind that seemed to grind the air's lens to the finest degree, giving it a kind of magnifying quality; even the front view's most distant visible trees were over-detailed, as in a pre-Raphaelite painting, instead of being the requisite blueish blur. More bright flowers were out – white, yellow, pink – and new leaves rustled in high-up, pale-green sweeps that had suddenly given substance to the deciduous parts of the slopes behind the house.

Nick wondered aloud, quite a few minutes after passing the Zone, what Jean-Luc would say to Lucy Sandler about the failed lawn. Jamie gave a short, sharp laugh: although he had not yet met the 'handyman', he found the subject amusing, for some reason. Nick had set the cherry tree upright and covered its roots again, a ten-minute spell of gardening which made him feel he should leave his job, sell up, retire to France and become a rural backwoodsman writing bestselling historical novels (while he hadn't written a line of fiction since school, his later essays had their moments).

There was the hint of a greenish tinge to the pool, they'd noticed in passing – its surface ruffled in spasms by the wind, blackened bits of nature floating within. We have not been assiduous enough, thought Sarah. There was a special vacuum in the shed, with a coiling, python-like pipe, but that was Jean-Luc's sphere. Nick begged the pool not to be naughty, which amused the girls.

'It needs a sacrifice,' said Jamie. 'Like a sacred lake.'

254

'After you, Jamie,' Nick cried in a jolly manner that produced only a mew of distaste in his son.

Following a good stretch, the poor elephant's fifty-four-year-old body taxed by several kilos of Beans who rode in the backpack like a stately Maharajah (Maharanee, Sarah corrected him), they stopped at a rock in the middle of the high heathy area with its wastes of broom and heather, munching on bread, dried sausage, sticks of celery, market cheese and ripe cherry tomatoes. The cherry tomatoes were a mistake, of course: one bite disembowelled them, their contents shooting out like shrapnel.

Slicing a nobbled *saucisson* with his curved, very sharp Thai knife, Jamie asked, after an unusual lull in their chatter: 'So what's in this murder deal at the house a few years back?'

Nick blinked in surprise. 'Come again, Jamie?'

'Yeah, this guy who was pushed off the roof at Les Fesses?'

'Les Fesses' was, in fact, Jamie's joke and not copied off Alan, whom he had never met; elucidating it to the girls (that 'Fesses' meant 'bottom' in French) had resulted in an entire afternoon of instability and near-insurrection.

'Pushed off the *woof*?' squealed Alicia, as if anywhere else might have been acceptable.

Tammy left a mouthful of celery half-chewed in her mouth because the noise might have drowned out something important.

'Yeah,' said Jamie, with an oracular smile.

Sarah suggested he meant the young member of the Resistance shot on the track.

'No, that's being shot and this is being pushed off the roof.'

'Sounds like a bit of local Gothic,' Nick said, deciding not to admit his prior knowledge.

'The shepherd told me. He's wiser than all of you Cambridge guys put together. He told me a lot about how to raise goats and sheep. Like, eating chestnuts helps them build up grease on their skin for the winter?'

'I didn't know you spoke French that *well*, Jamie.'

Sarah sounded genuinely surprised. She'd meant to emphasise *that*, in fact: a subtle difference. *That* well. It was a minor slip.

Jamie seemed to crouch, suddenly, without moving a muscle. He said *fuck* so quietly it might have been something else, a sigh or a groan. Then he looked up at her with a smile, emphasising his comments with the Thai knife. 'GCSE grade A French at fourteen but I'm not all up myself about it. I was really good at school until I was *fourteen*. Right up until the day of the triffid,' he added, because no one had said anything in between.

Triffid! Tammy's ears pricked. At fourteen Jamie had caught Helena's nickname for Sarah and run with it for several years until his father had exploded. Jamie had told Tammy all about it: the glass in the front door smashing, her father out of control, throwing things, hitting him. She could barely imagine it, because her father hardly ever lost his temper, and then he only shouted. Each time Jamie recounted it, it got worse, more violent: broken bones, by the end. The police. There was a secret Daddy she didn't know about, he implied. Tammy didn't want to know about it, but Jamie's version of the story was planted deep in her consciousness, nevertheless.

'No, sorry, sorry, correction,' said Nick, raising his hand and sounding like someone in Parliament. 'You started smoking cannabis *before* the separation. Dates, dates.'

'*Wha'*?' Jamie's face looked as if he were trying to make something out in a fierce wind.

'Is "murder" killing someone or just putting them in the junjun?' asked Alicia. She had a tomato-pip on the end of her nose.

Tammy pretended to laugh and it came out in a hideous cackle: 'Putting them in the dungeon! Bear with no brains.'

'Shall we change the subject?' suggested Sarah, brightly. 'Who's for an apple?'

'Not if it's got crumbs and earwigs and catkins all over it, as usual,' Tammy said, wrinkling her nose. She'd surprised herself with 'catkins'. Her brain was growing every day and it was wondrous to behold: she just let it.

Jamie watched his stepmother, only about twelve years older than himself and young-looking for her age ('the perpetual student', his mother would call her), peeling the apple for Beans. The wastes of broom stirred in a sudden gust all around them. Tammy was picking the skin off a slice of *saucisson*. Beans uncurled her fist to show a crushed splodge of Camembert peppered with the rock's grittiness and said, 'Shop. Maramama Beans.' It didn't ease the tension.

Sarah's eyes glinted with wet. 'Triffid' always did something intimately nasty inside her, like a school nickname.

'Girls, why don't you play hide-and-seek in the bushes?' she said, finding strength from somewhere, she never knew where. The broom was chest-high, it was a good idea. 'But Tammy, you'll have to hang on to Beans the whole time. OK?'

'Then that'll only be two of us doing it,' Tammy complained, already off the rock.

Alicia started counting down from thirty in her usual breath-less dirge; Beans and Tammy had already vanished. To the adults on the rock, there was nothing but the dark-green sprays of massed broom, shifting like a cartoon sea. In fact, Tammy was just behind the rock and she had her hand over Beans's mouth. The broom sprays covered them. It was like a small arched room. The dirge ended on minus three, as Tammy had just been doing minuses at school and they were a fascination to her sister, who was also said to be advanced for her age, although Tammy found her stupid.

'I'm coming, ready or not!' Alicia shouted; her voice, despite its decibels, taken by another gust. She also seemed to her parents to vanish, kept track of only by glimpses of her yellow hooded cardie, moving further and further away.

Now the adults thought they were alone. Tammy could just hear them over the wind rustling in the broom.

Jamie asked if they wanted him to carry on with the murder story.

'If you have to,' said Nick.

'That's it,' Jamie chuckled. 'That's all he'd say. *Il était poussé.* Kind of chatty guy?'

Although Nick knew the dead man was Bruno the shepherd's

brother, and called Raoul Lagrange, he pretended not to for Sarah's sake. 'Better that way,' he said.

'So you're not interested, Mr Historian?'

'I don't frankly believe it.'

'Because it's me telling you.'

'Nothing to do with you per se, Jamie. It's just that the evidence follows a conviction. Dangerous. You started out with a conviction that the house was negative and lo and behold here be the evidence. Remember Iraq and WMD?'

Jamie glared at his father with undisguised venom.

'He saw it happen. *J'étais là. Je l'ai vu. Il était poussé.* I was there. I saw it or him. He was pushed. Original research. Peter's always said that's your weak point, Nick.'

'Peter can go fuck himself,' said Nick, in a quiet, defeated tone.

There was a pause in which Sarah felt she might start trembling.

'That explains the funerary bouquet,' she said, in a jolly voice.

Bleak, complicated stories trailed away around her, leading to huddled figures in cowls in the middle of fields, to want and famine and disease.

The shepherd had made it clear to Nick that it was an accident: the man had used that very word. Jamie infuriated him with his elaborations and dramas, his embellishments, his fabulations. He cleared his throat, intent on dampening it all down, avoiding conflict. Jamie would win if there was outright conflict; he would destroy the sabbatical, the idyll. This was undoubtedly his twisted aim – on a mission from Helena, probably.

'You *sure*, Jamie, he wasn't talking about the young man murdered on the track by the Nazis?'

He could be so obtuse, Sarah thought.

'Found you!' came faintly from afar, desperate now.

'Even I know,' said Jamie, 'that a guy in his forties – that's roughly the shepherd's age, right? – is too young to have seen a guy being shot by the Nazis. It's like Helena says, you have

258

to position everyone around you as stupid. Maybe not Sarah but Sarah's just the skivvy, so that's OK.'

Ah, thought Nick. Helena is, after all, behind this one. He would go Zen. He would not let her win.

'I don't think skivvy's *quite* the word,' laughed Sarah, her eyebrows right up like a clown's.

The girls had all disappeared. Could Tammy be trusted with Beans? Voices were snatched away in the wind. The broom was a slur of wildness. The clouds were grey-black and piled up over the horizon, over the sea. Her hair was unmanageable, the shifting broom made her think of her hair, made unmanageable by the water here. She ought to do it every month, she reflected, but that's expensive. Everyone else has money. She had noticed silver threads in her comb, like a character in a fairy tale. Jamie was pathetic, in the end. He had nothing but his own wounded pride. He was to be pitied.

''Course I asked whodunnit,' Jamie pursued, 'but he kind of shrugged and held his lips between his fingers?'

Sarah nodded. 'So why did he mention it in the first place?'

'I told him the house was really, really negative.'

'Right,' said Nick. 'OK. That's nice to know.'

'That's bats,' muttered Sarah.

'Maybe we should ask the Chambords about this,' Nick suggested. 'On second thoughts, maybe we should just let it drop, if you'll excuse the pun.'

'He grabbed my elbow and was pretty excited,' Jamie pursued. 'He thinks you're all disgustingly rich and maybe American.'

'You put him right on that one?'

''Fraid my French isn't good enough.' This came with a self-consciously sly grin.

'Where are the girls?' asked Sarah, sing-song.

Tammy removed her hot hand from Beans's mouth and waited for release. Beans didn't make a sound, as if caught in a spell. The broom made its own swaddle, as in swaddling clothes. Tammy had already decided where the TV room would go, and the bunk-bedded bedroom. A wail went up from far away, barely carried to them on the wind.

'The lost soul,' said Nick, standing and waving.

'Essentially,' he said, on the plod back home – all of them anticipating a nice mug of tea and the chocolate cake Sarah had made with Alicia – 'history's made up of little bits sort of strung together, but each little bit isn't the past itself, it's only a memory of the past, and strictly verbal at that, so it's all pretty provisional and somehow loose, and my job – our job – is to tighten it up as far as it'll go. But the past – the living present of the past, I mean – is gone. Kaput. Finito. All that's left of the great lady is a necklace. Or a bit of the necklace. That's what people forget. Especially the archaeologists,' he added, checking Jamie was still listening.

Now and again father and son managed a truce in which messages were exchanged by carrier pigeon rather than crow. It often followed one of the nastier skirmishes. This present truce had begun with Jamie stating that his father's job was a waste of time, breath and money, and completely divorced from reality. Nick had asked him what he meant by 'reality', apart from Beans using one's head as a Congo bongo drum. Jamie had reckoned real 'reality' was something hidden behind what we think of as reality; he was into solitude, he said, because other people got in the way of real reality. The discussion then swerved into the meaning of history. Tammy was holding her father's hand and letting the words flow in and out of her head without capturing many. She was too low down to be heard: she'd tried, pulling on her father's large hand, but kept being interrupted.

Incessant gull-cries from behind: Alicia was tormenting Sarah by dragging back in her foot-slogging misery, describing in medical detail the state of her blisters (she hadn't any, her feet were as smooth as a peeled onion). Sarah, while irritated, was also marvelling. Only yesterday, it seemed, Alicia was not constructed, knew nothing of anything, not even pain or the pleasure of sleep overwhelming you at the end of a day. She was not, full stop. Sarah had made her so well that she could fabricate, fib, flirt.

'I wanted to be an archaeologist, yeah?' said Jamie. 'But the steering wheel kind of came off.'

He walked in a strange way. He dragged his feet and failed to keep a straight line. The bottoms of his trousers hit the ground around his boots and were scuffed to threads and shreds, or were maybe bought like that. You could see his underpants. His tee shirt had tiny holes in it and a large one exposing an underarm when he swung his hand up, and bore a discreet logo that said *Sticky Marks*.

'There's still time,' Nick suggested, without enough conviction. He'd never heard anything about Jamie wanting to be an archaeologist. 'Bags of time.'

'And you can open the bags when you need more time,' Tammy remarked, in a loud enough voice for once.

The trees either side were silent. Sometimes a track between trees could be menacing. There was only the crunch of their footsteps, now, as if they were eating their way to the house through a line of biscuits.

Did French birds sing in French?

These faint springtime whiffs of woodland darknesses were not English – even the resin from the pines was a foreign epiphany.

Yes, Sarah thought: there are these bad moments when you feel you are nothing but an intrusion. After we are all over, the creatures and the plants and the endlessly moving waters will breathe easy again. The historyless sigh of the seas.

The afternoon weather had turned: the gusts smelt of rain, while cracks of light sheathed the dark clouds so they resembled high, glistening cliffs towering to infinity. She looked up and was glad she was here, after all.

As soon as she was set down in the yard, Beans ran towards the new fence in her splay-legged, two-year-old's way. Alicia and

Tammy began to send out rescue craft in the form of leaves to insects failing to swim in the swimming pool, feebly battling against extinction.

'I don't suppose that's electric,' said Nick. 'The new fence there. He wouldn't go to that extreme.'

'There are these like really small magnetic forces,' Jamie continued, 'you measure with something called a torsion-balance?' He nodded at his own words. 'We've got the equivalent in our brains.'

Beans stopped within inches of the wire and turned round, grinning at them. 'She knows she shouldn't touch,' said Sarah, smiling. 'Cheeky thing. She's a terror.'

Nick agreed. 'Beans!' he called out, a touch snappishly. 'Don't touch the fence, will you? I know just that feeling,' he added.

Beans picked up a pebble and threw it in the air and grinned at them. Jamie was rolling a cigarette; Sarah assumed it wasn't a spliff. She was looking forward to the next trip to Aix, to the Centre des Archives d'Outre Mer, to the grown-up, polished haven of pinewood tables and stacked shelves, the order and the quiet, the secretly enthralled scholars, the oiled precision of a space in which no children were *permis*.

She started walking towards Beans. Nick followed her, the empty baby-chair at his side, spilling its straps and buckles and almost tripping him up. Beans ran away from the fence, teasing them, and her mother trotted after her, playing catch. Beans squealed in the full agony and delight of being chased as Tammy and Alicia played by the pool. The skin of the water prevented the insects – types of winged beetles or ants – from clambering aboard the rescue craft that were too far from the girls' hands to guide, although they stretched their arms as far as they could over the water.

They were told to stop and Tammy joined her father by the fence. He was contemplating the two low wires strung through the moulded hooks on each short post. He was listening. A soft, regular click, like someone tutting in their heads. He bent down and touched the upper wire with the tip of his finger.

The slight, if disagreeable, furry sensation he was used to from long-ago games of dare was not what happened. He'd fallen out of a tree and hit the ground shoulder-first. He was still doing so.

'Bloody hell!' he yelled, flapping his hand. 'That could kill someone!'

Sarah had caught Beans a few yards off and was squeezing her. 'You are joking, Nick. Tammy, don't touch.'

'I am not joking. I feel ill.' He took his pulse on his wrist. It was steady. 'He's mad. Completely insane. If the kids touch that, they'll be shot across the yard. Fried for breakfast.'

'You nearly let Beans touch it,' Sarah said, wonderingly.

'I didn't let her! I didn't know!'

Tammy was dying to touch it, but was told to retreat.

'What's the big issue?' asked Jamie, ambling up.

'The big issue,' said Sarah, as if ticking him off, 'is that the idiot French handyman has put up a massively powerful, potentially lethal electric fence knowing there are small kids around, with no warning, to keep wild boars off the owners' stupid prospective lawn.' She shook her head and snorted like a pony, she was so cross.

Jamie had an unlit roll-up in the middle of his mouth, caught by his teeth. 'The case for the defence is that they're pretty keen on having a lawn?'

'I don't care. It's unacceptable. We're paying them good money.'

'A capitalist contract,' said Jamie. 'By 2050 or probably 2030 the world's going to be uninhabitable except for the filthy rich thanks to the capitalist contract, yeah?'

Nick found the battery unit under a plastic cover on the house side of the fence, nestling inside a little shelter of breeze blocks. He used two long splints of wood like a claw to release one of the copper clips, which sparked furiously as he worked it off. He was scared. Another electric jolt was sniggering in the wings. He told the others to stand back, having some vague idea that electricity could arc through air.

'Wood doesn't conduct, does it?'

''Course not,' Tammy scoffed.

'We do have our fair share of troubles,' Sarah sighed.

'I wouldn't call them troubles,' said Nick, unnecessarily. 'I'd call them very minor incidents.'

The clicking stopped.

'Let's hope they stay that way,' said Sarah, involuntarily conjuring dark, skeletal figures in dust-storms, tarpaulined camps, flies on babies' cheeks.

Jamie said: 'I once knew this guy called Les Trubb and he was something like Hungarian or maybe Slovakian in the form below at school, and really up himself?'

'So what?' muttered Nick, easing off the other clip with his claws of wood, still not trusting the basic laws of circuitry.

'He'd be on the noticeboard for, y'know, exam results and so on as Trubb Les and I'd put a circle around it and write *spelling*, exclamation mark.'

The clip came off. Oddly, it sparked.

'Right,' said Nick, standing up, 'now for our *pronunciamento* to the gods.'

'What's that?' asked Tammy, glad that her father was still alive.

TWELVE

Lucy Sandler was in the bath when the call came; heady with Badedas, bubbles like the tops of clouds seen from a plane. They hid her body, in which she found fault. Or many faults. Fault lines, fissures, inadequate muscle tone. She'd given up massaging her breasts; a lot of effort for nothing. She'd once had the sharpest figure – the *sharpest* – of any of her circle: and the nicest hands. Now she looked, not like a Bonnard, but like the Lucian Freud in the glossy arts magazine she was trying not to get wet, a nude from the eighties whose 'sombre tones of sagging flesh, relieved only by the cranberry-tinted elbows laid in like bruises above the groin, mercilessly expose time's stake in life'. What pseudery, she thought. Despite the author of the article, Julian Dale, being an old friend. Who never talked like that in front of a painting; all he did was gossip, queer-gossip. But cranberry-tinted elbows, that was good, she had to admit. She glanced at her own elbow: pale and bumpy, like a pug's nose. Why so shiny?

She reached for the cordless, carrolling on the glass shelf. Important calls always came when you were in the bath, especially in the early evening. This was from the Fusspot family in France. Yet again. Fuss fuss. She felt it was somehow wrong, metaphysically wrong; they should have had some kind of intermediary. An agent. An agent of the Lord.

Mr and Mrs Fusspot and their three little girls – but she couldn't think of names, she'd be hopeless on that radio panel show whose sentence she could never remember. She was reasonably sure her mind was going, but terribly discreetly, like a retiring butler. Perhaps it was just age. The same was happening to Alan. Mr Fusspot was going on about an electric fence. An electric fence around the seed-bed, to keep the boars off.

'What a terrific idea,' she replied. 'Jean-Luc has at last shown some initiative. The French are short on initiative. Because of Napoleon, who had much too much. Unlike us, they haven't invented a thing, I don't believe.'

It didn't matter that she knew this was quite untrue. Cinema, photography, Marie Curie. She was a conversational mannerist. The distance-distorted voice went on about how powerful it was, the electric fence. Six thousand volts. That did sound rather a lot. The bubbles cleared to show a flat, unappetising breast. Can that really be mine? she mused. It was like a motorway service-station omelette. The fence could kill someone with a weak heart.

'What a clever way to get rid of one's husband,' she joked.

Oh, how he fussed. They had small children, he was saying, as if she didn't know it. Who might be grilled like fritters: she saw them sparking, their eyes popping, hair a star-shape, face black and smoking as in those violent cartoons.

'Then tell them not to touch it,' she sighed. 'They'll soon learn. Anyway, didn't you touch electric fences when you were their age? We had horses. I was always daring boys to touch them. The wires, I mean. It's called toughening up.'

Really, it was incredible, the way this intelligent man, this major don, was so dependent on her. The very epitome of the brilliant academic without a single life skill. She said a brusque goodbye, pretending she was in the middle of a meeting, and dropped the phone on the bath mat. Alan came in without knocking, half-naked, his peeling stomach showing through his dressing gown like a separate being, a surly bald servant in an experimental drama. Her cloud cover had mostly vanished to clear sky, exposing the ancient landscape below: he looked down upon it like a disapproving god.

'Lucy,' he said, 'I'm pulling out of Iraq.'

He showed her an email to 'Mister Shandler, Art deeler' that said all four of his limbs would be cut off. Not as clever as the one a few months back that said he could have a shorter penis, for free, from 'Al-Ka-ida'.

She handed it back with a grunt. 'Probably the silly boy next door,' she said. 'The one whose ball breaks our geraniums. He's Steiner-educated. They don't teach spelling. That's my construction on it.'

'You're building crap on spec,' he said, pensively folding the piece of paper. 'I'm going to pull out, Lucy. Before I fall apart. I don't even feel the hot breath of Interpol or the FBI on the back of my neck. I feel much worse.'

'Hmmm. Let me think.'

She let a little pause embed itself with a V in his forehead. Alan could not fall apart. Not the right term. Dissolve, maybe. Exfoliate to a quivering mush in the centre.

'Funnily enough,' she said, 'I've just been talking to France, sweetheart. Mr Fusspot. Jean-Luc has erected a massive, lethal electric fence. Perhaps you could crawl inside it.'

'Where?'

'Around my lawn. To keep off the boars. As in wild pig.' She prodded his stomach with her toe. 'The type with tusks and a big fat belly.'

'I'm pulling out of antiquities entirely,' he said, pushing her foot away so that it landed back in the water and splashed him with froth. 'Don't sound too interested.'

'You look like an epileptic,' she laughed, indicating the side of his mouth by touching hers.

He wiped the bubble-bath from his face with a hairy wrist. 'I'm telling you, I mean it. I didn't just come up to ogle you and say how about it.'

'Silly billy,' she said, 'of course you aren't quitting. You know too much.'

'Exactly.' He sat down on the edge of the bath, his huge exposed belly concealing his naughty bits like a Churchillian frown. 'I can't handle the Russians. My hair is falling out, my skin is crumbling. I think this is from the Russians. They always spell my name like that. They want the gypsum worshippers from Tell Asmar. Or at least, nice Mr Putin wants the gypsum worshippers, probably.'

'Yesterday it was the Iranians.'

'Tomorrow it'll be the Chinese. Or the Saudis, so help me God. I take a different route home each day, Lucy. They gouge out eyes with their thumbs. Out, vile jelly,' he went on, quoting flatly, 'where is thy lustre now? All I want is to live until I can have my own electric wheelchair and get my arse wiped for me.'

'I'm not stopping you,' she murmured, closing her eyes. Sometimes Alan's gargantuan wit grated on her aesthetic sensibilities, and he looked simply fat and revolting.

'Art Brut is back,' he said, quietly.

'Art Brut? Oh, come on, Alan.' She was genuinely surprised. Alan had gone potty.

'Zig says it's the coolest way to make a buck. We had lunch together today. You find some lunatic asylum somewhere dull like Iowa and take the art for a tiny donation. Even drawings in biro. Doodles. Crazy magazine collages by some mute psychotic. Sculpture, if you're lucky. Stuff stuck on in any old way by a dwarf toe-obsessive with a mental age of five.'

'Assemblages,' Lucy corrected him.

He drew a hand over his face as if clearing fog and sighed. 'Zig sold a crazy painting he found in a garbage tip and cleared, wait for it, twenty thousand dollars, last week. That gallery off Madison, owned by those twins. Twenty thousand dollars. All he did was some preliminary working-up in the local papers and local TV, then sourced it to his friends at the national level. Zig has a long ponytail, which helps.'

'Outsider Art,' said Lucy, without opening her eyes. 'If you want a ponytail you'll need my sewing machine, Alan.'

'Let's stick to the Frenchie name, it's more accurate. Raw. As in steak.'

'Sexier,' she said, contemptuously. 'As long as you say it with a French accent. Which you don't.'

'Art Brut is back and becoming very, very big, Lucy,' he

insisted, leaning forwards and persuading himself. She could smell the lunch with Zigismund Moritz on his breath. 'Everything else is tired. Tired and old and over-analysed,' he added, lifting her arm and pecking at it with his lips – ironically, she felt. 'What's really tomorrow's lunch is intimacy and feeling and paint and stuff, not the massive installation that is so up itself it thinks it's divine as in forever. That's yesterday's breakfast. And abstraction is so out you can only swear with it.'

He dropped her arm. It hovered.

'We need to talk about the fence. That's today.'

'We will talk about the fence,' he said, scratching his stomach and scattering a light fall of snow over the bathroom tiles.

He explained how Art Brut fulfilled people's need for the unmediated, the genuine; the primitive without the sub-colonial, tribal angle. She knew all this, she'd read the articles, but she let him continue because she felt pity for him. He was so boyish, so American. This was his latest gewgaw. It was going to be overplayed with, ruined, thrown out. 'The bottom's gone out of tribal. Everyone travels, these days. Where Barry would come back to LA half-dead from malaria with a crate full of juju stuff from places no white man had ever set foot in, retired couples take weekend breaks in those places. Practically. They have wheelchair access and twenty-four-hour parking.'

'I thought there was nothing left,' said Lucy, who'd once had a fervid fling with Barry Jordis.

'There isn't,' Alan confirmed. 'It's all fake, now. Even in the deep bush.'

'Wasn't it always?' she murmured, remembering the tiny, terrifying mask above Barry's great bed, with jagged white teeth and a coil of twine around it. The heat of LA shut out by a vast picture-window, the glacial breath of the air conditioning, the huge and tinkling whiskies on their bare bellies.

'Art Brut isn't fake. It can't be. It just is. That's the essence of it, in a world that is entirely fake, otherwise. That's why it's suddenly becoming *it*. The prices are following.'

'It's unmediated crap, Alan. It's amateur. The fag-end of this awful campaign against elitism. End of discussion. We have a serious lawn issue. Jean-Luc's put up this lethal fence and they're fussing. I can't find solutions to everything.'

She turned the hot tap with her painted big toe. The scalding water flushed warmth between her legs like exploring fingers.

'Amateur,' repeated Alan with a groan, shaking his head. 'What you've just said is very conservative. But the main point, Lucy bunny, is it's safe. I mean, I'll go home by the same route each day. I'll keep all of my limbs. My penis will remain the same size until the day you excite it, in whichever year that may come.'

'You Americans, you may run the whole show but you're so *brutally* naive,' Lucy laughed, working up the bubbles by paddling her hands, flecking his face again in the process. 'And such *cowards*!'

'I can't bear them. They're – oh – completely ghastly. Sort of autocratically callous,' Nick complained, several hours after the phone call to the Sandlers. 'They're heirs to Alexander III. They'd support serfdom like a shot.'

He had, much to his regret, re-established the current in the fence. They were to re-establish the current each evening, then disconnect it in the morning. Life was all about compromise. He had no desire to toughen up his children by the Lucy Sandler method. Or by any method.

Jamie was eating with them tonight, picking at the stew and knocking back the fairly decent Cahors at the top end of their budget (around six or seven euros), and commenting adversely on the music. First Sibelius, then the soft jazz, then the troubadours, then the Smiths. He shook his head each time and asked them how they could listen to it, it was depressing and/or geriatric. Sarah suggested Dylan and Jamie concurred, knowing that Nick didn't like Dylan very much: he found his wailing voice annoying. Nick was stung by all this, despite trying not to be: 'What you should be saying,' he declared, 'is that you *find* the music depressing or geriatric or whatever. It's called projection. The music in itself is not in the least depressing, it is uplifting – and to say any of it is geriatric is just risible.' Nick hadn't used the word 'risible' ever before in his life, he didn't think.

Jamie shook his head in disbelief, his contempt visually heightened by his wearing, for no apparent reason, a pair of small, round sunglasses that made him look creepy. He was back in his father's denims, too; he'd cut the jacket and jeans shorter and sewn a Union Jack onto the top pocket. Nick had commented on this adversely and Jamie had laughed: it was a punk insignia. Nick had missed punk by several years; already in his mid-twenties, embarrassingly old. Jamie wore the jacket open over a tee shirt that said, in discreet letters, *This Is My Clone*. Nick found it all slightly sad, slightly vulgar and slightly unsettling, but kept this to himself.

He was explaining his comment about projection: the latest research had found that habitual use of cannabis increased the chances of depression or even schizophrenia by fifty per cent. Thirty, Sarah corrected. Whatever, Nick went on; if you artificially stimulated the endomorphin gates you needed more and more to swing them open, and eventually they hung loose and there was no more endomorphin.

'I think you mean endorphin,' said Sarah, swaying slightly to her Dylan.

'Endorphin. The substance like morphine, anyway.'

Jamie reckoned someone had been reading crap newspaper articles and then half-remembering them and that this was no great advertisement for the speaker's professional rigour. He sounded like a much cleverer version of himself, sneering like this, and Nick lost his cool. He found it incredible that his son, of all people, belonging to a generation for whom the term 'recliner' was invented the better to accommodate an evolutionary twist in the upright biped, could accuse him of a lack of rigour.

Jamie sighed, rose from the table and walked off into the night without a torch, distantly slamming his eponymous door and breaking cobwebs instead of glass.

Tammy emerged, investigating the noise from the top of the stairs, and was rewarded with a finger-snapping command from her father to go back to bed. Sarah went up and placated Tammy as if she'd just been beaten about the head; she padded back to bed and clutched her long-haired troll that had once been Sarah's, when it was already retro.

Nick claimed, when Sarah returned, that kids these days were mollycoddled, over-protected, treated like porcelain. Sarah objected to this accusation and went quiet, even mournful. Once she'd got so depressed and tired when Alicia was a baby that she'd spent a morning yelling from the bedroom and throwing shoes at its locked door while Nick tried to reason with her.

The light flickered off his retreating hairline as he stared into the candle-flame, swallowing his darkness in more wine, costumed against his will in a frock coat and mutton-chop whiskers with a handy birch-rod at his side. The age gap had broadened between them: it usually did on these occasions, giving rise to all sorts of mutual assumptions and misreadings. The wine could not touch the venerable, solemn stuff they served on high table at college. He'd been spoilt, as fruit is spoilt. He no longer felt genial.

'Oh dear,' said Sarah, after a silence interrupted only by a night creature's moronic beep-like call, possibly an owl's. 'We should have gone to Finland after all. Or Brazzaville. We did consider Brazzaville, didn't we? Much more honest.'

'I've tried,' he said. 'I've done my very best.'

'I hate it when you say that, Nick. You sound like a doctor over the dying patient.'

'I don't think I'm the doctor,' he murmured, listlessly. 'Oh, let's play Scrabble. And let me beat you for once.'

Alicia appeared as they were undressing and informed them there was a cat purring in the girls' room. Not a cat, but the ghost of a cat. The noise turned out to be the beginnings of a wasps' nest in a crack in the beam; or perhaps last year's, reawakening. Nick stumbled on the stairs, going down for a roll of tape to put over the crack.

Jamie was sitting on the sofa. He'd returned from the blank of the night. His eyes were hidden behind his little round sunglasses; he had a leaf in his hair and a scratch on his cheek. Nick, passing into the kitchen, ignored him. On the way back he noticed the dusty bottle of wine and the full glass on the stool at Jamie's elbow.

'Oh. That's Alan Sandler's untouchable wine supply,' said Nick, who was more dismayed by this than anything else. 'Isn't it? That's incredibly out of order, Jamie. That's stealing from the gods.'

He picked the bottle up. A 1985 St-Émilion.

'Smells corked,' he said.

'You never took me skiing.'

'I didn't like skiing.'

'You still went skiing with your friends, right?'

'Your mother didn't want you to go. She objected. You'll have to replace this bottle, corked or no.'

Jamie nodded. 'Your version.'

'There's still time. I did offer.'

'Like once.'

'Better than never. You weren't interested. In fact, like your mother you ideologically objected.'

The little round sunglasses made Jamie look like a rock star being interviewed. His father saw himself in them, tiny and old. He told his son to switch off the lights when he was finished. He put the bottle down and took a sip from Jamie's glass, the ruby pocked by fragments of cork. A gorgeous berry richness disfigured by a zigzag of vinegar.

'Pity,' he said.

'Finished with what?'

'Being down here,' Nick mumbled, already tackling the stairs. One day they and their ilk would be impassable, the worst face of the Eiger. Maybe in under thirty years. He would have made Jamie pay for that bottle. He would have done, if it hadn't been corked.

273

'I know who killed him,' said Jamie.

He could see the top of his son's head in the murk of the under-lit room, the retied tribal knot like something on a bird, a suggestion of another socio-economic system, of causewayed enclosures and men coerced into building giant henges. It was unsettling.

He had to whisper it from halfway up, a harsh rasp that stirred his pseudopolyps: '*Killed who?*'

'The guy who fell off the roof.'

There was a sudden, unearthly scream from the girls' bedroom. 'We'll discuss it tomorrow,' said Nick, over his shoulder.

His hunch was correct: Alicia had been teasing the few sleepy wasps crawling about in the crack. Ointment from Sarah's emergency bag was applied. So was the tape. Alicia snivelled, stung on the finger. Beans wanted one, too. Tammy giggled away, for some reason.

The parents retreated into their bedroom's blackness. Sarah was a soft ledge of warmth Nick settled against. 'Jamie's downstairs. Stoned out of his head,' he told her, in a low murmur. 'Scratched his cheek. He's nicked one of Alan's bottles.'

'Jesus.'

'It's OK,' he smiled. 'It was corked.'

'But that's out-and-out theft.'

'He won't stay much longer, in that case.'

'The triumph of individualism,' she remarked softly, without turning. It might have been a shred of her sleep.

He stroked her edge, the child's landscape of her dip and curve, reaching the end of her nightie on a stretch of cool thigh, the knobble of bone at the side of a knee, like a bared boulder; stubble-fields of calf where she had recently shaved. The shin bone's exposed, asexual ridge. Unlike the foot. Sarah had beautiful arched feet. Its succulence underneath. He reached the summit of the little toe, the piled cairn. She flicked it out of his fingers, mewing her complaint.

'Love you,' he said.

'I'm sleepy.'

Sleepy was good: there was reconciliation in the word. *Tired* would have been bad.

'Maybe too sleepy,' she said, turning over to face him. He started exploring down below, nevertheless. 'I ought to go to Aix again, soon,' she added, following her thoughts. 'I'm in need of documents.'

His own thoughts that night were industrious, a big noisy factory above the river of dreams. He wouldn't be carried away. He was vaguely envious of Jamie knowing something more about the builder, but it might be hogwash, empty rumour. The shepherd was the poor man's brother; he had said nothing about a murder, only that he'd slipped off when it was wet, that you should never go up on a roof when it was wet. Unless his local accent had concealed something more in the interstices.

Jamie had been conducting some oral research, clearly. Original research. He had the time. Nick felt disgruntled about this. Original research had always been his Achilles heel: when he was young, it was theory that had dominated. You sluiced the dense matter of facts with the clear, invigorating waters of theory, Marxist or otherwise. It left him, now, with this traceable fault-line in his work, the fracture in his collected essays that might bring the whole arch tumbling down. Peter Osterhauser had no such fault-line: his very strength was the original research, its depth and breadth, each fact counterchecked and substantiated over and over. Once every ten years Peter Osterhauser would publish something remarkable, unassailable, with a great weight of learning that others marvelled over. Just when Nick felt his colleague had dried up, the waters came gushing forth and the world stood still. This was why Peter had been appointed professor, although he was not yet fifty. Even that stung.

After an hour or so he got up and opened the window. It was a clear, moonless night. The stars massed more thickly and then thicker still the longer he looked, their prehistoric glitter rendering even time's passage futile. Orion the hunter.

Venus a reddish-blueish sparkle. The owl or whatever was still beeping over and over, a hoot like an alarm clock, hardly animal. Otherwise it was silence, and there were no man-made lights. It might be Africa, he thought. The fragrant night air had a touch of warmth to it, a hint of the heat to come in a matter of weeks. He recalled a research trip he'd made for his thesis to the eastern highlands of the Bamenda peoples; not the wet, viscous air and thick forests of the coastal valleys but dry heat and horizons; short and feathery grass-cover in which he'd knelt one early morning and felt fulfilled.

An hour or so passed – very fast, as sleepless hours always do. He lay in bed and smiled grimly into the darkness as Sarah breathed evenly in sleep. All thoughts at this hour were crap. The moment you were born they handed you a spade to start digging your own grave.

The distant screams continued: harrowing, agonised, bewailing the ruin made of the world. He surfaced from a dream of screaming, pug-like faces with dirty teeth, like something out of Tolkien. Sarah was already awake: he clawed for the lamp and when it came on she looked bewildered.

It was two-thirty in the morning. Somebody was being stabbed. The kids.

Oh yes. The wasps, of course.

Sarah came back from her investigation while he was finding his feet. 'The kids are fine,' she said.

They listened. The hellish screams reminded Nick of something. A farm near his school, its dark and solid smell wafting over the playing fields. Smoking in a wintry hedge, sharing a delicious Number Six with his best friend Duncan, feeling huge and adult and furtive near the piggery. Heat and cold.

'The boars,' he said. 'The electric fence.'

'That's what I thought, maybe. It's horrible. They're in pain.'

They listened. Tortured souls touched by fire, racked on grid-dles, dismembered with rusty handsaws. Hog-headed sinners.

'They're cross, more like. I guess they'll learn, soon. Pigs are rather bright.'

There was a final screech that tore into bits, whisked away like embers. Then silence.

'You see? They've departed. Somewhat irritated,' he said, his legs trembling under the duvet.

'We could put one round the pool,' suggested Sarah.

'Erm, I think not. Anyway, it's too low. False security is the worst.'

Beans jabbered next door, singing an intermittent dirge to her cot's overcrowded soft-toy population above the synchronous owl hoot. Neither Alicia nor Tammy had woken up.

Nick felt a vague wake of discomfort at having agreed to switch the fence back on. The Sandlers were definitely the gods. Something mischievous and cruel. And Jean-Luc? If he were to look down at Jean-Luc's ankles he would see little wings on them. Hermes, who could pass through walls and alight anywhere; who guided the dead souls to the ferry-boat.

Oncle Fernand is very pleased with his nephew.

Jean-Luc spends the weekend, when he isn't staring into the river by his fishing rod or deep in a *Spirou*, working on the monument. He's only just realised – in the middle of the night, blinking into the darkness – that the monument is to Oncle Fernand. That is now its official name. *The Monument to Fernand Maille*. It was staring him in the face. He imagines the unveiling ceremony, with the mayor, the *conseil municipal*, the President of France. Of course this is a fantasy: he will never show it to anyone. The very idea makes him feel sick.

He also thinks of it as a bird, because of the feathers stuck along the handles. Oncle Fernand had fifty chickens, it was always said. His brother – Jean-Luc's father – thought chickens were stupid, demonstrating the fact in the usual way when one had to be slaughtered: headless, it still ran about.

Oncle Fernand, however, was different; he nursed a mutant chick with huge feet and a crooked spine and miniature wings.

It lived a year and when it died Oncle Fernand cried, apparently. He was twelve. His father – Jean-Luc's grandfather – was very worried by his boy and beat him, saying everything, good and bad, was merited. These were the stories that Jean-Luc was brought up with.

This isn't a monument, this is Oncle Fernand's mutant chick, Jean-Luc tells himself, laughing inside his head. The resurrection of the mutant chick.

He writes this out carefully in pencil on a piece of cardboard torn off a box. *La résurrection de la poule mutante*. Because it makes Oncle Fernand so happy, he glues the strip of cardboard along the side of the monument, from wheel to wheel. He doesn't like the look of his careful handwriting, it reminds him of school exercises and is still uneven, but he leaves it.

He doesn't know what to do with the photographs. He hasn't looked at them again since the woods, yesterday. Just looking at the plastic envelope scares him. It's because of Raoul Lagrange, hovering in the background. You can't get rid of ghosts, just like that. You can't shoot them, or make them transparent by adding chemicals, or keep them out with an electric fence.

He has a rival in love. It is like a Johnny Hallyday song. He has five Johnny CDs but the one he chooses now is the tape of best hits that he bought from the stall at St-Maurice five or six years ago. He opens his old tape recorder and puts in the cassette. He has to blow the dust off, and the side of the tape recorder is scotched up with tape that's peeling away, but the music still plays. He knows it all by heart, anyway: it's not Johnny promising his eyes when she can't see any more, the salt from the kisses of his mouth . . . it's Jean-Luc Maille. It's the honey from the touch of his own hand. It's his blood that is the same as hers, that is over and above any difference between him and her, between him and the Englishwoman, because face to face they resemble one another, we are blood for blood the same, we are just the same –

There is moaning from next door. A shout. He checks by putting his ear to the door. You never know. Last year she fell out of bed and fractured something and the bad-tempered nurse – not Elodie, back then – told him off for not responding to her cries. 'I wouldn't have a minute to myself if I did,' he replied. The nurse told him he'd regret it, after, when his mother was gone for good.

'I'm trying to sleep, stupid!'

'Too bad,' he shouts back.

'You'll kill me! I'll call the police!'

'After I've killed you, or before?'

She goes silent at that. He's noticed that sometimes he gains the upper hand. Perhaps he scares her with his jokes.

As the tape plays Johnny's best hits, Jean-Luc hangs the old greenish soup spoons by wire from the pink plastic handle; they are flowers on the bush, and you can see your face in a spoon. He used to make faces in his spoon, when he was small. His face all swollen and comical. He could cut out little faces from the magazines in his drawer and glue them into the bowl of each spoon, but he needs the Englishwoman's face, close up, for the prettiest flower. The one that made him smile in the picture book, when he was a little boy at school. He nips the wire with his red pliers: a satisfying click, each time.

And where is he going to find the Englishwoman's face, without asking her to pose? The face on the photos he took was too small each time.

Unless he cuts out the photo of her naked, standing by the pool, and sticks that on instead. Her whole body instead of her face. This idea appeals to him more and more. She'll be safe in the spoon, the heart of the flower. But the envelope scares him. It's because of Raoul Lagrange, standing at the back in his blue overalls, straining to lift his head on its broken neck. Watching, watching through eyes as white as the pieces of gravel the girls gave him. His rival in love. And he can't do anything about it: you can't get rid of someone who's already got rid of.

He sticks two of the pieces of gravel on the ends of the pink handle, holding each in the glue until it's dry enough and his finger aches. The duck has eyes, he laughs to himself.

Blind eyes. The eyes of the dead. It has to have the dead on it, being a monument.

He picks up the scissors, mustering his courage. But he's frightened to open the envelope. It's too strong.

His mother calls him again with a whine like a tom-cat on heat. It is Sunday morning, the nurse has been and gone, and now it is up to her son. The whine won't stop, she's thirsty, for a week now she hasn't been able to get down the stairs because of some kind of feebleness in her legs, and has only shuffled around her room once or twice.

He still has the scissors in his hand when he goes through. She's sitting in the winged easy chair, where the nurse left her.

'All I want is a glass of water,' she moans. 'My throat's as dry as a biscuit.'

'There's water on your bedside table.'

She grimaces and shakes her head, the folds of her throat wobbling like a chicken's. 'It's last night's.'

'Water doesn't go off that quickly,' he says, picking it up. He is saying things for the sake of it, he isn't really concentrating, his mind is on the monument. 'We could boil some white marrube flower in it,' he says. 'Clear you out. Spring cleaning.'

She grimaces. Jean-Luc wants to grimace, too. Every spring until he was eighteen, over three dreaded mornings before school, he'd been forced to drink an infusion of marrube, the bitterest drink there was, as his grandmother had made Maman do – to purge the liver, to clear the blood. They'd pick the ugly flowers in the summer in the hot fields below Aubain to dry over the winter and they would both grimace as they found them, they couldn't help it, it was memory working, it was the bitterness that had remained in their heads.

'It'd kill me,' she says, and immediately regrets it from the look of her.

He puts the glass down, remembering those harvests in the hot fields, the sun on his neck, the scents, the rush basket full of leaves and flowers, the sight of her skirt and her laddered, vein-knotted calves. She'd always wear the same blue working skirt, day in, day out, summer, winter. It smelt like a goats' pen. On the wall is his present to her when she was sixty: a duck in ceramic, with a bamboo frame. A real artist did it, selling stuff from his studio in St-Maurice. He was Dutch and wore a beret. She liked it. It was very well done, you could see the exact feathers, what type of duck it was: a mallard. He was glad she liked it. He was twenty, then.

'Why've you got those scissors?' she asks, with the same scared look.

'I thought you might need a haircut,' he smiles.

She crouches in the chair, her small, square-shaped body turning even smaller. Her hair is stuck patchily to her skull and cropped every month by one of the nurses. It looks like a worn flannel over her head; she strokes it. 'You're not touching it,' she says, as if guarding a treasure.

He laughs. He didn't even notice the scissors in his hand when he came into her room. He has a great urge to cut off all her hair, to take it back to the spotted skull. A nurse washes that balding head every week over the plastic bowl, as if they are in a proper hairdresser's; a towel draped around his mother's neck, the jug filled up in the tiny bathroom next to the kitchen. Up and down, up and down, the nurse goes. Much easier to have it all off.

'Much easier to cut it all off,' he says, smiling. He comes up to her and snips a curl above her ear. It lies in his hand like a tiny clump of fir needles. He shakes it away and it vanishes against the grey linoleum that was once patterned with blue and red spots.

'Murderer,' she whispers, her eyes expanding in their creased sockets.

'I haven't murdered anyone, Maman. But I'll murder you if you carry on like this.'

'I bet you would, too!' She looks both terrified and defiant, shrinking into the chair with its bald patches and grease stains as if she might melt into it, become the chair itself. One day the chair will be empty, and then what will he think?

It would be so easy, he realises. A quick plunge of the scissors into her chest, then another to make sure. Or into the throat, like the shepherds do with their goats or their sheep, slowly but firmly pressing the blade into the windpipe. Jean-Luc's father showed his boy how to do that, when they'd a few goats up at the back, the flies and the smell filling the kitchen.

She tripped up a few years ago and hit the radiator: blood spurted from the side of her head like a drinking fountain. He held his thumb against it until the ambulance arrived. The strange thing was, she'd carried on chatting to him, in a good mood, or maybe knocked into sense. Things were better then.

But Oncle Fernand is telling him not to be stupid, to go and get her a glass of fresh water. He has far more important actions to perform than putting his mother out of her misery. Or cutting off what's left of her hair.

He comes back to Les Fosses on his mobilette to check the fence. He's on his way to the Dutch couple's kidney dish of a pool and makes a small detour to see whether the fence has done its work. He half expects to see electrocuted boars littering the yard.

No one about, although it is mid-afternoon. The seeds lie like rice over the earth, blackened by heavy watering. Almost April, everything bursting out already, the cardousso on his own door as open as it can get, the time for sowing long past but he couldn't not have tried. He'd be fired, otherwise. Madame Sandler was quite clear about that, although he doesn't always believe her. But these people would be reporting back: she has spies, now. She'd realise he isn't pulling his weight, that he's been pulling the wool over her eyes for years. He hasn't been, in his own mind, but that's how she'd see it.

The very first thing she said to him on the phone, years back, was: 'Are you for hire?' Or maybe that was just her bad French. 'No,' he said. 'I'm not a car.' She liked that answer.

She phoned him up late at night, once, all the way from England, telling him to plant some red geraniums in pots either side of the door before they got there that weekend with her friends. She wanted to impress her friends. She didn't want the house to look unwelcoming. Ordinary large pots, Jean-Luc. He did what she'd said, but it was the wrong type of geranium and she was shocked by the pots. He'd chosen the fanciest ones he could find in Jardiland – shiny blue glazed pots imitating baskets, with basket-type handles. 'I said ordinary, Jean-Luc; these are disgusting pots!' Her friends laughed. She laughed. Monsieur Sandler laughed. Jean-Luc was upset: he couldn't see what was so disgusting about the pots he'd chosen.

They were thrown out and replaced by two very old terracotta pots from an antique shop, chipped and peeling like bad skin, with moulded heads sicking up leaves. They were expensive, even though they looked as if they were about to disintegrate. He had to come and water the flowers in these and the other pots she'd bought every other day: she didn't want a watering system with its little black pipes running everywhere. A year later the two antique pots were stolen. No doubt by one of the passing hunters, as nothing else was nicked. So he went to the café and told Louis in Marcel Lagrange's hearing, but all Marcel said was that some Arabs had stolen the chrome badge off his Cherokee when he was in town. They'd sell it back in Morocco, he grunted. They all need sending back, then we'll be comfortable again.

Madame Sandler was glad that nobody had broken in, when Jean-Luc told her on the phone. She hardly seemed to care, otherwise.

Yet she cared about her lawn.

The fence has worked. Jean-Luc feels good about this. There are fresh boar-spoors all the way along the margins. He senses an obscure triumph over the primitive forces of life, shadowing him from the woods. Oncle Fernand isn't talking today, or he'd have congratulated him. There was nothing said, even by the plaque. There are often days like that. Of rest. Yesterday Oncle Fernand chattered away, boring his nephew. Who has bought another throwaway camera, but not at the same shop. It's in one of the pockets against his thigh in his military-style hunting trousers: light, but he can feel it. He is armed.

A jay warns the others from the woods.

His ears prick to it, as in hunting days. He still has his gun at home, not touched now for four or five years, not even for the rabbits. It belonged to his father. One day he's going to dismantle it and oil it and put it back together again and shoot Marcel Lagrange. This is the fantasy he plays with in his thoughts for the fifteen minutes it takes him to fiddle about with the fence and the watering and the pool. The pool is slipping back to being green, a very diluted *menthe*, even though the filtering system is working. The English haven't done what he asked. He tests it: normal. That's not good, if it goes green for no reason. If it gets worse, he won't see her swimming for a few days at least. He thinks he sees tendrils of slime waving around the base of the filter.

He wants to see her again, suddenly – not close up and clothed, but secretly and distant and naked. It is the most valuable thing in his life, apart from the monument. And the two are linked by her. He can barely stand the idea of sinking to the normal level of life and talking to her about the house, jobs, the lawn, the pool, her mouth struggling with her bad French, her eyes looking impatiently at him.

The pool is in the balance, if he doesn't pour the chemicals in it might turn to pea soup by tomorrow and then take several days to return to transparency. As it is, he'll have to warn her not to swim for the next two days.

He stares at the water from the end of the pool nearest the woods: most of the liquid rectangle is white sky, interrupted by the dark line of the roof further up, the blackness of the house tipped upside down. He remembers swimming in the rivers, the pools that streams make, when he was a kid; there was something in him that was afraid of the depths, the slimy weeds that clung to your legs, the deep invisible pike. The same spots are no good now, there's less water and the rivers are lower and the pools are mostly standing and stagnant by early July. He hasn't swum in years.

He could give it a dose of copper sulphate and shock it with granules of chlorine, but he's no expert. That would condemn it for a couple of days. He can't not tell her. She might swallow some, or get a rash on her beautiful face. But how can he tell her without his voice trembling, giving away the fact that he knows she's been using the pool?

A breeze gets up and gusts over the water, combing all the shapes away in one sweep. When it settles he notices a big bird on the upside-down roof, a hunched silhouette like a vulture.

He looks up. It's not a bird: it's a human being.

He can't move a finger. His neck has seized.

The silhouette surveys him. His heart and lungs are confusing themselves. He forces himself to lower his head and looks only at the reflection. The main thing with ghosts is never to catch them in the eye, even if the eyes are not visible. He calls on Oncle Fernand and the Virgin to help him, to keep him from harm. But he has abandoned her Son. He doesn't know if the Virgin would want to help him. Oncle Fernand is out.

Someone (he noticed earlier) has taken the new cardousso off the front door: only the old, broken one is left. That's not enough. That's no protection at all.

But he prays, nevertheless, and the ghost of Raoul disappears, seems to grow smaller and melt into the roof. Jean-Luc lifts his head slowly to check. Nothing but the crest of the roof against the white sky. Jean-Luc squints to see better, to lighten the shadow. The bird has flown. He has trouble swallowing. He glances all around him and looks up again and then something, some pale and spectral movement, catches his terrified attention lower down, where the sunlight deepens the shadow over the back of the house: the cobwebs on the back door are fluttering, half-broken. This scares Jean-Luc almost more than the ghost of Raoul Lagrange, because Raoul was always nice to him. As nice as his brother is nasty.

Except that now, Raoul is Jean-Luc's rival. Jealousy is a bitter thing.

There's a munching of tyres on gravel as the car stops. The family are back.

The girls play near him as he stacks stones by the tumbled wall: he plans to attack it before the summer, but time is running out. They are building a hide-out on the edge of the woods, with their father's permission. He thinks they look healthier than when he first saw them. They wave to him, chattering, a few metres off.

He strolls up to look. The girls stand in the camp, a ridge of dead leaves, as if posing for a photograph. His new throw-away camera is in his pocket and he takes it out, surprising them. They laugh and so does he. The two eldest stand like policemen, the youngest is hiding her face. Two, three, four clicks, just a simple press of the finger: it thrills him, the way it works again, the way he shoots them and they get sucked into the camera to wait there until the laboratory does its bit and sends him the plastic envelope to open like the best present in the world. The middle one grabs the young one by the wrist, shaking it, trying to get her to look at the camera. They all laugh and then the youngest one points.

Their mother is walking towards them slowly from the house with her arms folded. Her face is divided in two: the top half is frowning and the bottom is smiling. He is embarrassed to see her, of course. He avoids her eyes as he goes back to stack the stones. She stands at a little distance and watches the children, who continue making the den. He is conscious of the sound of the stones clipping on each other as he stacks them in their various piles, small and medium and large, like the uneven beat of his own heart.

He remembers he has to tell her about the chemicals in the pool. He hurries up to the shed and takes out the plastic canisters and starts tipping the chemicals into the pool before she goes back inside; as the copper sulphate gurgles out of the bottle and spreads in curls of blue through the water, she turns and watches. He knows she'll come over and she does. She's like the little inquisitive robin. His heart warms to her, but all he does is acknowledge her with a nod. He can't help it, he's flushing so hot he has to wipe his brow on his sleeve.

She says, in her poor French, how toxic the chemicals look. All he has to do is say yes, they are, but after a couple of days the poisons are dispersed. So he says it. Then it's fine to swim, if we have to do this in the summer? Yes, he says. Come the summer, he goes on, he'll make sure he tells her when the treatment is done. His ears feel blocked with the rushing of blood: it's as if this conversation is not taking place right here and now.

He looks after her as she walks away, her arms still folded, the body he's so familiar with hidden by her clothes. The worst and best part being that she doesn't know.

He grows closer and closer to her over the next couple of weeks; especially when using the binoculars, with their nice leather smell reminding him of the animal skins stretched out at home in his father's time. Most days he has come up to the thickening spurge behind the hut, even if she only swims two or three times a week. He never forgets his brush knife, laying it within easy reach in case he needs an excuse for being here, ready to act the gardener and start cutting. One day she came out early but got straight into the car. She didn't come back, although he waited two or three hours. He wondered if she had left her husband. But no, two days later he watched and she came out of the house as good as new and swam. The ghost of Raoul Lagrange has not appeared again on the roof, although he keeps checking.

Today there is a violent, cold mistral and her appearance is unexpected. The overloaded stems of spurge splay and shift in the gusts. He has to be careful. The wind excites him. She strips, shivering, and he takes another picture to add to his collection as he'd once collect pebbles or moths.

There is an explosion of glitter and the sound of splashing, faint on the wind. It must be very cold in there, he thinks. It must be very cold against her bare skin, against the nipples on her breasts and the soft furry kitten below that he strokes in his dreams so that it purrs and purrs.

The low, uncertain sun flares off the water as it moves, so all he can see of her body is a dark shape among the flashes, a shadow that changes to white then back to black, until she turns at the end and swims in his direction, towards the woods. Then he can see her face chinning the water. It always looks surprised, happy and surprised at the same time. Ten lengths, no more nor less.

He takes another photograph as she climbs out. He takes no more than one or two each time. There are twenty-seven exposures and there are only thirteen remaining. Soon, he thinks, he won't bother at all and just take them with his brain.

She gleams all over, hugging herself. Then she straightens up side-on to him and spreads her arms wide like wings, with the sun full on her. She is still shivering, though. He can see tiny droplets winking all over her pale body. She has her eyes closed. The spurge sways again in a violent buffet and she gives a little delighted gasp. The kitten has glittery droplets on its head.

When the stems that hide him shift, he feels the early sun glancing off his face, spotting it and leaving dark marks on his vision. He wants to see the goosepimples on her skin and grabs the binoculars too eagerly before he's properly put the camera back in his top pocket; the camera falls down the front of his jacket as if down a cliff and clips a big stone with a surprisingly sharp report. His father always warned him about getting careless, when they were hunting together: in all the excitement of it.

She looks up and her mouth drops open under a puzzled frown.

She's looking straight at him with her black eyes, right through the swaying stems of spurge as if she's taking time to understand. She hides her breasts with an arm, squashing them.

He is stupefied. His heart pounds in his head, on the side of his head in the vein which is the only part of him moving, the rest of him hunter-still. Then her creased-up eyes shift slightly to the left and a bit further and he realises she has not separated him out from the plants after all, despite the early sunlight spotting him. He lets his breath out soundlessly. He must be invisible, he must have become the plants.

He sees her bend down to where her towel lies in a heap and reach for something spindly, putting it on her face; she straightens up with her spectacles on her nose, one lens flashing the sun in his eyes as she turns towards him.

He twists round and reaches for the brush knife in one dazed movement and then bursts clear with his back to her and begins hacking at the undergrowth behind the hut, at the tall, heavy-headed, milk-fat spurge.

He's the gardener. He ignores the clots and dribbles landing in gobs on his clothes and face as if he's being spat at. Never in his life would he normally have cut into spurge like this and the milk-sap is everywhere, as if a goat's udder has exploded. Beyond everything he can hear his father shouting at him, furious and scared, as he pants and grunts.

He waits for her voice behind him but it doesn't come. He goes on hacking without thought until that which is stinging is just that and storms into his brain and becomes the serpent.

Can eyes hiss? Jean-Luc's are hissing. He presses the flat of his palms against his sockets and bends right over but nothing quietens them and yet he still doesn't howl. It is something else that is howling into the air from his mouth.

Sarah grabbed at her little heap of clothes and pressed them against her as she backed off.

The undergrowth beyond the pool-shed had exploded into a man.

She wasn't sure who the man was but he was dressed like a soldier and he was crazed, he was swinging something like a machete with his back to her. She wanted to run but her legs had jellified, all she could do was back off step by step towards the house with her clothes pressed against her nakedness. It was so extraordinary, the sudden irruption of this terrible figure, that she considered herself in a kind of parallel existence from which she was observing the action unfold.

She could hear him grunting with effort, the plants falling with a rustle, the light smack of the blade as it flashed and made contact over and over; she could hear her own breathing as she walked backwards on trembling legs, leaving the pool-side and reaching the rough ground that was uncomfortable against her bare feet in this other universe. She felt she might reach the house unseen, that the man hadn't yet seen her although she knew elsewhere that he had been watching her, that this was as old as myth and would end badly for one or the other of them. She had met women in the Congo who had been raped by rebels or government troops or coltan miners, who had colostomy bags tied to their waists because of the damage done to their insides with bayonets or pieces of wood, and now they came vividly into her mind and she felt terrified again. She'd loved the forest in the Congo, it might have been a kind of teeming, humid paradise, but instead it had been made a hell.

This paradise had also been made hell in a matter of seconds – it was all the same: paradise, hell. Her legs were weak but she was almost there, crouched and stepping backwards with her clothes bundled against her, the huge stone wall of the side of the house beside her, the door just a few yards further, her children inside and the madman with the machete without.

She must scream for Nick, he must phone the police from the chair in the bathroom, she had forgotten the number, she should have written the number down precisely for this kind of eventuality in this remote place.

The man like a white mercenary had stopped swinging his machete. He was very still, bent over with his back to her – even from this distance she could see him clearly because the plants were now gone and the early sunlight splattered his tunic.

And then something between a whoop and a howl went up, freezing her before she got to the door.

The man went *yai-yai-yai-yai*, covering his face, and then howled in short, angry bursts, like a monkey defending its territory. He was mad. He had dropped his machete. He wasn't a killer or a rapist, he was Jean-Luc the handyman, staggering out with his hands pressed to his face, stumbling out towards the pool, blinded as if by some unearthly force of retribution.

THIRTEEN

Afterwards, Nick was to ask her why she hadn't at least pulled her knickers on. He was intrigued, not worried. 'I mean,' he added jocularly, 'I'm only asking from my metaposition as object-ive historian, not as interested husband.'

'I didn't have time, is the short answer. I thought the priority was to get him out of the water. And there is no metaposition. Only overlap.'

'Problematised metaposition,' he clarified.

The fact is, she didn't think. There were no priorities. There was only the action, the instinct. She had been in the netball team at school: the instinctive dart forward, the thrust, the body calculating height with its labyrinth of muscle and tendon before you knew you even had to jump. Nick had been bad at sports, shambling about the muddy field on his long legs. Even the running track had foxed him: he'd thought too much on the way instead of blanking everything out but the finishing line.

Once, while taking the art-club painting class in her enthu-siastic first year at Cambridge, the stark-naked life model – a good-looking guy in his late twenties with an improbably large willy – had wandered about in the breaks checking out the efforts, munching on his apple among the clothed without a care in the world. No one commented or turned a hair: but he didn't come back – the more radical feminists in the group had decided he was an exhibitionist, taking advantage of them, appropriating their space.

'It's all context,' she explained, rather needlessly. 'While he was posing, it was acceptable. But he crossed the invisible line, he entered the real world. He should have put on the dressing gown supplied.'

'How does this apply to our impromptu bather?'

'Let me think, Dr Mallinson. OK, I suppose what I'm saying is that in an emergency, the rules change. You don't notice. I didn't actually notice I was still at the birthday-suit stage. It must have looked fairly weird, like a scene from *Carry On Camping* or something. And I can tell you: I could hardly pull my knickers back on for the goose-bumps.'

Nick smiled: 'I think you being naked makes it Greek and heroic, rather than comic.'

'Wild differences of interpretation, as you would say yourself.'

All she'd had time for was to shout out a warning as Jean-Luc had advanced like a drunk towards the water, going *yai-yai-yai-yai*.

He'd toppled in like a felled tree; the splash had seemed to drill each of its white pips into the air in slow motion. She dropped her clothes – knickers, bra, shirt, socks, jeans, sweater – where she stood and darted forwards across the yard to try to help as the water slapped vigorously at the sides like applause. She was only aware of a film of cold covering her bare skin, particularly over her buttocks.

He seemed to be below the level of the water, his hair like a giant black sea-urchin. He might well have been surfacing, he might have made it out onto the side himself, without her help. She nearly fell in herself, reaching from the side for his shoulders and clasping the thick wet cloth of his tunic, pulling as hard as she could.

His hands began to move under the water, propelling him in the right direction so that his dead weight lessened. His face was above the water and somehow huger, like a giant's face, sheened with water and bright with cold. It struck her as being repellently physical, perhaps because his bent nose was streaming and his eyes were shut and in his open mouth she could see old fillings, strings of saliva or water connecting his bruised-looking lips, the unshaven little bristle-patches under each nostril that careless men never bother with but look so awful.

He was groaning rather than spluttering, so maybe in the end her efforts, which were in her view considerable and put at least one vertebra out in her back and strained a muscle in her right shoulder, were not essential. Whatever the facts, he didn't drown, but by the time he'd heaved himself out she had gained an impression of great weight caused by the water soaking his clothes, which was what she remembered about her swimming lessons, when the whole class had had to swim in their old clothes and learn how to hold someone in difficulties under the chin.

The real thing was confusing and messy, though; and embarrassing – not necessarily because she was starkers. She blushed when she thought about it, afterwards; the way she had shouted and flapped around him like a feeble bird, pulling not on his body but on his camouflage jacket so that it rose above his head until he'd managed to reach the side himself and she'd realised she was making things worse, and had let go, proffering only a hand in case he slipped back under.

When he sat on the side and opened his eyes, she was shocked; his eyes were red and swollen from the chlorine, as unseeing as a blind man's. For an instant of madness she thought she might have been too late, that he was in fact drowned and had turned into a zombie. He was in pain, though, and zombies never feel pain.

'*C'est les plantes,*' he groaned. '*Merde, putain, ces putains de plantes! Yai-yai-yai!*'

She understood, eventually: there were purplish patches on his hands and his face, the purple moving around strangely on the fish-cold surface of his skin. He flapped his hand as if expressing amazement, over and over. He was being rather brave. Sarah knew about the toxicity of oleanders, but not about those big, innocent-looking weeds. Supposing the girls had tried to pick them? They were pretty enough, in a clumsy sort of way. No, they were quite ugly, from another angle. Now they were almost all dealt with, anyway.

She told him in her turbid French that she was going to get dressed, and ran over to her clothes dumped near the door and pulled them on, while he just sat in a spreading glint of water on the side of the pool, shivering in the sharp, unpleasant gusts. He moaned as if in grief, forehead resting on his knees.

Once she was decent, she came back to his side and made him stop rubbing his eyes by pulling his hands away. His fluttering eyelids were even more puffed up, the eyeballs filmed over. Holding onto his wrist as he stood, she then guided him to the house. He was whimpering, now, holding his head down. Her hair was wetting her sweater's collar unpleasantly.

She felt the stiffness in his whole body through his wrist, the way he resisted her and then relented, letting her guide him, trusting her like a little boy. But when she considered the way he had been with her little girls and then today, skulking in the underbrush while she was bathing naked, she thought of him again as menacing. It was odd, leading someone menacing by the hand, like a child.

She didn't say anything about the menacing side to Nick, who was scratching his head sleepily when she burst into the bedroom to announce the emergency. All she told him was that Jean-Luc had lesions in his eyes from cutting the wrong plant. She knew the word 'lesions' from her child's emergency first-aid book, and it made her feel she was more in control of the situation.

'He's keeping his head under the kitchen tap, but it's not getting better. I think the chlorine made it worse.'

'Like sow thistles,' Nick remarked, hastily pulling on his trousers. 'I'll always remember that from school. The old field behind the pavilion, cutting sow thistles with our penknives then flicking them at the enemy ranks. And that itching powder stuff from the hedges. Great fun!'

'Whatever,' said Sarah, suddenly desperate for tea. 'That was boarding school, this is normal life.'

★   ★   ★

Nick drove him to the hospital in St-Maurice, while she had a hot shower. Jean-Luc had held his face under the kitchen tap for ages but his eyes were worse: the lids looked as if they were turned over and might burst in a spray of blood, while the eyeballs themselves were a filigree of tiny wriggling veins like an elaborate brooch in which the dark iris sat like a mute stone. His large knuckles were encircled in violent purple blotches, as if he'd been crushing blackberries.

The girls had stayed asleep throughout. She'd had a vague hope that the action might have brought Jamie down to help, but it hadn't. Jamie had been tenaciously semi-absent for the last two weeks, appearing at odd times to raid the fridge (they had padlocked the wine cellar). He'd carry a fragrance of woodsmoke, paraffin and cannabis, and would sleep for twelve hours in his cosy den of an attic: say, from nine in the morning to nine at night. He was living some parallel life. Reasonably friendly, he kept his other life a secret. The babysitting deal had been forgotten. Sarah was oddly unconcerned; she had placed Jamie in a part of her mind that was sealed off from the rest, like something boxed in lead.

Right now he was up in the attic, in a sleep phase. One day soon, perhaps tomorrow, Jamie would leave entirely, only to pop up again at Helena's cottage in Wales with wild stories of his father's and his stepmother's wickedness, merrily rewriting history, building castles of fantasy in some murky corner of his brain radioactive with jealousy and loathing. And Helena, as before, would write nasty, accusing emails to which the only possible reply was silence. Meanwhile they would have to clean up the mess in his den, empty the pan of stale piss, open the windows wide to release the stink. It was always like scouring out some underground animal's lair. That one day he would grow out of it, find a job, become an upright citizen and make lots of money, seemed less of a forlorn hope than that they would succeed in embracing his present self with the arms of selfless, parental love.

She occupied herself after the drama by cutting out paper

fish with the girls, because it was April Fool's Day later in the week and the French secretly stuck fish on each other's backs with sellotape, shouting out *Poisson d'avril* when the victims realised. They were looking up names of fish and writing them on the cut-outs in both English and French as an educational addition. Sarah felt Alicia and Tammy were advancing in leaps and bounds with their erratic home-learning: they were doing no more than two hours a day of actual 'classes' with either her or Nick, but it was peculiarly effective.

Goldfish. *Poisson Rouge*.

'Red's not gold,' said Alicia. They looked up 'gold'.

Shark. *Requin*.

She herself was walking about with a crab-shape that said *I Hate Jamie* scotched permanently on her back, and Jamie no doubt felt the same.

'Hate is such a strong word,' her hate-filled mother would always say.

This ugly part of Sarah that hated her stepson caused her to doubt herself. It undermined her self-belief: the objective, dispassionate historian. Jamie lurked in her mind: deep, almost recondite. Compared to Jamie, Jean-Luc was a paper fish that could be torn off.

'I met Georges Chambord in St-Maurice and had a wonder-fully intense chat,' said Nick, as they sat down to supper. 'He said that life consists of three things, like a game of poker: luck, strategy and guile. *Le hasard, la stratégie, et la ruse.* I had to look up *ruse*, because "ruse" isn't right. Guile, trickery. Good, hm? He's invited us to dinner on Friday, by the way.'

'Not with Des the Res, I hope.'

'Oh, presumably not.'

Jean-Luc hovered over their conversation, tainting it. By the end of the meal he was firmly squatting between them.

'As I've reiterated several times,' Nick sighed, 'he may simply have been birdwatching. He was coming here to do some work anyway and arrived early to bird watch. And got incredibly embarrassed. Although the absence of his van or mobilette, that's a weeny bit suspicious. Anyway, let's not think about causation before the evidence is absolutely solid. Or as solid as anything can be in this world of *apparence*.'

'Sometimes,' said Sarah, after a moment, 'I think Peter's sobriquet for you is rather a good one.'

'I don't want to know.'

'The Tortoise,' she said.

'I can think of worse,' Nick sighed, after a moment's silence. He was amazed at the way, whenever Peter Osterhauser's name was mentioned, a kind of flat-fish of venom would flip in his chest. Occasionally he would imagine himself as a professor in somewhere like Freiburg in the late 1930s, and Peter as a Jewish colleague. How hard not to have denounced him, or at least watched the poor man being taken away and not felt relish. The Tortoise!

He'd put a Yusef Lateef CD on the hi-fi: the sax skittered about over the urgent drums. Very urban, very somewhere else. He should, Nick thought, have become a jazz drummer. Jazz was utterly of the present moment. It was life itself. Professor Osterhauser played classical viola. Nick played CDs. The Smiths. The Bobo Stenson Trio.

'I don't see Tortoise,' he said, eventually. 'I don't get it.'

Sarah pulled a face, absently staring at the fire. She didn't like jazz very much. She always saw polished Fifties cars gleaming in rain under streetlamps.

'There isn't worse,' he all but pleaded. 'Is there?'

'Buttered Scone?'

'What?'

'A play on Mallinson. It's slang for number one in Bingo, apparently.'

'And so?' Nick's heart was hammering in anticipation: he could hear Peter's simpering laugh, like a bus's air-brakes.

'I'm not sure. A sort of cluster of subtle meanings, double-entendres. You know what he's like.'

'Like the Bourbons, like Jamie, he learns nothing and he forgets nothing.'

'It's not important, Nick. I think we should concentrate on the problem in hand. Can we change the music?'

'We've concentrated all day,' he replied, gloomily picturing his colleagues swapping nicknames for him in the buttery, spinning falsities about him in the dark corridors and dining halls of Fitzherbert College, panelled and floored with countless acres of English oak or plundered African mahogany. Really, it was just a miasma of jealous bickerings overlaid with a sheen of intellect. Dark castles of fantasy.

'Anyway,' he went on, 'at the risk of you calling me more names, I still think we should sift the evidence first.'

'Yes, Mr Holmes.'

They had sketched out two plausible scenarios over the Jean-Luc incident. Either he was innocent, the binoculars merely for bird-spotting or hunting purposes and the machete-like knife for cutting underbrush; or he was guilty of, at the least, voyeurism. The horrible hunters had binoculars, they had noticed. They had found the binoculars and the big knife amongst the cut plants on Nick's return from the hospital; they were careful not to touch the spattered traces of sap, still milky and wet in places.

As Nick's favourite phrase had it, history was 99 per cent lies and 1 per cent the awful truth.

Whatever its truth was, there was an ominous feel to the drama. Genuinely ominous, not as in 'That sounds ominous.' Omen, omened, of good or ill omen, ominous, ominously, ominousness. From the Latin. He had once written a schoolboy talk on historical omens such as comets, and (in the days when he would sit for hours in the school library, wondering what to be, educating himself into donhood) had been struck by the change of letter from 'e' to 'i': why did it change? Such things would beguile him back then. A strange boy, he supposed now, if he could meet him.

That's why he'd put on the jazz. Jazz was the opposite of ominous.

Jean-Luc would not be blind for ever, the hospital doctor had said. The poor man had to sport rather natty aviator-type dark glasses that changed his appearance entirely. He looked like a fashion victim, Nick joked. They had joked rather a lot about an incident that was full of pain and shame. Nick had been initially amazed to hear that Sarah had been secretly skinny-dipping.

'Perhaps you were making love with the gardener in the spurge,' he'd joked. '*The Gardener in the Spurge,*' he repeated, in a breathy, dramatic manner.

'Yup, and that's why he fell into the pool.'

'Water sports?'

Not just ominousness, but unpleasantness. Something soiled, even in the jokes. Something lost for good.

'There is this kind of burlesque side to it all,' he mused. 'There always is, somehow. Maybe not with the Holocaust or carpet bombing or slavery.' He was nodding thoughtfully, frowning a little. Sarah felt shut out, as usual; he was doing this more and more. Prelude to bumbliness. 'I have to say,' he suddenly announced, wide-eyed, 'that when you burst into the bedroom you looked like that famous scene in the James Bond film, when Britt Ekland, if it was Britt Ekland and not Raquel Welch, emerges from the sea with her tee shirt wet. An Aphrodite trope. It had me gagging as a schoolboy, anyway. It *was* James Bond, wasn't it?'

'I wasn't *that* wet,' she laughed.

'Just the hair, maybe.'

After a moment she said: 'I'd already told you I had my doubts about Jean-Luc.' The jazz had come to an end. The quiet was good.

'Meaning?'

She hesitated. Nick was suddenly ready to pounce: he had that glittering, raptor look in his eye. Or maybe it was just the candlelight.

'There's something unstable about him.'

'Evil, you mean. Unstable is just a euphemism.'

'It might not be. Evil is not a concept I trust. Unstable is.'

'For now,' said Nick.

Fifteen love, she thought. Their marriage gave her tennis elbow, an overdeveloped forearm.

Nick, digging in, wondered what she would call Mengele or Klaus Barbie. Unstable? Can you be icy and unstable?

'I used to think,' Sarah replied, deflecting his drive, 'that history's villains looked villainous. Then there was this silly thing on telly where they removed Hitler's moustache and no one recognised him; they all thought he looked trustworthy and rather sweet.' She chuckled, resting her chin on her knuckles. Nick nodded thoughtfully, finding her particularly beautiful like that.

'Hitler plus moustache definitely looks psychotic,' he said. 'Those eyebags. A bit like Saddam's. The strain of gorging with Old Nick,' he added, gamely smoothing his own pouches.

'Mao?'

'Baby face. Like a balloon with the features scribbled on. Creepy.'

She relaxed: he was enjoying the game, now. She proffered Stalin – a tricky one. He got up to change the music. Although it was not yet the right day, he had a large red-and-blue fish sellotaped to his back, flapping rather realistically. *COD*, Alicia had written across it, unaware of the pun.

'What you don't see in black and white is his yellow eyes,' he stated, sitting down again, the troubadours bewailing their impossible love behind. 'Just the avuncular grin and Dunhill pipe. This is a bit like that Monty Python cricket match.'

'Before my time,' she said. Advantage Sarah. 'Robespierre?'

'A repressed homosexual, foppish, hated smells, finicky, very pale. Not nice, despite a good start.'

'Whoo-er,' she said. 'Careful. Here's the man who supported an elective called Queer Theory?'

'Which brings us round to Jean-Luc,' he declared, with a satisfied smile she didn't like.

'Actually, I think you're way off beam there,' she said, the wine filling her head with a pleasant devil-may-care attitude to the match. 'I think he likes girls a *lot*, big or little, in skirts or out.'

'Ri-ight,' said Nick, nodding knowingly, with a possible tint of the sardonic that lit the electric grille in Sarah's chest. His lips pursed as he pondered. She felt cheap, in some way. She felt like hitting him over the head: she hated it when he pondered. He seemed to retreat, become someone else completely unattractive. A turn-off. She heard her own words echoing: cheap magazine stuff. It was such an effort not to sound like a cheap magazine, day in day out. Not to be her natural self, if that *was* her natural self. Sometimes she wish she'd married a businessman.

'So that's the final conclusion,' he murmured.

'There may be other unthought-of possibilities,' she said, quoting one of Nick's staple reflections as an historian. He smiled, and they caught each other's eye.

Of *course* she loved him. Together they had developed their own past, their own history. They could refer to it, even in irony, and no one else would understand. The silly little things, not just the earnest discussions about Fredric Jameson or Foucault.

'By the way,' said Nick, taking her hand, 'you've got what looks like a rotten turbot stuck on your back.'

Alan called out from the kitchen, where he had taken the call.

'Jean-Luc's had an accident.'

'Why? I mean how? Oh Lord.'

'Not fatal,' he cried. 'Just uncomfortable. A work accident. Hey, like the Crucifixion. That was also a work accident.'

He appeared in the doorway, beaming. 'Great joke, huh? This ex-Jesuit told it me. The Crucifixion –'

'Alan, breathe deeply. Think of your heart. Start again. Jean-Luc.' She was working on a gallery poster at the dining room table; she enjoyed the interruption.

'They think he was spying on Mrs Fusspot taking a skin-dip.'

'And? Oh God. Fallen off a ladder?'

'He was out with his brush knife, cutting back that plant that spits milk in your eyes and burns them hollow.'

'Spurge?'

'Or so he said. Do you need a pair of binos for clearing brush?'

'Oh, he's so silly. Silly man. They're all so ignorant.'

'They had to call an ambulance. He also had a brief encounter with the pool, unconnected with any leisure activity.'

'Lord, not drowned?'

'I think if he had been drowned I would have said that first, Lucy my lovely.'

'Not necessarily. Oh, shit. Blinded?'

'Temporarily. Burns to both eyeballs. The punishment matches the crime, I say. It's mythical. That goddess spied on. Jesus, which one? Begins with A. I'm losing it.'

'Arachne.'

'She's spiders.'

'Sounds more like a Mills & Boon,' said Lucy, who had once tried her hand at writing one in a financial lull and miserably failed. 'Isn't that how they're always punished in Mills & Boon?'

'You're thinking of Shakespeare,' said Alan. 'Or maybe Charlotte Brontë. Anyway, the goddess pulled him out, this time.'

Lucy stared at him, open-mouthed. 'Did he fall in? Or jump in?'

'Maybe he's Narcissus,' said Alan, brightly. 'Or Tiresias. Tiresias was blind, with wrinkled dugs.'

He stepped behind her and cupped his wife's breasts.

'Mine are not wrinkled,' she said, kissing his wrists. 'They have just seen better days.' The options for the new gallery poster were cool or violent. Neither pleased her. A third way – tasteful – was boring. It was vital to get it right. No artist was good enough, that was the trouble. Not one had any sincerity, it was all fake. 'Alan, you're teasing. It's too cold to swim, even for goddesses, naked or otherwise.'

He gave each concealed husk a gentle squeeze, as best he could, then moved away. In the old days she'd go without a bra and you couldn't tell.

'I am not teasing you, my angry queen. For once I am deadly *sérieux*.'

Lucy leaned forwards in the chair, hands between her thighs, sloping-shouldered. 'Fuck,' she said. 'More detail, please.'

Blindness terrified her. She required a cigarette. She had given up years ago, but the craving came and went and came again. It was a poison in her blood. It would never go completely. She had once, as a child, pricked her eyeball cutting roses, prior to boiling the petals in a forlorn attempt to make perfume for her mother, and had seen double for several days.

'There is no more detail,' said Alan, flipping an eraser on the back of his hand. 'There's only broad-stroke. I had the husband on the phone. He's crazy but he's a bright guy. He was very diplomatic, *très discret*.'

'Please stop talking French when you can't.'

'I have to start somewhere. Hey, he also claimed that Jean-Luc was pretty forward with their little girls. Picking them up and so forth. Nothing dramatic, though. They just had this hunch and then the voyeur struck.'

'What drivel,' said Lucy, as if Alan had filled her in minutely. 'Jean-Luc is French. The French admire attractive women and smile at children. It's normal. That's why I like going to France – men look at me.'

'Do they?'

'Don't sound surprised, Alan. Any moment now the last one will stop looking at me and no man will ever look at me again. Mrs Fusspot is pretty in an unambitious way, you said so yourself. It doesn't mean they're all rapists and paedophiliacs.'

'Paedophiles. I think this was more than Jean-Luc being avuncular. I think this was a lot like Jean-Luc being a complex of sinister, concealed desires.'

Alan was enjoying himself. He enjoyed the way the phrase about sinister desires moulded itself in his mouth, reminding him of his fine-tuned intelligence, his mastery of the word. He had long wanted to get rid of the guy, of whom he was weirdly jealous. Lucy was obsessed; he sometimes wondered if she and the handyman didn't fuck like monkeys in the barn when he – Alan – was out doing some dull, manly chore like taking out garbage to the end of the dirt road. The eraser bounced on the floor in that manic way of erasers and disappeared under the desk.

Lucy said nothing. She was staring down at a blood-red, silk-screened slice of apple with *moral indignation* and *good intentions* serendipitously scrawled across it in lime green. All so retro. Everything went in circles. Nothing progressed. Almost no men, in fact, now looked at her. She tapped the blank part of the mock-up where *Lucinda Gallery* was to appear in civilised dove-grey. She imagined the gendarmes arriving with squealing tyres, screams and yells, Jean-Luc bundled away under a blanket, the dreadful, soppy English family simpering in the house, clutching each other, so fiercely righteous and Victorian.

A harp played gently from the speakers, the sun was falling on polished surfaces, Alan had been grinding his coffee beans and sweetening the air, but elsewhere an angry knot of disaster scribbled itself. She lacked the thew to deal with it. She was fifty-nine. Her entire female reproductive apparatus had been removed five years ago. There was now nothing but air between her and sixty.

'I lack the thew,' she murmured. 'Did you mumble something about binoculars, Alan?'

'You know I never mumble, my sylph. Apart from maybe or maybe not molesting their little threesome, he had these binos. He spied on Mrs Fusspot taking a dip, stark naked. Imagine that. Imagine that woman stark naked. Svelte and small and dark. Yum yum.'

'State what happened again, sweetheart,' said Lucy, glumly, 'but without the lasciviousness. There are facts that have escaped me.'

Alan told her. Jean-Luc had watched Yum-Yum with his hunting binos and she'd spotted him and so he'd pretended to be cutting back the undergrowth with his brush knife. Yum-

Yum pretended she believed him, because she was scared he might go crazy and chop her up into juicy pieces. And then he'd got splashed by the milk. 'That was not pretending,' he added, with a throaty chortle.

And then he'd fallen in, but only temporarily.

Alan thrived on this sort of thing. He hadn't even bothered to dress this morning. He took calls in his long Arab pyjamas that hung off his stomach like a frock. He was on great form. He was moving out of Sumeria and Babylonia and Assyria as fast as his camel would take him, he'd joke, even if a little man were to offer him the equivalent of the Royal Graves of Ur in a backstreet shack.

He had always been nimble, despite his belly. If you follow the money you have to dance. He had started his career at high school, not in pictures but in books. He bought old childrens' books for peanuts and dismembered them, framed the illustrations and sold them at great profit: ten, twenty dollars. Then, later, it was older books. Really old books. Seventeenth century and earlier. Parchment. Medieval manuscripts. A wealth of illuminated pages turned to pictures for the walls of the rich. Collectors flocked over Alan like terns over herring.

You have to swerve in a ball game: he swerved, sprang out of medieval, scored with modern. His pure abstract period was a ball. He just followed the dollars. All-white canvases. Canvases that were just that: canvas. The world could not be fooled forever; he knew the bottom would fall out of abstract before it happened: he swivelled into Central African for about two days – it was too late, too many fakes – then into Near and Middle Eastern. Jackpot every time. You pulled the handle and stuck your hand out and something ancient dropped into it: cylinder seals, mostly, but who cares? It was an income stream. And then one day you see the most beautiful woman you have ever seen, in white marble. From Ur.

But even she was not worth his life or losing parts of his body for.

In the world according to Zig, Art Brut was beginning to

smell of crisp new bills of serious denominations. Get these words, Alan: figurative, emotion, narrative, honesty, natural, weird. Alan had worked the Art Brut scene for a week and was already more of an expert than Zig. At least when it came to prices, sources, contacts, and the names that mattered. The prices were stirring, on the rise, about to soar.

'Oh,' he kept saying to Lucy, 'there is something so comforting about artists who do not know they are artists.'

'That's because they aren't,' she'd reply.

It was Oz instead of LA. Art Brut was a kind of paradise filled with shaggy-haired mutes, wise-eyed grandmas and apple-pie hermits with lovable obsessions. There was once a postman who built a full-size imperial palace out of pebbles picked up on his round.

You discovered it for free. One hundred per cent profit on your returns. He had clients for whom he was only investing, buying and selling, who had no interest in art; they would leap at this. They would really leap.

She had never seen Alan so animated. It was second-life syndrome. He'd gone from hell to heaven, from Iraq to Oz, in so many hours. No mysterious midnight calls, no threatening emails, no heart flutters. Just a call from the wretched fusspots at Les Fosses, which seemed to delight him even more.

'We'll have to go down for a couple of days and sort them out,' she sighed. 'A break from London and its intrinsic malaise. We'll have to extract the key from the silly man.'

'I believe you can hire a contract killer for £2000,' Alan wheezed. 'Five hundred extra for a touch of torture before-hand. Bullets thrown in. Seriously.'

'And where did you find that out?' she smiled, stroking his hand.

'My friend from Bucharest.'

She pursed her lips before planting them on his knuckles. 'Bucharest. Now which part of London is that?'

'It used to be called Hammersmith.'

'No no, that's Cracow. Maybe it'll be on the news,' she

continued, now squeezing his hand quite hard, 'and there'll be shots of Les Fosses. Maybe she'll bring charges and the cops will have to search the house from top to bottom. Take it apart. Lots of attention. You know what they're like.'

She felt Alan's hand quiver under hers. He was deathly pale around the jowls. In one of the *caves*, the smallest one, locked with a combination padlock, lay the large metal box marked BOOKS. He muttered about it in his sleep. One layer of lousy novels and then the treasure, nestling there in Lucy's silk off-cuts; most of it having seeped, like scent gathered from the steam of boiled roses, out of the National Museum of Iraq about a month before the invasion. Chucked down the stairs, actually, judging from the fresh chips. His chief Dubai contact, the guy with the glass eye, had watched it happen. And was now dead.

'Promise me you are joking, Lucy.'

'Now there's a change of weather,' she said, on top of things again. 'That's why we need to go down, my big baby. Apart from paying poor Jean-Luc a visit and pinching him all over, silly boy.'

'Go down?'

'Go down Moses, go down,' she began to sing, smoothing out the poster mock-up unnecessarily.

The truth was, she was not surprised. The way Jean-Luc would look at her out of the corner of his eye when she was lying by the side of the pool, or bathing in her black two-piece. Flattering, at her age. 'Damage limitation. A little talk. Anyway, I want to see how my lovely English lawn's getting on. Before it's trampled by the media hordes.'

Alan groaned theatrically, drawing his bunched hands down his face as if peeling off a mask. 'Now I'm tense as hell,' he admitted. Over London's hum, a distant cluster of sirens sounded and swelled.

'Here they come,' joked Lucy, breaking into one of her more appealing laughs.

* * *

Apart from the casual information that Jean-Luc had hurt his eyes, the children had been kept entirely in the dark, which made Tammy's interrogation of her parents all the more surprising. A couple of days later she fell on their bed face forward before Beans and Alicia woke up, and talked into the bedclothes. They were sipping their tea in bed, reading.

'Has Jean-Luc stolen something, Mummy?'

'Why on earth do you say that?'

'Because I think he's done something naughty.'

'What makes you think that, sweetie? The poor thing's just had an accident.'

'It's the way you say his name. You don't feel sorry for him.'

Nick rolled his eyes.

'Rubbish,' said Sarah. 'Go down and watch a cartoon and stop being silly, Tammy.'

'Want Jamie.'

'He's sleeping, as usual.'

Having inadvertently overheard her parents discussing Jean-Luc in the kitchen, Tammy toyed with the idea of mentioning the big knife, but decided not to. Seized, nevertheless, with a reckless ardour she would not have been able to explain, she asked if he had shown his naughty bits. Since her eight-year-old mind believed babies emerged from the tummy-button, this gave a mistaken impression: her mother looked scared, suddenly.

'Why do you say that, Tammy?'

'Cos.'

'That's not an answer.'

Her father said, with an awkward grunt: 'You're not basing your suggestion on previous observation, I hope?'

'Wha'?'

There was a tense pause. Sarah's hands were nestled around her mug as if it had to be clung to in the whirlpool. Then Tammy started bouncing on the bed on her knees, waggling her head about and singing breathily, all but unvoiced: 'Jean-Luc, Jean-Luc, is showing his poo. Jean-Luc, Jean-Luc . . .'

Nick snapped at her – an unusual occurrence. He told her

to act her age. As she slid off in an unceremonious bundle of hurt, her foot caught on Sarah's tea and spilt it over the duvet.

Soundly yapped at, Tammy plodded down to the sitting room and sobbed on the sofa. Nick eventually joined her, holding her hand and explaining that if Jean-Luc ever showed his naughty bits, she was to say straightaway, but he was sure Jean-Luc would never do something like that.

'He took our photographs.'

'Well, he's allowed to. We're not in your school, here.' He told her that Jean-Luc was out of hospital and staying at home while the lesions got better, that he had to wear special dark glasses like an aviator's goggles.

'What's an aviator?'

'An old-fashioned pilot.'

She withdrew her hand and curled up against the cushions. It was cold. Nick covered her in a throw-over that smelt of dust and smoke and kissed her on the crown of her head, as thoroughly confused as she was.

He had just settled back in bed, reassuring Sarah, when Alicia came in and announced that Beans had jumped out of the window.

'April Fool!' she added, quickly, over the thumps of grown-up feet hitting the floor simultaneously either side of the bed.

Later that day, Tammy was wandering around the pool-shed imagining it as her hovel surrounded by toadstools, to which the prince was about to come and fall in love with her. She saw what she thought was a small box under the raised shed.

It was Jean-Luc's camera, wrapped in its jacket of goldeny card with *Fabriqué en Chine* on the bottom. It rattled when she shook it. The excitement she felt was that of someone who had made a great and secret discovery. She looked through the viewfinder, studied the lens. For some reason the camera had a rubber band round it. She felt she might be rewarded enormous sums, but on second thoughts decided not to tell anyone. She had a small camera of her own, not a digital but a chunky pink waterproof object with which she managed dissatisfying pictures taken so far apart she'd forget what most of them were of. This camera was like the ones they were supposed to take on school trips, because it didn't matter if you lost it. Somewhere inside it were her and her sisters, like miniature people, small as germs. She pointed the camera at the house and pressed the button. When it clicked, she gasped.

She checked Jamie wasn't watching from the roof; he'd wave to her from up there, sometimes. She wasn't to tell her parents he went up on the roof from his window, or they'd stop him. And he could see the sea. He could see further than anyone had ever seen. One day he'd take her up there, too, he'd promised.

He wasn't up there.

She ran into the barn with the camera and showed her sisters. It wasn't an April Fool, it was real. This was the most exciting event in her life so far: even Beans was frozen in wide-eyed appreciation, while Alicia was already contemplating the vast chest they'd have to use to bury it in on the desert island far from home, once they'd worked out a way to get there and back in time for tea and cream cakes. Their urgent whispers were furry little animals that crawled away and hid in the barn's most secret corners.

FOURTEEN

Jean-Luc likes himself in dark glasses.

He is preparing a mint tisane for his mother and the nurse, whom he likes to keep happy; he's afraid the care would be withdrawn otherwise, the patient too difficult. Maman would never agree to moving to a home. Part of him is afraid of her moving to a home, anyway. He can't picture himself alone in the house, for the first time in his life. However hard he tries, he can't picture it.

He thinks dark glasses suit him. He's never worn any in his life, and these are the medical type that go round the side and enclose your eyes entirely, but he likes them after a day or two, they change his face, they make him look powerful and strange in some way. His eyes still sting and feel as if they have crumbs under the lids, but each day they hurt less. It was so terrible to be blind, to think he had blinded himself, that when he realised he could see, in the hospital, he felt he had been given a second life.

She'd guided him by the wrist to the house. He barely recalled falling in the pool: the pain had smothered him and seemed to take him over. He'd felt the pain was a great hand wiggling his arms and bending his body and bursting out of his head.

Then a step that had met nothing and a terrible, icy blast of water so shocking he couldn't breathe. Hands pulling his jacket up beyond his head, making things worse. The blindness and the water combining to hunt him down and kill him.

Then her softness, her smell, her voice. The angel. The guiding angel. Through the agonising fog he'd sensed her as being completely naked, but he now felt that must have been his imagination.

The husband had asked him no questions in the car, where Jean-Luc sat panting in the front, his whole head soaked, hair plastered to his head, red weals appearing on his skin where his body was reacting to the sap. Each time he'd opened his eyes the light was a long blade pressed into the eyeball. It wasn't really light at all.

He'd still thought he was blinded and a terror took hold of him, and then a great sleepiness enfolded him. He'd been walked into the hospital through a galaxy of sounds that seemed to have nothing to do with him, they were voices and noises from somewhere else or from another time. He was entirely separate from everything but the pain, and the pain itself was a tiny beast shaped like the burr of a thistle, burrowing into him. Then the water and the special drops had sluiced it away, only for it to return as something worse, disintegrated into a million crumbs under his eyelids and under several places on his skin, where the burns were small but third-degree, the doctor told him, speaking as if he were deaf. His father had been right to warn him. He had reacted very badly, it was in the family.

He is reasonably sure they won't find the camera. Why should they? It fell into the undergrowth and then he cut the spurge; it would be hidden in the cut stems. As soon as he is better, he will go back and search for it. And the binoculars.

Supposing they *have* found the camera?

The future is as dark as how I see things now, he thinks. It's all up to the gods. The Virgin and the saints. Destiny.

He walks up the stairs carefully and knocks on the door. The nurse tells him to wait. He tries not to think of what is going on in there that is making him wait, but can't help imagining the soiled flesh, the dark-purple rashes, the intimate horrors. He hopes they will open the window, after.

He stands on the little landing holding the two cups in one hand, looking down into the darkness of the steep stairs made darker by his glasses, blurred by the lesions. The ceiling bulb with its faded, fly-blown shade is a dim moon. He can't distinguish the loose and worn lino runner his father had always talked about changing. The walls need a lick, but all he can see is a muddy swirl. His little finger is sticky from the sticky-back plastic that lines the cupboards in the kitchen. They are very old cupboards, painted dark brown, but his father, back in the Sixties, lined them inside – shelves and sides and back – with plastic patterned with big bright flowers. The plastic is peeling off in places, but the stickiness is still on the back. When you reach in, it catches you on the fingers or the side of the hand. One day he will empty the cupboards and strip the plastic away. It will take about half an hour. But then what? He can't picture the cupboards bare of those flowers, those patterns of once-bright petals. The cupboards have been like that ever since he has been on this earth, in the same way their smell never changes: old bread smells mixed up with biscuits and herbs and mice. You can bottle that smell and put it on my grave, he thinks.

Once he dreamt he was following that scent like a hunting dog all the way home; home turned out to be a giant man-size bowl full of washing soda and drowned wasps.

Eventually the door opens. The stink is as thick as slurry, he all but gags. He can't understand how the nurse puts up with it; today it is Colette with the curly orange hair and squashed nose. She takes the cups from him with a wink. She has a loud voice, broken by too much smoking, and a drinker's eyebags. The orange is dye.

Six or seven years ago, before she was nursing his mother, she got drunk at an Aubain *fête* and pulled him from the back of the village hall, where he was helping with the lights in the shadows, and pressed him to her in a slow dance. He tried to free himself at first, but she had a nurse's strong arms and he couldn't use too much force because everyone was watching, and some of them were laughing, although he didn't know if they were laughing at him. She was so drunk she asked him in his ear, after he'd stopped struggling, if he was afraid of women. It was a cool night in late February but he was sweating, his tee shirt clamped to his back. He felt her breasts on his chest, their moistness, and her breath was full of drink and bad teeth, roaring in his ear. He didn't reply, he just waited for the music to stop, but it was a long song by an English singer he recognised from a few years back. His face was in the curls of her fake-orange hair, her thumb stroking the nape of his neck. He kept stepping on her toes.

She asked him to guess her age and he said sixty, because that's what it felt like and because she was from Paris he had no history to go on. She pushed him away, staggering a bit, calling him names, but there were a lot of people about and no one noticed. Raoul Lagrange passed by on his way to the bar and she shouted at Raoul, her face flashing from green to blue to green like a witch's under the coloured lights: 'I'm forty-six! Do I look forty-six or what do I look?' And Raoul Lagrange laughed and put his arm round her and gave her a kiss and said, 'My sweetheart, my lovely, you look twenty-six.' She hugged him back, tight, and he made a funny face. They danced for a bit under the flashing lights, their faces turning blue then green then blue. She had to be carried home. Raoul's funeral was a week later.

Jean-Luc was back in the shadows while they were dancing. He felt sick, her cheap perfume on his clothes, a strand of orange hair on his shoulder, but he busied himself with the lights, the strobe. Fortunately, she has no memory of what happened that night. His own memory is of her warm, moist breasts and the thumb on the nape of his neck, but they are detached from the rest of her. The rest of her makes him want to run off, even now. But he has to keep her happy; she likes her mint tisane.

Now she is ribbing him in her usual way, just adding rubbish about how he looks like a sexy film star in his dark glasses. Or a gangster. She suggests next time he bring up a whisky as she smooths out the rubber sheet, his mother talking at the same time from the chair about how that would be a miracle, he hardly bothers to replace her glass of water – so that the two women's voices overlap and go on and on and drive him into his room like a pair of squawking vultures.

He's careful not to show his room when he opens the door. He's careful to slip in sideways each time so that no one notices the state of the walls, half-stripped of wallpaper, plaster crunching on the floor.

'Don't do anything I wouldn't do in there!' shouts Colette through the door, and he hears his mother laugh. The door shivers as Colette tries the handle, but the lock is firm. There's a silence. They are listening. Maybe they're afraid he might be about to blow his head off. Jean-Luc all over the walls. But the gun is in the cellar, needing an oil.

He's covered the monument with an old sheet. It is too big to hide anywhere, now. He sits on the bed and holds his head in his hand, easing the pain in his eyes, thinking of what his father would tell him about the Germans, how they'd put a beetle on each eyeball and stitch the lid over it, how you could hear the munching in your agony, munching back into the brain, how this happened to Resistance men his father knew before they were shot, how the shooting must have been a relief. Sometimes Jean-Luc is driven to think death must be a relief, even though he's never been tortured like that.

There's still a silence the other side of the door. He doesn't like that silence.

He frowns, suspicious. The working lock replaced a much older lock which still has its keyhole exposed. He crouches down to look through it and sees a dim, wet eyeball. There's an explosion of giggles through the panel. He searches about for something to stuff into the keyhole, furious, wanting to ram a sharp pencil in but settling for a page from his note-book, balled up and squeezed tight into the opening. He presses his ear to the door. Their voices are so piercing he can hear it all.

'He's got ten lovely girlfriends in there, your boy has!'

'I don't suppose they're alive. I wouldn't put it past him.'

'You shouldn't be saying that about your own son,' Colette chirps, as if it is all a joke.

They begin to talk about the nasty rape and murder of a teenage girl that has been first item all week on the telly news, squawking away so that Jean-Luc half-expects to see feathers floating in under the door. He opens the window despite the cool to let the smell out; although the smell is mostly on his clothes, it seeps in. There is no one on the street. Then a hooded boy – one of the Rodier tribe – goes by on a bicycle with something pale on the back of his black top. Jean-Luc squints through the blurred spots and makes out the shape of a fish.

Of course! The first of April! Jean-Luc laughs, feeling sorry for the Rodier boy, then with a stab of horror he reaches back with his hand and feels paper.

He rips its Sellotape off his jacket, stares at it. It's a fish cut out from pink card, with a red heart drawn in the middle. He feels his heart has dropped down to his stomach.

He never felt Colette stick it on. He hopes it was Colette, and that he hasn't been walking about with it all day. He went twice into the village, keeping his head down, to buy bread and collect the eye-drops from Dr Demarne. His face is flushed with shame. He doesn't remember anyone laughing at him, they just felt sorry for his eye allergy and made one or two jokes about the Mafia. It was bound to be Colette, the slag.

He looks out of the window again. No one, not for five or more minutes. Aubain might have been the victim of nuclear attack, or alien mass abduction. He takes the sheet off the monument and blocks the bottom of the door with it, like you are supposed to do in a fire. Then he sits on the bed and thinks about the missing camera, strange currents running through his body.

The photos of the girls are bound to be perfect, he's sure. Most things are, when they're out of your reach. He took the girls close up, not like the ones in the first film, when they'd been blurred or sticking their tongues out like frogs. Their faces would fit easily on the spoons. The only disappointment might be the eyes, reddened like a rabbit's caught in headlights. He's noticed that on wedding photos. The flash causes it.

He imagines cutting their heads out. The girls make him feel happy inside. What he likes most of all is that he can make them laugh, their brown eyes twinkling with happiness. He likes their fair hair, their pale skin, their strangely dark eyelashes, their chirrupy laughter like sparrows in the bushes. Suffer little children to come unto me. Their sweet little dresses and shoes. They would be perfect for the flowers, gazing out from the heart of each rose.

He thinks of himself snipping carefully round each face and sticking them onto the hanging spoons, pressing them into the spoons' bowls so the brown glue bulges up around the edges. The garden of roses. It's cruel, not to have the camera, not to have what it contains. He'll have to go back and find it.

It is quiet next door, but not suspiciously so; he hears Colette leave, saying goodbye to him through the door with a silly voice off the telly. Then: '*Poisson d'avril, Jean-Luc!*'

And he sits there, frozen, not reacting. Like a dead man. Not even letting the bed squeak.

Maman might be having her afternoon doze. He reaches under the mattress for the envelope and takes out the photos. Closing his left eye and swivelling his right downwards he can avoid the lesions like crystals, his nose bulking large in his view. He doesn't look at the one with Raoul's ghost at the back; he keeps it underneath the others, his heart thumping.

The girls' faces aren't so bad, after all, and he snips them out, squinting through his dark glasses. The scissors are too big for their miniature heads and his eyes hurt. In the end, the cut-out faces are tiny pale counters, no good at all. He's sliced one of them too low, so that the forehead's gone.

He blows them off the table and they land on the floor like drops of milk, like white sap.

When he moves the monument on its wheels, just a few centimetres forwards and back, the spoons tinkle against each other.

Oncle Fernand comes limping up behind and congratulates him. Once the girls' faces are on the spoons, along with their mother, it will be the finest monument he can imagine, even though it does look like a big white-eyed duck. He'll have to go back for the camera as soon as he can. Why not tonight? Because he can't see well enough to drive. But if he closes one eye he can go up to where he hid his mobilette, slowly, steadily. He'll take the big torch. He'll smell his way to the Mas des Fosses.

Legless Bibi can't run away from the fish-bone spider. The nails hurt her breasts, her navel. She complains. Ah, Jean-Luc! Ah! Ah!

'That's life,' Jean-Luc tells her.

He catches his hand on a feather and it falls off. No glue is ever good enough, he thinks. Only soldering works. And even then.

He pulls the pile of *Spirou* out from under the bed, but his eyes hurt too much to read. All he can do is skate over the pictures in the cartoon squares, one after the other. He knows most of the words by heart, anyway. He knows how each story is going to end, even over two-months' worth, as if he can predict the future. *Spirou Présente les Nouvelles du Monde Entier:* he even knows half of those articles by heart, and especially the one about the teenager crippled by polio who receives his lessons at home through a microphone and wires carried by a friend from class to class at Columbia University. He'd be in his sixties by now. Philip Smith, fat, with glasses. He's like an old, reliable mate.

Maman is calling for water. He feels so good about things that he fetches some for her almost straightaway, breathing carefully through his mouth. She rabbits on to him but his mind is elsewhere. He wonders if the monument is finished. He can always make another one. As many as he wants.

The Englishwoman never saw him spying on her. Her husband was very sorry about the accident. People are always falling into swimming pools. In the car, the husband went on about the time his eldest kid, when she was a baby, threw sand into his

face on some beach in England, how much it hurt. It was probably quite lucky you fell in the pool, he said, because it helped
wash the sap out. No mention of his wife swimming naked,
the binoculars, the camera. Jean-Luc told him through the pain,
just to be polite, that the sap of fig trees can give you serious
burns. You don't want to saw a fig tree until the dead of winter.
The husband didn't know that: he was very surprised. He asked
Jean-Luc if he could see anything at all. Just enough to know
you're driving on the left, Jean-Luc told him, peeping and
feeling the light scooping his eyes out.

'Sometimes I ask myself if you're gaga,' Maman snorts. 'Didn't
you hear what I was saying? Madame Sandler is coming.'

'Coming where?'

'Here! To the Mas!'

'The Mas isn't here. It's there.'

'You know what I mean, stupid. She phoned her English
friend in Valdaron, the one Gabrielle cleans for. Gabrielle told
Colette. Later this week, maybe even tomorrow. Now that's got
your bowels turning, I can see that.'

'So what? I've treated the pool. I did it last week.'

'And her lovely lawn? Nice and thick and green, is it?'

His mother seems to want him to fail. She's grinning over
her glass of water. On the sill is a jar with a spray of dried
flowers, including big teasels, their tiny hooks balled with dust
and stray hairs and flies. He pulls one out, scattering the rest,
and taps it on her nose, tickling her face. She squeals, because
the teasel's head is rough and prickly.

'Promise you'll be nice to me?'

'Yes, yes! Oh, why were you ever born?'

'Your fault, Maman.'

'An accident. Yow! A mistake.'

'No I wasn't. You tried for years.'

'But I never wanted *you*, did I? That's what your father always
said. He'd say: "Where did *he* come from? We never asked for
him."'

'He never said that.'

'He did. *Where did he come from?*' she repeated in a hiss, her head forward like a snake's.

'It was a joke!'

He's a little rough with the teasel, at this point. He doesn't realise how fragile her skin is, these days. It seems to peel off her cheek in tiny strips. Strangely, she doesn't notice. She just glares at him, now he's stopped. Beads of blood well under her eye, on her grazed cheek-bone.

'He never said that, Maman. Don't lie.'

She nods, slowly, instead of saying anything. The blood begins to run down and she puts a hand to its tickle. Then she looks at her fingers.

'You're mad,' she says. She seems to be pleased at the sight of the blood on her fingertips, as if it isn't hers. 'You ought to be locked up.'

Another day made it to the evening and Nick checked that the windows were properly closed, and locked the main door in the kitchen: leaving with her bedtime milk, Tammy heard the big key turn twice like someone starting to be sick. He'd never bothered to lock it before. She'd picked up that the gods were winging their way from London at the end of the week. And that locking up made no difference, as far as the Jean-Luc problem was concerned: Jean-Luc had a key. There were no bolts on the door.

After their bedtime story and the goodnight kisses, hearing her parents safely downstairs, Tammy produced the camera from under her pillow and took photos of her sisters with the flash. They stood on their beds and Alicia showed her tummy, and so did Beans; Tammy giggled so much she couldn't take any more.

She allowed Alicia to take one of her; she pretended to be very afraid in her bed, clutching the sheet to her neck and moving her face around like plasticine until it was the most terrified she could make it and signalling with her hand when it was ready. She didn't think the photo would come out, because

Alicia moved the camera down a little when she pressed the button. 'That'll be blurred,' she whispered. Beans watched with a very serious look from her metal cot. Then they got really scared, because they heard creaks from the attic, as if there was a monster or a ghost up there. Or perhaps Jean-Luc in his dark glasses.

'It's only Jamie,' Tammy remembered.

But she knew, watching her father checking the windows and hearing him lock up, that Jean-Luc was the real danger. She pictured, drifting into slumber, the big stone house surrounded by CCTV cameras like the ones outside her school, keeping them safe from any old Tom, Dick or Harry who might be inclined to (and here the voices of her teachers and of the nice policewoman who came round to explain the dangers of the outside world spiralled gently together into sleep).

The house rose around them in its shuttered, night-time guise, indifferent to it all, creaking and shuffling through the decades, the centuries. Nick was standing on the vast roof with an urgent letter to post and the rain was falling in light swathes, rendering the tiles as slippery as ice. He had no idea that this wasn't all as real as anything else, and was very afraid. Someone was about to push him, but he didn't know who. He began to slide anyhow and surfaced with a start as the verge slipped away from under him, replaced by depth. There was depth in life, after all, he was demonstrating to his students. His lectures were renowned because he gave practical demonstrations on slippery roofs. This was why he'd been made a professor.

He hadn't been. That was Peter Osterhauser. The darkness in the bedroom might have been the darkness of death, though they spoke of a point of light. His heart raced unevenly. The only light was the sickly green glow from the digital clock, recording the countdown with remorseless, if illusory, precision.

The point is, he heard himself thinking, who will know about your sacrifices, your trying to be good, to be just? There

are no teachers in the sky, no end-of-term marks, no congratu-
lations from the headmaster. It's the bullies and the nasties who
enjoy themselves, who gain, who seize the day and never pay
for it, after, because there is no after. It's Henton, Smythe and
Rollick. It's the greedy ones. The corporation rookers. The
traffickers of politics. The Hummer-cruising sniggerers. *Oile,
oleum, elaia.* Who cares about the judgement of history? They
don't, because they'll be dead.

It was as if he'd never kicked free of being fifteen, sixteen.

Last April, a year ago almost to the day, his old schoolfriend
Duncan drove all the way from Stafford, where he was a devoted
poverty campaigner, with a rope, a camping stool and a piece
of paper, to ancient Ickthin Forest in Devon, part of which
bordered his and Nick's old boarding school, Hilmorton Academy.
There he parked the car and walked some fifty yards into the
trees, unfolded the stool, and hanged himself from a mammoth
oak tree's lower limb, just high enough to take his feet off the
ground when he kicked the stool away. He had told nobody.
He was fifty-three. Everyone, as always in these circumstances,
was left stunned, bewildered, and riddled with guilt. Nick had
felt himself go cold inside.

Now, away from his work, away from the endless deadlines
and hassles and urgent messages, he had time to contemplate.
He stared, wide awake at three in the morning in a room in
France that had scarcely lost its strangeness, its foreign smell,
and contemplated the meaning of Duncan's suicide. Duncan
Haighley had been one of his closest and oldest friends. Why
had he driven all the way down, back to school? Why had that
been necessary? Duncan had not enjoyed Hilmorton, but neither
had he hated it; failing to shine as Nick had shone, Duncan had
been a quiet, unassuming boy of an underrated intelligence and
a tremendous social conscience that extended to a sometimes
tedious puritanism and tendentiousness, especially when he
embraced green politics. But how right Duncan had been all
along! And how wrong his friend!

Nick now imagined him hanging there like a flitch of bacon

and felt nauseous rather than tearful. A small girl had discovered Duncan, by ill luck, and run back to tell her parents about the man with the crooked head staring at her from the sky. And so the damage branches out, tremors through the air, passes from person to person. She will carry a little particle of Duncan's despair like a cancerous cell through her life, and maybe it will ruin that life, waking her in nightmare with an image she can scarcely trace – for surely her parents will never have mentioned it, hoping the growing mind would leave it behind, or not understand what it really meant.

But nothing is forgotten, Nick heard himself saying in the vaults of his own mind, staring into the blackness. *Nothing is forgotten.* What was that playful, slightly cocky phrase that opened his first important paper on the mandate system in Africa?

We would do well to remember that history is more about amnesia than memory.

He took half of one of his mild sleeping pills. Forced amnesia, he reflected.

When he woke up again, the clock face was in competition with a grey wash brimming the edges of the shutters. Nearly eight. Sarah was breathing gently, nothing visible but her glossy black-and-loganberry hair. He needed a pee.

Checking on the way back, he saw the girls had all got up: the bedroom was empty. It was like a trick of light, the kicked-back duvets about to become his daughters, sleeping.

He listened blearily at the top of the stairs for the sing-song murmur of Spot or Rupert or Thomas. Silence. Sarah stirred from under the duvet, seeking more air. He thought of waking her, saw her mouth open as if in sorrow or pain, her breath noisier, someone else's dead hand protruding, hanging off the edge. It was hers: the sparse light glinted on her golden rings. Beans had woken her up several times in the night.

His heart inflated and beat its swollen hammer against his upper ribs, fighting the backwash from the sleeping pill.

He saw, at the top of the narrow stairs, the low attic door

was open. He went up quietly. The fug brushed his face like a thick and familiar cloth. Jamie's sleeping bag on the mattress was zipped open, and he was not in it. It was thrown back violently, exposing the ructions of the bottom sheet, a small litter of broken matches and pellets of dirt and his white iPod. Otherwise, the attic was surprisingly clean, its swept boards still witness to Jamie's burst of energy. The parachute silk, strung between the far Velux and the door, gave the huge room a somewhat unearthly, luminous glow. A nice space.

The Velux window was slightly open, he noticed. It was speckled with raindrops: it must have rained in the night, but not much. He closed it in case it rained again. The window seemed to startle the attic with its rectangle of sky; through the slicked glass he saw the big new sun wobble in solution, like a soluble, orange tablet.

Nick wasn't sure whether to feel relieved or concerned. Now and again Jamie had done very strange things while on drugs: walked along the edge of a flat roof in Dunstable shouting at passers-by. Turned up to work in a despatch-rider's office with only his helmet on. Plucked a dead bird in the middle of a dual carriageway near Southport. He was not 100 per cent reliable.

Ominousness.

They weren't in the sitting room. They weren't in the kitchen. He checked out the few remaining rooms in the house, including the scullery with Jamie's Door, knowing that the silence made this all pointless. He wanted to burst into laughter, a fit of hilarity swelling in his belly. The kitchen door was unlocked, interestingly: a bird took off from a tree and flew away without a care in the world through the fresh morning air, which still smelt of wetness, of large wet clouds.

He said to himself: these things only happen in stories. His girls had been kidnapped. It would be in the news. Under the remorseless, lascivious, fantasising gaze of the British press, urging everything into simulacra. He really did have a desire to laugh. He dressed silently in two minutes flat, as he heard himself saying in the ensuing inquest. My wife slept on. I didn't want to wake my wife. He thought he might be going mad, entertaining such absurd and almost evilly nasty thoughts.

The plump sun, still low and reddish-orange, was split in two by a black pencil-line of cloud. Other clouds were dashed higgledy-piggledy in long snakes and puffy ladders, as livid as bruises. A solitary red squirrel flew over the yard and rippled vertically up a trunk into the leaves, chattering angrily. He stared after it. The dawn birds were a sea of thoughtful mutterings, with the occasional loud burst nearby that startled him each time.

The swimming pool was a block of dark green, reflecting the dark green slopes beyond. Its tiles shone with wet. The barn and goatshed were empty, with the kind of nonchalant vacuity that only mindless objects can conjure. It annoyed him. The fresh morning sunlight was flooding the yard either side of the house's broad shadow.

He stood by the pool, staring in. He wondered whether to shout. Jamie would be taking them on a harmless walk, that was all there was to it. Two sides of the same coin: one awful, one fine. It was a question of how life flicked it, how it fell.

He put his hand into the pool's water and to his surprise his fingers disappeared. The very water was dark green, as though someone had poured in a bucket of dye. Pea soup. Robin Hood's livery. Even darker than before it was cleaned.

An inch or so of transparency, then his hand vanished like a squid's tentacles into the depths. Jean-Luc might have done this, he thought, switching it on and off like a light. A fly struggled in the skin of it, the first victim of the day. His old-looking and scaled-down face, pasted onto his silhouetted head and shoulders, scowled up out of the gloom. It was like staring into himself at bad moments, when he felt like disappearing, dissolving.

Was this a very bad moment? He looked up and wondered

if he was being watched, not by security cameras, but by a pair of binoculars. It was only then that he noticed the shoes, abandoned by the metal steps: Alicia's pink, unbuckled pair were sitting on the edge, placed carefully side by side as if someone had sucked her right out of them. Or as if, cartoon-like, she had taken a dive, leaving a little puff of exhaust.

He pulled his sleeve right back and swirled his hand about in the water for a minute or so, until his flesh turned too cold.

He loped in a sudden fit of excitement right round the house. As long as he kept scurrying about, he could keep his terror in check. He hurtled through the archway and circled the house once, scuffling on his long legs, panting audibly, glancing into the car then up the track. He called out their names in turn, but not wildly. Sensibly. As if playing hide-and-seek. The countryside, so much wilder here than cosy England, didn't even bother to reply. He came back to the lifeless pool-hut and rapped on the window, as if they might have been hiding inside. His three girls. With Jamie. The pool began to scare him with glimpsed faces, white and sightless, pressed against the glass of the surface. He remembered the toad, mysteriously vanishing when the pool cleared.

The cellars! Hope flickered and burnt its little incandescent spot in his chest. He checked the three that weren't padlocked, slipping on the worn steps down, looking behind and into vats and barrels and the grape-crusher with its massive wooden screw. A worm-chewed ladder disintegrated in his hands. A horse-collar fell, huge and heavy with a flurry of straps and hooks and powdered by dust. He hadn't ever noticed the old bicycle, or the wooden hay-fork veiled like a bride in cobwebs. They were so motionless, and he was so busy. He coughed. He was wasting time. This was all plain silly.

The locked cellar, fastened by two combination padlocks on each bolt, had a tiny window with a thick grille at shin-level: there was nothing but blackness inside, like a solid cube.

He hurried across the yard and shouted into the woods,

standing uncertainly on the tumbled wall. His voice rose and shattered against the quiet. He repeated their names politely and waited, wobbling on the loose stones. His pseudopolyps stirred like a frayed collar.

The intense callousness of foliage.

The absolute indifference of the natural world.

The dense self-absorption of the beasts, pitiless, specialised. No wonder we wanted to take our revenge on it all.

He waited in the stillness, speckled only by birdsong. All these strangely meditative moments in a life: the sigh of the withdrawing surf before the breakers' crash, the anguish.

He came back to the pool, finding it harder and harder to breathe. The water gave nothing back. It was a screw-top lid. Jamie could swim, and Tammy too, but Alicia could only thrash with wings and Beans could only sink calmly, without any fuss.

He would have to wake Sarah. He couldn't stand the idea. All that panic, that anxiety, that bother.

And the three of them would still be floating. Or maybe not. Why did they dredge pools and rivers to find the dead? He picked up Alicia's pink shoes and smelt them like a tracker dog. Leather and sweat. No, plastic. He shouted their names again and his voice evaporated in his throat, already suffering.

He loped to the house and up the stairs in his shambling, long-limbed ungainliness. Sarah was standing in the bedroom in her nightie, blearily raising her eyebrows.

'Did you sleep badly or something? What are you doing with Alicia's shoes?'

'I think,' he said, hoarsely searching for breath, 'they've gone for a walk with Jamie.'

'Oh, he's re-emerged, has he? You *think*? Have you been jogging?'

'Actually, I'm conjecturing.' He took a deep breath and blew it out like smoke. 'I'm attempting not to panic.'

'I'm sure they're fine,' she said, already whipping off her nightie.

★   ★   ★

'Jamie's with them,' he said. 'I'm assuming.'

'Can we assume?' They were both hurrying down the stairs, if steadily. Sarah was white but calm. She was actually quite good in emergencies.

'Will they have gone up the track, Nick?'

'Which way?'

'You take one way, I'll take t'other,' she said, oddly like her mother in a good mood.

'We mustn't give Jamie the impression we're worried,' said Nick, by the main door. 'That we don't trust him.'

'He knows already, unless he's *really* thick.'

'He's not thick at all,' said Nick, surprised.

The house had them in its mouth, behind its teeth. It was grinning. But it was not biting. The yard looked like a great desert plain to be crossed without water.

'I'll go towards the road,' said Sarah. 'I'm going to shout their names.'

'Done that.'

'Of course everything's all right, really. We're all *so* paranoid. I'm in a state of dread most of the time. A waste of my life.'

'Several times,' he continued.

'We're completely over-dramatising,' she snorted. 'Did you check the barn *properly*, Nick? Check it again. Oh, *shit*.'

She shouted their names at the yard as if cross with it. He waited politely for the silence to draw down its curtain and confirmed he *had* checked the barn with great thoroughness. She pictured him picking through the barn's clutter with tweezers, when he had in fact nipped in and out.

'Oh. What's happened to the pool?'

She was standing on the edge. He had the impression it had got worse in less than twenty minutes. A rim of scum was now visible where the water lapped at the sides. Where it entered the water, the alarm's white pipe was smeared green. Nothing but shadows broke the surface as she dipped her hand in and swept it about, making the filters tut and mutter. He imagined her fingers touching something she wouldn't want to touch, but he hadn't yet told her exactly where he'd found the shoes.

'Pools do that, apparently,' he said. 'Overnight.'

'Jamie was floating in a pool in my dream last night and it was all murky,' she said, looking very round-shouldered.

'Sarah, don't even begin to go that way. Everything's fine. They've gone for a walk with Jamie.'

'Great,' she said, already moving off. 'They've gone for a walk with Jamie. Just great. Just *so* consoling. And Alicia's in bare feet. Scorpions? Snakes? Huge red ants?'

When he was four, Jamie would only do a poo if his father was present. This meant, when Nick had lectures, meetings or tutorials all day, his son would hold it in and develop stomach pains and scream and Helena would phone the college, leaving messages imploring him to come back home if only for ten minutes. Nick became a laughing stock among his colleagues: Sir John Seeley never suffered this. Helena would not use euphemisms, that was the trouble: she believed infants were closer to the arcane powers, that the planet should be run by children. Nick reckoned the planet run by Jamie would be proximate to the Third Reich, or perhaps the Central African Empire under Bokassa. But he would speed back on his bicycle from a seminar on 'The Role of British Intelligence in Imperialist Statism' and stand by the loo as Jamie, staring at his father with a strange little smile, would deliver the goods on his throne.

Now Jamie had the same expression, made more malignant by twenty-one years of practice. He was holding the tin with Alicia's chocolate cake inside. Nick had just been up the rear track almost to the rocks and back, calling and calling, lonely between the trees, feeling as if climate change – which had recently begun to give him sleepless nights – had been toppled from its Olympian status and replaced by something far worse.

'Jamie!'

'Yo.'

'Where are the girls, Jamie?'

'The girls,' Sarah echoed, unexpectedly just behind, the lid on her panic rattling.

Jamie said, putting the tin down on the kitchen table and raising his two hands in mock-placation, 'Why so unhappy, man?' They could smell him from the door. He must have been pretty much in the same clothes for the whole two-week sojourn in the attic.

'Oh for God's sake!' shouted Sarah, her glasses misting up from her hot, shiny face.

'The girls are missing,' snapped Nick. There was a pause while the awful finality of this statement, like a newspaper headline, sunk in. 'Alicia, Beans and Tammy,' he added, weakly. He felt thirsty and sick and wanted to cry.

Jamie planted a chunk of cake in his mouth as if nervous of it being taken away.

'Jamie,' said his stepmother, striding forwards with her glasses off until she was inches from his face, 'have you seen the girls this morning? Yes or no?'

'Ja-meee,' pleaded Nick.

His son nodded dramatically, his mouth full, indicating with his finger his inability to speak just at that moment.

They waited, Jamie ponderously chewing. He looked like a fox caught with a chicken in its mouth, his eyes looking up at them and yellowish. Sarah recommended that he stop *arsing around*. Her glasses were misting up again. She had never used that expression in her entire life, and it surprised her as much as Nick.

Jamie swallowed exaggeratedly as if it was incumbent on him to obey, his lips as dark as the one Goth in their Cambridge road. 'Yeah, making this den in the woods,' he said, looking off to one side, as if studying the fridge. 'It's called kids having fun.'

Nick felt a great flood of relief, which was why his voice went hoarse. 'You mean you left them in the woods on their own?'

'You want them back in their cage, right?'

'Oh for fuck's sake!' Sarah declared, equally relieved to be given a second life.

'Where did you leave them?' croaked Nick. 'We shouted. Didn't you hear us shout? Didn't you? We were both shouting.'

'You were the Romans,' Jamie explained, with an apologetic shrug. 'And we were the Gauls.'

'Jamie, you are a prize prick,' said Sarah, holding his face and grimacing with relief. He pulled his squashed cheeks from her with a look of disgust.

Outside it had started to rain again in a very unEnglish way: drifts of gauze like a pencil-sketch of a tropical storm.

'They must be getting wet,' Nick said, turning distractedly to the open door. 'Where are they playing, exactly?'

'About twenty yards in front of the house?' said Jamie, with an air of contempt.

They were crouched and sniggering on the third overgrown terrace below the house, just where Jamie had said they would be. The den was a circular wall of leaves, hidden from higher up by overhanging branches.

'Were you really mega-worriered?' asked Alicia, with a candid air of triumph.

'Nah,' Nick replied. He tossed her the shoes. She was in her socks, stuck all over with bits of nature's floor. 'You didn't trick me one bit.'

'Likkel window,' said Beans, pointing at a spot in the ceiling of leaves. 'Roof *big* voo!'

'Ssssh,' Tammy commanded with a threatening finger, unusually severe with her little sister.

'It wasn't a trick,' Alicia complained. 'I just took them off cos I'm a princess of the Gores.'

'Gauls,' said Tammy, who was suddenly embarrassed by the whole episode.

'Me queen,' shouted Beans, throwing up leaves.

Tammy was the sole witness at the court martial, during which Jamie fished a flat tin out of his pocket and prepared a roll-up on the kitchen table. He interrupted this to have a good scratch of his dirt-thickened hair. He'd wanted to be an astronomer at ten, Nick recalled. A golden boy with golden locks and a potentially golden future.

The girls had woken early – about six o'clock – and crept downstairs to rescue the baby boars from the electric fence. Jamie was on the sofa, taking a break from his self-imposed cell. The morning woods, the clear air, the great outdoors. The gift of life. The idyll. They'd built what Jamie called a 'sanctuary' out of dead leaves and heard their names being called out: it was the Romans, it was the colonisers, it was the beginning of the end. Jamie had slipped off to the kitchen for essential supplies and was caught by the unexpected return of Caesar's patrol.

He grinned, looking cheerily haggard. 'It was cool. A fun time was had by all. We kept our feet on the ground. They'll tell their grandchildren, right?'

'Not by *all*,' said Nick, studying his thumbs.

'You might have detected we were a teeny-weeny bit anxious?' suggested Sarah, calmly, in a voice fretted to a stick by fury. Relief was a distant memory, now. 'That's what really bothers me. Not you taking them out to have fun, but ignoring our anxiety.'

'A lot of anxiety,' Jamie agreed, nodding his head before licking the cigarette paper; but it was a reproach.

Nick rolled his eyes to the ceiling: anywhere but his son, the impenetrable concrete wall of his son's selfishness. 'I think we all deserve the proverbial cup of tea,' he said.

No one moved.

Tammy stared at a cleft in the table, into which crumbs had fallen. She was one of those crumbs. She had made her parents suffer. Never again would she do such a thing in her entire life, she decided.

'Like, you know when you screamed your head off at me, Sarah?' said Jamie, sticking the roll-up between his pouting lips.

'I shouted.'

'Screamed your head off. Not when you called me a prick, but the time before. Two weeks back.'

Sarah swallowed with difficulty. 'Under intense provocation, yes.'

'Provocation is an underrated instrument of power, historically speaking,' commented Nick, in a jovial tone. 'Underrated by *historians*, that is. As is not doing anything. Inaction as a form of violence.'

'Shut up, Nick,' Sarah muttered.

Jamie stood, ready to go outside and have his smoke. 'That's why I had to sort myself out on my own. Because of the shouting.'

'Maybe talk about this at some other time?' his father suggested, glancing Tammy's way.

Tammy thought Jamie seemed sad as he nodded, but when he turned his head she saw the other half of his face was smiling.

They had seen the sea. They had seen further than anyone had ever seen. The roof's slope had scared her, but it wasn't slippery, it was just huge, like a different land, and dark. They had all held hands and reached the top, holding on to the cool ridge. A bird had passed them and then they had seen the sun rise. They were the first in the world to see it rise. It was like an explosion without any sound and the redness filled their eyes up. Then Tammy felt little drops on her face: it was raining! It made the tiles shine. Alicia started whimpering and they had to creep back slowly across the tiles on shivery legs into the attic. That was the one and only time, Jamie told them. His face had gone white. That's because, on the way back, although it was only a few yards hand-in-hand, their shoes kept slipping on the tiles. The roof had changed. It wanted to throw them off.

Then they had fun on the ground. The ground's different, Jamie said. The ground's for kids. The air's for ghosts, right?

No one had told a lie, either. That's why half of Jamie's face was smiling, now.

FIFTEEN

The dinner with the Chambords was memorable, not just because the meal – foie gras *truffé*, very bloody *entrecôte* and a fiery rum baba, washed down with, among other delights, a dark, twenty-year-old Saint-Estèphe and a *trou normand* of Calvados between the cheese and the dessert – made even high-table banquets at college feel paltry. It was the relief that life could spare you and then yield magical, carefree and stimulating moments like these. The company was delightful, of mixed ages, and entirely continental: a quiet lawyer and his elegant architect wife; a young Belgian poet with his older librarian boyfriend; and a homeopathic doctor whose glamorous Spanish partner was a well-known flamenco teacher. Georges and Claudine conducted the proceedings without help, wafting away dishes and the slight language barrier with the same charm and facility.

It made Nick and Sarah feel more civilised than they'd felt in years. Thankfully, when it came to the inevitable politics, the robust discussion was even-handed, and the English contingent contributed their piece without too many fits and starts, itemising the dangers of Blairite liberalism. This shifted into a discussion of the merits of Modigliani with practised ease, the join barely detectable. The girls ate with the adults, to the former's astonishment – an astonishment so great that they did nothing but stare in vestal silence unless addressed, their eyes glittering in the candlelight.

'God, I love France,' said Sarah, on the drive back. 'How much have you drunk, by the way?'

'That's why I'm going very slowly,' said Nick. 'I have my family on board.'

'You're not going slowly,' said Sarah, who hadn't even minded when two of the party lit up. 'That's exactly my point.'

'They weren't really locals, though.'

'So?'

'In my Marxist days, I'd have conducted a class analysis and not enjoyed it.'

'Oh, who cares?' said Sarah, ambiguously. 'All we need is geniality and kindness. They were lovely to the kids.'

'And truth and justice,' declared Nick, over a silly song from the three at the back. 'Whatever they are. They're ideas. But we no longer need ideas, do we? Too difficult. All our leaders require is ego, massive self-esteem. And God, of course, their grins fed by God. Sssh, Tammy, I'm talking. So Blair can be mates with Berlusconi and Bono and not see any contradiction. Ditto Sarkozy. It's the inevitable continuation of Karl Mannheim's *freischwebende Intelligenz*. Emancipation from history and society, the old order, all that tricky oppositional crap. Hm? Very post-Sixties. Actually, I *will* tell you what truth and justice are,' he went on, as if Sarah had specifically not wished him to. 'They're wanting a habitable future for my children and their children and their children in turn – *please* try to keep the volume down, girls! OK? Thank you. It's called creation, not destruction. It's called deep reflection. It's called having ideas and convictions, then acting on them.'

Why so heavy? wondered Sarah, as they bumped onto the track. *Why is he always so heavy against himself?*

Fired by the Chambords, they realised they had never been to the local metropolis; that would be embarrassing in front of the Sandlers. So before the latter descended on them – Nick pictured a silvery UFO rippling the pool – the Famous Five (as Sarah put it) took themselves off to Nîmes for the first time since their arrival two months before.

Nîmes was hardly a city (let alone a metropolis) except in terms of antiquity, elegance and the usual surrounding fungi of big-box stores, car dealerships and (to the girls' satisfying groans) oily McDonald's.

They found a parking space in an underground car park playing Mozart and visited the huge Roman arena, watched the three-dimensional film in the intact Roman temple, regretfully gave the exhibition of neolithic burial customs in the Roman period a miss and climbed up through the Italianate garden to the Roman tower. The kids, by this time, were saturated in historical knowledge, bleeding it from the nose, and dreamed only of an ice lolly.

It was early April, but the sky was entirely clear and many of the surfaces in the old and rather lovely centre were of blindingly pale stone. Faced with the tower, a kind of vast molar with an inner spiral staircase and extraordinary views from a cramped balcony that caused Sarah much anxiety, Nick felt inspired. Maybe it was simple relief: that he wasn't the parent of missing children, that the path had forked and he had taken the right one.

He stood by a twisted old olive tree and felt a desire to paint. Or rather, he completely understood why people developed a passion for art – something he had never really felt in his life before. He saw cubism in the myriad planes of the tower's north-facing side, its south-facing, sunlit half turning the sky several shades of blue deeper. The same sky! He was actually thinking like a painter. Everything's perspective, he thought.

He tried to point out the visual effect to the girls – 'Look, look!' – but they told him he was being boring again; they punctured his enthusiasm, deflated him. He all but sulked after his epiphany, heading for the ice-cream stall down below.

Even Tammy would probably remember very few of the innumerable nuggets of knowledge he and (to a lesser extent) Sarah had proffered. Jamie had no recollection of the trip to Delphi with Helena, for instance, when he was seven. Yet Helena had stuffed him with elaborate, pseudo-mystical information and stroked his forehead with sacred water from a grassy spring by the temple of Apollo that turned out to have been the run-off from a gardener's hose.

The two youngest were treating Sarah like a washing line, pinning themselves to her in the busy streets, and Nick wondered if they hadn't all become a little hick out there in the sticks; it was a strain, keeping an eye on the girls after their rural sanctuary, and the ambient noise was deafening. Beans kept pointing at the roofs and wanting to go up on them, which was sweet. She also needed changing. His eye caught the English newspapers' headlines in an outside carousel, one of which – the *Guardian Weekly* – declared global warming to be 'worse than feared'.

He bought a copy and read it aloud to Sarah as they sunned themselves at a café in front of the cathedral. Since 2000, the carbon count had considerably increased. It had been anticipated that, faced with planetary catastrophe, the West would have invested in expensive carbon-capping technology. It hadn't.

'I'll read it later, Nick,' Sarah assured him. 'It's embarrassing, the English.'

City bonuses were at a record high. A shell had exploded near a Baghdad playground and a father had found the head of his five-year-old girl. His own little girl, called Safia. The accompanying photograph showed only a small, blood-spattered shoe.

He looked up and saw Alicia's head turning easily as she flicked the end of her straw at Tammy while Sarah was wiping Beans's fingers. 'Coco tummy *touch* Beans *here*,' his youngest was insisting, her grammar fructifying by the hour. She prised the top of her nappy away from her belly and Sarah's nose wrinkled. 'Oh dear me,' said Beans.

The newspaper ruined the rest of his day.

'We're possibly the most selfish generation ever to have walked this planet,' he informed Sarah late that evening, after a resumé of the main article over supper. 'No, forget the cautious historian's qualification. *The* most spoilt, and *the* most selfish. The baby-boomers! Ugh. We had everything on a plate and grabbed even more.'

Sometimes he never stopped talking, Sarah thought. Like the girls. An isolation tank had a lot to recommend it.

'Not counting yours,' he went on. 'The Thatcher brood now in their thirties and forties. We can't go on blaming our parents, you see. What a shame. Not to be able to blame our parents any more. They saved the world from the Nazis. We've failed to save the world from ourselves. No, listen. We need to get enlightened here. A spot of critical transcendence. There's this massive load-bearing wall in your house that's about to collapse. What do you do? At the very least you shore it up with props, then you start to rebuild it from the bottom up. Why are we doing nothing except applying the odd trowel-load of Polyfilla? Because we are not in the least interested. Today, we're having a ball.'

'Maybe the wall's a party wall,' Sarah observed, turning her spoon over and over so her distorted face kept appearing and disappearing. 'You know what neighbours are like. Noisy and selfish. Anyway, my parents were too young to fight the Nazis. They kept the peace in sandy pockets of the Empire.'

'If your neighbour does nothing,' Nick went on, 'you go round and do it yourself. If there isn't the time in hand to take him or her to court.'

'Supposing your neighbour's America, or China?'

Nick cradled his face in his hand. 'You go round with a shotgun. OK?'

'No, not really. It's called war.'

'Whatever, I feel completely and utterly ashamed. A waste of air-space.'

'You've really caught the sun, Nick. It shows up the nobbles on your forehead.'

'Are you listening, Sarah? I'm angry. I'm angry at myself.'

'You're writing. This is your field. Oil, oil and more oil.'

'To be read by how many people? We fly to places like Fez or Gdansk, pretending to be doing our academic duty, and read our papers to seven bored colleagues, who read their papers in turn in incomprehensible monotones, and then we all go out and get drunk. It's a farce.'

'And what did you do in the war, Mr Joyce? I wrote *Ulysses*.'

'You know the ones who win write the history,' he persisted, each set of long fingers glued together and tracing circles on the table. 'We're a side-show. Everything is power. The best candidate never *ever* wins. Why? Weak power base. So. Direct action. It's all that's left to the powerless. Combat their desire with our desire. A theoretical case for assassination. Take out the godfathers.'

'You sound horribly like a Bin Laden video strained through Marcuse.'

Nick said, in a mournful voice: 'I met my past, today. He went by looking somewhat under par and sort of accelerated away when I hailed him.'

'That's not Dylan, is it?'

'Praise indeed, I suppose. Thank you. Nicholas Mallinson, aged fifty-four.'

'Shooting stars burn brightest in the darkest night,' said Sarah.

'That has to be Dylan.'

'Sarah Allsopp, fifteen.'

'Gosh, well done,' he said, without mockery. He closed his eyes for a moment. 'Indignation and courage, that's what we need. A chemical reaction between the two. An unstoppable fizz. Bring down the money markets. You realise the weather is a revolutionary?'

Sarah laughed and was about to call him a reborn Trot, but Nick stayed serious.

'The Iraqi father found his little daughter's *head*,' he whispered, eyes open again and face thrust forward; he was fearful of small ears listening in. 'Her name was Safia.'

'I thought you weren't supposed to whisper.'

'It's in the paper,' he said, gesturing towards the sofa, where the *Guardian Weekly* lay like a crumpled charge-sheet of horrors. 'Imagine that. The kid was five years old. And all *completely* avoidable. None of it ever had to happen. Nothing ever does. That's the key! Safia could still be alive! They all could! And we *let* it happen! We could have stormed Downing Street instead of flaffing about in Hyde Park!'

'Faffing,' she corrected. 'And it's happening day after day,' she admitted, slumping a little. No, she couldn't imagine it. She could see it, but she couldn't feel it. It broke all the circuits.

There was a brief pause. He watched the fire struggling against its own smoke. 'You know what's going to happen, don't you? Sheer exhaustion will calm it down and we'll declare a victory, redeemed by history. The occupying forces staying on to keep the peace just as we'll do in Darfur. The oil will be ours, lots and lots, like the Chad field so conveniently next to Darfur. Iraq will sink into obscurity. And the five-year-old called Safia? A forgotten skull.'

'Nick . . .' Sarah complained.

'I'm haunted by my own helplessness,' he pursued. 'They gouge each other's eyes out, for God's sake.'

'Nick, do we *have* to?'

'And now we've got the deus ex machina descending on us tomorrow,' he groaned, eyes hiding behind his hand.

'Dei,' corrected Sarah.

Nick got like this sometimes. She termed these 'Nix fits'. It came of his having suppressed the early activist side with balance, footnotes and leak-proof substantiation. A side which had never been fulfilled beyond waving a fist next to his shoulder-length hair at cruise-missile demos and sitting on dull committees of regressive, sour-faced comrades.

She let it pass, stroking his knuckles on the table. They had polished off a whole bottle of strong Graves. He wished he hadn't mentioned the kid's head. She had her own unmentionables, too. Yesterday, collecting unwashed mugs from Jamie's room while he was out, she had spotted a sheet of paper carelessly folded on the broken chest of drawers. On it was scrawled, below *Cheap socks in market!* and *Must eat more fruit!* (among other touching memoranda):

> *Here I AM again*
> *I'm high up high uphighbird*
> *knifing the water far below/you there*
> *confectioning a stranger*
> *don't you remember?*
> *one to ten*
> *again again*
> *bitch in the dawn cold*
> *wannabe flesh*
> *gonnabe gonnabe*
> *now I'm lowdown a frown*
> *a broken city*

She always swam ten lengths, no more, no less. It was as if a curtain had been lifted on Jamie's consciousness, stoned or otherwise. Oddly, instead of anger or even shame, all she felt was a momentary pity. *Cheap socks in market!* He'd only had to ask.

Anyway, she knew she had taken a calculated risk: this wasn't a prelapsarian Eden, where nudity went unremarked. It was a fallen world, where you had to eat more fruit and wear socks.

Nick was saying, but calmly now: 'Remember that Buddhist monk, immolating himself in the square against Vietnam? Or Jan Palach? Where are they now, eh? When there's something far more serious?'

'Not here, I hope,' she grimaced.

When the smart, hired Audi arrived at the worst time (late, too near lunch, although the girls were playing happily in the barn), its tyres scrunchingly audible through the sitting room's open window, she hurried to the main door and knocked the Scrabble box off a side table by the fireplace: the sitting room, lovingly restored to its pristine pre-Mallinson state, was suddenly littered with a spray of letter tiles and a multitude of used score sheets.

She tried to sweep the Scrabble tiles into the tipped box, but they were peculiarly recalcitrant on the woven rug. Nick was already outside: she heard his deep voice greeting the Sandlers,

342

a peal of hearty laughter, footsteps over the gravel as she picked the squares up as fast as she could. B-L-A-Z-E-R, she read. O-N-Y-X. High-scoring words. Why did she feel so desperate, ready to burst into tears? What did it matter if there were Scrabble tiles on the sitting room floor? Why did she always have to prove something, claim the higher moral ground instead of relaxing into life, into life's haphazard and human ways? What did she care if she scored low in the Sandlers' eyes? It wasn't a thesis!

'I'll do that for you,' Jamie said, paused on the stairs.

Jamie never ever offered to help.

'Righty-ho. Oh. Thank you, Jamie. If you could.'

She went into the kitchen, closing the door into the sitting room to give him a little more time, and greeted the Sandlers with a shy, slightly embarrassed bonhomie. In fact, she reckoned they should have come down here to check everything before letting the place, anyway. She didn't feel all that guilty. And she felt more worried than guilty when it came to Jean-Luc. He lived alone with his ailing mother. He was a loner. He had spied on her naked body and photographed the girls, among other things. He had the right, sinister profile. She'd even begun to conjecture whether his impromptu plunge had not been quasi-deliberate, a piece of psychological theatre. The difficulty would be in the consequence: supposing he took revenge? Nick had dismissed that as paranoia, but it was easy to imagine him at the door, axe in hand: those deep-set eyes. The Dominici Affair all over again.

She'd always had her doubts about him: female instinct.

Lucy was chattering on emptily, and Lucy herself knew it. It was to cover a sudden feeling that her future was no longer something she could believe in; it had been obstructed, or taken over, by this family. Her idea had been that she and Alan would retire to the Mas des Fosses within the next two or three years, while they were still fit and compos mentis. It was now six years since they had bought it, but it felt like one or two. In six years she would be sixty-six, Alan an astonishing seventy. They would be officially old. The track was in an appalling state, it made the house seem even more remote. This family thrived here, however, she could see that. They all looked much healthier than back in December. They were still young. Even the senior Fusspot was relatively young beyond his hair-loss, his long-limbed, professorial awkwardness.

'You all look as if you're thriving,' she said, not unsourly.

'I think we might be,' Sarah agreed, modestly, which infuriated Lucy even more.

Alan's legs were aching, he had to jiggle them to restore circulation. 'I have seen the future of democracy,' he said, 'and it's called Ryanair.'

'The future of the planet, surely,' Nick ostensibly joked, beaming.

Lucy was surprised they hadn't been to various places she brought up in conversation as the coffee brewed, including a sweets museum and a 'jewel' of a Romanesque church. Sarah pointed out somewhat defensively that they still had bags of time and Nick said more soothingly how they'd been busy 'exploring' the local walks. Sarah noted Lucy's eyes noting the state of the kitchen (acceptable, surely).

'Is it very strong?' asked Lucy, as Sarah poured the coffee.

'Oh no,' said Sarah. It was decaff, but she didn't let on.

'In that case don't bother with me. I only like it the way the French do it, small and very strong.'

'That's me!' laughed Alan.

'Isn't that more Italian?' parried Sarah.

'No,' chuckled Lucy, gamely.

After Sarah had made a special brew for the woman, cramming the coffee to a solid bulk in the little espresso's filter, they all moved into the sitting room. Lucy was first through (she didn't see why she shouldn't treat the place as her own, when it was) and found herself brought up short by something on the tiled floor, directly in her path. It was a sentence made up of Scrabble letters.

I DIDNT FALL

I WAS

PUSHED

WHOOO OO OO

She stood stock still with her hand over her mouth, feeling a chill ripple through her over and over, very fast.

Nick was too used to seeing the kids' rubble on the floor to make anything of it, but as he moved forward Lucy laid a hand on his arm.

'Why in English?' she breathed.

He vaguely took in the fact that she had turned sheet-white. 'It's English Scrabble,' he said. Then Sarah appeared with Alan. They all looked down. The letter tiles were set a little crookedly, which made them curiously menacing, like a message snipped from newspaper print left by a killer.

'It's Jamie's little joke,' Sarah chuckled, sweeping the letters up with both hands. 'Nick's grown-up son.' Again, the letter tiles seemed to have a life of their own. She was conscious of being bent right over in front of the Sandlers, of the top of her buttocks being exposed, as she struggled with the tiles and looked around for the box. There was no box. Jamie had surpassed himself.

'Not so grown up,' chuckled Alan Sandler, eyes glued to the strip of honey-pale ass above the belt, cloven into blue shadow.

'Is he here?' asked Lucy, weakly.

Nick ignored her and addressed Alan: 'Oh, I don't know,' he said, involuntarily stung by his presumption. 'Jokes aren't exclusive to children.'

'He's here for a short break,' said Sarah, over her shoulder. 'He's a bit of a poet,' she added, to Nick's surprise.

Lucy sat down unsteadily in the cane chair as Sarah dumped the letters on the metal table with a clatter. She was cursing Jamie from her belly as she turned round and smiled.

'"Exclusive to children",' Alan repeated, musingly. 'Isn't English a truly weird language? I mean, you expect that to mean it's *forbidden* to children, but it means the opposite? Just on account of that little preposition?'

The reflection hung in the air for a moment as Nick grappled with the novel concept that Alan Sandler might be intelligent, might even be more intelligent than him.

'One of those Janus words,' Alan went on, hitting the sofa as only the owner could – with the insouciant force of his considerable weight. He had sat on the Scrabble game's 'Rules of Play' leaflet, and pulled it out from under him. 'Like, ah, *cleave. Sanction. Doubt.*'

'Are your legs better?' asked Nick, slyly.

'They're fine,' Alan replied, in a sing-song voice.

The girls were in the barn, probably hiding from the gods. Sarah decided to leave them. The French would have insisted on all three coming in for an elaborate greeting, but she was not French.

She queried *doubt* as she perched herself youthfully on the low firestool beside Lucy.

Nick broke in before Alan could reply. 'In Shakespeare, Sarah. To suspect and, well, to be undecided.' He glanced at her with a disappointed, even embarrassed look. 'Didn't you do *Hamlet* at A level?'

Sarah pointedly ignored him and turned to Lucy, who was leaning her forehead on her hand and blinking at the rug. 'Erm, are you all right?'

'*When one player has used all his tiles and the pool is empty, the game is at an end*,' read Alan from the buttock-creased 'Rules of Play'. 'I guess that's pretty final, if somewhat melancholy, even morbid.' His wheeze gave him the air of a campus poet. At any moment, thought Nick, he'll be quoting Robert Frost.

'*Weather*. Both wear away and endure,' Nick said, planting himself on the sofa next to Alan. Who was flicking through the leaflet brusquely, as if finding secrets within and nodding. He pointed at the word *horn* in the example and embarked on a childhood story, an intricate Michigan farm tale involving a game of Scrabble and a freckled girl that seemed intended only for Nick's ears, and so the latter felt privileged.

As this male session went on, Lucy stirred and asked Sarah, in a feeble voice, why her grown-up son thought the poor man was pushed.

'What poor man?'

Lucy looked at her. Alan was nudging Nick in the ribs, now into the naughty bit in the barn. Nick was manfully holding onto his decaff and laughing too loudly, as he himself had noted Englishmen tend to do. 'Hornier, very good,' he bellowed, and laughed. In fact, with one ear he was listening in to the women, hoping Lucy wouldn't tell Sarah about the builder who fell off the roof. He hadn't yet got round to pummelling Jamie in his thoughts.

'The poor man your son was referring to,' said Lucy, edgily.

'My *step*son was only referring to him*self*,' Sarah reassured her. 'He has no other criteria to go by, I'm afraid.' She wondered why she was being so disloyal to her clan. She had to stop herself pouring it all out to this hard, unattractive, superior woman. Sarah felt a need to divest herself, to sweep the surface free of struggling insects before they entered by her mouth and then came out again by her mouth, more and more of them, as if breeding inside her belly.

Lucy looked at her for a second with suspicious eyes. They were hooded by folds of skin that bore down on her eyelashes and would not have been there at all ten, twenty years ago. But she had not turned to fat, thought Sarah; the dreaded foot pump had not been connected. That was unusual, these days. It was almost to be admired. She was almost French in her slimline elegance, her sharpness. What poor man did she mean? Sarah had not really taken it in properly, she just wanted to get through it, reach the other side when they'd be gone: depressurise. What poor man?

'Really?' said Lucy, at last.

Sarah nodded, pulling a face. It was hard to keep the little sail of their conversation aloft in the gale from the men on the sofa. Jamie's joke struck her as harmless, suddenly. She was much too tough on him. She hoped it was harmless. She hoped it wasn't –

'Oh. A *mal entendu*,' said Lucy.

'We've had a bit of a row,' Sarah admitted, quietly. 'Nick and Jamie don't exactly see eye to eye. Jamie has not emerged from a tricky adolescence.'

'He's how old?'

'Oh, erm, twenty-four? Twenty-four.'

'I have two in their thirties who are equally irritating. Maybe I should meet him. You didn't mention him before, did you?'

Sarah confirmed that they hadn't and poked at the fire, whose unnecessary presence on this warmish spring day was intended to show the owners, via its ineffectual smokiness, the need to do something about it. The smoke ignited like dust in a mine-shaft, sparkling into vigorous flame, drawn up the chimney as if by some giant vacuum cleaner in the sky.

'The fire's always been terrific, of course,' said Lucy. 'Shall we take a tour of inspection outside, Alan? Look at those men.'

Alan's hand was on Nick's forearm and they were both in near-silent fits.

They toured the lawn, or rather the seed-bed. Sarah reminded them it had been completely ravaged by the boars. Alan began intoning a poem in an actorish lilt:

'And he, despite his terror, cannot cease
Ravening through century after century,
Ravening, raging, and – shit – up*rooting* that he may
    come, ah,
Into the desolation of – *reality*.'

'Impressive,' said Nick. 'Should I . . . ?'

'William Butler Yeats,' said Alan, still actorish. 'The great Yeats. A poem called "Meru". Meru, the sacred mountain of the Hindus. He's talking boars, for sure.'

'Of course,' said Nick, blinking rapidly. 'Wonderful stuff.'

'Mythologic,' said Alan.

Lucy realised Jean-Luc had lied to her. And so had the tenant, who had described the lawn as 'fantastic' on the phone some time ago. She was surprised at the depths her heart had abruptly sunk to when they'd rounded the corner of the house and seen nothing that resembled a lawn inside the low, mean-looking electric fence. She now sealed her disappointment from view by rolling her eyes and exaggerating it: 'Lord. All I want, for God's sake, is a blasted bloody lawn. Oh, Lordie me. Oh *really*.'

'Duck – and cover!' laughed Alan, while Mr Fusspot reacted by kneeling on the ground like a knight begging forgiveness of his queen.

In fact, some of the seeds had sprouted after a few days, encouraged by the recent warmth, and he was showing them that, from a very low angle, the area appeared hazed in green. It was a clear sky, with that southern sleekness of blue to it, and the sun was almost burning on their northern skins. It had already dried out the seeded earth, well soaked that morning. The girls were very quiet in the barn, no doubt peeping on the visitors. Which felt vaguely unauthorised, Nick thought. Tallish white flowers like cow-parsley had come from nowhere and were scattered quite thickly around the yard. He disliked the Sandlers being here, despite Alan's bonhomie. They smelt of interior furnishings in confined spaces, of stale urban perfume.

Nick was dressed in long, newly bought shorts and looked, to Lucy, ridiculous with his white legs, his bony shins, his sandalled socks. Only the English ever wore socks with sandals. He placed both hands on the ground, his chin almost touching the ground as he squinted.

Lucy was fed up. The Fusspots evidently felt bad, through their fusspottery, about dragging their landlord and lady all the way down here, and he was trying to cheer her up. It was a forlorn task: she saw, in her failure to grow a proper English lawn, far deeper failures. The tenants irritated her with their ingratiating smiles and genial falsities, although the wife (she felt) could pack a punch. They were like flies, to be swatted away. But she was nevertheless polite, diplomatic.

No one had yet mentioned Jean-Luc by name. She would have to see him in person. She would have to explain, like a mother to her son. This is what friends recognised about Lucy: that she was courageous and deep-feeling, in her own odd way.

If she hadn't been sent to boarding school at the age of six, she might (she would say) have been as sweet as glucose.

Alan volunteered to touch the electric wire, insisting it be switched on against Nick's advice; and claimed – tapping the tape three times with a 'Right?' after each touch – it was a mere tickle. This was embarrassing, given the panicked phone call the other day. Nick marvelled and looked sheepish: he'd felt the shock had pretty well amputated his limb.

'I was a farm boy, summers,' Alan explained. 'We played catch with balls of barbed wire.'

He tapped the tape again, looking at Nick with a boy's crooked smile, head on one side. 'Right?' You could see the shock pass across his eyes like tracing paper.

They also contemplated the pool's startling murk. Lucy groaned. Alan quoted Shakespeare, this time: 'The green mantle of the standing pool,' he intoned, waving a hand.

He glanced up at Nick as if throwing a ball. Nick fumbled it. '*Hamlet*. Fantastic.'

'*King Lear*. Poor Tom and his foul fiend.'

'You know your literature,' said Nick. 'I'm a history person, myself.'

'And who ended up a crooked dealer?' wheezed Alan, gripping Nick's elbow again so it hurt.

'He did his masters in Flann O'Connolly,' said Lucy, flatly, without raising her eyes from the murk. 'Harvard. And she was a fervent Catholic.'

'Flannery O'Connor, doll. A genius,' Alan went on. 'She knows her evil people.'

'Hey,' said Nick, like a freckled junior in an American movie. He wasn't quite sure whether he had heard of Flannery O'Connor. He felt he was threatening the reputation of the entire university. 'The Irish are great storytellers, of course,' he said.

'What's that got to do with O'Connor?' asked Alan, mischievously.

'Ah,' said Nick, and he actually blushed.

'My favourite story,' Alan pursued, 'is about the encyclopedia salesman who falls for this virginal spinster in her thirties with a wooden leg, and they sneak off to a remote barn and kiss and drink whiskey and she's swooning with love and he asks her to remove her wooden leg so that she can be kinda purer. Then what happens? Huh? The salesman is very young, a Tennessee country boy, very sweet and lickspittle.'

'I haven't read this one,' said Nick.

'They elope and live happily ever after?' suggests Sarah.

'No way. He steals it. The wooden leg. He grins evilly and puts it in his travelling case and tells her he's also stolen a girl's glass eyeball, and then leaves her stranded up in the loft of the barn, betrayed. End of story. He's the devil incarnate, you see. A liar and a villain. No scruples. O'Connor knew her evil. Given my own field, so do I,' he added, with a wink. 'And those people scare me.'

'Sounds like a parable for the invasion of Iraq, that story,' said Nick.

'Someone, we couldn't remember who,' said Sarah, hastily changing the subject, 'claimed swimming pools have no past and no future. We were discussing this the other day.' *Day* – the vowel edging towards 'die' to conceal any hint of privilege: a process started in her teens, never let go of. She was shy of it now, in front of Lucy's planed upper-middleness, the polish, the sheer towering wealth. She knew they were floundering in front of this couple, but this made her feel nicer as a person. 'Somebody French, we thought. Camus? You know, that they're pure present. Swimming pools. Not ordinary pools.'

'Lord, I hope this one has a future,' said Lucy.

Alan stood over the alarm with his hands on his hips, pursing his mouth.

'Oh yes,' said Sarah, 'did you find the code? It's probably best,' she added, with an apologetic grimace.

"'Tis sweet to hear the watch-dog's honest bark,' Alan proclaimed, 'bay deep-mouthed welcome as we draw near home.'

Nick nodded. 'You certainly know your Shakespeare.'

'Did the silly man actually fall right in?' asked Lucy, suddenly.

'Byron,' said Alan, with a smirk.

'I had to rescue him, pretty well,' said Sarah.

Lucy gave a little jerk of her head. 'How can you rescue someone "pretty well"? You either do or you don't.'

Sarah was mortified, as if she'd been unexpectedly ticked off by a favourite teacher. 'Well, I have to admit he helped himself a bit,' she murmured. 'I've a slight suspicion, anyway, he kind of fell in on purpose.'

'Silly man, spying on you like that. Taking photographs of *little girls*,' Lucy added, with a faux-shocked look. 'He's lived with his mother and never gone anywhere, not even Paris. Cats go dotty if they live with their mother, you know. He's gone stagnant,' she added, with a touching sigh, as if talking about her own son.

Nick didn't terribly like the generic, mocking appropriation of his children, but merely nodded. Sarah looked uneasy: Lucy was too much, a huge, thick dollop of meanings after the thin, two-month gruel of partly understood French. Alan was checking out the pool-shed, the pump, the system. The pool purred and clicked under the surrounding woodland murmurs.

'We haven't seen your children,' Lucy exclaimed, as if startled by the fact.

'No, they're playing in the barn. Their favourite place. Let sleeping dogs lie,' Sarah said, blushing for some reason, as if she'd committed a faux pas.

'They're remarkably quiet,' said Lucy. 'Are you sure they're not crushed under the old waggon or something?'

Sarah laughed, though she was shocked at the callousness. She spotted a tiny hand clasping the side of the barn's opening.

Lucy went on, in an altered, businesslike tone: 'We've had trouble at the gallery over people taking photos of our photos of nudes, and then sticking them on the Internet with different faces or something. Very postmodernist, I don't think.'

'What people won't do,' said Nick. He felt life had taken on a new lustre since the panic over the girls, but he knew it wouldn't last. The coin would be flipped again. It was flipping every day. Now London was sweeping through like a tidal flood, brown and dismal.

'The man's a disaster,' said Lucy, staring at the water. In fact, she was almost relieved by its snot-green state: it made getting rid of Jean-Luc that much easier. She had clung onto him in a way she now saw as pathetic and needy. He was useless, she reflected. That's all there was to it. He was useless and he was, in addition, creepy. He was probably into rubberwear or flag-ellation as well as little girls. You never knew with the French. She was lucky he hadn't grappled her to the ground and screwed the living daylights out of her (or worse) when Alan wasn't around. Oh, she was fed up, really fed up. 'God, don't you wish you were back in England?'

'You must be joking,' laughed Nick.

'Yes,' said Lucy, reflectively. 'With everyone getting fat.'

'Really?' said Sarah, as if she didn't know.

'Lord, yes. Ugly and fat. Ugh. Fatter and fatter by the day. Special hospital beds and crematoriums. You've probably heard. I say throw them out for the crows on special hills.' She talked of England as if they'd been away years; Sarah found it rather gratifying. In some ways, it did feel like years. Wasn't Alan Sandler fat? Or did she mean obese? 'Such awful *middle-middle* taste,' Lucy went on. 'Distinctly *middle-middle*, because that's what most of these urban designers are, it's all they know. I've met some of them. Twangy vowels. Middle-middle or *lower-middle*, even: style, I'm talking about. Design. All over the place, even in the trains. The whole of England carpeted with it, along with their ghastly music. Especially the countryside. I had to go up to Manchester last week.'

'Oh, yes. I like Manchester,' said Nick. 'I was following Engels about,' he added, chuckling.

'Used to be so wonderfully sombre,' Lucy pounded on. 'Proper working-class sombre with that mournful smell of coke. Now it's an indescribable municipal *vulgarity*. Giant screens, sex every-where. Aspiring proletarian, I call it. Appetite. Everything has to be crammed. Crammed with flavour, crammed with goodness. That's their favourite word. *Crammed*. More and more like that ghastly country Alan comes from, for whose sakes we're all going to go to hell in a handcart, along with the lovely animals and trees and beautiful flowers.'

'God bless America!' called out Alan from the pool-shed door.

'And now China,' sighed Lucy, still gazing into the murk, alarmingly unstoppable. 'The schlock shop of China. So seedy. Jettisoning the last shreds of their ancient wisdoms for the same old Americanised slush, without the freedom even to complain. Utter, utter vulgarity. Slush and sludge and slurry. Destroying nature for nothing but a dirty slurry of dollars. Greece is the same, of course, plus Greek *men*,' she added, with a shudder. 'Everywhere's the same, pretty much. *Even* Islamic countries and that lovely Arabic curve – replaced by straight lines in concrete. Oh, Lord. Don't you agree?'

'Oh yes,' said Nick, cocking his head like a parrot, unexpectedly warming to her. 'This is very much my line. The last days of Babylon.'

'We're all guilty of it,' Sarah interjected, conscious of her pedigree, that maybe it fell straight into the middle-middle category; thinking how all this was really an attack on them, the genteely impoverished Mallinsons. 'We all have to make an effort. It's not that we're above it or innocent ourselves.'

Lucy looked at her as if she had popped up from somewhere lower down. Nick suggested jovially (perhaps unaware) that they'd better start thinking about lunch. Which was unsubtle code for: Sarah, get on with it.

Sarah went into the house while Alan checked the *caves* for whatever reason. Lucy and Nick entered the barn – where the girls were hiding, their position given away by snorts and giggles. Nick found it on the cusp of cheeky, but Lucy seemed reasonably amused. She discussed projects for the barn with him. He felt it would be a cinch, to be an architect. He was full of ideas and she told him he was very clever. Something about Lucy's withering honesty attracted Nick, despite the snobbery. Or even, in the darkest depths of his soul, *because* of the snobbery.

Alan followed Sarah into the house, having inspected the cellars alone. One cellar in particular, its door yielding to his combination sequences like a djinn's spell. He checked no one was watching, pushed his dark glasses up on his forehead and stepped in. The metal box was still in the corner, untouched. He didn't unlock it. It excited him even more, not looking. The white-marble beauty concealed. Five thousand years pulsing unseen. It was a kind of magnetic core to all of life.

He talked to her in the kitchen about the history of Sumer, checking out behind his re-established dark glasses the inimitable slopes of her breasts as they descended into the fashionably low-cut top perilously close, by his calculation, to the nipple. They had a good, smooth shape, the colour of clover honey, and he wondered whether they were helped by a bra or were buoyed up naturally by their own muscle. Furtive sex acts shadow-played in the back of his head as he talked Gilgamesh, Ur, Uruk and the goddess of Love, Astarte. He bet her lanky, intellectual husband was no great shakes in bed. Even without Viagra, he would have been hard put not to try it on, not to break through the crust of her diffident, cerebral Englishness to the hot lava beneath. If only he had his life over again. If only he could halve his weight, suck out the flab with a pump.

She grilled thyme-sprinkled chèvres on toast and tossed the salad, criss-crossing it with honey: a light, tasteful, local-produce lunch, with rolls of expensive organic ham patterned with *corni- chons*. Although she felt less uncomfortable than she'd expected to, the idea that the Sandlers had flown down to 'sort things out', like parents or teachers, preyed on her equanimity. She was worried about Jean-Luc, about what he would do when told he was fired; the Sandlers were not worried. Local handymen were always being relieved of their posts.

It was, nevertheless, like a visit by a ghastly royal couple, and it made Sarah feel she was a guest, suddenly. No, a skivvy preparing lunch, cleaning up, fearful lest something be in the wrong place or damaged by the kids. They hadn't, for instance, replaced the bottle in the wine cellar – corked or no.

Alan Sandler was interesting on Sumerian art, although he was quite clearly eyeing her up. Or maybe that was just his manner. It was a burst of something other, suddenly, in their rural fastness. It was almost a relief. Lemon juice discovered an unknown scratch on her finger.

'What's that?' she asked, interrupting him.

Alan cocked his head. A series of trills, warbles and sudden heart-rending wails, like something being torn, was dimly audible. Sarah opened the door and it appeared to flood the kitchen in unstoppable swirls.

'Oh, that's the crazy nightingale,' said Alan. 'Same place every year, just beyond the washing line. No volume control. That's why we avoid April and May,' he added, chortling wheezily.

'I thought they sang at night. Wow. It's lovely.'

'All day, all night. Trying to get a woman. I know the feeling.'

The girls had emerged from the barn and she called them over; their interest in the nightingale's performance lasted a few minutes. It seemed not to be bothered by them approaching and trying to spot it, although they were forbidden (on pain of horrendous reprisals) not to disturb it physically. It remained invisible in the undergrowth, as if by magic.

Lunch was a success, in the end, if tiring. The kids behaved, mostly, although Beans chose the moment of serving to go bright red, as if blowing up a balloon, and surreptitiously fill her nappy. Alan had descended to the wine cellar and, instead of running back screaming 'Thief!', emerged with a dust-shouldered bottle of 1987 Morgon. It was not corked. A mixture of fresh wet grass, crushed acorns and plum. Nick put a CD of Mozart string quartets on the stereo.

'Of course, you barely need to touch these ingredients,' said Lucy, cutting into her rolled-up ham, its *crème fraiche* fill spurting beyond the plate's verge and the *cornichon* dice tumbling, too small to bother with.

Jamie was nowhere to be seen and continued thus, which was a relief. Sarah did not find his Scrabble joke funny, in the context. A few more days and he would be gone; he had actually agreed to this. The idea of resuming life here without Jamie was dream-like, filled her with anticipation. You repeatedly struck your head against a wall to know the pleasure of stopping. After a good few solitary joints in front of a camp-fire, he would decide to resume where he'd left off: depart, in other words. This had been the pattern, so far. He even had his own wind-up torch. He was, in some ways, resourceful.

The Sandlers, it turned out, were going to their favourite and very smart restaurant near Valdaron. They had not suggested the Mallinsons accompany them, nor accepted the offer of being cooked for again. The first would have been awkward whether they had picked up the considerable bill or not, but their refusal to sample Sarah's cooking – duck *à l'orange* for the main dish, the zest having been soaked overnight in Grand Marnier – smacked of snootiness. Her efforts were a bit show-off in their complexity, she realised, as a banquet for the royal progress would have had to have been.

They held back the duck for the following day and retreated to pancakes, savoury and sweet, made with the girls' help in what Sarah called a 'dedicated pan' bought in St-Maurice. Supper was early and felt vaguely bereft, although Sarah was growing weary of Alan's friendly hand on various bared parts of her body. The Sandlers had enjoyed lunch, it seemed, but didn't quite say so enough. It had looked a touch contrived, she now realised. Middle-middle, straining too hard. Only the wine was class. Unequivocal transcendence.

Now the guests were out and the Mallinsons were settling again, although the house felt curiously estranged from them, literally filled with the Sandlers' respective scents. The master bedroom, to which they had retired to change, was the head-quarters of the entire world perfume industry, Nick commented with a laugh. As for the pancakes, Beans and Alicia would only eat the sweet ones. Lemon squirted into the former's eye. The latter part of supper was in the shadow of her intermittent screams. 'Like living near Heathrow,' Nick joked. He was strangely perky, tonight.

'I prefer the nightingale,' said Sarah.

'Really boring, that bird,' said Tammy. 'It's going to drive me mental.'

She asked why Jamie was staying so long upstairs.

'He's not upstairs, he's out,' said Sarah. 'Making his camp.'

'He *is* upstairs,' Tammy insisted. 'We heard him on top of us.'

'Toppa toppa toppa toppa,' Beans intoned. 'Toppa toppa top –'

Sarah shushed her with an unthinking abruptness that froze her face in shock. 'Are you sure he's up there, seriously, you two?'

'We *did*,' said Alicia, thrusting her head forward, her lips glittering with sugar.

'That's a relief,' said Nick, who tended to worry when Jamie was absent after leaving loaded messages. This one was particularly loaded, even though it must refer to the poor builder. *I didn't fall, I was pushed. Whooooooo.* At the back of his mind, it had reminded him of the suicide note that poor Duncan Haighley had left last year: *'No one's fault. I climbed too high. Sorry.'*

'Shall I call him for supper?' asked Sarah.

'Why not?'

Beans, after meditating on the hurt, began to quiver her lower lip.

'I'll do it!' Tammy and Alicia yelled, simultaneously. There was a brief scrap which ended in something underhand and possibly vicious, from which Tammy emerged victorious and Alicia in apparent agony, clutching her tummy. Tammy yelled up from the bottom of the stairs over Alicia's wails, which had stymied Beans's. There was no response.

'Are you sure he's there? Please, Alicia.'

'I'm very *very* sure, Mummy.'

'He's sulking,' said Nick. He went up to check, not by rattling the attic door but by standing in his and Sarah's bedroom. There were creaks and thumps from the ceiling. He tiptoed up the crooked stairs. He had the suggestion of a headache from the red wine at lunch.

'Jamie,' he called through the attic door in a businesslike way, 'it's supper. Pancakes.'

Jamie loved pancakes. He can't be asleep, Nick thought, listening to the silence. When he wasn't asleep, he would always respond, if only with a grunt.

It was a strange silence. This was the silence, not of an empty theatre, but of a full theatre at a moment of suspense. Breathless. Except that it went on and on.

Jamie had shut himself away before – for five days once, in Cambridge – so they weren't unduly worried. In the morning the three pancakes left over for the girls' breakfast had gone. 'The mouse has been,' joked Sarah, who was nettled, especially as the mouse had left an empty glass of wine in the sitting room and the sticky, sugary plate on the kitchen table. There'd been a couple of creaks above their heads as they'd dressed, but otherwise neither had detected any sounds in the night, although the non-stop nightingale – joined by several others further off – hampered their listening.

There were no sounds, either, from the master bedroom, except an intermittent rumble through the ill-fitting door which they presumed was Alan, snoring.

The Sandlers had got back at midnight, moments before the Mallinsons had finished the washing up prior to heading upstairs to escape them. The nightingale, after a break in the afternoon, had been burbling, trilling and tearfully wailing all evening.

'Take a break!' Alan shouted.

Both couples had drunk too much, the Sandlers' perfumes battling with a haze of expensive wine and a tint of cigars, the Mallinsons content with local plonk bought at the market, whose only merit was its organic nature. Alan had insisted on a nightcap – brandy – to round off a session that had begun with pre-supper whiskies; the conversation in the sitting room was equable, even after Nick, following a remark from Lucy about the French liking to be different from everyone else, had praised their tenacity over Iraq.

'OK,' Alan said, his white jacket impossibly crumpled, 'you know what I think? I think life is a flowing stream and we all flow with it. I was at Woodstock, Nick, and I dreamed my dream, I thought the world was turning the corner; I saw Jimi Hendrix play the guitar with his teeth in the rain but I was wrong, the world is not full of nice, caring people, only the nice, caring people keep thinking it is and allow the crazy and evil guys all the mileage and *complain* –' here he leaned forward menacingly, '*complain* when the realistic, practical guys go in and do more than just make *caring* noises, while cashing in on the liberal, democratic and capitalist miracle.'

Nick stared at him through a fug of alcohol and tiredness, astonished. 'You were at *Woodstock*, Alan?'

'You glimpse me in the film. You've seen the film? I am glimpsed by history. I am the thin, handsome, long-haired, bearded youth near the stage for one shot of approximately two seconds, only the world is not looking at me, it's looking at Jimi's teeth-work on his Fender's A string.'

'I am physically green with envy,' said Nick.

The two women were smiling inanely, half-asleep. 'Maybe the pool's envious, too,' said Lucy, dreamily. 'Envious of the stream.'

As they were saying goodnight to each other – an awkward moment, as neither couple wished to go up simultaneously, although desperate for sleep – a whoozy Lucy had whispered to Nick in his ear, her hand firmly around his forearm, 'Whatever you do, darling, don't, don't, don't, *don't* mention Vietnam. Woodstock's just fine.'

The girls woke up at seven o'clock the next morning; they'd been told to keep as quiet as possible, but their fierce stage whispers on the landing were almost worse. Bursts of giggles sounded like explosions. Nick and Sarah, feeling somewhat hungover, also kept whispering to each other, despite the thickness of the walls. The final decision over Jamie was to leave him be, saying nothing about it to the Sandlers; the latter were due to see Jean-Luc later in the morning – he was always home at midday 'in true French fashion', as Lucy had asserted the previous evening. They would pay him off with a bonus he didn't deserve, and the Mallinsons would not be bothered again. Alan was to spend the rest of the day in the area's various junk shops, mental hospitals and care homes.

This had intrigued the Mallinsons, as intended: he was, as he'd explained over the pre-prandial whiskies in the sitting room early the previous evening, branching out into a new and very profitable field.

'Art Brut.'

'Oh yes,' Nick had said, vaguely. The twilight was purple through the window-glass. 'Um, André Breton, was it? Or do you mean the aftershave?' he joked, regretting this immediately.

'Art that does not have any idea that it is art.'

'It does really,' Lucy slipped in, 'it just pretends it doesn't.'

'That's *fake* Art Brut, sweetie-pie. We are not interested in fakery, only in the true and the innocent. What I am talking about is the purest expression of the interior soul, the unmediated creative current splashing outward and unsullied by the intellect.'

'Oh, the intellect,' Nick said, in a mock-sepulchral tone, 'that dreaded beast from the vaults.'

Alan Sandler dabbed his plump, shining face with a tissue, unsure how to take the irony. 'You got it. How would you define history, Mr Oxford Professor?'

'Cambridge. And not yet a professor. Only doctor.'

'Cambridge. Doctor.'

'Oh,' said Nick, crossing his endless legs at the ankles, 'as a series of vague and soiled snapshots you try to form a narrative from? Interpret? Will that do?'

'Art Brut is art that is bashful of history,' said Alan, creasing his eyes like a cowboy used to long horizons.

He took another gulp of the Glenlivet they'd brought along with them and sieved it through his teeth in a silent snarl. He was on his third. The hearth-fire roared as it had done from the moment they'd arrived and it was too hot. He had donned a white jacket and trousers and looked like a seedy, retired vice-consul somewhere tropical before the war.

Lucy said, 'What he really means by "unsullied" is that he can acquire it for free and sell it for a fortune. It's the latest craze in New York, you see. Feelings and intimacy are in. Amateur nonsense, *actually*.'

'Amateur implies auteur,' Alan objected, jabbing a finger at his wife across the rug. 'Implies self-consciousness. Has meaning only in relation, be that of denial, with its twin – the professional. The fatal dialectic. This is much purer. This is as pure as cave art.'

Nick wondered how this sodden slob in the sofa could think so sharply and eloquently. It excited him, this contact with a corrupt intelligence, out there in the real world of wheelers and dealers.

'Supposing I were to scribble on a newspaper with a biro,' Sarah had said, flatly; she was snatching fifteen minutes while Tammy read to the other two upstairs: a fresh venture that had the merit of the novel.

Alan looked at her, wheezing through his nose. 'You are not innocent. You have eaten of the tree.'

'Oh, I don't know.'

'You most certainly have,' he said. 'I *hope* you have.'

'Here we go,' said Lucy. 'Drink up, Alan. Din-dins. We've booked the table for seven-thirty. It's Jean-Luc tomorrow, we don't want to be knackered. I believe in face-to-face.'

'You are afraid of it, Sarah,' said Alan, scratching his pocked, bun-like nose. 'Of your own *opulence*.'

'Gosh,' said Sarah, raising her eyebrows and setting her head back awkwardly, as if she'd just seen something unpleasant.

Nick wondered what he should say or even do as he kept on smiling inanely. Lucy was on her feet.

'He's a terror,' she said, indulgently. 'Come on, Mr Charm itself.'

'Opulence,' said Mr Charm itself, rising unsteadily with a brief, improvident noise like a flapped newspaper that might have been a fart or the sofa's old springs. 'Sheer unadulterated opulence,' he reiterated, gazing for a second or two on Sarah's modest cleavage. Any doubts about the noise were quashed by an additional sequence of reports, sounding as if someone were hammering steadily from within his considerable lower regions.

Lucy talked over it about keys while Sarah pretended there was a squall upstairs – when there was (for once) flat calm. Alan's gaze followed her hungrily as she rose from the chair. Nick felt proud rather than annoyed. Both men watched her mount the stairs, a bustle of maternal bother, her best skirt rippling above her ankles as if in pursuit, the image only dampened by the gradual modulation of the air by Alan's interior, long-suffering recesses. The smell seemed to putrefy Nick's thoughts as effectively as a high-frequency scream.

'Cliffs of fall, frightful, sheer, no-man-fathomed,' said Alan, quietly, still gazing up. 'Hold them cheap may who ne'er *hung* there.'

History – or the interesting bit – is in the surplus luggage, Nick would tell his students; or what we call 'legacy'. The snapshots image had come to him on the instant, it was entirely off the cuff. Or due to the whisky.

Just before the Sandlers went off to 'deal with' Jean-Luc, when Alan and Nick were checking the progress of the cherry tree (very poor) and some other dubieties under the hapless Jean-Luc's aegis (the wood-treating of the pool's shed; a short stone path from it to the pool's tiles; the pool itself), Iraq came up again. It came up yet again because Alan said, staring at the uneven, un-cemented stones of the path, 'I'll tell you the real reason the French blocked the invasion. They don't like hard work.'

Nick gave a stage-groan. Iraq's bed of nails was the very defin-ition of legacy. It made the Suez crisis look like a comfy old sofa; on the other hand, regarded from his position as an oil historian specialising in Chad, it was a triumph, pure strategic brilliance. Chad and Iraq: the same massive undrilled fields, the same trope. All the US had to do was dirty France's name in

Chad through some covert operation or other, then fight it out with China. In Iraq, there wasn't even China – or Russia. A game of poker, yes – luck, strategy and guile – but the luck factor was a masquerade, the chaos a double-bluff.

Sometimes Nick was tempted to believe again in universal, transcendent laws, so distinct was the pattern in the carpet. As for justice: there was so little of it, but that was not the historian's purview. Collecting the evidence and making sense of it, inductively and deductively, then turning it into coherent narrative, as close to the 'truth' as possible: that was all (post-Michelet) one was required to do. The rest had to be put in the deep-rage room, where it smoked and smouldered but never caught – must never catch.

That is to say: he no longer believed in the Revolution. Or in any kind of redemption, much. His very body felt ramshackle.

And he had this sense, more and more often, that this was a reflection of something greater, or perhaps deeper, than simple age. By carelessness more than design, he had accepted to play a minor role in the college's links with the 'Guild of Cambridge Benefactors', shaking hands with owners of international construction companies, slick-haired property investors and corpulent oil sheikhs who had slid a considerable number of dinars into the university fund. Even closer to home – aware that no one was disposable these days – he helped to entertain wealthy alumni at small, fancy dinners in the Master's Lodge; one of the Master's current prospects was – according to the Internet – an arms dealer as well as a constructor of rigs. The bolts on Nick's ideological framework were so loose as to be useless: in 1997 he had voted for Blair, the ultimate hollow man.

But when Alan claimed, after Nick's pained groan, that the invasion would be judged as a fine, honourable decision in a hundred years' time, and that any other view was a failure of historical imagination, Nick had to object. He was stung by 'fine', he was provoked by 'honourable', he kept seeing that little girl's head rolling away to the father's feet, or however it had happened. Safia.

They had moved over to the pool, looking for any improvement that might be the consequence of Nick's half-improvised cocktail of shock chlorine and clarifier two days ago.

'A smart, cold-blooded oil-grab, maybe,' said Nick, 'of vast advantage to the survival of America's unfortunate lifestyle, but you just cannot say there's anything fine or honourable about something that, if it *hadn't* happened, would have left hundreds of thousands of people, including small children, with their lives intact and still, presumably, to be enjoyed.'

He was tired of Alan's swaggering mind; he was worried about Jamie; his pseudopolyps had transformed into a soreness he felt might have tumorous ambitions.

'What did you think of Star Wars?' asked Alan, folding his arms by the filter. 'And I don't mean the film.'

'Star Wars? Lunatic. A dim cowboy's wet dream.'

Alan gave a low chortle. 'First, Ronald Reagan was not dim, as his diaries prove. I've just read them. His dimness was a front and you swallowed it. Second, his policies broke the Soviets without a shot being fired. Yet I'll bet my bottom cent you were manning the barricades against him with all those crazy lesbians, sure in your own virtue. Like Stalin. Like Hitler. Like Saddam. Like Bin Laden. Like Pol *Pot*. Actually, like Che Guevara. Che shot defenceless people. He shot prisoners in the back of the neck. I'll bet you didn't know that. Did you know that? In Cuba?'

'He was a guerilla fighter,' shrugged Nick. He knew so much about what his old hero had got up to that he didn't know where to start, it would be embarrassing. 'I wrote a book about it, actually. He was killed in Bolivia fighting a vicious drugs junta, a junta run by the likes of Klaus Barbie and backed to the hilt by the CIA.'

'Let's readjust that,' said Alan, who seemed not to have heard the latter part. 'He was a mass-murdering leftist guerilla fighter therefore we forgive him.'

'Erm, not *quite* fair . . .' Nick had never been able to handle arguments over intricate matters when they were slapped on with a wallpaper brush. He preferred to back off, even when (as now) his heart was thumping with rage.

Alan turned on his heel with a snort and walked away, joining Lucy at the door of the house. He had a hangover, he was cross, he was fat and grumpy. The nightingale abruptly switched itself on and he told it to shut up yet again, but yet again it ignored him.

'Where are the hunters when you need them?' shouted Alan, and the women laughed.

Nick stared into the murk, with the odd sensation that he was dressed in pyjamas. He breathed in deeply and blew out slowly. Reagan himself was not his field, that was the trouble. The diaries had not yet been published in Britain. He had skim-read the odd review in American journals; he'd been busy, deprived of sleep. Perhaps he would send Alan one of the numerous remaindered copies of his short book, *The Violent Stage: Che Guevara and the Cuban Revolution*. The shooting of the prisoners occupied a chapter unravelling and defining complex social and ideological forces: too general, he now thought.

The pool was an even deeper green, with khaki highlights and ringlets and curls of foam like patterns in wood. It smelt of old, damp belfries. The scum by the surface had rooted as slime, waving its tiny suckers on the sides. Every life, he considered, tends towards this murk. It is all such a huge and continuing effort, retaining clarity, keeping it running clean. Had they all been so wrong?

He watched Alan and Lucy Sandler heading for their car, Sarah nodding with Tammy at the kitchen door. The nightingale's voice seemed to be growing in volume, ecstatic and heartbreaking at the same time, echoed by others beyond, so that he got a sense of a kind of conspiratorial desire to keep it all going, to trigger the seasons despite humanity.

He decided that, when Jamie finally emerged from his sulk, he would pour love onto him. He would not assume that his son was a hard-luck story. He would treat him like a miracle. More or less.

SIXTEEN

Jean-Luc has not found the camera. Three days ago he set off long before dawn on foot, with the big key to the Mas in his tunic pocket. He hadn't brought his dark glasses because it was dark anyway, but the small patch in the blur he could see through was not really enough, it was hard to make out the road, what was surface and what was ditch. He nearly tripped over a badger, a big black-and-white fuzz crossing the lane in the usual spot, lit by the shivering beam from his torch. When he was a kid it was the same spot, same time – but not the same badger, he assumed.

They have a nasty bite, Janno. Their back paws step exactly where their front paws have been, see? Their setts are hundreds of years old, boy, like myself.

He misses his father, suddenly.

The walk through the woods, once he'd found his mobilette in the usual place and cut across, was possible only because the sky was lightening up, a deep green flushed with blue that danced about like fireworks in his head. Not having his dark glasses, he kept his eyes almost shut. The dawn chorus was set off by the loud whirr of a wren, probably his doing. The nightingales would be here any day. He liked them talking to him, over and over.

The house was a black cliff, approached from the north. He thought he heard kids' voices over the chirps and trills and kept very still, crouched in the undergrowth under the holm oaks. When the high voices faded (if that's what they were), he advanced slowly towards the area where he'd cut the spurge, the light and the shadows fusing in his creased-up eyes, soldered together then splitting apart. This is probably how animals see, he thought. Sounds and smells, sharper. Sometimes he was on all fours.

He would have liked to have been an animal. A big cat. A puma. Light on his paws.

It was hopeless. There was no camera, although he peered all around by the pool-shed, crouched, fearful of being spotted from the windows. A blackbird yelled out suddenly and made him jump. He had the key to the house but he didn't feel like sneaking in, disturbing someone.

He made it back to Aubain on the mobilette by seven-thirty and a woman shouted at him in the main street, but he didn't see who. He just slipped back into the house as if he hadn't heard. The street already smelt of coffee and bread, and he'd detected shampoo from the neighbour's steamed-up bathroom window, one floor up: his nose was hunting-dog sharp.

Three days later, and he's lying on his bed as if he's crash-landed from off a roof. They must have found it, along with the binoculars and the brush knife. Maybe the film is being developed right now, exposing him. Three or four days: that's enough. He lies on his bed in his room and sees himself sprawled broken on the ground. People are coming up to him, running, and he can't move. Maman is still asleep: he put an extra sleeping pill in her tisane and she never tasted it. She is knocked right out. He does this more and more often, especially when he needs to slip out early. He didn't, not this morning, but who cares? It's a mercy for everyone.

When the new nurse comes, she has trouble waking Maman up.

His eyes are inspected in the kitchen. They're already healing, she says, and wipes them and squeezes in some eye-drops. 'You're a right pair,' she says.

'What, my eyes are?'

'No,' she laughs, 'you and your mum.'

She's young, early twenties, with big front teeth like the ends of celery stalks in a pretty, plumpish face; she smells of lilac scent, toothpaste and pure alcohol. She's called Marion. She has the narrowest waist he has ever seen: he can spot it even under her uniform, even through his injured eyes. He would like to squeeze it as she bends over him and presses her thigh against his hip, breathes on his face, touches his cheek with her pointy finger-pads. He likes the way her big teeth rest on her lower lip. He likes her dimples.

Afterwards, he wonders if he imagined her waist, because Bibi's waist is also very narrow, rising to sharp breasts. His eyes sting with the drops. Or maybe he's crying. He's sorrowing for the missing camera, he feels angry that they've kept it. It's his business, what he takes photos of. And he can't finish the monument. He needs the pictures of the English girls, their smiling faces, their pretty little flower-faces on the spoons. He seethes inside with frustration; he's done nothing but mooch about for three days, not even able to watch telly.

He puts on his most recent Johnny Hallyday very loud, ignoring his mother's wails. It's the song about blood, about the lovers being the same in their blood, about exchanging silence and now we're face to face we resemble one another, blood for blood, and he can see himself with the Englishwoman and how their blood's 100 per cent the same – Johnny makes it possible, and Jean-Luc knows all the words, he sings along in a whisper, in a murmur, rocking his head and wanting to sob and wail like Johnny, full up with love.

The whole village must be hearing it, he thinks, but no one complains. They're all dead. They're all zombies, sitting there in the café and talking about him, because he's the only one who's still alive. The rest of the world is dead, apart from him and the animals and the plants.

'Jean-Luc, you stupid oaf, turn it down!'

He shouts through the door, over the music: 'You're dead, Maman! The dead can't hear!' And then hits the door with his fist, because if he didn't hit the door he'd open it and hit her instead, over and over again. He thinks of his father's dog whose insides were ripped out by the boar, who went on whimpering and then lifted its head and smelt its own intestines, blood gleaming on its nose. He saw it for himself. He was ten or eleven.

This morning he sat in front of the monument and pleaded with Oncle Fernand to talk to him, but Oncle Fernand has gone silent. He is afraid of the Germans. The SS, not any old Germans. He's hiding so he won't have to take them to the Mas des Fosses. He didn't hide when they kicked the door open in the café, looking for someone to take them to the Mas des Fosses, to take them to the boys. He didn't hide because he didn't have time. Or maybe because he didn't think he'd be chosen. Of course he had time to hide! Everyone knew the SS were coming! They knew from three, four hours before! The news came up along the roads, the goat-tracks, over the hills from down below, all the way from Nîmes long before dawn, when the SS had left their barracks to cleanse the mountains of riff-raff, of trouble. Johnny Hallyday would have kept them at bay, singing his heart out. But Oncle Fernand was only twenty years old and had never heard of Johnny Hallyday. Johnny Hallyday was only just born, probably.

'I told you, Maman, if you don't shut your mouth I'll shut it for you! For good!'

Oh, how she squeals! Then nothing. Muttering, maybe, her false teeth loose. She could choke on her teeth, the nurse said. Jean-Luc feels he's smelling his own intestines, looking after Maman.

Let me think, he thinks, swaying as the next song starts, promising her his eyes if he can't see any more, the salt from the kisses on his mouth, the honey from the touch of his hand.

Oncle Fernand is still afraid, that's the trouble. He didn't hide because he hadn't any reason to; he'd done nothing, he'd always kept his distance from the Resistance boys, he just kept his head down and worked quietly at the tannery in St-Maurice, walking there and back with his limp, two hours each way. They waited for the SS to arrive and arrive they did, a hundred or more of them roaring into Aubain, ten times louder than Serge Faure

370

on his big motorbike. And when they kicked open the door of the café, asking someone to show them the way to the Mas des Fosses, Oncle Fernand didn't put his hand up. Although he did know the way, of course; he knew the way like the back of his hand from long before the boys made their camp there. He helped on the farm, that's why, as a lad, when they needed an extra pair of young hands. No other reason. They were distant cousins, that lot. Blood thicker than water. By rights, Jean-Luc thought, I should be living at the farm. By blood rights.

So who volunteered Oncle Fernand for the job?

Old Père Lagrange, that's who. Or that's what Maman has always told him, via Tante Alice. Tante Alice being Oncle Fernand's sister. Whom Jean-Luc never knew.

Old Père Lagrange, that's who. He was pissed as usual on fig brandy fetched from the straw in his cellar for old François Bouillon's birthday, who was eighty. They were all pissed, the old men, except for Oncle Fernand. Because he wasn't old, then. He was twenty. You were younger than I am now, thought Jean-Luc. By sixteen years. Seventeen.

And when the Germans asked – waving their automatic rifles about, guns that had shot dead whole families elsewhere (Poland, he was told), lined up in rows and falling like ninepins in front of their houses and barns – old Père Lagrange pointed at Oncle Fernand up at the bar, having his coffee after his Saturday morning at the tannery, and said, 'There's your man, Captain.'

There's your man.

There's your man, Captain.

Knowing the boys would be gone. The Resistance boys. Because Old Père Lagrange would supply paraffin for them, from his stores. Knowing how angry the Boches would be when they got there and discovered the boys had gone, had been gone for two days. Knowing that, most like. And still he pointed at Oncle Fernand, all innocent up at the bar, having his coffee in the very same café the great-grandson Marcel Lagrange goes to, and Raoul Lagrange used to go to, and all the other grandsons and great-grandsons and great-great-grandsons of old Père Lagrange still go to, unashamed. And signed Oncle Fernand's death warrant with that pointing finger, as if it had a nib on the end of it. And yet old Père Lagrange was a bit of a hero, after the war, for helping the boys. Helping them at his age, and with a dent in his forehead from the trenches. An article in the paper, all yellow now, when he hit a hundred. On show in a frame, for a while, in the *mairie*. Jean-Luc saw it, as a kid. The hero of two wars. A piss-yellow clipping from 1970, the year Jean-Luc was born.

Prodded him over the edge. Old Père Lagrange, the good-for-nothing bully who was sozzled by noon whether it was anyone's birthday or not, prodded Oncle Fernand over the edge with that pointing finger.

And Jean-Luc feels more and more enraged, reflecting on this for the umpteenth time, without Oncle Fernand's voice to calm him down. He finds that he's been scratching with the biro on the table. Faces, lines, bullets, circles and slits gushing blood. How many bullets did they pump into Oncle Fernand when they found the Mas empty? One, they reckon. Out of an automatic rifle.

They found the Mas empty, but there were potato and onion peelings in the kitchen and beds of bracken in the sitting room and cigarette stubs by the windows with the look-out views onto the valley and in the fireplace there was a big heap of ash, still warm in the middle when they kicked it.

They walked back with him halfway along the track to the lane and then they pressed the rifle to the back of his neck and the bullet came out through his face at the level of the nostrils, getting rid of it. Faceless Oncle Fernand, aged twenty. Did he cry when they jerked him round to look the other way? Did he cry and plead with them? Did he tell them, on the way back, that he'd had no idea the boys were ever even there? Did they kick him all the way back to where they shot him? Did they take his eyes out before they blew away his face?

Jean-Luc squeezes his own eyes tight, feeling the pain of it, of Oncle Fernand's innocence and the foreigners' guilt. Johnny Hallyday is singing his heart out at the song's end, giving him courage, believing like an innocent child who believes in the sky, promising her fire instead of a gun, salt from the kisses of his mouth, honey from the touch of his hand. My mouth, my hand. Her.

If the Germans were to come into Aubain now – he imagines this clearly enough, with all the war films that have been on the telly – he would take them out before they took him out. He wouldn't wait to be killed like a dog. He grips the monument and moves it from side to side so the spoons tinkle, empty except for one. The blind-eyed duck floating on the pond. This wouldn't float, though.

The missing camera is an agony. He can no longer watch the Englishwoman bathing in the nude. His life is a mess, he thinks. Oncle Fernand has run away so the Germans can't get him, leaving Jean-Luc to take his place, to face them alone. He wouldn't have let old Père Lagrange point him to his death. He'd have whipped out his father's hunting rifle and leapt up onto the bar and shot the SS captain – look at his surprised expression! – and then peppered old Père Lagrange, gurgling blood into his fig brandy, and then as many of the Germans as he could before their bullets tore him up like a hero, like all dead heroes, dead for France, dying on a sweet smell of fig brandy from the exploded bottle as Johnny's song fades in turn, guitar and voice and drums all fading at the end of the song.

Jean-Luc, exhausted, fists clenched around the monument, sees his own soul disappearing like the scut of a hare escaping into the trees. He sees himself as a marble monument, naked, snow-white, draped on a sheet. He would like to end up like that, he thinks.

But the next song starts like a heart beat, like life coming back, just the drums on their own, and then the guitar, and then Johnny wailing into the dark: *Oh, my pretty Sarah, how much more time?*

And then Maman yells. He covers his ears. He can hear her

yelling again through Johnny's pain and desire. There's someone at the door. He looks through the window and swears and leaps immediately to stop the music.

The Sandlers arrived at Jean-Luc's at midday. They felt midday was good because all French people, in their estimation, scuttled back home to eat at that precise hour, if they didn't have a rendezvous in a restaurant. It was unlikely Jean-Luc had a rendezvous in a restaurant, even if he hadn't been half-blind.

They were surprised to hear loud music belting from his house. It was audible as a murmur from halfway down the narrow main street of Aubain, but it had never occurred to either of them (they'd walked from the parking place in front of the church) that it might be coming from Jean-Luc's house. They had never, in the six years of employing him as a handyman and gardener, visited his house before. In fact, they weren't even sure which one it was until they asked a young girl with piercings, carrying a letter: most of the houses had no numbers on their doors, and there was no *Maille* visible next to what doorbells existed. When they realised the music – some awful French type of rock or *variété* – was emanating from the indicated house, they doubted the girl, but by then she'd disappeared.

There was a bell to press, somehow furred-looking and green about the gills. Lucy tried it. Alan was standing a little apart, looking grumpy and red in the face, with his felt homburg tilted against the bright sun. He thought the hat made him look distinguished: it was a recent thing. He hadn't wanted to come, but he was her minder. He couldn't understand why a simple phone call wouldn't suffice; if the key was the main issue, they could add a Yale to the door. He was tired from the travelling and the late night and felt there'd have been nothing wrong with a simple call.

Lucy believed in doing things face-to-face, however awkward; this stemmed from her gallery experience, working with difficult artists, dealers, members of the public. She visited studios and was loved for it, even by the many unattractive, sour-faced, linguistically challenged artists she had to deal with. She felt she could abate whatever anger or desire for revenge might rise in Jean-Luc simply by being present in front of him, carefully explaining the matter in her reasonable, accurate, schoolgirl French. She didn't want to be a village pariah. She didn't want to be put in the same box as those awful English types without a word of the language, using locals like pawns in some thoughtless game.

And the key worried her, in some deep way. It was a very old lock, the main lock to the house. Handing over the key would be a symbolic act of renunciation.

Behind it all, she wanted to see Jean-Luc's house.

When their dishy and reliable builder had fallen off the roof – reliable if you were behind him all the time, that is – she'd felt a wall of hostility from the village. Nothing was said: it was just one great silent wall. The funeral happened so quickly that it was over before she and Alan could even book a flight. They were still in shock. The man should have been wearing a safety harness, following EU norms. When the family tried to sue, she left it all to the lawyer. Horribly, for a moment it looked as if the family might win, might claim untold amounts, simply because he had been employed on the black. It was like the burglar falling into the pool: everything was on the side of the victim. She saw them sitting around an oilcloth-covered table, formidable in shawls and baggy clothes, gradually eating her for breakfast. She was fifty, sixty years out of date. They probably had a dishwasher.

Then, at the height of the stress, it all went quiet. He should never have gone up in the wet, the deep-voiced lawyer told her. No roofer ever goes up on a tiled roof in the wet, not down here: there's no grip on the curved barrel tiles, none at all. The sun was out that day, but it had rained in the night. The tiles hadn't dried, they were greasy, they were a skating-rink on a slope. You didn't push him to finish, did you? Put pressure on him? That's the rumour, here.

'No more than any other owner might,' Lucy said, from her

mobile in the back room of the gallery. 'You know what it's like.'

'You put no pressure on him at all, OK? Madame Sandler? *Nous sommes bien d'accord?* No pressure at all.'

The lawyer's sexy, chain-smoker's voice was unutterably soothing. She could marry this man, see themselves safely into old age, leave Alan to his mad mullahs.

'OK,' she agreed. 'It's clear.'

And that was that. They flew over. Everything left in place for weeks, as if time had stopped: the old tiles still stacked on the ground, beautifully stained with moss and lichen, ready to hide the new ones. The finished part ending just where, she supposed, he'd started to slide three or four feet from the bottom verge; a few little stacks of tiles up there like miniature chimneys, ready to lay; one tile loose and crooked, like a dramatic clue. It was horrible.

Standing in the attic, under the transparent plastic sheeting, she was just inches away from the actual moment, she felt. She thought she could hear his last grunt of surprise. Then Alan spotted, near the ladder leaning on the beam, a flask of coffee and a plastic tub. The coffee was spotted with green slime; the tub was a writhing mass of maggots. The lunch, no doubt prepared by his wife, that he never tasted. It gave her the worst migraine of her life.

Because of the music upstairs, she had no idea whether the bell had worked. She was suddenly a lot more nervous and glanced at Alan, who was peering upwards from the empty middle of the street, scratching his brow under the hat like a *film noir* detective. The house was narrow, squeezed in between other narrow houses, and rendered in a sallow limewash that was peeling to stone in places; its net curtains were yellowed and shrunk-looking, gave nothing away except that there was mystery beyond the rows of little lace dairy-maids: the mystery of poverty and neglect. She felt faintly adventurous. She hadn't had anything to do with poverty and neglect since her voluntary days with the soup kitchen in Paddington. The sunlight was bright as a polished knife; the street contrived to look shadowy.

Jean-Luc wouldn't like them to visit: this was sacred ground, like a dark temple. For all she knew, domestic privacy might be a major tradition in this area, even more major than in England. No proper local with local roots had ever invited her to their home here, she realised. She felt like a trespasser. A snooper.

'Maybe this isn't such a good idea,' she said, moving over to Alan.

'Sounds like he's having a ball,' Alan replied. 'Welcome to the *discothèque d'Aubain*.'

'Aubain does not rhyme with pain, Alan.'

'Doesn't it? Looks pretty gouty to me. I think we should retire to Malibu. Somewhere in the third millennium, not the first. I think he might be bats.'

'And get burnt up in a forest fire,' said Lucy. 'Forget it, sweetheart.'

'I think the curtain just twitched, up there.'

The music stopped suddenly in the middle of a song and didn't start again. Lucy had pretty well sprung for the bell before she'd had time to reflect. It sounded, decisively, from somewhere deep within. As if the house were clearing its throat.

'You know the stories of Edgar Allan Poe . . . ?' she murmured, with a wry grimace that Alan shared as a chuckle, folding his hands in front of the door and rocking back on his heels.

'Ooh la la,' he said, inconsequentially. He had little red shadows on each cheek, like blusher.

Jean-Luc received them in the kitchen, which the front door opened straight into. Steep stairs disappeared into darkness.

He looked as if he'd been awake for many nights, face stubbled around his off-putting wrap-around sunglasses in which no eyes were visible. Lucy didn't smell drink off him, however: Jean-Luc was not a drinker, she knew that. Most other men in the village, of his age or older, were drinkers, she reckoned.

At least, when they got close (usually in the summer, which perhaps wasn't fair) they carried with them a fragrance of alcohol, like walking gardenias.

He shook their hands and motioned to them to sit down. He was polite enough, if a little grim. You forgot he wasn't a blind man. She'd half-expected him to yell at them. The kitchen was gloomy, so goodness knows how he saw anything. As far as she could make out, almost every surface had been covered in vinyl – but a very long time ago, with flowery washable wallpaper between the cupboards that ought to have been put in a museum of Sixties memorabilia. The table's off-white vinyl was rippled, worn and holed by burns. Ditto the dark lino on the floor.

Then the darkness fled into dismal corners, banished by the neon above their heads. She blinked to adjust. One door on the wall cupboard was hidden behind faded coloured postcards from places like the Île d'Oléron and, surprisingly, a joke card from Guadeloupe with a row of palm trees under snow. Unless it snowed in Guadeloupe? The old, bulbous fridge gurgled and growled. There was a microwave, she noted, and a smell of coarse coffee and drains. She felt she had arrived, in some way. She would tell friends about it, how she had sat in the kitchen of a *paysan*, with nothing fake in it whatsoever. She wouldn't mention the postcard from Guadeloupe. Her account would supersede the visit to the Hopi house on the Arizona bluff thirty years ago, where she had admired a Bang & Olufsen stereo – which she did mention, as the sort of comic highlight.

'That's better,' she said, in French.

He hadn't yet smiled. His proffered palm had been rough-skinned. He definitely had an air of the unwashed. He sat down with a scrape of the metal chair and folded his hands in front of him. She couldn't see where exactly he was looking, he might have been sitting in a cave. He didn't offer them anything, which was disappointing. It marred Lucy's opinion of French hospitality. His mother was shouting in a high voice from up the very narrow, vertiginous stairs. He said something over his shoulder as if chucking it at her, an unintelligible rasping shout. The working classes were half-deaf: Lucy had always thought that. The mother shut up.

'Well, Jean-Luc,' she said, hearing the English words in her head before the French came out, simultaneously translating herself, 'we must speak of these problems.'

He nodded. Then he asked what problems. She itemised the lawn and the pool, the fact that the water was green and the lawn a disaster. Her vocabulary was more limited than she'd realised, it was always the same. She'd rehearsed this several times, but now that she was on stage the script dried up. She could barely think of any words other than those homonymically parallel, like *désastre*, or beginner-simple, like *vert*. It all needed oiling.

Jean-Luc kept his head bent, his hands trembling a little. She didn't think that was a good sign. His knuckles were raw as if gnawed and the skin blotched a cranberry red: not just the allergic reaction to the spurge, perhaps. Dry skin like laminate. Real poverty was ugly, she remembered. Jean-Luc was probably not even that poor: he worked for lots of people. At least a dozen. She'd met others at parties in the summer who joked about him, tolerating his foibles, one or two (certainly the very wealthy Danish couple with gilded skin and hair) who said he was indispensable, in so many words.

Jean-Luc explained about the pool and the lawn in his usual mumbled way, making no concessions with his accent. She nodded as Alan yawned and looked around him, an unhealthy colour under the neon: it was like sitting in an airport, where everyone looked ravaged, whatever their age. Alan didn't like Jean-Luc, she reminded herself: jealousy, mostly.

She said, picking words from her French hoard like one of those claw-grabs in a funfair, her pronunciation turning them plastic and cheap: 'I think there's a problem also with the English family, with what passed three days ago, with your relationship with them. I think you know of what I talk, Jean-Luc,' she added, smearing over an awkward sentence connection with

379

something between a sigh and a mumble so that the effect was weakened – not quite what she'd intended. It was a mistake to come here. Alan was right: he would have been quite prepared for a simple call. She had culturally misjudged. The lady never visited the peasant.

He paused and then said, in clearer French than usual: 'You should have had the alarm activated, Madame.'

It struck her in a flash, like a blow in the chest, what he was driving at. Alan, looking suspiciously at him, was sweating in his dark leather jacket, she could see the gloss on his cheese-white brow under the raised hat-brim.

'Jean-Luc, that was your responsibility,' she pointed out.

'It's always the responsibility of the owners, Madame.'

'You were saved,' she said, partly because it was the simplest way of saying it. If they'd been talking in English, she'd have said: 'This is irrelevant. You were fished out unharmed. Don't talk rubbish, mate.'

'I could report you,' he went on. 'I could sue you for damages. I have been ill for three days, swallowing the water. The chlorine and other products made my eyes worse. I've lost work.'

'What's he saying?' snapped Alan, in English. 'Is he saying he's gonna screw us? What a nerve.'

Lucy felt out of her depth: this wasn't the Jean-Luc she'd expected. He had revealed a cold, calculating side which was new to her. This must be the French thing. The remorseless logic of the Napoleonic law and so on. She felt very threatened, she wanted to see his eyes. It was like talking to a Mafia hoodlum.

She waved at Alan to shut up and turned to see herself twice over in the double screen of the dark glasses. Tiny and withered, like a sad old lady on television. 'You know there's no point, Jean-Luc. I have to say that I will be looking for another gardener, now. I'm very sorry. But I'm sure there are other people who have need of someone. It's best like that. Thank you for all you've done. I want to pay you –' she searched for the equivalent of 'properly' but couldn't find it, *proprement* might mean 'cleanly', so she petered out. 'Up to now,' she added, feebly. Lord, this was exhausting. *Jusque* or *jusqu'à maintenant*. Or *présent*, even, instead of *maintenant*? Oh, sod it.

His mother was calling again. He looked up as if cocking his ears, obeying a signal from beyond.

'She wants to say hello to you,' he said, with a faint smile. 'We have to go up. Hello and goodbye.'

'He's not going to sue us, period,' said Alan, staring at Lucy. He looked sillier in his hat, indoors. 'I think we should go. I'm thirsty. You and your face-to-face.'

'We have to greet his bedridden mother, Alan,' said Lucy, in as even a tone as possible.

'Why?'

'Because this is France and the French have their customs. They are not uncouth like us. We met her when we bought the house, if you recall. She was only lame, then. She came along with Jean-Luc. She was going to clean for us. He's accepted the situation, thank you.'

She turned to Jean-Luc; although he had kept his head very still, she felt he'd been listening. Listening without understanding. An upper-class Parisian friend had once told her that speaking English in front of a French person not in command of the language was the very pinnacle of rudeness.

'Do you want to give us our key, before we visit your mother?' she said, in French.

He stood with a scrape of the chair and reached up to an old, iron hook where a large number of keys hung on their strings. He handed over the one for the Mas des Fosses without a word.

Lucy thanked him neutrally, immensely relieved, and slipped the big key into her bag. It was a lot easier than she'd anticipated: it probably happened to him quite a lot. They went upstairs, Jean-Luc letting them go first. The stairs were very steep and the runner was loose. Alan was wheezing by the time they got to the room.

She went in all smiles. The air was appalling. The woman

was clearly incontinent. She had a broad, unexpected grin cut into her face that reminded Lucy of the jagged splits in a Hallowe'en pumpkin. Her face was entirely grey and shiny, with undefined knobbles and swellings through which her main features struggled to be noticed. Her hair was white and thin and wild. She stared as if aghast at their royal bearing. They shook hands with her in turn, Alan politely taking off his hat and booming a greeting in his hopelessly American accent that had her wide-eyed and marvelling. Jean-Luc was leaning against the wall, arms folded, with an odd expression of triumph.

Oh, Lord.

Madame Maille clutched Lucy's hand in both of hers and held on. Her eyes were wide and watery and her hands had been pulled from a bucket of ice. The only decorations in the room were a piece of sampler work in lace, framed behind cracked glass, and some ghastly ceramic thing with a bamboo surround featuring a duck. The wallpaper would once have been very loud, with a spatter effect and the embossed vertical treads of tanks. She clearly worshipped her son's employers. 'Adored' them, was how Lucy was going to put it back home.

'I hope you get better soon, Madame Maille,' said Lucy, conscious that this was special, a special moment she would share, embellished, with her friends.

She was also desperate to leave, to pull her hand from the icy grip and get into her car and speed away to a mug of builder's tea at home in London with Radio 4 or 3 murmuring in the background. It was embarrassing. Jean-Luc had bested them. They were firing her son and his mother had no idea. They were the wicked landlords, the cruel foreigners, the wealthy, hypocritical tosspots. She hated this. She hated not being in control of her own perfidy. Cornwall would have been better. Wales, even. No, not Wales.

Alan, hatless, was wiping his brow on a tissue, looking awful. The air was virtually non-existent, crammed with odours and Lord knows what germs. There was a little table on wheels full of medications and creams and, next to it, a commode. The cloudy white plastic bottle on the bedside cupboard contained dark liquid she imagined would be yellow if poured out. She felt sick. She would be like this herself in under twenty years. Twenty years was nothing. She must join a gym and eat nothing but nuts and berries. Madame Maille let go of her hand and sank back on the bolster, a slight frown on her speckled forehead, broad with hair-loss. The corners of her lips held gum. Old people are so detailed, Lucy thought.

'You're so good to my Jean-Luc,' said the loving mother. 'He doesn't deserve it.'

Jean-Luc laughed, a kind of yelp. '*Ils m'ont viré, Maman,*' he said, so clearly that even Alain could understand. *Viré*: it sounded as if they'd injected him with a deadly disease. He pointed to his dark glasses. Of course they hadn't sacked him because of that. Preposterous. It was at times like this that she desperately, desperately desired a cigarette, although it was five or six years since she'd stopped.

He went to the door and closed it. Then he leaned against it and folded his arms again with that menacing look his face took on in repose. Lucy's heart began to race. Madame Maille's frown deepened and her eyes, darkening, shifted their gaze from Lucy to Alan and back again.

'*C'est pas vrai,*' she said, in husky bewilderment.

Alan said, 'Let's go, Lucy. Excuse me, *monsieur.*' He was attempting to reach the door-handle past Jean-Luc's waist, without success. His hand hovered and fell. 'Lucy, let's go. He's blocking the door. He's bats. I told you.' Alan's hand was now up and shaking the air. 'Lucy, he's blocking the fucking door. Will you tell him? Will you tell him to stop fucking — to stop blocking the door? I'm thirsty. I can't stay here. I have to go.'

'I think we must go, Jean-Luc,' Lucy said, addressing the over-large dark glasses. Looking him in the eyes, or at least where she guessed them to be, she added a '*s'il vous plaît*', although she'd been *tutoy*ing him for years. It must have spoken volumes. Such an awkward language. She was not unafraid, she noted. The sickroom's fug had overwhelmed her underarm deodorant and she felt the tickle of sweat on her ribs.

He comes away from the door without a word and keeps his arms folded and watches them leave behind the mask of his dark glasses; they mutter and chirrup like birds, like parrots. He watches them descend the stairs, dark shapes in the darker darkness, emerging into the square of light cast by the kitchen neon. He stays upstairs. It is the rudest, most offensive thing he can think of doing, not to show them out, not even to shake their hands goodbye. He hasn't opened his mouth since he came away from the door. They were troubled, he could see that. Maman is talking away to him but he ignores her.

He slips quickly into his room because he wants to watch them go up the street, catch the way they look as best he can. He has power over them, still. They are running away. He has chased them away without raising his voice, without waving a gun at them as always happens in films.

Madame Sandler emerges in the street, and he concentrates hard on threading his vision through the hole in his lesions. His eyes burn, but on a low flame now. His eyelids scratch away at each blink, so he tries to blink as little as possible. She emerges, but her fat husband does not. She glances up, and Jean-Luc retracts his head from the net curtain, thick with plaster dust and gnats. Maman is talking away, as if to herself, accusing him of this and that.

He wonders why Monsieur Sandler has not appeared in the street below. Maybe he's dared to use the toilet. He glances down at the sheeted monument and has an urgent desire to look at it. He carefully removes the stained cloth, which he throws onto the bed. Then – the hunter's instinct – he glances over his shoulder at the door, which he hadn't bothered to lock.

The door has swung open. Monsieur Sandler is standing in the bedroom doorway, staring at him. Staring not at him, in fact, but at the monument. Monsieur Sandler's mouth is open.

Jean-Luc leaps to hide the monument with his body, biting his tongue in the shock. Monsieur Sandler says something in clumsy French about forgetting his hat, even though his hat is on his head. Jean-Luc shouts, now. He shouts at the man to get out. He can taste the blood from his tongue. Monsieur Sandler's plump hands come up and he says something else. Something about seeing, wanting to see, stepping forwards and craning to see the monument.

Jean-Luc raises his own hands and rests them on Monsieur Sandler's shoulders and pushes him towards the door. Monsieur Sandler resists, as heavy as a sleeping or even a dead man. He places his hands on Jean-Luc's wrists. Jean-Luc has to push him hard so that the man totters with tiny backward steps until he is over the threshold, his eyes continually on the monument and the scribbled-over sheets of paper around it. He has a surprising strength for a fat man. Every second that his eyes are on the monument rouses an anger in Jean-Luc that is not so far from grief. Last night he dreamt of a fish gasping for water on a riverbank.

Jean-Luc slams the door and locks it, gasping for air.

'He's a murderer!' screams his mother.

Jean-Luc doesn't know whether she's referring to him, or to the madman who broke into his sanctuary.

He looks at the monument.

Someone has swapped the original for a dead thing, a ridiculous contraption in which the toy pram is triumphant: just a toy pram stuck over with junk, with feathers and rubbish. No wonder Oncle Fernand has stopped talking to him: he must be disgusted and ashamed and angry.

Jean-Luc feels tears tickling his cheeks, causing him wasp-stings of pain. The salt mixes with the blood from his tongue. I can promise you the salt from the kisses of my mouth. Jean-Luc sings Johnny! The music's still ringing in his ears.

There is no one to kiss, or to promise anything to.

He removes his dark glasses and waits until the pain subsides, creasing his eyes against the bright light. His mother is complaining to Monsieur Sandler, a chuntering through the door like an old engine. He looks down at the street. Madame Sandler has disappeared. Or maybe that is Madame Sandler next door and not his mother. Both at once, now. She must have come upstairs. No, she's calling from downstairs. She appears to be angry with someone. Her husband replies, muffled, and the door rattles against its lock. How dare they? He would like to be alone in the hills, on the wooded and grassy heights, crunching on raw chestnut, talking to the birds.

Then there is quiet. Perhaps they have all torn each other apart, like rats in a sack. His name, once: Maman's voice. A question. Jean-Luc? She sounds worried. Maybe she thinks he's about to blow his head off like Jules Fabre did next door after Sunday lunch, upstairs. His eyeball recovered in the corner by the wardrobe. But he hasn't got his gun, his father's gun. It's in the cellar, needing an oil.

He looks down at the monument on the table and picks it up in both hands.

It is surprisingly light, as if he'd expected his efforts to have added weight. He waits for a while. Then he lifts it as high as he can over his head. A spoon drops off and bounces against his skull. He hurls Oncle Fernand's monument against the sword-shaped rips of the stripped wall on the far side of the room. The water is hitting his ears again; it's the same crash, as if the pool is entering his head and smashing through his body. Bibi goes flying up among the feathers and the spoons; a puff of plaster dust floats into the ray of sunlight and turns it into the solid arm of God. The sieve rolls to his feet. There is no sign of the fish-bone spider.

And then he sees it, leapt onto his bed.

The arm of God is as muscular as a body-builder's. It squirms with a million souls. The fish-bone spider is a fish-bone: no, that's his own tiny spine on the bed, plucked clean out. He's got a new spine, now. With a slight feeling of alarm, he realises it is Oncle Fernand's.

★   ★   ★

386

Something had gone awry with Jamie very early on. Before birth, perhaps. In the seed. Astrologically (Helena would reassure Nick), the moment of their son's procreation was amazingly auspicious. He was a magical child. But Helena had also consulted her charts before choosing her house in Wales, a decommissioned, black-granite chapel regularly under two feet of water and downwind from a piggery. And what was she now, with the personal aid of the subtle forces? An agoraphobe who couldn't go out to buy a box of matches without consulting the I Ching, and who regarded Nick as the nodal point of darkness in her hysteric's cosmic scheme. The Saudi Arabia of her personal planet.

The nodal point of darkness was now outside the attic door, attempting to persuade the magical child to emerge. He and Sarah had decided that enough was enough after returning from their morning walk to find lunch mostly consumed and the freezer door slightly open, the fridge throbbing gallantly, ice already bunching up. Sarah threw a wobbly which impressed the kids so much they fell quiet, having ceaselessly nattered all the way to the rocks and back. Sarah throwing a wobbly meant shouting for two minutes, breaking a mug and then bursting into tears. It was always a mug, never a glass. Fortunately, there were not usually more than two wobblies a year.

The attic was not responding. Nick was giving it an ultim-atum along with a generous offer of financial aid, but with an air of helplessness, because the attic remained silent. He would have loved to have got inside Jamie's head at some point in his childhood and readjusted the connections, like a nanoengineer. Now it was too late. Jamie's aim was to shipwreck this little domestic enterprise called the Mallinson family. There he stood, on the rocks, flashing his lamp. The original wrecker.

Nick remembered that this morning he had decided to love his son unconditionally. To pour love onto him. It had seemed a great idea at the time. To embrace him. To see him as a miracle and not – how had he put it to himself . . . ? *Somebody to be pitied*. Was that it? He was Jamie's only father. He looked down at his feet. He'd changed back into his sandals from his walking boots. Maybe he shouldn't ever wear sandals, with or without socks. He needed the permanent authority of boots. But the Roman army had done pretty well in sandals. The Indian sages in nothing at all. Maybe he needed to frighten Jamie. Put the boot in. As his own father had done with his lanky, over-cerebral son. Damaged by the war, his father. The effects of shell-blast. Head with a continual miniscule wobble. At least he'd kept his head, unlike the five-year-olds in Iraq. How his dad had seen the world, life, living history! The noise of war had damaged his ears, a tin whistle in each one; as he'd put it to Mum – long-suffering, diminutive Mum, the ultimate domestic ritualist: 'At least I can't hear you give me orders.'

What had damaged Nick's ears? Rock music. Led Zep at full volume one famous day in Duncan's room.

All he had done was bleed his life away in words. Bearded Che still up in his study, as on Malcolm McDowell's wall in *If* . . . ; only now it was ironic, a referential wink for the young men and women passing through. His whole generation a façade, a film set. Indulgent mannequins. Baby-boomers continually squalling for attention. Somewhat on the fag-end of it, he was, but still a member of the club. He'd watched *If* . . . again recently and sided with the teachers, the well-meaning headmaster. It was terrifying.

'Jamie? I don't blame you. I'm sorry. I'm sorry, I really am. Let's try to move on?' he added, adopting that same upwards inflection and sounding fake.

Silence. He had always been apologising to Jamie, come to think of it. Or worse: *for* Jamie.

He wasn't unusual. Thousands of Japanese teenagers shut themselves in their rooms, sometimes for decades. It had a name. *Kiryoko* or something. A modern condition.

Suddenly the door opened, just missing Nick's nose. Jamie might have been standing there the whole time. The attic beyond him looked rather snug: reasonably tidy, even. The headquarters of the mission, scented with dope. Cosy, warm from the sun on the tiles and the paraffin heater.

'You're selling something?'

'Toothbrushes,' said Nick, grimly. 'No, insurance.'

The floorboards were bare, swept clean. Maybe Jamie had hoovered when they were out. Or used a broom. Maybe he was, after all, monkish. His eyes were a little red.

'Life insurance?'

'Life can't be insured,' said Nick. 'It's priceless.'

'Wow, thought for the day again.'

Nick was nettled by this. His voice hardened. 'Just to say, Jamie, that our guests did not appreciate your Scrabble joke and we did not appreciate finding our fridge raided.'

'It wasn't a joke. It was serious. They were upset?'

'Why, Jamie? What's the point?'

'Because they pushed him.'

Nick looked pained. 'What?'

'That's what the shepherd said, and at least two other people in the village. Original research, Nick. The Sandlers pushed him. *Poussé.*'

'Not literally,' said Nick, with an exasperated snort.

'Like, we're not *literally* pushing the planet over the edge?'

Nick sighed, easing the grey force flowing from his chest straight to the knuckles of his right fist. 'So they just put pressure on him to finish, like you have to, generally. With builders.'

'*With builders.* Listen to yourself, Nick. I'd have had more respect for you if you'd *started out* a total fucking Tory.'

'Hey, that's –'

Jamie slammed the door in his father's face, genuinely angry, so that Nick had to retract his stabbing finger an instant before it got broken. *Out of order* was what he had been going to say. He saw the words swinging on the door, like a sign nailed to its wood.

Nick waited a moment, until his own rage subsided. It was no doubt mostly his fault, anyway: Jamie had always been tricky, he was born tricky, but had been made even trickier by their hopeless parenting – the fads and fetishes, the careless self-seeking disguised as revolt. He went downstairs feeling utterly mortified and defeated. He dreaded a confrontation with Sarah: she would accuse him of weediness, as usual. Of not standing up to his son. And she'd be right to accuse him. He only ever went so far. In everything, probably.

Fortunately, the Sandlers were back. They were in the kitchen. Alan Sandler was sweaty, red-faced, very excited, a walking exclamation mark. Nick thought, as he waved hello: they pushed the man to finish, to finish the roof. It was their doing. *Regrets*.

'The guy's an artist! I saw it on the table! This – what do we call it, Lucy? –'

'Assemblage,' said Lucy, who looked depressed.

'Assemblage! An incredibly genuine example of raw art! Art Brut! Worth thousands, tens of thousands! A photo of your wife was on it! A nude study, stuck to a soup spoon? I recognised the hair. On the head, I mean! Did she *pose* for him?'

'No, she did not,' Sarah sighed.

'Sorry,' said Nick, confused, 'this was something Jean-Luc had made himself?'

'He's seeing Art Brut everywhere,' said Lucy, gloomily. 'One does, when one starts. Like seeing faces in a blot. It's really just Bad Art, capital *B*, capital *A*. And Bad Art is everywhere. He even saw it in Luton airport, not surprisingly. Braques don't grow on trees, darling.'

'Lucy, this had a title. A real whacky title. It was a self-conscious act. I wrote the title down in the car.'

'I know you did, sweetheart. You've told me already. Jean-Luc manhandled him, by the way,' she told them. 'Really manhandled him.'

'Oh dear,' said Sarah, who even through her dismay realised that these types' lives were probably always like this: dramatic, hysterical, rather interesting.

'Exaggerated,' said Alan, pulling a bit of paper from his coat pocket. 'Here it is, translated from the French by my loving wife: *The Resurrection of the Mutant Chicken*. It was on the assemblage. On a strip of cardboard. That guy is a genius. He's bats, but he's a genius.'

'It seems Jean-Luc's an artist in his spare time,' Sarah explained, addressing Nick. 'There was this sort of eccentric sculpture of a chicken on the table in his bedroom. With a photo of me skinny-dipping, it appears. Proof he was spying.'

'On a spoon,' repeated Alan.

'How very unscrupulous of him,' said Nick. Jamie's words boomed through his head: *Listen to yourself.* 'What was the title again?'

'*The Resurrection of the Mutant Chicken,*' Alan cried, flapping one hand. 'Genius! Another Damien Hirst!'

'That man is very much *not* Art Brut,' said Lucy, sourly. 'That is calculated Saatchi and Saatchi art. You don't know what you're talking about.'

'Exaggerated,' said Alan, pointing at her.

Sarah waited for the tea to brew, standing by the sink with folded arms, manufacturing a sympathetic look as the Sandlers argued. She had the curious impression that she was unclothed, again. That Jean-Luc had permanently stolen her clothes and left her naked and vulnerable, even though she was no longer worried. He was creative; creativity was an outlet for darker forces. She had always been fascinated by really creative people, people who didn't worry about the mesh of argument and substantiation, about everything having to be tucked in and ticked off, folded in on itself, concluded. Jean-Luc wasn't a disturbed voyeur, he was an artist. Things made sense, now. She didn't mind hanging from his spoon, she thought: feeling magnanimous in thinking it. She herself had painted in her first year at Cambridge, but it was terrible: the life models looked like shop mannequins, in her versions. It takes all sorts, as her mother would say.

Lucy wanted to leave Jean-Luc alone, having sacked him: Alan wanted to solicit him, or at least investigate further. Sarah wanted lunch, but Jamie had consumed all the bread apart from half a baguette in the freezer; the Sandlers had gone out for a 'bite' after seeing Jean-Luc, to a restaurant near the village that the Mallinsons' budget would never match. They were wreathed in the fragrance of wine and garlic and looked slightly too big. All they wanted now, they said, was a good old English cuppa. Sarah had the feeling that two parallel timetables had entangled themselves. She'd come here to escape timetables. On the hob simmered an apologetic pan full of pasta shapes.

The sun seemed to have gone in. The kids were hunched in front of a video next door, stopping up their hunger with a bowl of French crisps (which, they complained, tasted 'boring'). She had not yet completed so much as a leaf collage with them from *Exciting Things To Do With Nature*. What she had to do was find her inner space, a calm within, or she would scream. But she was too tired to find her inner space. And if she did succeed in finding her inner space, smiling benignly inside it as tall as a house, one of the kids would be found floating face-down in the swimming pool. Or whatever.

Lucy kept referring to their meeting with Jean-Luc as an 'escapade'. He might have done much worse than just *shove* Alan out of the bedroom! 'He didn't really shove, doll,' Alan interrupted, 'he just pushed.' She'd been genuinely frightened. Her eyes were bright. Supposing you'd been stabbed, with that awful poor bedridden woman looking on? Like something out of your own Fanny Connor, sweetheart. Flannery O'Connor, he corrected.

Their voices trailed over Sarah's mind like jets. 'But he didn't stab him,' she pointed out, pouring the tea.

'But he might have done,' Lucy insisted, with an element of relish.

'You can say that about anything. Milk?'

'We historians call them counter-factuals,' Nick proffered, clocking Sarah's irritation and wanting to deflect attention. 'The great *what if?*'

'I can't believe what I saw,' Alan insisted. 'The truly genuine article.'

'What if the United States had not joined the Allies,' Nick went on, regardless, 'in 1917? And so on. What if young Hitler had not failed to enter the Vienna Arts –'

'Weird, to be secretly photographed,' said Sarah, with a slight shudder.

'Or Bobby Kennedy – this is *very* interesting – had survived the shooting in Los Angeles?'

'Ah, dear Bobby Kennedy,' said Lucy, sipping her tea.

'Exactly.'

'I am so excited,' Alan crowed. '*So* excited.'

'But Bobby Kennedy didn't survive,' said Sarah, quietly. 'Jean-Luc didn't shoot Alan.'

'Stab,' said Lucy. 'There was no gun.'

'He just snapped me in the pink,' Sarah finished, almost inaudibly.

But it did frighten her, sometimes, considering the hypotheticals, the infinity of possibilities branching out like neural pathways, fired finally on only one track. And this idea she had at the back of her mind that everyone was, in the end, theoretically defenceless against the very worst possibility – that it was all purely a matter of chance; that you really were one tiny mote among billions, as the Earth itself was one tiny mote among billions. Was this all that coming here had done? Exposed a void at the back of her mind, open to the bottomless plunge of the over-starry nights?

Jean-Luc had threatened to sue because he'd fallen in and there was no alarm. Nick didn't know that. She looked across at him as the Sandlers rabbited on like uncharitable academic colleagues would do at meetings designed for everyone to participate; she saw, from the way he moved his eyebrows at her, that he'd got nowhere with Jamie, either.

'I'm forbidding you to go anywhere near him, sweetheart,' said Lucy.

Alan stared her down. They were alone by the liverish pool, which nevertheless smelt of bleach. 'I'm forbidding you to give me such orders. Hey, I'm going to offer him money, a career, fame and fortune. Without him moving.'

'I don't suppose that's the point,' she said.

'The point, as you know, is that he keeps on being Jean-Luc. The genuine article of gouty Aubain. There were drawings all over the table. The walls were half-stripped and he had scribbled on the plaster. The whole room was art. The room of an artist who doesn't know he is one.'

'Or the room of a psychotic,' she suggested, already losing the argument.

'I'm surprised at you,' he said. 'In suggesting there might be a difference.'

This time, *she* would be *his* minder. He promised not to pursue things if they turned threatening. He mopped his brow and looked up at the sky, which had a murky vapour over it that wasn't quite cloud. 'You know,' he said, 'as his hands were on my clavicles, pushing me out, I felt our fates were intertwined. And I loved him at that moment.'

'Alan sweetheart,' Lucy groaned, 'please, whatever you do, don't do American.'

They drove to Aubain in almost total silence. The holm oaks on the way were horribly gloomy, a kind of gunmetal grey. They needed sunlight, in which their leaves shone and all but glittered. She was rehearsing what she had to say. 'Happened': *se passer*. She was considering the idea that this offer of Alan's might neutralise any tendency towards revenge in the unknown part of Jean-Luc. The main street was just as empty as before.

She had the vague idea that they were re-running the same scene, as in an experimental film. The weather didn't help: it seemed to have turned English. Bad continuity.

This time, when he opened the door, he kept a blank, expressionless face around his dark glasses. Lucy stuck all sorts of worrying possibilities onto it, as she remembered sticking plastic features on potatoes long ago. He didn't seem surprised to see them, anyway. Alan beamed at him, clutching his homburg. Jean-Luc retreated to the other side of the table. He appeared to have hurt his foot. At least, he had a pronounced limp.

'Sorry, Jean-Luc, but we have a very interesting offer to discuss with you,' she said, feeling ridiculous. 'A very interesting offer.'

Alan beamed some more, nodding.

Again, Jean-Luc wordlessly motioned them to sit around the vinyl-covered table. It was four o'clock. It seemed like a different day but it wasn't.

On Alan's behalf, Lucy explained what he had realised, when he had gone back upstairs for his hat (Alan raised the hat from the table, still beaming and nodding, his breath audible in his throat): that what he had seen upstairs in the room proved that Jean-Luc was an artist.

Un artiste. Or was it *une?* She stuck with *un.*

Jean-Luc kept very still behind his wrap-around dark glasses.

That although there was a lot of *sous* in that sort of art, they realised this wasn't why he made his art. '*Les dollars,*' put in Alan, rhyming with 'bars'.

The man still didn't move, not even to nod; this wasn't how any artist she had ever known behaved, especially at the mention of money.

That Alan would very much like to see what else Jean-Luc had done. Everything that had 'happened' (*ce qui s'est passé*) was explained: it was all for the purpose of creation: *pour la création.* Throughout her discourse Jean-Luc retained his expressionless expression, hands folded in front of him. It was to do with the eyes being hidden, the mouth so firmly set in the dark stubble. But she saw the beat of the vein on the side of his neck; the muscles of his unshaven throat detach and settle separately from his swallowing.

Finally, she stopped. Jean-Luc waited a few moments and then he opened his mouth and began to laugh, but very softly, like a duck heard in the far distance. Then he shook his head once and said something extraordinary.

'Oh,' said Lucy.

Alan asked for a translation. He'd heard something about being 'nuked' and was confused.

'"You remind me of the Germans when they shot me in the back of the neck,"' said Lucy. 'I believe that's what he said, sweetheart.'

'They shot him in the back of the neck? Hey, that's serious. Maybe it was Che Guevara did it.'

Lucy translated somewhat apologetically from Jean-Luc's static mumble: 'He lost his face. On the way, they promised Jean-Luc a woman. Instead, they shot him in the back of the neck and the bullets came out at the level of his nostrils. I don't think,' she added, with a meaningful look, 'this actually happened.'

Jean-Luc said some more.

'Hm,' said Lucy, nodding. 'Here goes, Alan. They shot away everything but my eyes. Not the eyes, but everything below. The jaw, the mouth, the nose. Everything but my eyes. I'm translating as precisely as I can. He's definitely saying "my", Alan. Perhaps we should leave?'

'He's bats,' said Alan, quietly. 'He's beautifully, beautifully bats.'

'Bats in the belfry, definitely,' Lucy agreed, behind a mask of agreeableness. '*N'est-ce-pas?*' she added, inconsequentially.

And then she saw the gun, leaning against the soiled cooker. Its slim, metallic barrel shone, its wooden parts gleamed. Perfectly normal, she thought, in hunter land. Jean-Luc had caught her looking at it, that ripple of shock. He tensed minutely in his chair.

'*Vous partez à la chasse?*' she asked, sweetly and benignly. Dread filled her torso like a dark-green liquid mounting higher. 'Perhaps we shouldn't be here,' she said, in a high voice, out of the corner of her mouth, as Jean-Luc rose without a word and picked up the gun by its dark barrel.

'What do they call it in Japan?' asked Nick, washing up after their unsatisfactory, late pasta lunch. 'You know, this modern phenomenon of teenagers locking themselves in their room for years.'

'Until they're no longer teenagers,' Sarah pointed out, wearily. 'I've no idea.'

'Something beginning with *K*,' he said. 'I think.'

'We know too much,' she sighed, pondering Beans's porridge-encrusted bib. Could it last another day without being washed? What was the point of life? *Interrupted nights are the seed-bed of depression:* she remembered the phrase from the *Guardian*. 'We know far too much, and comprehendeth nothing.'

'The global democracy of knowledge,' he observed. 'Horror stories from the war zones, in your living room now. And every day and every night, 24/7. Depthless surface. A sort of unicellular murk. Unembraceable; as, of course –'

'Jameson said. Probably. Or maybe we're just seeing it through the dominant paradigm,' she added, with a slight mocking lilt.

She binned the bib. It was frayed. It had been Tammy's, then Alicia's. There was already a history, artefacts, evidence. Destruction and obliteration and forgetting. 'The Sandlers are exhausting,' she said, after a moment. She checked she hadn't put Nick into a sulk. She hadn't. 'I can't wait for them to go back. It's the pressure.'

'They are. Tomorrow. We'll breathe again.'

'Sounds as though Jean-Luc's sorted, anyway. One less worry.'

Tammy asked if they could go out and play. As usual, Sarah gave them strict orders to go nowhere near the pool, and to keep a permanent eye on Beans. She was so annoyed with the Sandlers and their nonchalance about the alarm. The girls ran out. She approached Nick from behind and hugged him around the waist. This calmed her, so she hung on as he scrubbed the dishes.

'That's nice,' he said. 'You're not too traumatised, then?'

'About what?'

'Oh, then you're clearly not.'

'The nude photo? I think I'm sticking to the *Carry On Camping* perspective. This is my new resolution. To be lighter on my feet.'

'Fantastic, Sarah.'

She squeezed him again as the dishes clattered.

'I hope they don't come back too soon,' she murmured.

'Oh, they have to give Jean-Luc time to knock something

up for Tate Modern,' he joked, keeping in the spirit. In fact, he was deeply troubled by Jean-Luc's snooping. He would have liked to have confiscated the photos of his naked wife, but was fearful of the consequences. Not a single action was without consequences, despite each generation's mass delusion that it was otherwise.

He placed a spoon on the back of a plate, then the scrubbing-brush across the spoon, then a tea-strainer. 'There we go. It's called *Thinking About Lenin on a Rainy Day*. One of Nick Mallinson's earlier works. Yours for a million.'

'Wowee, genius.' Sarah squeezed him tighter. 'I'm the one who's always saying I could do it better myself.'

'But you do everything well,' he said, meaning it. 'And I mean it,' he added, in case she had in fact taken it the wrong way, despite his voice being full of love.

SEVENTEEN

It is easy for Oncle Fernand to force the Sandlers upstairs at gunpoint, because Oncle Fernand was in the war and was forced like that himself. Now it's his turn. The Sandlers babble as they stumble upstairs, especially Madame. He prods her buttocks with the barrel. Oncle Fernand thinks women shouldn't wear trousers, anyway. Jean-Luc watches him do everything from another part of his head; his head is like a tank, which Oncle Fernand is commanding, staring through the gun-slits. Jean-Luc is just part of the crew. A young, scared gunner crouched below in his desert goggles.

When the two pass Maman's bed, covered in splashes of blood, they make strange gurgling noises and go quiet. He should have removed the big scissors, still sticking out of her throat. He pressed one of the blades in slowly as far as it would go. Her mouth is still wide open, her blank eyes staring up at the damp patches on the ceiling. She couldn't believe that he would do it, but he did. Oncle Fernand can do anything, despite his limp. He's never liked his sister-in-law.

The Sandlers crouch in his bedroom, very white, trembling as if freezing cold. 'Dollars, dollars,' repeats the husband; Madame is unable to speak. Oncle Fernand makes the husband tear the top sheet into strips and tie one of the strips around his wife's mouth and the other around her wrists. Then Oncle Fernand, who has seen prisoners of the Germans tied up this way, ties the husband up himself, so tight that the veins swell on the wrists and the teeth push out from the stained cotton. The Sandlers' grin like toothpaste advertisements and gurgle. The cloth gets wet quickly. Their eyes are huge and frightened. They remind him of owls.

He pushes them onto his bed with the gun's barrel, where he discusses with Jean-Luc what to do. Everything that was on the monument must be replaced, quickly. The evening nurse is Colette. They have about an hour before she comes. It feels good, having no one watching them from the keyhole, no shrieks and orders and moans.

First, he must replace Bibi. The nails he used for her are too small. There are nails in the wall, for pictures, which he removes with the pliers on the table. Five of them. That will do, says Oncle Fernand. The hammer is also on the table. The toy pram lies where it fell the other side of the bed.

Oncle Fernand asks Jean-Luc to put on the Johnny Hallyday very loud again, which he does. But it is Oncle Fernand who unbuttons Madame Sandler's silk blouse; he rips it off, in the end, because her hands are tied. Oncle Fernand has a great deal of trouble unclasping her bra at the back. She's crying. Her breasts are not pointed like Bibi's. Her husband makes a move and Oncle Fernand lifts the butt of the gun and brings it down on the gagged mouth. There's a crack. The wet cloth reddens as if binding a wound. The husband whimpers and groans on the floor. Oncle Fernand, just to be sure, kicks him in the belly very hard because that's what the SS soldiers did to him when they found the boys had gone from the Mas. The husband has trouble getting his breath, now.

Oncle Fernand doesn't bother with Madame Sandler's jeans, because Bibi is legless. He only undoes the top two buttons, to show the navel properly. A few hairs curl over and Jean-Luc feels his frog plump its cheeks up, wanting to croak, but ignores it.

He ties her wrists to the bed's frame at the head and her ankles to the frame at the foot. Then he fetches the bloodstained top sheet from next door and tears that, too, into strips. This is the cobweb, says Oncle Fernand. For a joke, he retrieves the sieve from the floor and places it on his head. They all had helmets, he says; they made fun of my limp, their helmets wobbling on their foreign heads. The sieve falls off and hits the husband on the nose as he lies there, still trying to catch his breath.

Oncle Fernand has difficulties driving the short nails home through the rubbery nipples, even though he keeps his knees firmly either side, pressing on Madame Sandler's armpits, pinning her down. Tap, tap. Tough beef-gristle.

The navel is easier, although Oncle Fernand feels the long nail should have been even longer; the navel is less like beef-gristle and more like punching a hole in an old dry orange. He doesn't bang it all the way in, fearing he might otherwise kill her. Her muffled screams can hardly be heard under the music. My love is 100 per cent, blood for blood. Our blood is the same. She lies there like the wounded Christ, bleeding at the nails in her nipples and her navel. The last two nails are driven into her palms, but the picture-nails are more like tacks and fall out as the hands squirm.

He ties the husband, who has made a mess in his trousers, by his fat neck to the foot of the bed. His gag is bright red. The eyes stare at him, bigger than ever, as the next song begins. They are dark brown. Maybe he's whimpering through the music. Oncle Fernand picks up two of the oxidised spoons and uses one for each eye, placing his free hand firmly on the forehead and holding the face still. It is like removing plum-stones, although Oncle Fernand's hand is shaking. It reminds him of what people did in the war, on both sides, French and German, even French and French. The eyeless husband roars in his throat like a distant boar, his sockets big and black and dribbling blood. Then he falls very quiet, quivering from head to foot.

The eyeballs sit in each spoon like stolen birds' eggs. It is no different, Jean-Luc thinks as he watches, from removing the eyes of a fish.

Which reminds him about the spider, the fish-bone spine that was the spider. Oncle Fernand ponders. The spine will have to be exposed. Eight legs. Fortunately, Oncle Fernand (like Jean-Luc) has flayed many a hare or rabbit or tough, bristly boar in his time: old Gabriele, Jean-Luc's grandfather, taught Fernand and his brother Elie, and Elie taught Jean-Luc. Who still remembers the smell of the hides.

Elie's brother takes his nephew's sharpest Opinel and begins at the shoulders with little nicks like stitches. The honey on the kisses of my mouth, Jean-Luc whistles as he watches from the back of his head. The skin has blemishes, spots, warts, the blood running past them down to the underpants exposed above the belt.

When the skin is tugged hard, coming away like a fishing net, the spine is not much more than a line of creamy nobbles under the blood and purplish matter, but Oncle Fernand says they haven't time to do it any better, they still have to drive over to the Mas des Fosses and finish off there.

'I'd like to go via Marcel Lagrange's place, he's usually there after five,' says Jean-Luc.

Oncle Fernand agrees, of course. He remembers old Père Lagrange pointing him out in the café to the SS captain, but they can't go digging up Père Lagrange. Marcel will do.

Jean-Luc thinks the husband might have passed out, because he has hardly resisted, wriggling only when the skin was tugged and jerked away; the fatty film underneath, more like a chicken's than a hare's, worked through sharply by the blade.

Jean-Luc feels the man's pulse through the streaks of blood and can't find it. The man's dead. He must have had a heart attack from the pain. He's certainly not a true martyr like the suffering saints flayed for their goodness, then, Jean-Luc jokes. The woman is panting, Jean-Luc sees it in her nail-nippled chest, her nailed belly going in and out. Her eyes are fixed on the ceiling, like Maman's, but gleaming with tears. There is as much blood as when they'd slaughter a pig in the old days, back in the Sixties. Like the Arabs, Jean-Luc thinks. Like the Muslims and their goats. All over the walls.

Changed into blue overalls, his face and hands washed, Oncle Fernand has to reach the van just outside the door without being recognised. Because of Jean-Luc's eye problem, Oncle Fernand is driving. He has perfect sight. Colette will be coming in fifteen minutes: she has her own key.

Jean-Luc watches out through the kitchen net until there's

no one in sight, and then bolts with Oncle Fernand to the van, parked just in front of the Sandlers' hired car, a few long metres up the street. The limp is a nuisance, it slows him up, the street stretches away with all its difficult buildings. Old Lucille spots him from her door. He's carrying the gun, but she doesn't lift a hair.

'Save some rabbit for me, Jean-Luc!' she calls.

Despite Jamie's manifold problems, they appeared not to be of a sexual nature because, as even Helena had once commented in a moment of despair, Jamie was a neuter. At least, he had never shown any interest in either gender. Helena, who'd always had a fondness for the subject and at one time (before the iceberg of Aids) had preached an earnest and rather exhausting form of free love as the key to a higher awareness, was left perplexed. Her attempts to throw pretty girls at him, or broach the gay question, had got nowhere. It was, in fact, the aspect of her son that most disturbed her. She even wondered, in a moment of revelation, if his rest-less dissatisfaction wasn't because his life-role was to be a monk, and offered to pay for a retreat in a Carthusian monastery in its Alpine fastness. Nick would simply refer to him as their resident Bakunin, who was not only the founder of anarchism but also impotent, pouring his frustration into revolutionary activity and destructiveness.

Now, however, with the girls temporarily out of earshot, playing at the back of the house (Nick had briefly checked them – happy as lambs in front of the barn), they could worry the subject a little more, and Sarah reasserted her opinion that Jamie had been screwed up by his mother's total anarchy on the sexual front. She and some of her more advanced partners would wander around the house nude, Nick had told her. There was even this cultural idea that children could be in on it all, being 'magical'. Cherubs, faeries, elves, all that. ('Yuk,' Sarah had commented. 'What a deluded generation you were.' And Nick had earnestly pointed out that he was nothing to do with all that free-love stuff, that he'd been petrified of girls until he was about twenty.)

'What I'm trying to say, Nick, is that I'm reasonably certain Jamie watched me skinny-dip.'

'OK. So did Jean-Luc. Maybe half the village were watching.'

'Right, thanks a lot. But do you see my point? Maybe I'm some of the problem. Maybe he's attracted to me. Jamie, I mean,' she added, glancing towards the door into the sitting room.

'As Bakunin was to one of his sisters.'

'Well, I'm not actually *related* to him, but I am forbidden fruit and not much more than ten or eleven years older. You're almost nineteen years older than me.'

Nick scratched his thinning hair and pretended to look agonised. He did, in fact, feel fairly agonised, although this was not the first time they had discussed the possibility of a kind of vegetal attraction. 'So what's the solution? Put me in a nursing home and marry Jamie?'

'Try to be objective, Nick.'

He huffed and puffed. 'Maybe we should ask Alan to hire Jamie as an Art Brut chaser,' he said. 'He'd be rather good, smelling out naivety and oddity.'

'Did I hear a noise?' Sarah asked, lifting her head like a hunting dog. 'From the back?'

They listened. Their nightingale was taking a break: they hardly noticed it, now. Nothing but slight gusts under the lintel. Nick rose and opened the door and looked. 'They must be in the barn,' he said. 'Do you want me to check?'

'Oh,' said Sarah, 'let's be chilled out. Light on our feet. They're fine. In the old days they'd have just roamed, wouldn't they?'

'Not at two years old, methinks.' But they might have done even at two, back then. You'd have to research the yearly statistics for child accidents, drownings in pools and rivers. Like road accidents in the Twenties: appalling. You'd probably be surprised.

But he didn't say this to Sarah. Instead he said, 'Yeah. We've lost our primary innocence,' remembering the way he'd roam in the fields himself, as a boy. Adulthood was like a photograph that wasn't quite as good as the real thing.

The axe is already in the back of the van. It slides about among coils of rope and old sacks and various other tools as Oncle Fernand races around the corners. Jean-Luc is surprised Oncle Fernand can drive at all, let alone like this. Papa always said that his brother was timid, hardly drank, wouldn't harm a fly, just gave off whiffs of the tannery.

Fortunately, no one else is on the road. There is no one at Marcel's house, either, so Jean-Luc blows the yapping dog off its chain at point-blank range then boots the bungalow's feeble door open for Oncle Fernand to go in and turn all the cooker's gas taps on. Marcel would usually have a fag in his mouth. If his wife, Cécile, arrives first, or one of his horrible kids, too bad. There'll be nothing much left of the house, if it goes up. Their fault, for having a gas canister under the cooker. Against the European norms, that.

They just have time to nip into the main bedroom for Oncle Fernand to piss all over the double bed before the gas drives them out.

Marcel Lagrange is on the drive, locking his four-by-four, eyeing the van suspiciously. He turns as they emerge and his jaw drops, his cigarette stuck to his lip. The gun is pointing at his head, which ends up a second later as a bright red smear over the four-by-four's side window as Jean-Luc's ears buzz from the shot. Marcel slides down as if drunk, the top half of his face blown off to the nasal bone, then manages to fall onto his hands. He waits there, on all fours, wrecked head dangling. He is still breathing; they can hear the whistle of it.

'It's because he's got no brain,' Jean-Luc laughs.

Oncle Fernand tips Marcel over with his foot. He rolls onto his back and the short, muscular arms subside slowly, quivering for a bit on the ground. The belly sticks up like Mont Blanc. The cigarette is still glued to the bottom lip. There is nothing much above it, to speak of. They can smell the gas a bit, even out here.

'Pretty picture,' says Oncle Fernand, rearranging the limbs as if Marcel Lagrange were a shot animal. 'Don't want to break with tradition, do we?'

They bump up the Mas's track and stop in front of the plaque and Oncle Fernand attacks its stone with the edge of the hammer. The woods ring like a bell, like the village bell that has rung every quarter-hour of Jean-Luc's life. The air is as dry as cigarette paper, the heat's around the corner. Another summer.

When the name *Fernand Maille* has gone, they cut across on foot through the trees to come out by the tumbled wall, axe and rope in hand. Jean-Luc points out in a whisper that he never managed to get the kids' heads satisfactorily, they were either blurred or too small. And now he's lost the camera. Oncle Fernand tells him not to worry. It takes a moment before they hear the voices, understand them as human.

High, excited voices in the barn. Jean-Luc stumbles along with Oncle Fernand, whose limp doesn't slow him that much after all. The long-handled axe is heavy; they leave the gun propped behind the pool-shed. He's not so sure about Oncle Fernand's ideas, now, but he is the tank commander, he does know best. The monument has to be made. What's been lost has to be made up for. Years and years.

The pool is crystal clear, now, better than a mirror. There is a toad, sitting at the bottom as if surprised. 'Pools are like that,' says Jean-Luc, studying his own face. 'Dirty as hell one day, transparent as heaven the next.'

The girls are playing in the middle of the dark barn, beyond the chopping block. This is the hardest part, he thinks, but Oncle Fernand urges him on. It is for the sake of the monument. Without the faces, it would not be complete. Jean-Luc wonders whether it matters if it is not complete, but he is not the commander, he has to obey. They fire cannon and spit fire and blast buildings to smithereens. They destroy whole cities for the sake of the monument. They get rid of the riff-raff.

The girls laugh at him because he is talking to Oncle Fernand, saying *Yes, of course, you must do it for the sake of the monument.* They think he is here to play, they clutch his trouser legs and pull on his hand and he has to shield the axe with his body, putting it behind him because the blade is greased and sharp. Oncle Fernand doesn't know the girls, he doesn't even like children. This is a surprise, because Jean-Luc's father always said how good Fernand was with children in the village, showing them simple tricks with cards in his timid way. How his eyes would light up and he would put on funny voices like an actor and make them laugh.

Oncle Fernand puts on one of his funny voices and tells them to hide in the barn, only in the barn; but they must hide so well that they can't see each other. Then he'll try to find them. They run off separately, squealing, as Oncle Fernand counts up to ten.

'The key to it all is this word *interpretation*,' Nick said, anticipating supper by several hours and chopping up veg. He was on the courgettes, slicing them lengthways into four then, holding the four parts together, slicing them crossways so he ended up – theoretically, at least – with four small quarters per section. 'Interpretation can be transparent or opaque. When it's transparent, it's like a top interpreter translating from another language. When it's opaque – shit.' He had cut his finger. No, he hadn't. Not even a bead of blood.

'All right?'

'Yup. I thought I'd cut my finger. Blood with the stew, but no. So when it's opaque, it's like when someone says, "You're interpreting my thoughts." With negative implications, usually. You're actually imposing something. History can't exist without interpretation. Actually, nothing does. We're interpreting all the time. But with history it's very fraught. It's not just a matter of translating from another language, transparently. It's imposing your own order on a confusion of facts. Hm?'

Sarah grunted, half in her book. 'Who said that originally? History's a confusion of facts?'

'Isn't that mine?'

''Fraid not,' said Sarah. 'I mean, someone said it before you. Vico?'

She was looking through *Exciting Things To Do With Nature* in a rare moment of quiet while Nick prepared supper early so it could stew happily while they went for a walk before (if the girls let them!) an hour or two of work. She was succeeding in not fretting too much about the girls when they were out of sight and sound. She was not a security-camera operator. She would, she thought, put that in her secret journal later this afternoon. They were imbibing the freedom of a natural environment. Tammy could be trusted, she was nearly nine, after all. Nine! Impossibly mature. She herself was left hours on her own in Aden, with pool and all. As long as the faint squeals were there, like the tiny bubbles in the kitchen window's original glass, she would not worry. She was even successfully forcing herself not to look through the glass every two minutes. She was letting go of her anxieties, media-fed, manipulated by the status quo.

The journal was secret because it was emotional, not intellectual; it went against the Nick Regulations. It was growing more and more honest.

'Anyway,' he went on, untroubled by Vico, 'a historian is always opaque, but strives for transparency. How do you think all that pans out, for the intro?'

'Pretty good,' said Sarah, wondering whether the pine-cone mobile would be feasible, given past experience. They'd found some very dry pine cones in the attic, before clearing it out for Jamie. She thought they were in one of the *caves*, now, for extra kindling.

'Where are those pine cones we found in the attic, Nick?'

'Pine cones? I burnt them last week.'

'Oh bother.'

'There are plenty in the pine wood, beyond the holm oaks.'

'They need to be very dry and light. It doesn't matter. The

kids sound as though they're having a wild time,' she observed. 'I think it's your turn to check, Nick. I caught Beans really devouring one of the picture books, by the way. She's obviously going to be a *reader*, like Tammy. Alicia's more into the spatial, physical thing. But it's early days.'

'When I've done this last courgette,' he muttered, somewhat miffed that she hadn't listened properly to what was so important to him.

Oncle Fernand hunts them down, one by one.

He finds the youngest first, who has not really hidden at all. She's standing behind the huge, old, orange-painted beam dumped there by the builders years ago. He brings her gently to the chopping block and lays her head on it and tells her to listen to the wood, it's telling her something deep inside. As she presses her ear to the grain, excited, the axe blade swings down with its own full weight and bites through the neck with a snap. The head's expression is still excited as it bounces, rolling to rest at Oncle Fernand's feet.

He kicks it away. The blood pumps out of the torso in little snuffles, sounding like a hedgehog.

They find the next youngest crouched behind a mouldering bale with her eyes tightly shut; she looks up at Oncle Fernand with a mischievous smile, as if he's only pretending to be cross. He swings the axe down on her skull and it bursts open, exploding like a shot-at watermelon, like a bull Jean-Luc once saw pierced messily in the corrida in Nîmes. Another two swings remove the head. Then he looks up and sees the eldest in the hayloft, staring down. She has the worst look of terror and shock Jean-Luc has ever seen. But Oncle Fernand is used to this, he was in the war. He has been in every war since then, he says. They're all the same.

He climbs up the ladder to the hayloft. The old ladder squeaks like a trapped rabbit. The eldest is now crouched in the corner, screaming with her small fists pressed to her chin. The noise is too loud for safety, but Oncle Fernand acts swiftly. His hands are like a boxer's red gloves. They close white-knuckled on the axe and bring it swirling low round his body as she scampers off, catching her deeply on the tendons under the right knee, so that they whip up like elastic bands. She falls and starts to wail. The axe handle is slippery with sweat, it looks like. It takes three swings, unfortunately, to remove her head, and the head has the same look of terror as it did when she was staring down. It only stopped making a racket on the third swing.

He hears a man's voice from the yard. The father is calling out their names like an alarm – running towards the barn, from the sound of his voice. Oncle Fernand makes it down to the ground off the ladder as the father appears in the entrance, a silhouette in the huge bright blazing square of the missing doors. The father hesitates for a moment, probably blinded by the barn's shadow after the sunlight, or maybe seeing the small head by the chopping block and not understanding it.

They can hear his breath, he must have run hard. Not good at his age. He stretches his arms out either side, as if to greet them.

Afterwards, Oncle Fernand will tell Jean-Luc that you must never hesitate in war. The father understands the head and opens his mouth but his huge, high *AAAAAAAH* is interrupted before it gets to the *H*. The axe cleaves him through on one side with a single stroke, with no time even to bring his arms up to shield himself. Jean-Luc hears the blade crack on the hip-bone, from what he can see of the angle. A hand flies up and lands on the ground by Jean-Luc's feet. He's not sure how the writhing man is finally despatched, but it reminds him of the time his father's dog was gored by the boar, steam rising from the warm entrails.

He and Oncle Fernand slip in them a bit as they leave the barn and cross at a hop to the pool and splash their hands and faces, the blood snaking away in threads; then Oncle Fernand grabs the gun by the shed and they run together to the house. There is no time to lose. The boys have gone and the foreign riff-raff are still in occupation. If a single person is left, Oncle Fernand will be forced back up the track and shot through the nape once more. The only monument will be a sad, stupid stone with plastic flowers on top.

The Englishwoman is in the kitchen, reading a book. Of course, she screams and screams when she sees Oncle Fernand with blood all over his jacket, pointing the gun at her. She has to be whole, Jean-Luc reminds Oncle Fernand. She has to be naked and whole.

She runs off into the sitting room and up the stairs, but it is not difficult to hunt her down. Jean-Luc knows the rooms in the house back to front. Jean-Luc is scared of meeting his rival in love, Raoul Lagrange, because ghosts are not like flesh and bone, an axe or bullet or pellets go straight through them like fog. Raoul does not appear, though. He's probably scared stiff himself, because Oncle Fernand is more powerful than most ordinary ghosts, staring through his tank-captain's goggles. It's the difference between a pig and a wild boar, Jean-Luc reckons.

They corner the Englishwoman in the attic, hearing the creaks from the landing. The big space is still nothing but dust and spider webs and a sack of pine cones for the fire, dry as bone by now, and a couple of ancient crates full of empty bottles. The attic's dust rises in clouds and makes Oncle Fernand cough, and Jean-Luc hits his head on one of the low beams. He swears and kicks at some old newspapers the colour of piss. He glances at the big black headlines on the nearest one. *The Allies Bomb the Northern Ports*, he reads. *France-Soir*, March 1943. The window in the roof is glazed over with dust and bird-muck. There's bracken heaped on the floor: Jean-Luc knows what that is. The Englishwoman sobs.

They force her out at gunpoint all the way to the pool. She is wringing her hands and pleading with them, weeping so much that her nose runs and her nice black top is soaked at the collar. She is calling for her husband, whom she hasn't realised is the pile of red rubbish in front of the barn. She has the attic's dust on her skirt. As Jean-Luc watches, Oncle Fernand makes her take off her clothes down to the undies and then her undies, too. He doesn't misbehave as she stands there, clasping herself

411

and shivering: he prods her with the gun until she half-falls, half-jumps into the pool. Each time she swims to the side and holds it, pleading, he stamps on her fingers. The water is cold. She is gasping. Oncle Fernand can't shoot her or she would not be whole. Now and again she calls out for help in English. She calls out her husband's name, then her children's. The woods take no notice. Birds sing in the pauses. Blackbirds, wrens, chiffchaffs.

After less than half an hour she turns quiet; she wearies and lies on her back instead of paddling. She is blue with cold and shivering, making little ripples that finally hit the sides. She lies on her back and slowly the clear, clean water covers her mouth, her nose. A bubble touches the surface and bursts, and then another, smaller, rising from her mouth. Then nothing. She is stretched out flat on her back, eyes wide open, naked from head to foot, and the water covers her completely like a plastic sheet. She is dead, thinks Jean-Luc. It is better than the photo he used on the monument.

He bends his head and cups the clear water in his palm and sucks it up between his lips, noisily. It doesn't taste of chlorine: it tastes of her – her sweat, her hair. His throat welcomes the water.

This is all Oncle Fernand's achievement. The last square is always her naked body, stretched out under the surface, with the water rippling over her and making her body quiver. It melts at the edges like ice. He uses the heel of his hand to make it melt more and still more. As he does so there is a distant boom, suddenly, like a bomb has been dropped or a plane has broken the sound barrier. The water trembles a little over the white flesh. Oncle Fernand lifts his head, and so does Jean-Luc. A patch of dark, low cloud drifts into view over the trees, smudging the clear sky.

'That's smoke,' says Oncle Fernand.

'That's Marcel Lagrange,' Jean-Luc grins.

And they both laugh fit to bust.

EIGHTEEN

'We had absolutely no alternative,' says Lucy.

The bright, burning sun is full on her face, the pool's reflection rippling on the creamed-up skin. She suits being a widow, that is the general view. The melancholy of it, the depth. 'He was a danger to himself, in the end, let alone to others.' There is the odd gust of wind that seems even hotter than the still air in which even bare concrete wilts. Not that she can see any bare concrete here, of course. The tiles are like upturned flat-irons turned to max. They make one's unsandalled feet hop.

The cicadas are quieter, today. Sometimes they are so loud one has to shout. They go on and on, indefatigably: insanely repetitive. All sexual, apparently, rubbing their back legs up in the trees in desperation. However would you paint that noise? It washes over you, shutting itself out, and then you wake up to it again and want to gnash your teeth.

There is a splash and she half-squeals, half-laughs as the drops scatter on her bared legs, unfortunately growing varicose and slightly swollen under the knees. She can't believe her thighs, these days. They have enlarged themselves without her permission; they have the consistency and texture of old butter left out of its dish in the fridge. She misses Alan greatly. She wonders if her headaches are simple grief, or a deadly tumour caused by grief. The grief surprised her. It still seems to have nowhere to go, and from that point of view is probably causing mischief. She talks to Alan, which means she talks to herself. She's gone a little dotty. Or even dottier, her friends would like to say. That'll be a *good* sign, when they say it. Unravelling his deals was the worst. In the end, he was too soft, too sweet.

It's the middle daughter who's jumped in, attempting to dive. She keeps getting the names muddled up. Alicia, Tammy, Beans. Now whichever – Alicia or Tammy – is squealing with delight because Nick is bearing down on her, the long stretch of him flat out on the inflatable crocodile.

'It's really quite frightening, that crocodile,' she says, because Sarah hasn't replied to her statement about Jean-Luc, which in itself was a rejoinder to something Sarah had said: 'I feel so bad about Jean-Luc,' she'd sighed. 'It was probably all my fault.'

And although Lucy had felt an immediate stab of pain because Alan might still have been here had they not come over to sort things out (yet Sarah had made no mention of him, only Jean-Luc), she had kept her reply studiously diplomatic. It was, in some ways, all the Mallinsons' fault. But so much is really one's *own* fault, in the end, willy-nilly. For instance, she absolutely drew the line at being in any way implicated in the other business, the falling-off-the-roof business. That poor, dishy man was simply careless, he should've known better. They take on too much, that's the trouble. It's greed, really. Everyone likes to find someone to blame.

The Greeks had it right. Hubris. Fate. The awful, spoilt gods.

But the Mallinsons were very good to her, after Alan's death. It must have been exhausting, organising his return to London. In the hold instead of in the cabin. Who would ever have guessed, just days before? She carried on, somehow, in a sort of fog. Completing his deals, selling most of his collection, even the ones he never wanted to part with. The two little gypsum worshippers from Tell Asmar and the white marble head from Ur turned out to be exquisite Saddam-era fakes, as did half the Sumerian pots. The rest nearly got her into very deep waters, although she pleaded ignorance. Maybe it was just as well he didn't live to see all that.

It wasn't so much Jean-Luc picking up the hunting rifle and handing it to Alan, anyway, as Alan's excitement over that wretched Art Brut business. Alan was American: he was used to guns, especially in the kitchen. He'd been in Vietnam as a nineteen-year-old. Even when Jean-Luc placed the barrel against his own nape and asked Alan, holding the butt, to press the trigger, Alan had looked more excited than scared.

'I can't do that, Jean-Luc,' said Alan. 'Assisted suicide is a punishable offence. Even in France, I guess.'

When Lucy translated, Jean-Luc laughed. Then he sat down and removed his dark glasses, head sunk on his folded arms.

'You can't kill a man twice,' he rumbled. 'Only once.'

'That's correct, Jean-Luc,' Lucy said, butting in and feeling scared.

Jean-Luc turned to his left and began talking in a low mumble to the air, but there was no sign of a mobile or an earpiece.

'Alan, let's go,' Lucy murmured, in English (she remembered every word, more or less). 'I'm going to let the doctor know someone here is keen on self-harm. Or worse.'

'Already? When it's just getting interesting? The gun's not even loaded, by the way. It's a game. Tell him I want to take just the tiniest little peep at his art, Lucy. Seriously tiny. A glimpse.'

'Alan, that's enough,' she said. Quite firmly. Perhaps too firmly. *That's enough!*

Jean-Luc was muttering again into his shoulder, pausing as if on the phone. The name 'Jean-Luc' came up several times, with a sense of urgency. Alan leaned forwards across the table, slightly off the chair, straining to listen. His face lit up, as if the French was comprehensible. There was a pause — was there really a pause? — and then what sounded like a long growl of pleasure from his throat; his head tipped forwards and struck the table like a knuckled call to order before he slid backwards and sideways and onto the floor in a muddle of limbs.

Lucy thought, completely illogically, he was reaching for a dropped pen or his wallet. Jean-Luc looked up, frowning, his eyes creased against the light. He was fumbling for his dark glasses.

By the time Lucy was crouched down in the cramped kitchen,

Alan had opened his eyes as if startled, along with his mouth. His hands were tucked into his groin. She lifted his head and called his name because she saw that he was a very long way away and he was not blinking. Jean-Luc stared through his dark glasses, saying nothing.

Lucy called her darling husband's name again, as if over a phone connection that had been cut off. Then she started shouting at Jean-Luc to call an ambulance. Alan's head lolled heavy in her hands and she was positioned badly so her back ached. He was obviously dead and her chief reaction was one of annoyance. She shook him as if to snap him out of it. She was aware she was shouting again, but she was still annoyed, even furious. He had done it on purpose. He had left without saying 'thank you' or even 'goodbye'. In a minute he would wake up and say, 'Hey, being dead was interesting.'

Jean-Luc was just sitting there, staring into space.

She yanked open the door and screamed up the empty street. *'Au secours! Au secours!'* was all she could muster. But it had the desired effect. Boots came running, she pictured medieval boots and people in cloaks in her blotched, half-blinded vision. She kneeled again next to Alan. There were other shouts. Dr Demarne appeared, like a great dog. Or perhaps it *was* his dog. Someone had placed a pillow under Alan's head. His eyes were still open. Time was swirling along, either slowly or very fast. She was surrounded by a forest of chair-legs and awful shoes, there was no room to move her feet where cramp was biting. *Whoops*, she wanted him to say. A stethoscope was coming out of his chest with Dr Demarne's ears at the other end of it. How could you look jolly with such a moustache? She was a widow, she thought. Someone from Iraq or Saudi Arabia or Washington had given Alan a lethal injection as Dr Demarne was giving him a lethal injection, right now. Madame Maille was standing on the stairs, wild-haired, as if risen from the grave. She looked exultant. Lucy could smell her even above the injection.

Now Lucy was sitting in a chair outside, visible to all the world. The fresh air was a shock. As were the bystanders, concerned-looking. She was the centre of attention in the village. It was the most important event in the village, possibly ever. Dr Demarne was pumping her darling's chest inside the house, she could hear it, she could hear a kind of thumping that may have been her own heart. 'Oh dearie me,' she said, just like her mother. She had a bottle of lavender essence in her hand, she didn't know why, and a woman's arm was on her shoulder. She was completely integrated into the life of this charming village. She smiled faintly at the people standing about, watching, not knowing what to do. She felt great love and affection for them, for all of humanity. She counted ten, eleven living members of the human race, including the man who ran the café. What was his name? She felt faintly heroic and fulfilled. Laurence or Loopy or something. He had a tea towel on his shoulder, as they always do. Not very hygienic, she thought.

The ambulance came like a horrid disappointment, its erratic siren bouncing in dread spasms off the winding street's walls. After a kerfuffle of apologies she followed Alan, who was calm on a stretcher, into the vehicle. She was supposed to sit with him. They did all sorts of urgent electrical things in the back of the ambulance. Alan juddered under the oxygen mask, but refused to play the game. It was embarrassing.

'Sorry,' she said. 'I'm so sorry. *Je m'excuse.*'

It was so completely annoying, having to speak French. It was an extra punishment. The medical staff in their white coats looked about twenty-three, with smooth, shiny faces. They ignored her when she said sorry, they were too busy or perhaps shy. She wondered if they were trained or were just pretending. One, of course, was very handsome. The vehicle was surprisingly roomy. She felt thirsty, she felt like having a swig of pure vodka. Funny, Jean-Luc never offering them anything to drink. Them! She felt tears welling up right behind her jaw, and couldn't stop herself.

Alan did not react at all. Not a twitch. Her poor sweetheart was a wordless, voiceless, mindless smudge, whose last word was 'enough'. No, that was her word. The last word he heard, then. His was 'peep'. Was it?

Enough! You couldn't put that in a novel. The pretty nurse gave her a tissue but it was a meagre bulwark against the floods.

She has spent the last half an hour, while the girls splashed about (the eldest is now sitting wrapped in her towel on the edge, slightly shivery despite the temperature, like a serious-minded Buddha), describing her visit to Jean-Luc's 'new place' in Nîmes, which is much better than the previous one in St-Maurice. A very nice man called Xavier with a bald patch like a monk's tonsure showed her round; the walls are gaily painted, and the inmates each have a largish room they can decorate as they please. Great emphasis is laid on self-expression, she tells Sarah, who is keeping half an eye on Beans, paddling happily with her Mickey Mouse water wings in the big-eyed duck inflatable, her little elbows resting on the swollen ring. 'A healthy emphasis, to my mind.'

'Jean-Luc's room,' she goes on informing Sarah, in a lower voice (Alicia — Sarah has just called her name — plump Alicia is ready to dive nearby), 'Jean-Luc's room was covered, absolutely *plastered*, in his drawings.' Xavier told her they were always the same, done in the same order, with very little variation, tending to the apocalyptic, the violent. 'They are basically cartoons,' says Lucy, as Alicia delivers another cool sprinkling on the legs stretched out on the recliner, legs Lucy has difficulty recognising as her own.

'Basically cartoons,' repeats Sarah, sleepily, adjusting her bikini at the nipple.

She wishes Lucy would stop talking. The bikini top might as well be a thick cardigan: the cloth feels starchy with heat, the hem actually all but burning her. The air smells faintly, for some reason, of caraway seeds. She has, she reminds herself, plastered the girls with total sunblock, and it is past four o'clock. The water blinds her in flashes as it moves.

'Yes,' says Lucy, 'most of them coloured with crayons or chalks, the kind of big fat chalk pastels I still adore to use myself. He never uses paints. He absolutely refuses to use paints. Xavier says he always depicts the same story, because it is like a cartoon story. He thinks the ladder with the head next to it is symbolic of the afterlife. I mean, Jean-Luc's subconscious take on the afterlife. They have to spray his efforts with fixative when he uses chalks – actually, hairspray. So his room smells like a cheap hairdresser's, it's very disconcerting.' Poor Alan, she wants to say: he'd have been so intrigued. But she can't trust herself not to crack, and the sun and the heat, the spangle and glitter of the blue water, are so delightful and happy.

'Certainly like cartoons,' Sarah says.

She knows what the pictures look like, in fact, because she visited Jean-Luc herself with Jamie a few times last year, when they were properly here. Pretty brave of her, but therapeutic on all sides, too: she felt a sense of responsibility – and he was on antipsychotics, so there was no danger. He looked a bit like a teacher, with silver-rimmed spectacles and very short hair and a clean jaw, but never spoke, just fiddled with things on the table or drew his cartoons. Now and again, his mouth made bizarre, contorted movements and he flicked his tongue like a lizard. Apparently, this was just a side effect of his medication.

She never thought, however, to ask much about the pictures themselves, not even with Jamie.

Jamie, to everyone's surprise, rose to the occasion.

He emerged from the attic one morning during the post-Alan crisis and visited Jean-Luc every day for the remainder of the sabbatical, hitching or taking the bus to St-Maurice or, sometimes, a lift with his father: they talked together alone in the car, Nick and Jamie, and it was all very positive. The perfect training, anyway, for her stepson's present incarnation as a geriatric care assistant in Devon, clearing up vomit and making the old girls laugh with his silly jokes. Long may it last, Sarah thinks. 'Don't we get the Poles to do that sort of thing, these days?' was Lucy's sole remark.

Perhaps it was the fact that Jean-Luc never said anything, never judged; he and Jamie sitting there in the home's lounge like a couple of Carthusian monks, mute as stone, each sporting their dark glasses.

Anyway, the so-called art just looked like a primary kid's scribbles to her, except for a weirdly sexual and violent content in places. Nudes and guns and axes and fire, blood spurting out of necks, scrawled words over and over in French, a big MIEL SUR MES LÈVRES in block capitals over what resembled a hammer and nails next to something like a dartboard or a round whirlpool. Prams. Huge round eyes. Spoons. *Aaaaaah*s, of course. A bubble from a mouth with nothing written in it, covered over in wriggling snakes of blue chalk. The last square always a huge explosion, clearly sexual. The staff just say that, whatever the content, the work in the art room is an integral part of the treatment.

Neither she nor Nick have ever exactly wished to examine them closely, anyway. Strip-cartoons or no, they're fairly distressing. Certainly not art, Brut or therapeutic or otherwise.

'Always in the same order,' Lucy repeats, as if obsessing about it herself.

'What exactly *is* the story, though?' asks Sarah, who feels she isn't engaging enough in Lucy's never-ending conversation.

She really doesn't want Lucy to feel she's being used, that she's not getting the company the poor woman no doubt craves out here, staying six months at a time now she's sold the gallery. Or that is the plan. The kids have been very tiring and noisy, overexcited by the familiar place. Somewhat disconcerting, it's been, coming back.

'There's the rub, darling. As he never speaks, as he's gone mute, partly bcause of the drugs, no one *knows* what the story is,' Lucy replies. 'But woe betide anyone trying to change it. Xavier received a black eye, you know, attempting to suggest to Jean-Luc that he draw a tree in the cartoon square where there's usually a dog on a chain before the page with nothing but ovens and lots of *S*s. Obviously to do with the war.'

'And the end's still the same? The explosion?'

'Always the same. A blue rectangle in crayon, with a sort of tiny female figure in the middle, and then the big bang overflowing its square. They changed his drugs because of some

420

potentially fatal reaction to do with blood cells, but the pictures stayed the same and in the same order. Make of it what you will,' she sighs.

'I couldn't, much.'

I could certainly understand the photos, though, Sarah thought to herself.

She had discovered the camera under Tammy's bed. A throwaway type. She was vacuuming a few days after Lucy had returned to London with the coffin and a metal box from one of the *caves* – Alan's stuff, was all she'd say. Vacuuming and polishing and cooking were good therapy, for some reason. Tammy denied any knowledge with great fervour and the camera was sent off to be developed.

It wasn't the indistinct nude shots of herself bathing – more than twenty of them – that disturbed her most, it was the images of the girls: not the ones he'd taken in the yard (which she had already known about, having spotted him), but the ones in their bedroom, showing their tummies; and ending on a terrified Tammy, crouched on her bed. The fact she was blurred from camera-shake made it worse. To spare the children more trauma, they decided not to approach them, assuming that Jean-Luc hadn't taken it and that Tammy was fibbing. What was alarming was not only that tiny seed of doubt but the fact that Tammy could fib so successfully.

They burnt the photos in the fire: acrid smell and hallucinogenic colours.

'There goes the evidence,' Nick had said. 'And good riddance, too.'

'All terribly Freudian, obviously,' Lucy went on, stirring Sarah from semi-consciousness. 'Symbolic totems and so forth. He won't let me take a single one away, and no one else can either. Xavier – I call him *Frère* Xavier, he's so like a monk – says the poor man knows where every page of drawings is, and he's done hundreds. When each series is finished, he stacks it on the pile before raiding it for his walls a week or so later. One page of squares takes him five days to finish. What are we now: a year and three months, is it, since he was incarcerated?'

Sarah nods, her eyes closed. She is half-drifting off again, deliciously – despite the drone of Lucy's low-pitched voice and the squeals from the girls. Nick is with them, she thinks: she can relax, let go. Beans has this habit of slipping through the hole in the duck, then tipping it onto herself and disappearing under. But Nick is with them in the water.

Lucy's mobile rings: an irritating fragment of Verdi. Sarah relaxes, thinking for a moment it was theirs, with its similar start to the ringtone. She remembers, as Lucy natters impatiently, their first sight in June last year of the new mast, rising from the trees a few kilometres away, utterly tactless in its white boniness.

'We can't have that,' she remembers Nick saying, aghast at the bedroom window.

As if they owned the beauty that had been spread before them for months; absorbed it as part of their birthright. 'It's the work of Satan,' he added, half-seriously. And then shouted this out, so that it echoed over the valley and the view, its perfection split like schist at a single, casual tap; the lines running all the way back to a child sloshing in mud in the Congo, to dead gorillas. Life was all about compromise, as her mother would say, fanning herself in Aden.

She briefly checks Tammy with a shift of the head, feeling the sun find the shadowed half of her face: Tammy is very all right, performing somersaults on the lawn.

Lucy has come off the mobile and watches the girl, smiling. Oh, the softness of the lawn. The success.

The new gardener – a dishy young Parisian called Damien, employee of a big landscaping company, a younger version of poor careless Raoul – hired an excavator and dug out the whole yard to a depth of ten centimetres, then shoved in fresh earth and compost and the richest black peat from (apparently) the diminishing bogs of Estonia. Although there was no seed sown until the autumn storms had been and gone, the sprinklers worked night and day keeping the soil fresh right through the late summer until the water table got sucked too low, so Lucy – thanks to Alan's life insurance – hired a water-lorry up to when the rains came, rather late, at the end of November.

The result is a lush sward from barn to house to pool, kept thus by a complex web of pipes watering four hours a day and framed by huge pots sporting luxurious mounds of English lavender (so much prettier) and thick sprays of jasmine, red geraniums and others she's forgotten the name of, with an oleander hedge on one side – every single bit of which is highly poisonous, she heard Sarah telling her girls. A new cherry tree has flourished, and already given a modest crop. The tumbled wall is now a perfectly pointed and levelled-off stone bulwark against the woods. Lucy feels she has achieved something of a miracle, and the boars are kept from mischief with the same fence Jean-Luc installed, simply enlarged. She had the men add a little gate. It isn't perfect, the fence looks silly rather than civilised, the gate twee, but there was no choice. The boars love lushness, especially in the dry scorch of July and August, when the hills themselves seem to shrivel up, the air cracks like a wafer. She can't even paint in the summer, under the trees: the cicadas drive her insane.

'*One* day we might know what the story is,' she says, as Nick's thin, mottled body emerges into view, varnished with wet. She closes her eyes, politely smiling as the white flesh passes her to find its towel spread out on the succulent lawn.

She feels very generous, anyway, inviting the Mallinsons back for a fortnight, only a year after they left, given what happened to Alan. But it would have happened anyway, probably: his heart worse than she'd thought – a sieve, they told her: full of leaks. He was overweight and never took exercise, had chain-smoked as a younger man. You can't escape the punishment of your own history. Not these days.

And she likes the Mallinsons. The collection of essays Nick edited has been quietly successful, won some prize or other, caused a brief stir to do with African oil and Esso or whatever, but no one tried to bump him off, as they'd threatened to with Alan. My poor sweetheart.

As for Sarah! Her published 'journal', *French Lessons in Skinny-Dipping*, has shot her into overnight prominence as one of the favourite reads of whatever that book-club couple are called on the box. Fortunately, all the names are changed. Except for Alan's, in the dedication. That was touching. And the end of the Jean-Luc business was, happily, rejigged – out of consideration for the poor man's feelings. The reviewers thought the book was exaggerated, made up. But of course it wasn't, it was honesty itself, and the end was charming: the placing of real, fresh flowers on that memorial plaque on the track as they left for the last time. Completely withered, now, but the same ones.

One never *quite* knows where any story will end, if there ever is an end. Certainly not where you expect it to, Lucy thinks, as a sudden commotion in the water makes her look up, as if startled.

ACKNOWLEDGEMENTS

My grateful thanks to Zoë Swenson-Wright for her unerring eye and detailed advice; to Jas and Sylvie Elsner for the inspiration; to my editor Robin Robertson and my agent Lucy Luck for support and suggestions; to Nick Miedema for his reflections; to Mike Lewis for allowing me to plunder his paper on imperial hydraulics; to Alexis Abbou, Bernard Pignero and Didier Goethals for their help and friendship; to Alex Bowler, Hannah Ross and all at Jonathan Cape; to Sylvie Wheatley for her last-minute advice; to all those who gave me technical help on everything from swimming pools to electric fences; to Aimé Vielzeuf, *ancien Résistant*, for his published war memories – and to those who have, over the years, recounted similar experiences to me in conversation; to my late father Barney Thorpe for his Francophilia and much-missed enthusiasm; to Josh, Sacha and Anna for the guidance of youth; and above all to my wife Jo for her patience and wise counsel.